Praise for the novels of Hazel Beck

"The magical world of St. Cyprian is one readers will never want to leave. *Small Town, Big Magic* is an absolute triumph of a debut... Hazel Beck has created the perfect blend of magic, humor, world-ending peril, friendship and romance, brewed into a spellbinding combination that readers will adore, and that will have them desperate for the next book!"

—*New York Times* bestselling author Maisey Yates

"Emerson Wilde is a smart, funny protagonist whose unshakeable belief in herself will charm the reader from the very first page of *Small Town, Big Magic*. A diverse coven of witches, an enchanted history, and a dangerous adversary all add up to an absolute delight of a magical tale."

—Louisa Morgan, author of *The Age of Witches*

"A fresh, fun, zany spin on paranormal romance, *Small Town, Big Magic* casts a big spell. Take one girlboss witch, add a magical journey of healing and self-discovery, and sprinkle in a dash of romance, and you've got an enchanting read perfect for fans of *The Ex Hex* and *Payback's a Witch*."

—Ashley Winstead, author of *Fool Me Once*

"[A] spellbinding magic-infused rom-com... Beck delivers a wonderfully realized heroine with a voice so clear readers will feel like one of her friends. This is sure to be a hit with any fan of paranormal romance."

—*Publishers Weekly*

"Beck's second entry in the 'Witchlore' series brings back a charming cast of characters and offers a heart-rending story of personal strength, growth, and fated love."

—*Library Journal*

Also by Hazel Beck

Small Town, Big Magic

Big Little Spells

Truly Madly Magically

DRAGON FIRES EVERYWHERE

HAZEL BECK

Recycling programs
for this product may
not exist in your area.

ISBN-13: 978-1-525-80474-8

Dragon Fires Everywhere

Copyright © 2025 by Megan Crane and Nicole Helm

All rights reserved. No part of this book may be used or reproduced in any manner whatsoever without written permission.

Without limiting the author's and publisher's exclusive rights, any unauthorized use of this publication to train generative artificial intelligence (AI) technologies is expressly prohibited.

This is a work of fiction. Names, characters, places and incidents are either the product of the author's imagination or are used fictitiously. Any resemblance to actual persons, living or dead, businesses, companies, events or locales is entirely coincidental.

® is a trademark of Harlequin Enterprises ULC.

Graydon House
22 Adelaide St. West, 41st Floor
Toronto, Ontario M5H 4E3, Canada
www.GraydonHouseBooks.com

HarperCollins Publishers
Macken House, 39/40 Mayor Street Upper,
Dublin 1, D01 C9W8, Ireland
www.HarperCollins.com

Printed in U.S.A.

This book is dedicated to you—all you marvelous citizens of St. Cyprian, the best little river town in all of witchdom... and the Midwest.

May you keep the witchlore close to your heart, even if you have to keep it safe from the world.

May you always listen to the wisdom of crows, your loved ones lost and yet with you, and the truth you carry inside.

May you find your magic when you most need it.

And may you always believe that love is on its way to you and that you never need to shrink yourself or hide away to deserve it.

Stay safe on the bricks, witchlings.

We'll see you there.

DRAGON FIRES EVERYWHERE

1

THE NUMBER OF CROWS EVERYWHERE WOULD be a little bit alarming—since there are far more than a mere murder, in every tree, strutting in the roads, wheeling lazily in the late November sky above all the shops—if I wasn't so close to home.

And so happy to be back on the pretty bricks of St. Cyprian.

It feels like I've been away longer than I have. I've spent the weeks since Samhain traveling around the world, gathering the magical keys to the witchlore archives that poor, deceased Happy Ambrose (spoiler alert: he was never all that happy) left littered about.

The Joywood—the ruling coven we basically dethroned, who would like to make our ascension into rulers as difficult and challenging as possible—claimed it was a *mistake*. An *accident* caused by poor Happy's unfortunate fate at Samhain.

Because otherwise, he totally would have gathered the keys himself and handed them over to me once the Joywood well and truly lost the ascension trials in October. *Sure.*

I liked traveling, I won't lie. But I missed home. I missed my friends and coven. And as much as I'm primed and ready to be

Georgie Pendell, Historian of the Riverwood Coven, it still feels a bit like a costume I'm wearing. A little too special for the likes of *me*.

It'll feel real once we fully take over at Yule.

I'm almost sure of it.

I could have transported myself anywhere from my last stop in Merry Olde England when it was time to come back home, but I came to Main Street first. I wanted to take a moment to fully bask in this town I've always loved, no matter how difficult the last year has been.

After weeks of not hard, but tedious, work put in place by the pettiest witches I know, I wanted to remind myself why, exactly, we all fought so hard to save this place from the evil coven that came before us.

The evil coven that had no intention of stepping down until we forced the issue.

I wanted exactly what I do now—to walk down the street that I would know if I was blind, with all the magical bricks and historic houses that are now shops and restaurants that draw in witches and humans alike.

St. Cyprian has been the center of the witching world since witches decided that Salem was the last witch hunt they planned to live through and came here, to a then-frontier town at the magical intersection of three mighty rivers—only two of which are visible to human eyes—to build a safe place where magical folks could hide in plain sight, safe from the burning torches and Puritan fantasies that had come for too many of our forebears.

And speaking of those Puritans, it's Thanksgiving. A holiday with its own questionable roots, but still the one I love best as it plays no favorites. No rituals, no gifts. Just food and the people you love.

I miss my people. My best friends, who are like family to me because my family of origin is complicated—whose isn't—and who are now the coven known as the Riverwood. The new ruling coven. And everyone is aware of that, I think, as people on the street catch my eye and nod or smile greetings in a way they definitely didn't do before we went through the ascension trials and were officially voted in.

Clearly things have shifted here at home while I've been away.

I walk faster.

And remind myself that I also miss my boyfriend. Obviously. I'll go see Sage, of course. Maybe tomorrow.

But first, I'm headed to my people, the Riverwood. They'll be excited to know I gathered all the keys quicker than expected. The Joywood told us I'd be lucky to find them all before I'm supposed to open the archives at the Cold Moon Ceremony at the start of December, next week. I therefore decided I would be so lucky, I'd do it *fast*.

This ceremony is meant to kick off the Yule season and our last weeks into full ascension. Though we won the ascension trials, that isn't the end of our fight with the Joywood. They're evil. And are no doubt planning to unleash their usual terrifying nonsense on us between now and our full ascension on the winter solstice.

No one can remember the last time there was a transfer of ruling coven power, suggesting to anyone who's paying attention that the Joywood really are as bad as we've pretty much always known they are. Playing with collective memories is just one example. Even now, after we beat them fair and square, every step we take toward assuming power seems to lead to more steps. I know this annoys my friends, and it's not that I'm *not* annoyed, but I'm a Historian. We're used to the twists and turns and hidden paths of history and lore.

No doubt the Joywood will continue to try to obscure things, hide important information, and outright thwart us. We *know* they have access to black magic—our Healer has been busy cleaning up black magic attacks since Samhain—so even though we've *won*, there's no certainty it's *over*.

But they never really have understood who they're dealing with when it comes to us. My friends and I grew up under their rule. We watched them steal our friend and leader's power and memory. Her sister's freedom and magic. We watched them lie and change the lore. We fought back when they attacked us again and again and again, straight on and in secret. We tracked their offenses—and sometimes I think we only know the half of it.

The secrets tucked away in the archives only the leading coven has access to will tell me the truth, and then there won't be so much uncertainty. We'll know the exact steps we need to take. We'll know how to protect ourselves, what unsettling dreams about crows might mean, and a whole slew of other things.

I can't wait.

This thought brings a smile to my face as I decide to head to Wilde House first. I want to drop off my things and magic them into place. It might not *appear* like I'm organized, but I certainly am. One witch's mess is another's system. I also want to check to see if my cat familiar, the delightfully lazy and gloriously orange Octavius, is about.

Wilde House is dark and empty when I transport myself in right at the front door. For a moment I just stand in the foyer and breathe.

Home.

Of course, Wilde House isn't really *my* home, even though I've lived here since I was eighteen. Truth is, I don't know how much longer I can justify staying here. I'm not a scared teenager moving in here to support my best friend who no longer remembers the truth about her magic anymore. I'm not the girl who lied to said friend about my family life so she would *insist* on me moving in. I'm not even a Wilde. Emerson and Rebekah, who are, spend more time with their significant others these days than in their ancestral home.

Wilde House has always been a special place because it's lovely and old and represents one of the founding families that made St. Cyprian what it is. It's also had over a century of protections built into its very walls and floors. These days it stands as a monument to the much-prophesied Wilde sisters, who were deemed disappointments at eighteen but are now two of the most powerful witches alive.

Someone should be here until we take over actual ruling coven duties full-time.

But after the holiday season is over, I'm going to need to find my own way. Maybe by then I'll be ready to move in with Sage, the way he's been asking me to do for months now.

I wait for images of us together like that to sweep through me and charm me. I've *been* waiting. And like always, I find it impossible to picture. It's just a blank, when I've always had an incredibly rich fantasy life.

Too rich, some might say. And often have.

"This is a sign of maturity," I mutter to myself, because a rich fantasy life really only ever got me in trouble. I'm maturing, and just in time, as this ruling coven costume needs to fit me better. Not being able to daydream about my future with Sage probably means that I'm growing into all those *good adult habits* my mother despaired of me ever finding.

Mind you, I can and happily have imagined all those scenarios for my friends—all now coupled up in our coven. Emerson and Jacob ruling St. Cyprian and the world with Emerson's might and fairness and Jacob's calm and certainty. Rebekah and Frost tucked up in Frost's glamoured Victorian on the hill (with Frost's enviable library) being snarky and beautifully in love in spite of it. I have thought more about Ellowyn and Zander's baby and the parents they'll be more than anyone has a right to, probably.

But Sage and me? Nothing.

Facts, not fantasy, are what make good Historians, my mother always told me. *You keep letting your head run away with you, Georgina, and you might lose it.*

She's never made it clear if she means that literally.

I drift toward the stairs and my attic garret rooms—my preferred description, though there's nothing *garrety* about the third floor of Wilde House and the actual lovely turret I get to live in. I smile at the sometimes grinning, sometimes scowling newel post, depending on who you ask. I've always found the carved wooden dragon's expression more interesting than fearsome. The glittering onyx eyes seem to pay attention, and I like that. And occasionally, the effect of whatever enchantment exists around the newel post means you can hear it say something in your head.

Hello, Azrael. I've returned home. Hope you've been well.

He says nothing in return this time—no surprise there. Dragons, even inanimate ones, do what and how they will. That's only one reason that many of my favorite daydreams involve great fire-breathing creatures of legend.

Where good old Azrael might make others uneasy, likely because he's been known to give off the occasional electric shock, I find his presence at the bottom of the stairs comforting. Like a sentry guarding anyone who resides upstairs.

Namely me.

My hand glides along the intricately carved head, warm and silken under my palm, and it offers a kind of deep purr in return. The only welcome home I need.

But the word *home* makes me feel anxious again. I hurry up the stairs, feeling out with my magic for Octavius, but I don't sense him. He's either enjoying Thanksgiving with the rest of the coven over at Jacob's farmhouse across the river, or he's off doing whatever it is familiars—and cats—do when left to their own devices.

I drop my things off, putting them back into their specific places. Especially my travel crystals, which need a good recharge. To anyone else, my room and my library in the next room look like towering, haphazard mishmashes of everything I love—books, old things, all kinds of crystals—but my system is as ruthlessly organized as the best archives and libraries around the world.

I don't like to let people see how my brain works.

I don't think that's weird.

Once satisfied, I'm even more excited to see my friends. I could transport myself over to what's no doubt a delicious Thanksgiving feast, but I decide to fly. To get a taste of the cold November night, the stars pulsing bright and beautiful. To enjoy the sight of St. Cyprian below me, twinkling in the late fall dark. And to take in the confluence of three rivers and all its magic that my friends and I once saved.

After I get across the river to where St. Cyprian's cemetery resides and the North Farm sits in rolling fields dotted with pretty farm buildings, I touch down outside in the yard. I see Murphy, Jacob's stag familiar, grazing in a field in the distance in the moonlight. I hear the ruffling of feathers—no doubt Zander's and Ellowyn's bird familiars settled into a branch somewhere. Maybe even Frost's raven, Coronis.

And through a big picture window in the front of the house, I see everyone else gathered around a very full dining room table.

I should go right in. But I don't. I stop. I watch.

My friends are eating, chatting, laughing. The dog and cat familiars are sprawled out around them, including my bored-looking orange Octavius. I try to step forward—I'm almost certain I do—but it's like something . . . stops me.

It's like there's a little bubble around the house. Not a real one. Not the sort of magic encasements I've seen and used before. It's just a figment of my imagination and I know that. *I know it.*

Just like I know that if I walk in there, my friends will greet me with excitement. They'll make space for me. They love me.

But the table is crowded. And from the outside looking in, it doesn't seem like there's space for me. Not just because they've only pulled up as many chairs as they need, but because . . . everyone is so happy, and it isn't the wine. They're smiling, laughing, and enjoying each other.

Three pairs of perfect couples.

They're balanced. And if I go in there, I'll upend that balance.

I shake my head, out here by myself. It's a silly thought. Particularly considering a coven is made of seven. This is my coven. I belong with them.

But Thanksgiving isn't about covens or witches or St. Cyprian. It's just . . . giving thanks. And they're all having plenty of thanks without me.

Because you weren't supposed to be back yet. Because you decided to make your return a surprise.

No amount of reason gets me to move my feet. I just stand here, feeling like I don't belong. And when I reach into my pocket, curling my fingers around the crystals that always guide me, I get nothing. I frown and touch the necklace I often wear—a teardrop-shaped piece of prehnite I've worn on a delicate gold chain since the day of my pubertatum, when my mother gave it to me. It's the only time my mother has ever given me a present that made me feel like she was trying to understand *me* instead of the daughter she wished I was.

Tonight it offers nothing but a kind of bleakness that sinks in deep.

Which is a sign in and of itself, I decide. I should have gone to see Sage first.

So that's what I do instead.

2

SAGE IS THE ONE WHO MISSED ME THE MOST, as he told me every single day I was gone. He sent me more little presents on the road than Emerson did—and that's saying something, because Emerson is hard to beat.

Sage has been increasingly concerned I'm focusing too much on work, and he's right, isn't he? I can see that now. The past few weeks have been all work. If I went into Jacob's house right now, it would devolve into work talk. Riverwood plans for the Cold Moon Ceremony. More speeches about our plans and priorities. More dark imaginings about what the Joywood had planned if all their machinations had actually worked.

All of it worth discussing, but still, all of it work.

This is supposed to be a holiday for *everyone*, even the ruling coven, so I decide I'll see my friends in the morning.

I know they'll be happy to see me then. And will be as excited as I am that I found everything I needed on an accelerated schedule. We'll dive deeper into all things Riverwood, and the rest of the steps that need to be taken before and after the Cold Moon. *Tomorrow.*

Tonight, I'll go see my boyfriend like a normal person. I'll go live a life that is independent and mine, instead of trailing after Emerson like a puppy.

That's how Sage characterized my relationship with her before I left. But then he apologized for getting negative. For letting the prospect of missing me cloud his thinking.

I don't fly this time. I picture Sage's place—a converted carriage house separated from his parents' beautiful Romantic Revival–style house up off Main. The Osburns weren't part of the original witch settlers to St. Cyprian. They arrived in the early 1900s, after the town was set up to be the capital of witchdom, so they're a little removed from the bricks.

I set myself down just outside his door, because my boyfriend likes rules and propriety. I've never dropped in on him unannounced before, and I'm sure that even though he'll be happy to see me, he'll be a lot happier if I knock.

Society has rules for a reason, I have heard him tell his students at the high school with great seriousness. And I'm a Historian while he's a Praeceptor *of* history. We have rules for everything and we swear by them. We like rules, Sage and me.

Even if, sometimes, I dream of life-altering love that could shake the stars loose with its intensity—

That is not realistic, I lecture myself. *And also it is childish. It's time to grow up and live in the real world.*

I should be grateful for what I have. I should treat my daydreams like intrusive thoughts. This is the last stretch of a long year, and it's past time I get with reality.

I go to knock, very properly, on his door—but I don't.

Something is wrong. I feel it dance over my skin like a shiver of warning. It's not a premonition. It's nothing that specific, just a very generic *off* feeling that even the most out-of-touch humans might feel when something *isn't right*.

I let my hand fall. Then I stand there, trying to figure out what feels so *wrong*. It's not the kind of black, choking evil that

I've encountered entirely too many times over the past year—*that* feels oily and gross. This is just . . . *off*.

I frown at the porch. Sage's bicycle is there, but it isn't neatly locked to the Fenrir-shaped spigot as usual. It's lying on its side, like he haphazardly left it out like that. But Sage is the least *haphazard* person I know, and that's a high bar when you're a Pendell who's best friends with Emerson Wilde.

There's no window to peer through. There's only this shivery certainty that something isn't adding up. I look over my shoulder at the little alley that stretches between two of the bigger roads. I hear a crow squawk from its branch in one of the trees, which sends that shiver deeper.

It reminds me of the dream Ellowyn had that she told us about—with princesses riding dragons and a crow army, not unlike a fairy-tale book I loved as a child. But that *certainly* has no place in the here and now.

I scowl at the alley. There are usually a few cars and trucks parked there, and tonight is no exception. But the one that sticks out as odd is a big black SUV.

One I recognize. Because Cailee Blanchard owns a little boutique shop on Main Street close to Emerson's Confluence Books and is forever parking it on the street right in front of Emerson's shop instead of her own or in the alley behind the shops.

I've had many conversations with Sage about her because her oldest was a holy terror in one of Sage's classes last year. Her husband, Dane, was a staunch Joywood supporter at the ascension trials, but Cailee is the type that doesn't believe a woman's place is *politics* when she has children to care for and a hobby business to run. I know this because she tells everyone this, without solicitation. She and Dane live way off the bricks, in the part of town where all the historical buildings were razed for cookie-cutter McMansions.

There's no reason her car should be *here*.

I turn back to Sage's door, the *off* feeling digging deeper, making my breathing a little unsteady as my heart trips over itself.

Her car being in this neighborhood could mean a million things, I tell myself.

But it's like I know, even though I refuse to consider anything *directly*.

Because I don't knock. I use magic to open the door.

And it's the sound of laughter—hers and his—that hits me first. The image of them grappling on the couch isn't as bad as that laughter, because anything "intimate" between Sage and me was supposed to be *serious*. We had to engage in endless conversations about consent and power dynamics, with many asides involving lectures on the importance of extensive communication.

We didn't laugh much, is the thing.

I stare. I could just . . . go home. I could pretend I'm not back in town, that I never saw what I'm seeing right now, including Cailee's tattoo of Daffy Duck right there on her ass. I'd like to do just that. I'd like to mutter a spell to forget the whole thing.

But I'm rooted to the spot.

Sage once scolded me for daring to kiss his cheek in the kitchen. And here he is . . . *humping away* at a woman in his *living room*.

A *married* woman.

With the TV playing some action movie when he claimed he watched nothing but select PBS documentaries, and only when he could take notes.

While *laughing*. Like sex is *a delight*.

That last part is the betrayal that feels like a knife in the gut. Not the *fact* of it as much as the *lighthearted execution*.

I slam the door closed behind me with a surge of magic, and the two tangled, half-naked bodies scramble off each other.

Cailee with a shriek, Sage with a choking kind of sound as he struggles to get his pants back up.

"Happy Thanksgiving," I offer, pulling out the ditzy smile I've perfected over the years. "Did I miss a breakup conversation?" I look from Sage to Cailee. "Or a divorce hearing?"

They both make a lot of noises, but no words, and it's like that shivery *off* feeling has coalesced into something else. Like the spine I've pretended I don't have since last spring, when Sage approached me at a high school dance. When I told myself it was time to grow up and stop inventing fairy tales about what my life was going to be like. When I gave up on the wild, impossible passion I've longed for all my life. When I chose to agree with my mother, at last, that nothing *special* was coming for me.

I saw what I needed to see. Now I need to . . . not be anywhere near these people.

But much as I'd prefer to simply catapult myself out of here, I feel like all the magic just seeped out of me and is currently located somewhere near Cailee's contextually disturbing tattoo. So I turn on a heel and walk out instead.

"Georgie!"

Sage is on my heels. I can't imagine *why*, but he is. He catches up and darts in front of me.

He's *mussed up* when I've never seen him anything but *perfectly pressed*, with not a hair out of place.

"It's not what it looks like," he blusters.

Such a ridiculous statement that it makes me laugh when I'm pretty sure I ought to be crying.

"Georgie." This time he says my name in his *firm teacher* voice, which, no, he never used in bed, where it might actually have been hot. "We need to talk about this."

I look at him. Really look.

I think about my friends hinting at me that he wasn't right for me. That he was punching above his weight. I think about them trying so hard to understand him or what I saw in him, but they're not Pendells. They didn't grow up with a steady stream of commentary about what's *realistic* and what's *acceptable* and what it *means* to not simply be Historians but to be *Pendells*, who have always stood for *timeless order*.

But now the truth is like a big, hot, bright light glaring in my face. I was always out of *his* league, exactly as my friends never *quite* said out loud. At least not to me.

And *he's* the one cheating.

I don't even feel angry. Just gross. Slimy and weird and a little sick to my stomach. Why does everything feel so off today?

Well. I did just see my boyfriend *inside* a married woman I have never liked, and in a *frenzy*. That would put anyone off.

"There's nothing to talk about, Sage."

"Georgie, you don't understand," he begins in that *lecturey* tone, and all I can think is that I let this man talk to me like this. For *months*. I murmured assenting noises, tuned out, and told myself that *relationships are about compromise, not sparks and romance*.

"I don't want to understand," I reply.

Because he never understood *me*. And the fact I stayed with him anyway? That's on me.

But him cheating certainly isn't.

That gives me the strength I need to get myself out of here. "I don't want to hear from you ever again."

Then I picture Wilde House, and let my magic take me there.

And once I'm home, I prepare to let myself cry.

But I don't.

Which somehow feels even worse.

3

I LEAN AGAINST THE FRONT DOOR OF WILDE House, staring at the grand staircase that will lead me upstairs. I feel like I've run a marathon. I feel an aching, awful pain in my chest.

It's not my heart that hurts, though. It's my pride. And a million other things.

I'm not sad I'll never kiss Sage again, or hold his hand, or get one of his thoughtfully precise presents. I'm devastated I'm going to have to admit to my friends they were right. I'm furious he *cheated* on me, when I thought . . .

When I *knew*.

If Sage was punching above his weight, that also means I was punching down. And I tried to convince myself that wasn't true. I *tried*.

Because even though I've been trying so hard to heed my mother's advice to let all my romantic dreams go, I still had this fleeting thought that there *might* be something special about me, about the Riverwood Historian I'm going to be.

But a man I didn't even love *cheated* on me, having the kind of *fun* with someone else he never had with me. Like I meant nothing at all.

That's when the tears start. And it's a relief. I'm not afraid of crying, unlike my entire family and most of my friends. I welcome the cleansing magic of a good cry. But I'm not going to let anyone see me cry over *Sage Osburn*.

It's better to get it out here and now while I'm still alone. When no one has to be concerned about my hurt feelings.

They wouldn't understand them anyway. Wildes are *important*. Goods are *a scene*. Norths and Rivers are *upstanding* and *respectable*. I don't know what Frosts are because our Frost has outlived them all, but I somehow doubt the arrogant former immortal ever worried about who he was meant to be. He just . . . became it.

Meanwhile, I'm the only redheaded Pendell, which has always been viewed as an affront. As if my hair was a sign from day one that I was going to disappoint my cold, buttoned-up family no matter how hard I tried to be the right kind of Historian. And daughter.

I push away from the door, wiping at my face. I need my room so I can have my things around me and my crystals glowing in my hands. I need to feel and process these emotions and have them appropriately worked through before I see my friends tomorrow.

They're going to be so *careful*, and that makes a little sob catch in my throat. They all told me, indirectly, that they didn't think Sage was right for me. But no one is going to guess, no matter how little they liked him, that he *cheated on me*. With Cailee Blanchard, of all people.

So there will be outrage, but also confusion. *Careful* outrage. *Careful* confusion. Those shared behind-my-back looks of *what do we do?*

I prefer to be part of said sharing looks behind backs. Being the *subject* of them sucks.

I want to fly back to Sage's and punch him just for that. Or curse him and his inadequate genitals that I pretended were lovely. But none of those things will fix *this*.

I want to turn back time, but I know better than that. *If you steal time, you lose time*, according to the nursery rhymes. The only choice is figuring out how to handle this so that my friends *aren't* careful and sympathetic, because I know I won't deal with that well.

And even my usual go-to routine of acting like a space cadet is unlikely to help.

I move for the stairs but come up short as I take the first one. A book that was definitely not there a moment ago is now sitting on the second stair. The same book from my childhood that I keep trying to give away, but can't. I gave it to Ellowyn as a baby gift after we found out she was pregnant, but it doesn't seem to want to stay put. I keep assuring her—and me—that it will stay with her once the baby is born. Once it understands it's not mine anymore.

Though I'm starting to wonder.

I know I didn't leave it on the stairs. I didn't leave it in this house at all. And I doubt Ellowyn dropped it off in anticipation of my early return when she doesn't know I'm here.

I flop onto the stairs and pull my knees to my chest. Then I stare at the book accusingly, because it's like salt to the wound, rubbed in hard to make sure it stings.

It's the concentrated version of all those childhood fantasies I was finally leaving behind.

I consider marching over to the fireplace and burning the book until it's nothing but ash, because surely then it will leave me alone. Except I am a firm believer that no book should be burned, ever. Except I gave it to Ellowyn as a gift for the baby who will be here soon. Except Sage was the one who made fun of me for my favorite book being a *fairy tale*, and I will make *myself* into ash before giving him a say now.

I pick up the offensive tome. "This. This was the bill of goods I let myself believe in," I say aloud, arriving at the page I used to sigh over.

"*I am yours*," I read aloud.

I don't even have to look at the words. I memorized them a long time ago, back when I still lived next door. I used to recite them in my mirror, pretending I was the heroine of my own novel. That somewhere, dragons and epic battles were waiting for me. That I had somehow lived through them before, like maybe *I* was the lone witch in all of witchdom special enough to have lived many lives.

That my entire existence would be marked by great passion and epic adventures.

I keep reciting the book, looking at the pages but thinking of the little girl I'd been back then, knowing full well I'd get in trouble if my mother found this book in my possession again. Pendells, she told me over and over, distinguished themselves by leaving *special* to others.

I keep saying the words anyway. *"You are mine. Our souls intertwine. I would lay down my life for you, but even then I would not die. Because love cannot be torn asunder."*

I snort at that. I stare down at the illustration of a red-haired woman I used to tell myself looked like me, since no one else in my family did. At her sword and her tiara and a dragon winging its way through the sky with a pack of crows fanned out behind it. "What utter bullshit."

Or is it that I want it to be bullshit, because then it wouldn't hurt? Because my friends have significant others, and I have witnessed their love. Real, beautiful love. Love that I have never once felt myself, not in the daylight.

No matter how many times I dream until my heart hurts at night.

I say the last part, the part that used to make me swoon, in nothing more than a choked whisper. *"Love will set us free."*

I used to trace my fingers over those letters again and again and again while my mother icily tore apart my father downstairs. Having what she claimed were not *fights* but the *honest conversations* that he always allowed. And he said little in return but, *Now, Cadence. That's not fair.*

Maybe the real Pendell legacy is that we think love comes with interrogations that feel like barbed wire.

Before I can sink into that sea of self-pity, something trembles beneath me. The stairs shake, like an earthquake. But it doesn't remind me of the one I remember when I was a kid—waking up to a vague shaking kind of feeling and then going back to sleep because this is Missouri. We might have a fault line, but it's not California.

This is deeper than any *earthquake*. It's the house, not the ground beneath me. Wilde House is . . . undulating. Like contractions. The mermaid-shaped chandelier in the entryway shakes and tinkles and sounds almost like someone's shrieking.

Maybe the Joywood are up to something evil. Again.

I should get to my friends—but before I can push myself to my feet, I watch as a crack snakes down the length of the spindle holding up the newel post. Then the wood of the newel post seems to . . . peel back.

Away from those onyx eyes, and then something in deep, swirling blues and greens *smokes* out of the opening. The familiar onyx eyes are moving with it.

I should say some kind of protection spell. Call out for help. Do *something* other than watch the smoke engulf the foyer in front of me beneath the chandelier. Do anything but *watch* as it begins to form a body. Claws.

Scales.

I must be dreaming. Hallucinating? Maybe the magic I've always thought was in tears is going a little haywire tonight, because Azrael isn't *real*.

He's a charmed carving, that's all—but it sure looks like he just . . . escaped the newel post. While I sat on this stair and watched.

Now there's a living, breathing dragon in front of me, filling up the entire front hall of Wilde House with its high ceilings and graceful dimensions, though there is nothing *graceful* about a *dragon* who *can't be real*—

"Why wouldn't I be real?"

The voice is smooth and silky and decidedly male.

And clearly came from the *dragon* that's formed before me. With sharp white teeth and gold-and-onyx eyes and a tail. And *wings*. And *talons*.

Actual talons.

I'm dreaming. Sleepwalking, per usual, and the dreams have gotten really, really realistic. I'll wake up with a crick in my neck on the stairs like I always do, but then I can talk about *this* with my friends tomorrow instead of Sage.

But his voice is sleek and sharp and *real*. It reverberates through the room and me. "I thought you were better than this, Georgina."

"Better than what?" I find myself asking.

As if I am actually having a conversation with the *dragon* that materialized out of a *newel post*. A newel post that's just been sitting there, very much a newel post and nothing *but* a newel post—okay, one with a little enchantment, sure—since I was a *child*.

"The kind of witch who can't believe in *true* magic." He huffs out a strange *dragon* breath that sizzles into the hazy smoke still hanging in the air.

I want to laugh. Maybe this is hysteria, and actually, that's comforting. I've had a break with reality, that's all. I am magic, all on my own, but this isn't magic. This is *dragons*, and *dragons* don't exist.

And while most things that you'll find in the witchlore existed at *some* point, it is common, accepted knowledge that dragons and unicorns and the like went extinct long before witches set foot in St. Cyprian. Or Salem, for that matter.

But there is a dragon looming there before me, and I am *not* waking up. I push myself to my feet, wondering if that'll get the dream to stop.

He looks up to the ceiling like he's seeing the chandelier for the first time and blinks his large golden eyes. Then the scales begin to melt away, and he shrinks down, slowly morphing from scaled, winged dragon to . . . a man.

A big man—a very big man—but still. A *man*. Dark-haired and -eyed, though there's still gold in his gaze. And somehow he seems just as dangerous now that he's no longer the size of the entire room.

He's tall. And broad. Muscled in ways it would be rude to study more closely. It's as if he's still carved, only now in flesh, not wood.

More importantly, he's still *here*, not fading away into dream or imagination.

I take a breath and I can feel it in my lungs, laced with smoke so it tickles, and there's no way *that's* a dream.

And I think, very distinctly, *Oh. At last. It's him.*

It hits me so hard I don't know how I'm still standing. It's *him*. It's all my daydreams come to glorious life. Passion and loud, wild sex and the way my friends take care of each other and *life-altering* kisses and intensity and *him*—

But before I can take that on, my friends appear. My coven. The Riverwood, the new leaders of the witching world.

All six of them land around me, looking alarmed and *pissed* and ready to fight. They look around, as if searching out an enemy—

"No one's here," I manage to croak out through the thunder inside me.

"Georgie! You're home early." Emerson tosses her arms around me and squeezes. "We felt a very strange disturbance and came . . ."

She trails off as she seems to realize there's someone else in the foyer with us.

"Did you bring home . . . a guy?" Rebekah asks, sounding impressed.

"A *hot* guy at that," Ellowyn mutters to Rebekah, and I try to take comfort in the fact that since she can't lie, Azrael is not only real, but really and truly *that* hot. "Can you say *upgrade*?"

"I'm *right here*," Zander complains.

"Yeah, yeah. You're hot too." She waves him off, one hand resting on her ever-expanding belly. She smiles at me. "So, are you going to introduce us?"

But before I can think of even one word to say, because *oh it's the dragon newel post come to life* seems like not enough, Nicholas Frost steps forward.

The unknowable former immortal witch turned Riverwood coven member narrowly regards Azrael—apparently not just a newel post any longer.

Then they speak the same word at the same time, fury and hate sparking off each other.

"You."

4

"YOU KNOW A DRAGON?" I ASK FROST. INcredulously.

"A dragon?" Emerson demands, casting a suspicious glance at Azrael. Then back at me. "What do you mean, *a dragon*?"

I mean things I don't know how to put into words, and I don't even try. I look at Azrael, who stands there, notably *not* looking like a dragon. He's dressed like a regular guy—if that guy happened to be *that* tall, *that* cut, and *that* ridiculously hot. He's also lounging against the far wall instead of filling the whole foyer, examining his hand as if it's of tremendous fascination to him.

Which is fair, because it's not a *human*-looking hand like the rest of him. It was a humanish hand a moment ago, I'm sure it was, but now it's a claw. A dangerous-looking claw, though it's smaller than the whole talony thing I saw on him earlier.

It's clearly meant to intimidate Frost.

I'm not sure it works, or if Frost is even capable of being intimidated in the first place, but if they know each other . . .

"Georgie, I hate to break it to you, but that's just a guy," Zander tells me, gently.

Like I'm fragile.

I want to scowl at him, but Emerson has moved over to the shattered newel post. She touches one sharp shard. "What happened here?"

"Well." I saw the whole thing transpire, but I still don't have the words to describe it. To explain it. Certainly not in a way that's going to make sense. And that's not getting into how it *feels*. I glance at Azrael. In his . . . man form, I guess. His absurdly attractive man form—but I tell myself to focus.

Because he *was* a dragon there for a few minutes.

I saw it. It's real.

Dragons.

Are.

Real.

His mouth curves into a smile, and that may be a *man's* gorgeous face, but the grin is all dragon. Everyone sees it. I can tell, because they stiffen. "Greetings, witches. You can call me Azrael. Don't worry, I won't eat anyone." His dark gold gaze slides to Frost. "Anyone important, anyway."

"Dragons are a scourge," Frost says coldly. "So much so, I forgot they even existed."

"Is that why you killed so many of us?"

"I never killed a dragon." The affront is clear in his tone.

"My mistake." Azrael's smile shifts, but not to anything remotely humanish. And I have to wonder if he actually looks . . . hungry. "Unicorns were your victims of choice."

Frost frowns. He doesn't immediately reject Azrael's accusation, which is . . . not great, but he doesn't seem to agree, either. "I don't remember unicorns . . ."

He rubs at his temple. Becoming mortal did a number on his memory, and as much as I mourn the access to *all* that firsthand knowledge, he did it to save Rebekah. To make sure we all lived through our second pubertatum test this summer when the Joywood was ready to kill us off, and almost had enough support to do it.

"Let's take a step back," Emerson says, eyeing the way

Rebekah moves closer to Frost, as if fully prepared to take the newcomer on herself. "You're Azrael? As in the dragon in the newel post? But now a real dragon. A dragon Frost knows because he was alive back before dragons went extinct?"

Emerson is clearly trying to put all this information together. She's doing a better job of it than me. I keep getting stuck on *dark gold* and all those *muscles*.

"He looks like any average guy to me," Zander says, apparently not stuck.

But he's also wrong. Azrael does *not* look like any average anything, but that's really neither here nor there. I decide Zander's lucky the dragon ignores him.

"Extinct?" Azrael scoffs at the word Emerson used. "Hardly."

"Not extinct then," Emerson corrects herself, but she's not patronizing him. She's trying to understand. "You . . . became a newel post? And then a man? But how did a newel post become a dragon?"

"A better question would be, how did a dragon become a newel post?" Azrael returns. He pushes off the wall, and his claw is a hand again. "Not all of us could be killed off." He slides a pointed look at Frost. "Some of us were just cursed."

"And by *us* you mean . . . dragons?" Jacob asks from where he stands, solid and strong, next to Emerson.

"I mean magical creatures of all kinds." Azrael gestures upward, and we all look at the grand foyer's mermaid chandelier. A chandelier I have seen just about every day my whole life and have never paid that much attention to. Lights, crystals, a vaguely nautical vibe, sure. But that's not magical. Is it?

"You're telling me there's an actual mermaid trapped in that chandelier?" Zander asks, peering up with interest. Maybe too much interest. When Ellowyn elbows him in the stomach, the chandelier seems to dance.

Azrael only shrugs. "Naturally. Though in Melisande's case, maybe that's for the best. She can be so melodramatic."

As we watch, the crystals on the chandelier . . . shimmer.

"So someone cursed you into our newel post?" Rebekah asks, not as interested in the shimmering. Likely because Azrael was making threats toward her beloved, however vague. "And a mermaid into our chandelier?"

"Not *someone*. The Joywood. They wiped out who they could, including their own." Azrael looks pointedly at Frost. "Then they cursed the rest of us. They couldn't actually exterminate the most powerful among us, but they could trap us in place. So they did." Another shrug, though there's nothing lazy about it this time. "Assholes."

The Joywood. Of course, the Joywood. I try to sift through everything I learned about dragons, mermaids, unicorns, and all the rest of the various magical creatures that supposedly once populated witchdom. The things I learned when I was young and could sneak such tales under my mother's nose. She thought it was pointless to worry about extinct beings—and suggested that maybe they had never existed at all, that these were just more fantasy stories that people told children.

I thought I remembered them. Which I didn't. I couldn't.

Most witches accept that magical creatures once lived side by side with witches, but long ago. Maybe back when Byzantium was a thing, not recently enough that the Joywood could have killed and cursed them and installed them in various artistic flourishes around a house.

But when did the Joywood actually start their reign of terror? They've made sure to obscure our understanding. Once I unlock all of the witchlore archives, I'll know. I'll finally know all the Joywood's dirty secrets, because the archives aren't like human history that changes with the victor of every war. They are many things, but one of those things is a neutral collection of every last *fact*.

"How did this curse break, exactly?" Emerson asks, studying the broken newel post again.

Azrael turns his gaze to me, his eyes direct and rimmed in that gold while otherwise black like onyx. "You tell me," he says.

"How would I know?"

He doesn't break that intense stare. "You're the one who did it."

I didn't do anything. I was just sitting there feeling pathetic and . . . "All I did was . . ." I glance back at the stairs. At the newel post that's now in smithereens.

"What did you do?" Emerson presses when I don't immediately explain. But I don't want to tell them the whole story. It's embarrassing, and they'll get that *poor Georgie* look that has been ramping up since I started dating Sage.

Who I'm no longer dating. A topic we can broach later. Much later.

You know, once we figure out how there's a *dragon* in the foyer.

"I was reading that book." I point at it, because it's still sitting there on the stairs where I dropped it.

"I thought *I* had that book," Ellowyn says, tilting her head slightly, like she expects the book to rush at her.

"I did too," I tell her. "But it was sitting there, and I just . . ." I don't want to tell them, but I remember that I'm Georgie Pendell, who has been known to chase moonbeams and dance skyclad in the back garden, because I long ago decided that if I couldn't be perfect then I might as well embrace the weird. Before I tried to grow up, anyway. And still I use that fantasy girl as a weapon or deflection when I need to.

It's better than touching that live-wire thing inside me that keeps reminding me *it's him*.

I smile. "It wanted me to read it. Out loud. I think maybe it was lonely."

I hope they think about that, a lonely book, rather than why ditzy, airy me was wafting about by myself in Wilde House on Thanksgiving.

Meanwhile, I think about what I actually said out loud. Words about love. Promises. No spell. Nothing magical. Just the old words of some fairy tale.

And I'm pretty sure I said them all with as much disdain as I could manage.

I push on, keeping ahead of any potentially embarrassing questions or my own traitorously pounding heart and giddy head. "Then everything started to shake." I explain Azrael's sudden appearance in detail, because I know Emerson will demand it if I don't. "I don't think I actually did anything. Reading the book out loud has to be a coincidence."

"A book is a spell even a human can cast," Azrael says, as if it's simple enough. And as if he's chiding me a little while he says it. "A universal magic."

"I . . ." I say that all the time. Exactly that, and especially to witches who get sniffy about humans.

But Azrael has turned away from me. From all of us. He's walking for the door.

"If you'll excuse me, I have Joywood members to incinerate. I've been waiting to rain fire upon them for a long, long time." He says this offhandedly.

Half of my friends are still staring at what used to be a newel post. The rest of us are close to gaping at the magical creature, the *dragon*, that erupted from it.

And is now sauntering off to commit a few revenge murders, like he suggested taking high tea.

He walks straight out the door. He doesn't even close it behind him.

I assume we're all rendered totally speechless and immobile, because I am.

But Emerson grabs me. "You have to stop him."

"Why me?" In what world would *I* be able to stop a *dragon*?

Besides, I'm all for him incinerating the Joywood. Shouldn't we all be?

Emerson shakes her head. "You broke him out."

I don't think I actually did, but there's no use arguing with Emerson *and* a dragon. "So what? I didn't do it on purpose."

"I think that means he's yours," Rebekah offers. "Like a chinchilla."

I don't know how I feel about the word *yours*, or how it shifts inside of me—hard—but I suppose she has a point. I was the one who was here.

Besides, her mention of chinchillas, historically a fraught topic between them, diverts Emerson's attention from me.

"He won't be able to incinerate them," Frost says darkly. There's something torn in his expression. "He doesn't understand what's changed."

"Do you?" I ask.

His eyebrows draw together. "Not fully."

Because why would anything be that easy? I sigh. I've unleashed the dragon, allegedly, so somehow it's up to me to *re*-leash him before he makes a mess.

Or a bigger mess than . . . whatever's happening in me.

That makes me want to laugh, but I rush outside into the bitter cold of the dark November night instead. I'm getting ready to try a quick spell to locate him, but I don't have to. He's stopped before the gate that leads out to the sidewalk.

And he's still in the form of a man, looking up at a bright crescent moon.

Like he's drinking it all in, and I suppose if he's really been trapped in a newel post for what has to be at least a hundred years he should. Fresh, cold air. The rivers murmuring all around us. Moonlight. Magic and life and movement.

I take the moment to try to reason with him. With *a dragon*, because every myth I've ever read suggests *that's* a possibility.

"Azrael. You can't go incinerate the Joywood," I tell him. Not that I think he'll listen to me, but I don't know how else to talk to supernatural creatures.

He's still staring up at the moon, and the fact that he's only wearing a T-shirt while the cold wind cuts through us doesn't seem to bother him in the least. "Why not?"

"If they cursed you once already, won't they just curse you again?"

"Only if they know I'm coming," Azrael says, with a lack of concern that I should find alarming.

But I don't. All that offhanded confidence makes something in me . . . *hum*.

"Maybe they do know you're coming," I point out, ignoring any *humming* and focusing on my rational, reasonable approach to an ancient, powerful *dragon*. Because I might not understand that burst of fate and *him* and passion and *mine*, but reason and rationality I can do. Reason and rationality are who I am. "Maybe they felt it the same way my friends did. Wilde House is protected, but we don't actually know if they've got eyes on *you*. Maybe the mermaid is a spy."

Azrael scowls at this. "She would be. She likes a grudge, does Melisande."

The way he says that makes me think—but I shove images of dragons wrapped up with mermaids in a variety of acrobatic poses aside. Facts are what matter, not fantasies. Something I keep trying to learn.

Besides, there are far more important questions to ask him. "Why did they curse you in the first place?"

Azrael doesn't spare me a glance. "For their own shitty and nefarious reasons, Georgina. Obviously."

He turns to look at me then. Really look at me. I feel those dark gold eyes on every inch of my skin. And the strangest part is that it's not all that different than when he was in the newel post, because he always felt real, no matter how much I told myself he wasn't.

Did I sleepwalk as much as I tell myself I did . . . or did I just like to sit with him? With *him*.

Night after night after night?

I know I should be thinking about the Joywood and the implications of magical creatures being cursed so that we all believed they were mythical or lost. But instead I'm thinking about all the ways I've unloaded my most private thoughts over the years on what I *thought* was a charmed inanimate object that, sure, spoke every now and then. But charmed things do that.

My cheeks heat, embarrassment ripe.

His smile goes sharp and self-satisfied, like he knows why. "I was very cognizant of everything happening around me during my time as a post."

I want to melt into the ground, but it's frozen solid beneath my feet. "Ah."

"He isn't worth your tears, you know."

I stiffen. This day really couldn't get worse. A dragon saw me cry and thinks it was about my lame ex-boyfriend. "I do know, thank you," I say, sounding prim to my own ears. "I wasn't crying for him."

"Good." Azrael studies me for a moment, then looks out at the night again. A crow caws from somewhere up above, and Azrael's eyes sharpen. He takes a deep breath. When he exhales, the cold air turns into a big puff of smoke. "Perhaps you're right. Going head-on at the Joywood is never the answer. It's what got us into this mess in the first place. This calls for subterfuge. And them not knowing their curse can be broken."

He breathes out another puff of smoke, a ring this time. He watches it disappear into the night as if fascinated. Hot air meets cold and makes condensation. It's simple science. Not magic. But Azrael seems delighted.

Then he turns to face me head-on again, and he has a kind of battle light in his eyes that reminds me of Emerson.

If Emerson were a large man who's really a dragon.

"The truth is, Georgina Pendell, Riverwood Historian, you need me." That jolts in me in a way I tell myself I don't love, but he keeps going. "You all need me. We need to have one of those meetings your Wilde sister is so fond of. We have work to do."

Then he strides back inside, like he was never going off to *incinerate* the Joywood at all.

Like he's . . . one of us.

I'm left out in the cold once again, and unlike him, I'm shivering against it. And trying, furiously, to catch up with how the past few hours have completely flipped every script there ever was.

I glance over at my childhood home next door. The lights are off. It's late. No doubt my parents are asleep in their separate rooms, lost somewhere in their chilly life together.

Beyond the house, the holiday lights of St. Cyprian shine down on the bricks that are supposed to keep us all safe.

And dragons are real.

I might not understand how this is at all possible, or what it means for the Riverwood and our plans to take on our new positions with as little drama as possible, but I laugh in spite of myself.

This man straight out of my daydreams is here. He's really *here*.

More importantly, the dragons I've always dreamed of are *real*.

And somehow, the most unlikely person in the world—me—has gone and set one free.

5

WHEN I MAKE IT BACK INSIDE, MY FRIENDS ARE still standing in the foyer, but Azrael isn't with them. Frost is glaring toward the archway that leads into the living room, while Rebekah is eyeing him like she expects an explosion. Zander and Ellowyn are studying Emerson, who looks . . .

Thunderstruck.

Not something we often see on our fearless leader.

"He . . . A dragon just called a meeting of the Riverwood." She blinks a few times, then shakes her head. "*I* call the meetings. *I* am the Confluence Warrior. Even when I didn't know who I was, I called the meetings."

Jacob rubs her back sympathetically, but his expression is amused. It's not often someone comes along and tries to upend the natural order of Emerson.

"Shake a leg, witches. We don't have *forever*," Azrael calls from the large living room where we often hold our meetings.

Emerson's stricken look quickly changes into her usual focus mixed with irritation, and woe betide the dragon who gets in her way. She marches into the living room and the rest of us exchange a look, then follow.

Azrael is standing in front of the stone hearth that now has a robust fire crackling in it when I know it didn't before. More than that, he's standing in Emerson's usual spot.

I get the strangest feeling he knows that.

But she marches right up to him. "Azrael," she says, and her voice is calm. Reasonable. Even friendly, which is one of the reasons she's so good at local, human-facing politics too. "I am the leader of this coven. A coven that certainly wants to help you, as we all want an end to the Joywood's reign of terror. But you've been stuck in a newel post for quite some time. You don't know—"

"You're right. I've been stuck in that newel post for a century or more." He waves at the shattered remains of it at the foot of the stairs, just visible from where he stands. "But I have seen and heard everything that's gone on around me. If it was anywhere near the stairs, I saw it. And I've heard pretty much everything that's been spoken on this ground floor. You're not exactly quiet, Emerson." Then he looks at me, and I don't know what I'm supposed to do with the ways his *glances* shiver through me. "Dragons have excellent hearing."

"How excellent?" Ellowyn demands suspiciously.

Azrael offers her a look, that dragony grin taking over his mouth. "Irrelevant, though should you ever see your ghosts again, you might want to let them know that although most of the people in the house can't see them, *I* certainly could."

Ellowyn's jaw kind of drops, and Zander gets a look like horror on his face. They both met their ghostly ancestors last month after a summoning gone awry, and were fond of them, so I'm not sure why they're having this kind of reaction—

But Azrael is already moving on. "The first order of business has to be—"

Emerson makes a sound. Kind of like a shriek, but with more temper. "You can't decide the order of—"

"—obtaining a new Praeceptor. Because Nicholas Frost, traitor to magic, won't do."

We all straighten at that, less amused than before.

Frost says nothing. He looks dark and stormy, as usual.

But Rebekah crosses her arms over her chest, her eyes narrowed and fury radiating off her. "Or we could get rid of the asshole dragon who literally *just* appeared after having been *kindling* for the past century."

"Azrael. Clearly you don't understand what happened on Litha," I offer, trying to find some rational ground here. "None of us would be here without Frost. He—"

"Sacrificed himself?" Azrael shrugs as if it was nothing. "After a literal millennium of living as an immortal. Something he was able to do because he was an integral part of a dark, sick coven who used evil for their own gain."

Everyone looks at Frost, who still denies nothing. Whether that's because he doesn't remember, or doesn't want to, I'm not sure—but I can't remember him ever defending himself, even when he could remember all the things he's done.

Emerson butts in again, sounding less patient than before. "We appreciate your support, and we'll protect you in whatever ways we can, but you don't have a say in the makeup of our coven."

He nods. "*Our* coven."

She frowns at him. "That's what I said."

Azrael shakes his head. "You can't become the ruling coven without a magical creature. And you can't live forever without sacrificing the magical creature in your coven after ruling for a hundred years, even if it's a lowly *ramidreju* weasel."

We all frown at that, as if a weasel should mean something to us. As if it does. I have come to suspect that this sort of thing is another little bit of evidence that the Joywood have messed with something.

But Azrael is still speaking. "This is the reason why the Joywood killed or cursed us all. They wanted to make sure they were the last coven that could achieve immortality, ever. They wanted to be the last ones standing."

He says this like it's a law. Like it's common knowledge.

When we all look at him blankly, he's clearly baffled. "You don't *know* this? I thought you were just making do because you couldn't find any of us."

"I don't buy it," Rebekah says then. She's clearly angry. And it's no surprise why. She doesn't just love Frost. She knows he risked everything to save her.

"I don't think he's wrong," Frost says. Stiffly. "I was part of a ruling coven. I don't remember anything about what we did to become one or what became of my coven, but I do not think he's wrong."

Azrael looks around with satisfaction, but I don't think any of us feel satisfied. I certainly don't. We'd be lost without Frost, no matter what misdeeds he might have done during his long, long life.

"It doesn't matter," Emerson says quietly. "What happened is in the past. We'd all make terrible mistakes if given a millennium to make them. What's important is the here and now, and that means making sure the Joywood are well and truly stopped. Frost is our Praeceptor."

"Then I will not be your dragon."

"I'm not certain we need a dragon," Emerson says, but not meanly. She's trying to be careful. A fair leader. "But we will protect you all the same."

He snorts, a very dragon kind of noise. "I do not need protection from a bunch of *witches*."

"If the Joywood wanted to wipe out all magical creatures, it isn't safe for you," I say, sounding a little too much like Rebekah just did. Angry. I laugh, trying to be the airhead I'm not. "I mean . . . is it?"

His gaze lifts to mine, and I can't read these dark gold dragon glances. I'm usually good at taking the temperature of any room I enter and every person I meet, making sure I project the image I want them to take away. But he's different.

I can't read him at all.

"You'll find the answers, Georgina," he tells me in that silken, knowing way of his. "And then you'll understand that you need me."

Everyone looks at me. And I feel that *fatefulness* rising inside me—but I shove it down. This is about *reason*. "Of course I'll do research on the matter. The way I always do."

He nods, as if he's won here. It's disconcerting. "Very well. Once you prove what I already know to be true, we'll reconvene."

I think Emerson's head might be ready to explode, but when she speaks, she's still her calm self, every inch the leader. "Azrael, for your own safety, you should probably go back into the newel post until—"

"Try it," he suggests, with clear, dark, and malicious intent. "And see what happens."

Jacob's eyes glow in clear warning at that. He's a quiet one, our Healer, but he doesn't take threats to our Warrior—his fiancée—kindly.

I have to solve this. "You can't just saunter down Main Street as a dragon. Or even go wandering around in your *man* costume."

"I do not wear costumes. I am not a Halloween party trick. I am an ancient and unknowable force that cannot be contained in a single—"

"Shifters," Frost says, as if he's tired. And possibly bored. When Azrael glares at him, it's his turn to shrug. "That's the word they use to describe what it is you and the other magical creatures do. You *shift*."

How he manages to make the delivery of that information an insult is its own master class, but I'm focused on the dragon, who looks like his temper might get the better of him and turn flamey at any moment.

"The Joywood will know, if they don't already," I say softly. And since they haven't appeared to strike him down, I assume they don't yet. But they *could*. "They'll figure it out. That's what they do."

His eyes are more gold than they were before, and I feel all the hairs on the back of my neck prickle. "I will not be cursed and trapped again."

"That's fair," I say hurriedly, because my friends didn't see him in his dragon form. They don't know what all that gold means. And they clearly can't *feel* it like I can. "But what about a compromise? I'm assuming you can't do some kind of glamour, or you all would have done that to keep from getting killed and cursed."

"With access to dark magic, powerful witches can sense our magic, no matter what," Azrael says mirthlessly, looking Frost's way again, but at least there's slightly less gold in his gaze. "They feed off it."

"What if we all did a spell?" Emerson suggests when it looks like Rebekah, always *this close* to chaos, might try to take a swing at him. "We can pool all our magic together to create a tighter, more armored glamour. To actually hide what you are. Maybe even strong enough to ward off their dark magic. We've had plenty of run-ins with it this year. We can fight it."

Ellowyn, who hid her own pregnancy for months, studies Azrael dubiously. I can't help but do the same. Hiding *all that* seems unlikely.

More than unlikely—undoable.

"It's possible." Frost takes a moment to say that, as if he's going through that glorious library of his in his head. "With our power and the right spell."

"I wouldn't trust you to make me dinner," Azrael growls.

Frost actually smiles at that, a cold curve of his admittedly beautiful face. "I might not remember everything, but I know better than to break bread with a fire-breathing worm."

"I'll work with Frost to create the spell," I jump in then, before the serpent in question decides to demonstrate his fire.

I'm not sure why I think Frost trusts me. But he does. Or he always acts as if he *might*, which with Frost is as good as the real thing. "I'll make sure it's correct. We'll cast it together. And if it works, then we can say you're some . . . long-lost Wilde cousin, or something."

"The Joywood have access to all the family trees by way of your foolish witchlore archives." Azrael studies me even more intently. "As will you once the Cold Moon rises and you get access to the archives. They'll know I'm no Wilde." I'm not certain why it seems like he's leaving off a bit of information there, but what am I certain about when it comes to him?

"Georgie can say that she brought a human home from England." I look at Ellowyn when she says that. She is decidedly *not* looking at me. "She can tell everyone he followed her back to St. Cyprian," she continues merrily. "That it was love at first sight in the British archives or whatever and *such* a strong connection that they couldn't be parted."

She waves a hand and smiles, guilelessly. When she is never *guileless*.

"You want me to pretend to be in love with a dragon," I say flatly. I do not look at the dragon in question. I tamp down the mess in me even more ruthlessly. "And vice versa. Is this a pregnancy brain lapse or something more serious?"

"What about Sage?" Emerson asks before I can laugh uproariously.

And she asks it *gently*.

I want to scowl. Instead, I plaster on my best dreamy smile, because if they try to console me, I will lose it. "Funny you should mention that," I murmur. "Sage and I have mutually decided to part ways."

Maybe I can keep the cheating a secret. Especially the part involving the dreadful Cailee.

Emerson frowns at me. "When did this happen?"

"Gradually," I say, happy that I do not share Ellowyn's inability to lie. "But coming home finalized the feeling of having grown apart." Emerson reaches out for me, but I just keep smiling. And don't let her touch me. "It's fine. For the best, obviously. A good experience, but one I'll move on from now. Ellowyn's plan is great."

It's not. It's horrible. Pretending I'm in love with a *dragon*? While also pretending he's not a *dragon*? It sounds like a recipe for disaster.

Particularly when it's *this* dragon.

When it's *him*.

Yet somehow, it's better than everyone being *careful* around me over a man I thought I *should* date, who didn't break my heart, but betrayed me all the same.

"Tomorrow I'll go to Frost's library, and we'll try to come up with a spell," I say. "But for tonight? You guys, I'm exhausted. And it's Thanksgiving."

Everyone murmurs assent at that, more or less. But before I can magic myself away from this mess and up into my bedroom, Emerson takes me by the arm and steers me deeper into the room, so it's just the two of us having a conversation while everyone else . . . flees.

Okay, maybe they just pair off and leave, but it looks a lot like *fleeing* when I can't do it myself.

"Are you sure you're okay? I know you really . . . *liked* him," Emerson offers.

Because she's a good friend. My *best* friend.

I smile at her. Not too brightly. Just enough to make it look like I'm *sadly brave* but not fully heartbroken. "I'm okay. It really was the best thing."

"I'm glad you figured that out. You deserve so much better." She hugs me tight, and I know she means *so well*.

But I'm lying to her, so her meaning well just makes me feel awful.

"I really am exhausted, Em. It's been a long day."

"Get some rest. And . . . I can come up with a different idea. You don't have to pretend to be in love with a man-dragon."

I wish I believed that was in the cards, but I'm not going to argue with Emerson. "We'll see. Good night."

I don't magic myself to my room after she leaves. I look around, half expecting—

The house is quiet. Everyone's gone.

I sigh, and decide to walk up the stairs because it's such a habit. I like to put my hand over Azrael as I go. Maybe talk to him a little bit.

But there's just a broken newel post now, and I stare at it.

He's real. He's a whole dragon. It's all *real*.

And I need some serious sleep before I can even begin to figure out how to deal with that. I take the steps with a certain resoluteness, as if the act of climbing them is how I'll shake off this day. I make it to the third-floor turret and walk down the hall, running my hand over the half-cracked door to my library as I pass it. Once I finally make it to my room at the far end, cozy and light and *home*, I'm ready to just collapse into bed and sleep for twelve hours straight.

But my room isn't empty.

Azrael is standing in the middle of it with his arms crossed over his impressive chest.

And he smiles at me, but it doesn't feel like happiness or joy or even kindness.

It feels like passion. It feels like danger. It feels like the wildest daydreams I've ever had.

All over me.

6

"WHAT . . . ARE YOU DOING IN HERE?" I MANAGE to ask him, despite that shivery sensation that's making my skin prickle. "This is *my* room." I remind myself that he's been living in a newel post for at least a century, apparently, so he might not know where to go. "I'll find a room on the second floor for you to—"

"I've always wondered what your room looked like." He wanders from one side of the room to the other, studying the crystals littered on every surface, the stacks of books, the old photographs propped up everywhere and pinned to the walls, and the dried-out flower wreaths hanging from ancient hooks.

"Why?" I hear myself ask, because I cannot fathom why a *dragon* would have even the slightest interest in my *room*.

"You can tell a lot about a witch by the place they rest and practice their most intimate magic." He doesn't look at me when he says that, so there's no reason for me to feel suddenly overwarm. He's obviously only talking about spellwork. Azrael looks over at me then, his eyes gleaming. "I always make it a habit to study the private domains of my Historians."

My Historians. "What do you mean, *your* Historians?"

"Dragons are always assigned to protect Historians." When I only stare back at him, his expression shifts into that same astonishment. "Not even this has survived as common knowledge?"

I shake my head. The idea of a protector is ludicrous—who would bother with a Historian enough for them to need protecting? From what? Bookworms and dust?

And even if I thought that reading was more fraught with peril than it is, here's what I know for a fact: Every single one of the women in my coven has been directly targeted by the Joywood this past year . . . if not over the course of their whole lives.

Except me.

No one cares what Historians do. Why would magical creatures?

I try not to sound as dubious as I feel. "All dragons protected all Historians? Throughout history, even though that's lost to us?"

"No, not all." He settles back on his feet, and I think about his dragon form, all sinuous, gleaming muscles and talons, not so much *standing* in the front hall as *conquering* it. "Not all Historians are worthy of protection, and no one can tell a dragon what to do if they do not wish to do it."

He stares at me then, something pulsing between us that feels just out of my grasp.

"I was the protector of another Wilde Historian, once upon a time," he says very quietly, studying me with an intensity that makes me feel like someone else entirely. "Why do you think I got cursed into this house?"

But I can't think of one Wilde that's ever been a Historian. Not in the last century or the five before. "What Wilde Historian? When?"

That intensity morphs into irritation. "How can there be so much you do not know?" he demands. "I gave the lot of you far too much credit, I think, from my position as observer."

His frustration pokes at my temper. Normally I would say

I don't have one, because I know how to control it. It was that or be like my parents, and I would rather my entire family think I'm a dingbat than be too much like them.

But the more tired I am, the more *pushed* I am, the more I have to admit that the truth is, I'm more like my mother than I want to admit.

I have a *terrible* temper.

It just takes a while to get me there.

And as I feel it boiling within me, I struggle to keep in mind that this is a *dragon*. I don't have to have vast experience with the species to suspect that blasting one with my entire and usually hidden temper is probably unwise. "We're just stupid, of course. I'm surprised that wasn't obvious from the newel post."

He makes a dragonish sort of scoffing sound, and I swear I see a little puff of flame snake out of his mouth as he does. "Witches are so touchy."

"Witches have been dealing with the psychotic, powerful, and tangled web of lies the Joywood has had in place for who knows how long," I shoot back at him. "The Joywood have obscured and changed what they could. Records go missing. Books that should exist don't. Frost has some of the missing pieces in his library, but you have to know what to look for to find it. It's hard to know what's hidden and what's an outright lie when it's not only all you've ever known, but they've done everything they can to wipe away the memories they don't want any of us to have." Like *dragons* and *mermaids*. "Take you and Melisande, the mermaid." A thought occurs to me, and I frown at him. "Is there . . . anyone else in Wilde House?"

"I don't know." He sounds unconcerned. "Melisande was the only one I could see."

I try a different tack. "What magical creatures were here in town with you before the killings? The curses?"

"Too many to name." But he considers. "In St. Cyprian,

specifically, there was a Fenrir, a handful of fairies, centaurs, basilisks, griffins, and so on."

I think about all the things around town in the shape of these creatures. Sage's spigot. A post on Main Street in the shape of a griffin. There's a little fairy trapped in stained glass in my childhood bedroom. I can see her from my window here in Wilde House.

It's so much to take in.

Because it's not just another secret—I think if it was *one* dragon in *one* newel post, I'd be able to cope with it more easily. Even with all the ramifications.

But we're not talking about a single act. We're talking about the Joywood targeting all the magical creatures there were. Killing them outright. Cursing them into hiding, and then erasing them from history. Turning them into fairy tales or dinosaurs, little more than acts of imagination on the part of children before they grow up. Not just to gain immortality, but to ensure they're the only ones who can.

I already thought the Joywood were evil.

But this is next-level.

"When I go to Frost's tomorrow to work on the spell for your glamour, I'll see if he has any books about magical creatures. Perhaps that will help fill in some blanks."

Azrael scowls at me. "You trust Frost. A murderer."

I blow out a breath. "Frost has never pretended to be a good man. We all knew from the start that you don't become an immortal from doing good things. Maybe that's why I trust him. There's no bluster, no pretension. Has your life been blameless, Azrael?"

Another scoffing sound. "Dragons don't believe in blame."

"But it sounds like you blame Frost when there's the whole Joywood wandering around, ripe for a little blame of their own. They're the ones who actually cursed you, aren't they?"

"Dragons don't blame *ourselves*. Dragons, by definition, are blameless." That grin of his is a weapon. I'm not sure he needs the smoke and flame, the claws and the tail. These things I can feel all around us, even though I can't see them. "Witches, on the other hand, we can and do blame for everything. You deserve it."

I roll my eyes. What ridiculousness.

And only after I finish the eye-rolling do I think to question what he might blame me for, since I'm the only witch in the room.

"You said you were tired," he reminds me, and then he smiles with a kindness I don't trust for one second. "You should rest."

I would love to agree, but there's something about the way he says it. About the way he's studying my window. "And what are you going to do?"

He flicks a wrist and my window opens, though it is not an opening kind of window and shouldn't have obeyed someone else's magic anyway. I have wards to prevent that.

"I'm going to fly." And he's starting to change . . . scales and smoke and eyes of gold. "Are you coming with me?"

I think to myself that I have never wanted anything more in all my life.

And it sears through me like scalding heat.

I tell myself it's irritation.

"Azrael, you cannot go around *flying* in your dragon form. The Joywood will see it or sense it or—"

"Then I'll go alone."

I can't let him do that, for reasons that feel like more of that scalding heat, but I rush forward anyway. With the idea that I'll reach out and somehow hold him in place, but he's smoke.

But it's not *just* smoke, because the smoke grabs me. Out the window I go, somehow, against my will. Or it would be against my will, surely, if I had access to anything that felt like will instead of that heat that is like a pulse in me, deep and wild.

And as we go, the smoke and scales come together to form that gigantic dragon I first saw erupt from the newel post.

I can feel him become corporeal. I can feel the strength of him, the heat. It meets that pulse in me and adds to it, like we're both a part of that *humming*.

And then we're flying. Soaring through the dark night sky, him with his wings stretched out wide and me on his back like I belong there. Like I've done this a million times before.

Something in me seems to shift, then settle at that, like I really have.

But all I can think is that I am *flying* on a *dragon*.

And I want to laugh. I want to throw my arms up toward the stars, the moon. I want to *sing*.

It's just like my book, I think.

Except better. Much, much better than any fairy tale could ever describe. Because I finally feel . . . at home.

Like I was made for this. For him.

This soaring, scalding, pulsing *yes* that turns me inside out, and I love it.

It's not just the pretty lights of St. Cyprian and all the other towns along the river that sparkle down below us. It's not the simple truth that flying and the magic that lets us all do it are wonderful things to experience on their own—because this is nothing like that.

Flying on a dragon's back is nothing like flying on my own.

Flying on this *dragon's back*, I correct myself, because I know with a certainty that feels old and weathered within me that this is an experience that is singular to him.

To him and me.

Like I've been waiting to finally meet him all my life, and all this heat and *certainty* inside me is recognition.

Azrael dips and rolls, and I can feel *his* delight, *his* freedom. He makes no noise, so I don't either. We're nothing but wings and his raw, earthy magic, starshine and moonlight.

We're *us*.

We rise and plummet, soar and roll, and I think, *Finally. We're* us.

Maybe the Joywood *can't* feel this, and wouldn't even if we flew straight at them. That even if they could feel us up here, they wouldn't understand it.

Because what do they know about a joy so deep and encompassing that it feels like an ache? Something almost like grief. Something that wide and exhaustive, but threaded through with dragon gold.

I don't know how far we go or how long we're gone. It could be a string of forevers, all that same sweet rush of tumbling through the sky.

It feels as if we've lived each one. A thick and colorful bouquet of lives, the two of us intertwined—

Though witches don't believe in reincarnation. That's for other beings, perhaps, but not us. We live too long, some say. We are already too magical, claim others, and cherish our ability to go to the other side and still affect those back here.

Eventually Azrael circles back from forever to St. Cyprian and to Wilde House, rising up from its part of Main Street with all of its usual authority and grace. And just as I was pulled out of my bedroom in the first place, I'm swept back in on a wave of blue-and-green smoke that morphs from scale to man as we go.

It's exhilarating. It *aches*. It's too much.

Now we're standing in my room once more, but we're both a little windswept. Our eyes are shining from the cold air and glowing from all that magic. I can see myself in my mirror. I can see it all over him.

And his eyes are gold and on me.

The way he's looked at me a thousand times before, I think—

But no. That's not possible.

Too many emotions are battering around inside of me, almost too much to bear. If he were anyone else, I'd probably let myself cry, because sometimes tears are the only way to get things out. But Azrael isn't anyone else.

I don't know what to do with him.

He moves toward me, two meaningful strides that almost have us *touching*—

But I move back because everything in his gold-and-onyx eyes is too much, too confronting. Too much *recognition*, when this morning I *knew* that dragons weren't real.

Trouble is, there's nowhere to go.

I run into the wall. I'm trapped unless I want to magic myself away, and that seems a bit risky with my heart trembling inside my chest.

And when the only thing in my head, in my heart, in every part of my body, is him.

He leans forward, so close I can feel the dragon heat of him, the way I did out there beneath the moon. Not just the heat in me, but the heat he gives off, like a furnace.

Deep inside, underneath all my layers of body and magic, something in me relaxes, as if it's finally found a soft place to land.

Home, I think again.

His eyes glitter. "You are brave, Georgina Pendell, though you try to hide it."

"Don't be ridiculous," I tell him. "I'm a Historian."

Not brave. Not *special*, Hecate forbid. Just . . . smart and organized and careful.

The way a Historian is supposed to be. Just ask my entire family tree.

"Careful," he sniffs, apparently reading my mind. Again. Which is a thought I can't quite take on board in the middle of this moment. When he moves away from me, I tell myself I'm relieved. "You would do well to accept yourself, Georgina. Denying who you really are gets us nowhere."

Us.

I'm standing there with my back pressed up against the wall, and he's prowling through my room. I think maybe he's going to leave, and I'm wondering which room in this house he'd consider an appropriate place for an ancient mythic dragon to sleep now that he's real—

But then, in an elegant move that makes my mouth go dry, Azrael stretches out on my bed instead.

On *my* bed.

He links his fingers behind his head, closes his eyes, and lets out one long sigh. Like he's . . . going to sleep.

Like he's *already* halfway there.

Like he . . . expects me to crawl right up next to him and snuggle in like he's my cat familiar and not . . . *him*?

"That's my *bed*," I say incredulously.

But I'm quite certain he's already happily asleep. And even if he wasn't, he doesn't care one bit.

7

LATER, TUCKED INTO ONE OF THE GUEST bedrooms a floor down, I don't think about how long I stood there, just staring at Azrael in my bed. I don't think about that scalding heat or that wildfire recognition that is still wreaking havoc on me.

Just like that pulse keeps kicking at me, like it's whispering, *Us. Us. Us.*

I don't think about soaring through the sky or that odd, shivery sensation that suggests none of this is *new*. Not really.

I tell myself that I'm being brave. Because it was rational and reasonable and *right* to remove myself from the situation. I was exercising the Pendell caution my mother has spent my life trying to instill in me.

I repeat that to myself until it almost drowns out that ache inside me, those little gleaming threads that I pretend I can't see, reaching out toward a conclusion I don't want to draw while I can still feel us gliding through the cold night like we make our own heat—

That's all future Georgie's problem, I tell myself as I let my eyes close on the longest Thanksgiving I can remember.

I quickly fall into a hard and dreamless sleep. When I wake up to morning light pouring in through the windows, I push myself into sitting position. I stretch and yawn, and then stop mid-stretch.

Because crystals dance in the air above me. *My* crystals.

Except I didn't enchant them to dance above me—though maybe I should have, because clearly they're the source of my amazing sleep.

It's just the type of thing Emerson would do. But I know her. More importantly, I know the crystals she'd choose for something like this, and it wouldn't occur to her to have them *dance* in the air above me. And not just because of the energy that would require.

She would have them ruthlessly organized around the bed. She would have chosen the *obvious* ones for good, protected sleep. Amethyst, quartz, citrine. Instead, the stones humming above my bed are in all blacks, greens, and blues. Like a *dragon* chose and charmed the onyx, tourmaline, serpentine, and sodalite.

I study them, recognize them. These crystals were all gifts. Anonymous gifts after moving into Wilde House. After I'd had bad nights, was upset about something or another, these crystals had just appeared in my collection over the years.

I thought they were sweet gestures from Emerson, who knows how hard I've tried to pretend my mother's disapproval doesn't get to me.

Now, in dragon colors dancing around me, I wonder.

I watch them for a minute, and then, before I can decide what to do, they all fall with a soft *thud* at the end of the mattress, just narrowly missing my feet. Almost at the same time, the door slams open, and Azrael stands there. In all his man-but-dragon state. "Finally."

"Do you *mind*?"

"Not at all." He prowls in like he owns the place. Perhaps

it doesn't occur to a dragon that he doesn't. He pokes around this room much the same way he did mine. Like every corner is fascinating.

"You charmed my sleep."

"You're welcome."

As if this reminds him, he sweeps a hand up, and the crystals rise up too. He closes his fist and they huddle together. Then, with a snap, they're gone.

I frown at him. And will obviously have to replace all my traitorous stones. Except . . . maybe they were never really mine. "You . . . gave me those. Over the years."

"You spent those years telling me your secrets and sorrows," he returns with an easy shrug. "You like stones. They cheered you up."

This is not an answer, but I find I suddenly don't want one. Not while he's looking at me with such . . . *intent*. Not when it feels like the kind of sweet gesture someone who knows me would make, but how could he know me?

He's been cursed in a newel post.

I'm distracted when Octavius hops up onto the bed with his usual orange potbellied *thunk*. He walks in three circles and then settles himself on my lap. It's his version of a welcome home, so I scratch his head until he purrs.

It's the first time I've felt actually *settled* since coming home. Unlike all the other familiars I know of, Octavius doesn't communicate with me. At least, not in my head with words. It's more I can . . . *feel* what he's thinking, and vice versa.

"Are you going to rise?" Azrael asks me irritably. He's staring at Octavius with a look I can't quite name. It's not predatory . . . *exactly*. It's *almost* the way he looks at Frost.

"Are you going to leave me be so I can do so in privacy?"

"Privacy." Azrael makes a scoffing noise, and a puff of his dragon smoke. "What about him?" He points at Octavius curled up in my lap.

"He's a familiar. He's a *cat*."

Azrael and Octavius regard each other. It's a strange standoff I can't quite figure out. Then Azrael stalks out of the room.

"As much as I don't like to be rushed, I do have a lot to do today. Luckily, the museum is closed for the holiday weekend. It'll give me some extra time to come up with this spell," I murmur to Octavius as I magic myself ready and catch him up on the happenings of my trip and return.

I don't mention Sage, but then, Octavius never cared for Sage. Much in the same way my friends didn't. Not with hisses or claws, but with careful distance.

Once I'm dressed and satisfied with the wildness of my hair, always a curly red problem, I call on a few of my crystals—the ones I found on my travels. They appear in my hand. I ask the amethyst for its calm and intuition, aquamarine for truth and clarity, and black tourmaline to shield me against negativity.

Including my own.

This is my usual morning ritual, and I enjoy it. When I'm done, I brace myself for all that *dragon* awaiting me. "I'm headed to Frost's library today," I tell Octavius as I open the bedroom door. "It's up to you whether you'd like to come with me or stay he—"

As I move into the hall, looking over my shoulder at Octavius, I slam right into a hard, hot wall of *muscle*.

Dragon muscle. In the shape of man.

I might have fallen back a bit at the contact, but Azrael's hand is on my arm. And he is holding me steady. And close.

Very close.

Close enough that I'm not sure I'm breathing. I don't even know how to characterize the reactions going on inside of my body. They're so *foreign*. They can't possibly be *me*. And yet, there's also that same strange *belonging* feeling from last night, centered in the very heart of me where I've always known my magic resides.

Confirming that no, I didn't make this up.

He feels like *home*. We feel like *us*. He gave me crystals to cheer me up. For years.

I don't know what to say or what to do—but that's enough to have me trying to pull away. For a moment, Azrael's grip tightens. He holds me even closer, and I swear to Hecate he just . . . sniffed my hair?

I should be appalled, but that is not how I would categorize the sensation that dances through me then, a bit of fuel to that deep, scalding fire.

Before I can comment on any part of that, his hand drops. And he's merrily off down the stairs, calling back to me as he goes. "Something smells delicious. Do you know how long I've been dreaming of these breakfasts you lot cook up?"

I can't seem to do anything but stand there in the hallway, completely and utterly at a loss. The past twelve hours have been nothing but new strange thing after new strange thing. The whole past year has been like this, so really, I should be used to it.

I'm a member of the ruling coven now. I've got to get myself together.

This is happening.

Which means I need to get to work. And trust Emerson and Jacob to entertain a dragon for the morning.

Besides, I'm too hopped up on crystals and flight to eat.

I could fly to Frost's, but I walk out into the morning instead because I clearly need some grounding. I take deep breaths in the cold air and amuse myself with exhalations that make clouds and look like dragon smoke.

This walk is good for me. I can feel my body respond to the movement, the cold. The fresh air on my face. I walk down Main Street toward Frost's eyesore on the hill and take these few minutes to find my inner self. The Historian in me. The researcher. Everything I've been up until now. Everything I am.

The river murmurs along in my peripheral vision the way it always does. The river that makes this a river town. The river that joins two others and tangles into a knot of power.

The water calls to me, and while it always does, even this winter version of it seems to have more pull than usual.

I tell myself that this is just another reaction to the *dragon* of it all.

That the reality of dragons and magical creatures and curses doesn't change anything for me, even if it feels like Azrael is trying to make it seem like it might, what with *dragon rides* and this . . . *reaction* to him.

I can still feel that heat inside me, prickling just beneath my skin.

I climb the stairs in the hill up to Frost's house. When I make it to his glamoured door, feeling windswept and cold but hopefully clear of mind, I don't have to knock. The door opens for me. No one's waiting there, but I know how to find the way.

Even though the hallways shift about at their leisure, if I keep my destination in mind, they deliver me where I need to go.

When I make it to the library, Rebekah is already there, slouched down in a chair at one of the intricately wrought, polished wooden tables. No sign of Frost, though I look around like he might be hanging from the chandelier or something. She smiles when she sees me and waves for me to come closer.

"We've been pulling books," Rebekah tells me. "Anything we think might apply. Nicholas will let you take some of them. Others are charmed to remain here—but you know the drill. He came across something about a book somewhere in Germany he thinks will help, so he went to get it. He'll be back soon." She tips her head toward the books stacked up on the long table before her. "For now, you can look through these to your heart's content."

I glance at the stack of books with some relief. *This* is normal. *This* is where I shine. No dreamy smiles required—I can just read and let what I have always believed is the best part of my magic lead me where I need to go.

I take the first book off the top of the stack, open it, and begin to read through a compendium of the magical creatures that were said to have existed within witchdom, if only once upon a time.

Most I've heard of, if only in fairy tales. A few are entirely new to me. But when I make it to *unicorn*, I can't sink into the information the way I did with the rest. I look up at Rebekah, who's drawing on her tablet. Maybe I shouldn't ask, but . . .

"Do you think he really killed a unicorn?"

Rebekah looks up at me, setting down her pen. She's considering. Thoughtful. Not mad the way I half thought she might be—but then, she knows who her man is. "He doesn't remember anything, but I know *he* thinks he did." Rebekah sighs. "And, hey, it makes sense, right? Immortality requires terrible acts and, if the dragon is telling the truth, specifically *that* terrible act."

"We won't hold it against him. I hope he knows that. He's proven himself redeemed."

I thought that would have been obvious, but Rebekah takes her time nodding. "*We* won't hold it against him. But your dragon will. He already does."

It feels a bit unfair, this ownership. I didn't *mean* to free him, even if it was somehow me and that damn book. I ignore that growing feeling of *belonging* inside me when I think of him. I concentrate on *reality*. "He's not *my* dragon."

Rebekah's eyebrows rise, her expression going carefully bland. "I'm sure it was someone else riding on his back last night, then."

I can only stare at her. I have no quick lies. No ditzy smile. She . . . saw?

"Coronis," she offers, with a slight smile.

Frost's familiar. I don't know how I didn't see a giant, ancient raven trolling about the heavens, but I guess I was a little busy being wildly joyful that Azrael was wheeling me around and around the night sky.

Rebekah sets her tablet aside and comes to stand beside me. She puts her hand on my shoulder and looks down at me, her face not blank anymore.

I think what I see is compassion. I'm afraid it might be pity.

"Be careful, Georgie," she says quietly. "We don't know enough about dragons, and Nicholas certainly doesn't trust this one."

I try not to frown. "I'm always careful." Isn't the fact that I'm here poring over old tomes a case in point? The dragon ride was just . . . Azrael.

I tell myself that, stoutly. And then keep going. What am I supposed to do? Refuse a dragon? I tried, didn't I?

No one has to know about that pulse in me. *Us.* No one has to get the faintest hint that this all feels as familiar to me as if I've known him all my life. As if his appearance made all my years make sense at last.

Facts, I tell myself. *Not fiction and fairy tales.*

I open the next book, wanting to get back to where I'm comfortable. The text is written in very old German script, and years of going through old books mean I don't even have to mutter a translation spell to understand it. But still, it's very dry and boring.

I place my hands on the ancient pages, and let myself *feel*. The history, the power, the magic. I internally say the words that tend to help me find what I need.

Words of old, knowledge told, lead me to what must be exposed.

I let my eyes drift closed, the magic within me humming. And this feels *familiar* in a way that doesn't make me ache. *Good* when the past day has been so weird. For a moment, I feel the way I usually do. *Careful* and *rooted*. Once again—at last—I know exactly what and who I am, and have been.

Especially when my hands lift and pages turn of their own accord, then settle.

I open my eyes and survey the page the book wishes to show me. It's a drawing or a diagram of sorts. A rectangle that almost looks like it's meant to represent a table. In a very old language, it announces that this is the shape of a true coven.

For a second, I think of that Thanksgiving table I saw from outside. A full and happy table without me. How adding myself felt like an imbalance. I'm half afraid to look at the list of designations at each place along the table, for fear I won't be represented in any *true coven*.

But there are *eight* meticulously labeled places at this table, not the proper seven that I was always taught a coven needed, or even the six I was afraid were all that were really needed last night.

I stare at the page, feeling my pulse pick up as I try to take in what I'm seeing.

A Warrior is at the head. That's no surprise. On either side sit a Healer and a Diviner. Then a Guardian and a Revelare are the next two, seated across from each other in the middle seats. Then a Praeceptor and a Historian in the last two seats. On the end is a *fabulae*. A very, *very* old witch word for a magical creature.

Now whatever's happening with my pulse is making my heart slam against my ribs.

I scan down to the paragraph beneath the diagram. *A true coven is made up of its leader at the head and a fabulae at the end. They're buttressed on one side by hope: the future, the past, and the connection to both in the middle. On the other side, practicality: knowledge, healing, protection.*

I feel like I can hardly breathe. It's proof that Azrael is right. But more than that, it's a different understanding of what a coven is than we've ever had.

Because, a voice in me says with great authority, *they didn't want you to know. They didn't want anyone to know.*

Before I can beckon Rebekah over, Frost appears. He's holding a giant, ancient book that looks like it hasn't been opened in centuries, and might have been produced by hand. He drops it on the table in a way that makes the archivist in me wince.

"I think I've found a spell in this one that should work to shroud a magical creature's power," he says. "Should your dragon deign to trust us."

He's not my dragon. But I won't protest too much. I refuse.

And besides, there's that aching *thing* in me that makes a protest feel like a betrayal.

"Look at this," I say to the both of them. I point to the diagram and watch as he mutters a spell to translate it for Rebekah.

"This feels familiar," he says. Then he nods. "If this is right, and true, Azrael needs protection now more than ever. The Joywood certainly won't want us to have access to him. They won't want us to have the opportunity to become a *true* coven, whatever that means."

It's hard to think of Azrael as being in trouble, considering the size and strength of him in *man* form, let alone his dragon form. But if the Joywood cursed him once, they can do it again. Last night was a risk, a bad risk.

So Frost is right. He needs protection, whether he wants it or not.

Before I can think about that, or deal with the shrouding spell Nicholas has brought, my gaze lands on a stack of books. On the top is the same slim little paperback fairy tale I've had since I was small.

Only instead of the usual scene on the cover, the dragon isn't flying.

He's falling. And *bleeding*.

And I don't think.

I don't do anything but *react*.

I'm back in Wilde House in the blink of an eye—a literal blink. I look around wildly, dropping my stack of books in much the same way Frost dropped the ancient one just minutes ago.

I don't see or hear anyone, so I shout out. "Azrael?"

No response. My heart is beating triple-time as I pulse out my magic to feel him, find him. *Save him.*

I feel nothing and I can barely breathe, the panic is so sharp. I transport myself into my room to grab my clear quartz wand and my athame, my mind geared for a fight. But when I arrive in my turret, I realize it is not empty.

Octavius is curled up on my window seat, calm and sleepy. And Azrael is right there. I get the impression of a huge, scaled tail swirling around the room, long and sinuous, but it's only an impression. As if I'm seeing it without actually seeing it.

He's lounging on my bed, reading one of my books. My crystals are scattered . . . everywhere. On the bed, on the floor, in the air.

And he is not bleeding. He does not appear hurt in any way. He looks as if he's relaxing and having a grand old time with *my things*.

"You're . . . okay?" I'm panting, willing my heart rate to slow, trying to find some much-needed calm amidst the panic—

And I'm not sure I want to parse the *levels* of my panic, either.

I'm afraid they would answer each and every question I don't want to ask.

He lifts an eyebrow, studying me with those golden onyx eyes. "Was there some doubt?"

"I . . ." I'd feel stupid if I wasn't still trying to catch my breath. I look down at my hands, and while I dropped all the other books in the foyer, I'm still holding the slim fairy-tale book in one hand. I don't know what else to do but hold out the cover, so he can see what I saw.

Azrael sits up, a lazy demonstration of his impossible physique, and studies the picture. He doesn't seem alarmed or upset in any way. He nods. As if to say, *Of course, there it is.* "Gruesome."

"It changed," I tell him, with a little too much heat, because he should *get* this, surely. "You—"

But just because there's a dragon and a girl with red hair on the cover, it doesn't mean they're *us*.

Embarrassment crashes over me, pushing past the worry and panic.

Azrael rises up from the bed in a manner that manages to be athletic and graceful at once, and crosses to me. He takes the book, then steers me to the cozy chair in the corner of the room that looks toward the turret windows. I like to curl up here, read, and drink my tea. He nudges me to sit down, and then a mug of tea appears on the little table next to the chair.

Like he's . . . taking care of me. *Nurturing* me, even. Which makes zero sense.

"Why are you . . ."

I don't even know how to finish the sentence. Because it's the strangest situation I've ever been in—and I've dealt with ghosts and muting hexes and talking statues this year, just to name a few of the highlights.

It's clear Azrael does as he pleases, but something about *me* and helping *me* seems to be what he pleases.

I don't know what to do with this. Or I do know, but I won't. Particularly when he crouches next to the chair so we're almost eye level, lifts the teacup, and hands it to me. There's gold threaded in the black of his gaze. And there's danger and mayhem stamped all over him, but something different at the center. Something calm and sure and . . .

"You've been a faithful friend to me, Georgina," he says, very seriously.

My heartbeat kicks up again. "I didn't know you were *real*."

He cocks his head, looking almost amused. Almost. "Didn't you?"

I don't know how to answer that. I always thought he was an

enchantment because that's what made the most sense. A spell, not a *dragon*. A magical newel post, not a sentient being.

But if I sit here and think on it, whether the realistic Historian part of me tried to rationalize it away or not, I treated him like he was real. Having *conversations* with him. Calling it sleepwalking when I knew full well what I was doing. What I was dreaming.

What I've been dreaming my whole life. Innocently, when I was small.

Much less innocently as I came of age.

And it was *real*, because he left me trinkets to cheer me up. Because when he spoke in my head, however infrequently, it was *him*. Real this whole time.

Mine this whole time.

He pushes the tea at me once more. I take it, breaking his gaze because it feels like all that black and gold has rearranged something inside of me. Or maybe burned away some strange little walls I didn't know were there, keeping all my selves compartmentalized.

Be more *fanciful, Georgie*, I tell myself harshly, the way my mother would. And I take a big, bracing sip of the too-hot tea.

"Georgie?"

It's Rebekah shouting from downstairs. *We're coming*, I tell her in our inner coven channel.

I put down the teacup. "Rebekah and Frost were with me." I push to my feet. "I'm sure they're worried too."

Azrael makes a noise that is *not* agreement, but he doesn't argue. He follows me out of the room, shooting an irritable glance at Octavius when he winds his way in front so that he's walking between us.

We head downstairs and find Rebekah and Frost in the entryway. Frost has the giant ancient book from Germany that I left behind. Rebekah looks ready to fight, until she sees Azrael behind me.

"Everything's okay, I take it?"

"For now," Azrael says, holding up the book. "I suppose you all think this means I've been threatened."

"Sort of a rational conclusion to draw," Rebekah returns.

But Frost shakes his head. "That book is not dark magic. It's no friend to the Joywood. What it *could* be is a harbinger of what's to come. So, not a threat. A warning."

Azrael looks at the cover again, considering the illustration. "It would take considerable magic to kill me. If the Joywood could have managed it, they would have done so years ago, and with great glee." He looks up, that dragon grin on his face. "They did not."

Frost lifts a shoulder. "Unless all their dabbling in dark magic has made them stronger than they were when they cursed you. Or since it's *only* you now, instead of the entirety of some magical creature populace, it would be easy."

"You would know how that works, of course," Azrael responds silkily.

But Frost doesn't rise to the bait. "We should do the spell to shroud you sooner rather than later," he says. "Unless you wish to test this theory of yours."

Azrael laughs, but it's a bitter sound as he comes around me as if preparing to fight. "Let's not pretend you care about my fate."

"I care about the fate of the Riverwood." Frost looks grim then, not his usual coolly sardonic self. "And it's clear from the books and from what little I can remember that you're right, dragon. The fate of the Riverwood rests on having a magical creature as part of its coven."

I take a deep breath. Then I reach out and put my hand on the big, muscled, dragony shoulder that is still higher than mine, though he's two steps below me.

I will catalog the wildfire that roars in me at that touch later. I will analyze the fact that my palm feels scalded. I will probably dream about the slow way he turns, and the hunger in his dark gaze when it meets mine.

I will spend a long time sifting through the feeling of *fate* in my veins, like desire.

But right now I need him to understand, truly, that he's a target. And that we need him to live.

That *I* do, though I'm not ready to think about that either. "And, Azrael, you're the only magical creature we've got."

8

FROST AND I SPEND THE AFTERNOON WORKING on the spell while Rebekah, Smudge, and Octavius do their best to keep Azrael occupied.

I remind myself, repeatedly, that while he didn't exactly pledge himself to our cause earlier when I pointed out that he was our only magical creature, he . . . looked at me, very intensely, for a long while. Then nodded—a quiet acquiescence that would be a whole pep rally of support from someone else.

Though I can't think of anyone else who's ever simply *nodded* at me and made me feel something alarmingly close to giddy.

Even hours later.

When Emerson gets home from Confluence Books, I'm alone in the kitchen making brownies for the meeting we'll have—by hand, not magic, as handmade brownies are a critical component of all coven gatherings. Grandma Wilde passed this recipe on to me, and I take the making of them as seriously as she did.

I am definitely not avoiding Rebekah's too-knowing glances my way, or any dragons or post-immortals.

My best friend comes charging into the kitchen the way she

has a million times before in our lives, and we fall into the patterns we've had as friends and housemates. She tells me about her Black Friday sale as a small, independent bookstore owner, and the crowds on the street that make her hopeful that more people are shopping local this year.

There might be a few fist pumps, as punctuation.

In turn, I catch her up on the happenings of the day. Not just the spell Frost and I have worked on for hours, but the *true coven* and *fabulae* business. I draw her the diagram we found, there in the air between us.

Emerson leans against the counter, running her finger through the batter in the bowl now that I've got the brownies in the oven, then licking it off. "The dragon really wasn't making that up."

She sounds surprised. I tell myself I have no reason to be *this* surprised at her surprise, but I am. "Why would you assume he was?"

Emerson laughs. "It's been a long year, Georgie. Even I can't drum up automatic trust for a dragon that pops out of my newel post. Particularly when he spent the morning telling me how *important* he is. That's rarely the case for truth."

I have to nod at that. "Fair."

We shift back to a discussion of chamber of commerce concerns—concerns I suspect Emerson will have to set aside once she's fully vested as the new head of the ruling coven, but no one dares get between Em and her beloved St. Cyprian festivals. Or skyrocketing tourist rates. And as she's telling me her plans for this year's Christmas Around the World extravaganza, I feel Azrael coming before he appears.

Don't be so silly, I chide myself. It's just a prickle on the back of my neck. It's late November, and this is an old house, so it's probably just a draft.

But then there he is, prowling his way into the sweet old kitchen that holds approximately 98 percent of my happy childhood memories, thanks to Emerson's late grandma.

The remaining happy memories from way back involve libraries.

"Are we ever going to get this nonsense started?" he asks.

"Some of us have jobs, Azrael," Emerson responds, but merrily, as if he should think that's fun and wish he had a job too.

I doubt very much he thinks or wishes anything of the kind when he studies her the way he does. "How *human*."

He peers at the bowl in Emerson's grasp, but most of the leftover batter is gone. I swear I see his wide shoulders sink fractionally, so I hand him the mixer paddles, and he lights up again.

I will not analyze why that gives me the warm fuzzies.

And the *much hotters* along with it.

After more Azrael complaints in the same vein—through mouthfuls of batter, which somewhat undercuts the *mighty and terrifying dragon* thing—the rest of the coven begins to trickle in. As he often does, Zander comes last and on the verge of late, muttering that the ferry schedules are demanding. We all know that's true. Since witches first showed up here, his family have been guarding the three rivers that form the confluence that gives this area its power and magic.

But he's also gotten more help in the nearly six months since his mother, Zelda, died. These days, his dad is doing much better, and they've hired a few more Guardians to help with things. That means Zander is looking ahead and making time not just to be part of the leading coven, but to be a father to the baby he and Ellowyn have coming.

If I think about how much things are changing, I might get dizzy—actually dizzy, not Georgie ditzy—so I don't.

We meet in the living room the way we always do, and everyone settles into their typical positions throughout the space. Everyone except me, that is. The leather armchair I usually curl up in with Octavius is just . . . not there.

"Where's the old armchair?" I ask, trying not to sound violated.

It's not *my* chair. This isn't *my* house.

Emerson waves a hand. "Oh, Mom said something about wanting to see how it fits in one of their reception rooms over at the embassy in Germany."

So . . . I have nowhere to sit.

That's silly, and I know it. There are plenty of other places to sit, like the rickety bench in the far corner. Away from the fire and the group. *It's fine.* I make my way over and refuse to admit to myself that it feels like I've been sent to the corner like some kind of naughty toddler.

I also refuse to admit I don't love that no one else seems to notice I've been relegated to the outskirts.

What I *can* admit is that I'm not fond of this much self-pity. It's flooding me like a rising river, and I hate it. I refuse to indulge it. I've never been one to wallow, and I'm not really sure why I can't seem to stop now.

I lounge on the bench like it's *five times* as comfortable as my usual seat.

"I have a sad announcement to make," Emerson says, and everyone stills. She blows out a heavy breath. "I won't be doing my traditional advent calendars this year."

For a moment, we all sit with that. I don't think I'm the only one who expects a follow-up, like a goblin attack or the rise of killer reindeer, but she doesn't go on.

"Um." I clear my throat. "Why, Em? You used to put so much work into them."

Her advent calendars were a whole event. Gift deliveries, flowers, once an entire costumed a cappella concert at each of our windows.

She smiles. "The work was the fun part," she says quietly. "I liked the idea that I could make Christmas magical for you guys. Now I have magic. It doesn't feel the same."

I feel my eyes tear up a little at that. Even Ellowyn looks suspiciously misty-eyed. Because getting her magic back has transformed Emerson, and us. It has turned us into the Riverwood. But there are losses too—even these silly ones.

I won't miss being assaulted by Christmas cheer at a different time every day in the lead-up to the big day, but part of me will always miss thinks-she's-human Emerson's delight in giving us her version of heedless holiday joy like that.

"Back to business," Emerson says in a brisker tone, and then dives into a quick recap of everything we know so far, catching up those who weren't around today. While the rest of us are seated and *never more* comfortable, indulging in the brownies and other snacks and pizza from Redbrick, Azrael paces restlessly around the room. I find myself watching him far more than I'm paying full attention to one of Emerson's *we've got this* monologues, even though this one is sprinkled with all the holiday glitter and cheer we won't be getting as a live advent situation this year.

But Azrael looks more like a dragon than a being in a supposedly humanish form should. He's just so . . . *dangerous*. And out of the corner of my eye, I can see the blue-and-green smoke, and the immensity of the real him. The tail and long, muscular body.

"When should we do the spell?" Emerson asks Frost.

"You can do a spell whenever you like, but without *him*," Azrael interrupts before Frost can answer. "I don't want him to be a part of it."

"He *needs* to be a part of it. He's part of the Riverwood. It will take our full power, all of our magic melding together to shroud a *dragon*," I say, hoping that appealing to the dragon-size ego in there will move the needle.

Azrael considers this for approximately zero seconds. "No."

"Maybe the Joywood can curse you into the ground this time," Rebekah offers with a sharp smile.

Azrael scowls at her. His pacing has led him closer to me, so I stand and put my hand on his arm, feeling the desperate need to get him to agree. I'm about ready to plead. "You trust me." *You've been a faithful friend.* "So trust me. Nothing bad will happen to you."

It's a big leap of a promise, because who knows what might happen? Magic is a temperamental thing, even when you know it in your soul. And that's not taking into account the dragon factor. Or the Joywood.

His dark eyes are on me, while threads of gold seem to dance. I feel that dance inside me, where my magic glows hot.

Ready for a spell, I tell myself. That's all it is.

But it's hard to remember that we're not alone.

"If you want to be part of the Riverwood, part of what comes next, part of defeating the Joywood once and for all, we'll need you in fighting form, Azrael," Emerson says. "Which means you cannot have a target on your back. They have to believe you're harmless."

Big ask. It's Azrael's voice inside my head. He hasn't done that since he was a newel post. It's significantly more disconcerting now, since the newel post wasn't the best conversationalist.

But we both turn to Emerson, my hand still on his arm. He gives the faintest of nods, and Emerson looks at Frost.

"Better to get it done now than wait for a special time," Frost says. "Every moment he's unshrouded is a ticking time bomb. Much like the dragon himself."

I feel Azrael's impressive biceps tense underneath my hand, which is distracting enough. Then he turns that dark, hot gaze on me. *I trust you, Georgina. Only you.*

My heart does that *thing* that only Azrael brings out in me. It's like panic and fear mixed with hope and joy, all of it wrapped up in *grief* and *yes* and that recognition I still want to deny. I don't like it at all. Too many complicated emotions when I prefer them to be straightforward. I can be sad or mad or happy or nervous, but I don't want to be *all of them.*

At the same time.

Though the way Azrael looks at me, it's hard not to think that complication might not be so bad . . .

I hear Emerson clear her throat. She's looking at me meaningfully, like we're going to have a talk later.

But not yet.

"I think we need to put a bubble around the room," I tell the coven, as if I've been thinking of nothing else. Certainly not how complicated I might need to get with Azrael, purely for research purposes. To see how much I dislike it . . . or don't. "Not just the normal protections around Wilde House, but a specific, obscuring bubble around this room to make sure no one can catch the slightest hint of what we're doing. Or why."

Everyone offers their agreement. Frost, who agreed with me on this earlier, nods. "The familiars will hold it for us."

As if they've been listening, they begin to appear. Not necessarily *in* this room, but around Wilde House. We can feel them out there—layers of protection against anything that might wish us ill, anyone that might betray us.

We arrange ourselves in our normal circle, then all kind of stop . . . because we need to make room for a new member. A very large member.

Which reminds me of the most amazing thing we learned today.

"Let's arrange ourselves like the table. The book." I flick a wrist toward the hearth and act like I'm Emerson, projecting a witch PowerPoint of sorts above the fire. The image is the same as the one I saw in the book in Frost's library and the diagram I drew Emerson in the kitchen, with all the Old High German labels translated into English.

"The spell said a circle," Frost points out.

The way he did all afternoon.

I nod because, in the normal way of things, he's right. A circle is balance. It's power. It's *protection*. We've done so much in a circle this past year because it is the most centered way to use our magic.

But this is what I told him, so this is what I tell everyone else now. "I think this is an adjustment we have to make. We're a true coven now. We need to behave as a true coven."

I could be wrong. Frost didn't offer me his opinion on that. All he said was that we should put it to a coven-wide vote. I suspect because he's oversensitive to any faint hint that he might be acting outside of the lines. And good for him on that.

Still, I don't think I'm wrong on this. And if there's anything that being Emerson's best friend since we were small has taught me, it's that doubting yourself never gets you where you need to go. Belief has a power all its own.

"It makes sense," Emerson agrees with a nod, and looks around to make sure everyone's on board. When they all indicate that they are, she turns back. "Do we need a table?"

"No, I think the floor is fine," I say, moving more into the center of the room. "Think of the rug like a table. Emerson, you're at the head."

She takes a seat on the hardwood floor at the edge of the rug.

A rug that I only now realize, all these years after staring at it and not seeing its pattern, depicts a *nachtkrapp*, an old German fairy-tale creature that looks like a raven, but without eyes and with holes in its wings. I glance at Azrael. Could this be . . . ?

He shrugs negligently, neither affirming nor denying that this rug could be yet another cursed magical creature.

I suppose it doesn't matter. Not until we know how to free them all.

Everyone else has taken their place, even Azrael. I'm still standing, though, and now everyone is looking at me, so I hurry to my spot.

Emerson starts off by taking Jacob's and Rebekah's hands on either side of her, starting the chain. It moves on, Jacob to Zander. Rebekah to Ellowyn. Zander to Frost. Ellowyn to me. Me to Azrael. Azrael to—

Frost's hand is outstretched, but Azrael is only scowling at it. I squeeze his hand and try to speak to him in his head.

I've never tried before. I've always talked out loud to him as a newel post. But if he can be in my head, if he can be real, I can be in his.

Please.

His gaze shoots to mine, onyx with very little gold, but too much heat.

With great reluctance, he puts his hand in Frost's.

And I swear the heat between our hands grows then, his and mine. One more connection.

Complication, I correct myself.

We whisper the words of protection, of shrouding the room from the Joywood and any who would wish us harm. A spell we can all do on our own, but when it matters most, we do it together to make the protection *that much more* airtight.

When the room is protected and fully shrouded from anything without, our familiars hold the bubble of safety around us, obscuring our magic from any passerby.

And then we begin the ancient spell. Together. As one.

"Moon above, earth below, grant us your strength and your power in this uncertain hour."

Magic swirls around us, in ways I can see and feel and even taste.

"Hide the dragon's intensity, shroud his immensity, give all the propensity to see only a man. A threat to none. Overlooked by all."

I *see* bands of black and gray swirling around Azrael, while his eyes glow gold. I can see the dragon he really is, like a projection behind him.

We've done powerful, amazing things in the past year, but this feels different. Not bigger, not more important. Saving the confluence, saving ourselves, surviving the Undine—these were all *bigger* things, but there's something *settled* about this magic.

Ancient.

Powerful.

A true coven, Azrael whispers inside me.

With careful words, we close the spell.

"With our words as one, our magic hold, to all who see."

And when the last word shimmers in the space between us, then disappears, we all sit in a reverent kind of quiet. The spell took a lot of energy, and we're tired, but I suspect we're all thinking the same thing.

It will be impossible to know if it *really* worked until we test it around the Joywood. Not a fun thought.

But something in me feels as ancient and powerful as the spell. Something in me knows it worked, the same way I know Azrael. Something in me insists that a *true coven* is a force the Joywood never wanted to reckon with.

After all, if they don't have a magical creature—if they killed or cursed their own, if Happy is truly dead—that means they're not acting as a true coven in this period between us winning the ascension trials and us fully ascending on the solstice.

Emerson is the first to speak. "Us shop owners have a big day tomorrow. We should get some rest."

She gets to her feet and Jacob goes to her, slinging an arm across her shoulders. She smiles up at him, and that's how it goes. Rebekah and Frost swirl off, looking at each other in a way that reminds me that they are both far freer spirits than I've ever been. Ellowyn grumbles her way to the bathroom, muttering about her *giant belly*, but Zander makes her laugh when she comes back, then takes her hand and magicks them away.

The couples pair off, back to their lives together. Something that has become regular and a little depressing . . . except this time, I'm not left alone.

Because Azrael stays here with me, as if he's mine.

We should rest, I tell myself piously, even though neither one of us is a shop owner. I should tell him what room to sleep in so I can have mine back, so I can give my crystals a good cleanse and figure out what's going on there.

Instead, he turns that dragon smile on me, and I feel it like his mouth all over my heated skin. "It's very dark, Georgina. No moon to be seen. How about a ride?"

And I should say no. I should scold him. I'm not convinced the spell shrouding his magic works if he's off flying around in his dragon form, and I certainly shouldn't *encourage* that kind of behavior, especially when there's a gossipy ancient raven wandering about keeping tabs on such things.

But I don't.

9

I WAKE UP IN MY BED WITH NO REAL MEMORY of how I got here. But I can tell I'm in *my* bed, with my soft down comforter and approximately twelve thousand throw pillows. So warm and cozy, like the sweetest cloud, that I don't want to open my eyes and face the day. I want to snuggle in and sleep some more and—

But something moves. And not a warm, fuzzy thing like Octavius.

My eyes fly open, and Azrael is *right there* beside me.

His eyes are closed, his breathing even. He's asleep.

In my bed.

Next to me.

I scramble up and out of bed so fast, I trip over my nightstand. The crystals and books littered on the surface shake and rattle, some of them even clattering across the hardwood floor.

Azrael opens one eye. Then the other. "Are you always so loud in the morning?" he asks sleepily.

From my bed. *My* bed. Where *I* slept.

With him?

I have no words. The last thing I remember from the night

before is another wild, joyous free-wheeling ride through the cloudy night. I cast my mind around, but I don't really remember coming back. Did I fall asleep mid-flight?

Am I hallucinating my entire life?

Because *how* did we end up in bed together? *How* am I in *pajamas*? I know I was tired, but . . .

Azrael is regarding me with a smug kind of interest. And there's something about his smugness that has me straightening.

I'm overreacting. He's a dragon. He doesn't understand boundaries. I should explain them to him.

Like a parent to a toddler. Maybe if I do, I will start reacting to him like that and less like . . . *this*.

But my voice still doesn't want to work.

With ease and grace, he moves out of *my* bed and around it toward me. My instinct is to scramble back, but all that smug helps me hold my ground.

Give him a firm, fair scolding. Explain the overstep, and set a boundary he is not allowed to cross. "Azrael. This is *my* bed. *My* room. And—"

"Of course it is," he agrees, moving past me. But he doesn't do so without *touching* me. His hand trails down my spine as he passes, and it's not *sexual*—even if my body has a *reaction*—it's . . . affectionate. The kind of thoughtless gesture I see Jacob and Emerson give each other.

But *not* the kind of careless gestures Emerson and I give each other. The affection isn't *friendly*. It's intimate.

It's *inappropriate*, I assure myself.

"I'm *starving*," he says, already halfway out the door. "Do you think we can have some of those cinnamon rolls you're always on about?"

I could run after him and try my hand at scolding him, but I don't. I stand where I am. Breathe. Then pick up my crystals and attempt to move through my morning ritual, a little too aware that my panic isn't because I *don't* want to wake up with him.

It's more that I know that when I do, after a longer night I can remember fully, that will be that.

It's that recognition. It's that ache. It's a sense of *finality* that goes along with that *finally* I felt when I saw him take form.

It's fate, I think.

It makes me shiver. It makes me wonder. It makes me question my sanity—but only when he's not in front of me.

And I certainly want to *remember* what happens between us once it does.

Tonight we'll sit down, no midnight rides, and discuss the boundaries of my room, my space, my *bed*. Maybe if I give him rules, I'll feel more in control of this *thing* that already feels as if it's been forever. When it's been two nights, two long days, and this morning.

I could ask him about it. I know he feels it too. But I don't want that.

It's like I know that if I do, there will be no going back.

Not that I want to *go back*. But I don't know that I'm ready to give up the option, either.

Today, however, we have Small Business Saturday to help with. I pick up some amazonite I got in Australia and put on my bracelet made of blue lace agate that I may have once told spell-dim Emerson was my version of a wristwatch. We made our own fun in those dark days. Today the stones are for communication and patience, which I'm going to need in spades. And not just for demanding shop customers.

When I make it to the kitchen, Azrael is the only inhabitant, but a large breakfast spread has been left behind. Though I think, based on the amount of plates and food in front of him, that Azrael has made quite the dent.

I grab my own plate. There are indeed cinnamon rolls, so I take two and some coffee and sit down at the kitchen table. *Across* from Azrael, rather than next to him. I think this will offer a better mode of communication.

What are we communicating?

I frown at him. He shouldn't be all up in my thoughts like this. Another boundary we will need to discuss. *Tonight*, I think firmly. Tonight I will figure out how to handle this. Him.

Me, something in me whispers.

"I'm going to Ellowyn's shop this morning to help out," I tell him. Firmly. "Tea & No Sympathy gets more traffic in the mornings, and always does a booming business this weekend. Then Rebekah will take my place, and I'll head over to Confluence Books to help Emerson."

He eyes the last cinnamon roll on the platter. "I can't wait."

"Azrael, you have to stay put."

But he takes his time eating the cinnamon roll, clearly *reveling in it*, and though I have always loved a cinnamon roll myself, his enjoyment is almost—

I shake that off. And have to blow out a breath to settle myself.

"I thought the entire point of the spell last night was so that I did not have to stay put," he says.

"We don't know if it worked."

He regards me with steady onyx eyes, the gold threads gleaming. "Yes, we do."

I look down at my plate. "Look. I'm not saying you have to stay hidden in the house forever, but I think it's best if you're careful. You . . . you need some better understanding of how the witch world works before you go dragon-stomping through it."

"I am part of your coven, Georgina. I am part of your life." That seems to sound inside me, deep. Maybe it rings in both of us, this breathless inevitability that I have wanted my whole life—but not *right now*. Maybe that's why he softens. "I was part of the witching world long before you. Perhaps you do not understand since the memory of magical creatures has been wiped away, but it is rude to treat us like something to hide."

I look at him, feeling somehow both contrite *and* offended. "You know perfectly well that I'm being *safe*, not rude."

"I know nothing of the kind. Besides, if the ruse is I'm a human who followed you home from England in a desperate love stupor, shouldn't people start seeing us together?"

Then he smiles at me.

And in that smile, I know I'm toast. There's no way to argue with it. Not when it dances and *shimmers* inside of me the way it does, and I could feign ignorance . . .

But it's real. This is happening. He is *waiting*. I am *resisting*.

It feels like a dance, and one I know the steps to, though I shouldn't.

"Want to dance?" he asks me now, his voice a temptation and fire in his eyes.

I do. Oh, how I do.

But instead, *not dancing* is how I leave Wilde House with a dragon in tow. We walk to Tea & No Sympathy down the length of Main Street, which is bustling today. It snowed early this morning, just enough to give everything a festive dusting that makes St. Cyprian look like a snow globe. I catch glimpses of the gleaming winter river through the alleyways that lead from town to the riverbank. Every time I see the glimmer of the water, I slow.

It feels like it's trying to tell me something in a whisper, in a song. Impart some wisdom. But if so, it's just out of reach.

I want to reach for it. I can feel a longing in me—

A crow caws from its perch on one of the stores, and it jerks me away from that sound.

"What are you looking at?"

I drag my gaze from the water to Azrael. "Just communing with the river."

He frowns at me, and I get the strangest feeling there's *concern* in the way his eyebrows draw together. But I keep marching forward. I don't have time for *river riddles* today.

My dragon is riddle enough as it is.

St. Cyprian is out in force this cold, bright morning, streaming in and out of shops decked out for the holiday season. Once again, I get the kind of attention I never did before this year. Everyone makes sure to smile and say hello, like they're trying to curry favor. This must be what it's been like to be Emerson all these years.

And I keep waiting for someone to point at Azrael and reveal him. I don't know how anyone could look at Azrael and think he's anything other than pure magic. A big, powerful dragon wrapped in a ridiculously hot male human form that I can't believe people don't see straight through.

But I can tell as we pass people on the street—witches and humans alike—that no one looks at him and thinks *dragon*. They do think *hot*. I stop counting the second glances and flirtatious smiles when I pass fifty.

And no, I don't like that at all.

"You'll need a human name," I say to him, maybe a little more forcefully than necessary, when a pack of women literally blocks the bricks to gape at him. "I'm sure the Joywood know your real name, and we don't want them to make that connection. We don't want them to think much of you at all. So it needs to be something boring."

He is smiling at three octogenarian witches who cast little sparkler spells at him, all googly-eyed, then turns that smile on me. "I am never boring, Georgina."

I ignore the smile. "*Nigel* is kind of a British name."

He makes a scoffing noise.

"Edmund?"

"That sounds like someone I would eat."

We go back and forth, not coming to any agreement as we reach Tea & No Sympathy. The shop is packed, which is a good sign, but after I weave through the crowd with Azrael prowling along behind me, I get to Ellowyn at the cash register, and she looks like *she* might start breathing fire on every single customer in her shop.

She sees me, and her eyes narrow. "I want to commit multiple murders," she announces, loud enough that quite a few customers hear.

The regulars laugh, because Ellowyn's grumpiness is part of the charm.

Some of the humans who've never been in here before, clearly, look concerned.

I skirt the counter and nudge Ellowyn out of the way. "I'll take over the register. Maybe you can find some way to put *Pete* to work," I say, jutting my chin meaningfully toward Azrael, who is surveying the crowd with a certain kind of hunger in his gaze that can't be good.

At the sound of the name, he shifts that gaze to me.

He has no boundaries, so why shouldn't *I* choose a name without his approval?

"Pete?" Ellowyn asks.

It's my human name for him. Cute, right?

Ellowyn snorts. *He doesn't look like a* Pete, *Georgie. Or a human. Nor is he cute.*

She leaves the register and makes her way to Azrael. I decide if anyone can handle a dragon, it's Ellowyn. Even pregnant. Maybe *especially* pregnant. So I focus on the job I can actually do here.

I check people out, listen to complaints about the price and the crowd. I deal with people trying to haggle or return unreturnable things. I don't *love* customer service, but with the right ditzy, *I'm sure I didn't hear you correctly* smile, I find it endurable.

Or at least, I don't feel the need to murder anyone. There's a kind of satisfaction in never letting anyone ruffle my exterior feathers, no matter how some try.

As noon approaches, the crowd begins to dwindle a bit.

People are no doubt flooding into all the restaurants and snack shops. I'm able to step away from the register for a few minutes, so I take the opportunity. I glance over to find Azrael with his head bowed toward a customer so he can actually speak at her level. He's telling her all sorts of things about the tea, with grand gestures and much enthusiasm.

Ellowyn's sitting in a chair by the window, her feet elevated. "He's got a talent for this," she tells me when I come over, sounding almost proud. "I've watched him talk at least ten women into twice the purchase they came in here to make."

I try not to wrinkle my nose at the fact they're all *women*. Ellowyn's clientele is primarily women.

I check the customer out with my sunny smile. Azrael comes behind the counter and stands entirely too close to me, but if I make a point of moving away from him, he'll see that as a win. So I don't.

"In another life, I would have made an excellent merchant, don't you think?" he asks me lazily after the woman leaves.

"Did you charm her into buying all that?"

"Of course."

I shake my head. "You can't use magic to get people to buy things."

"Why not?"

"It's . . . not right."

"She wanted tea. I convinced her to get the tea she needed. Ellowyn earns money from the purchase she made. Explain to me how this is not right?"

"You didn't give the woman a choice."

"I knew what she wanted."

"I'm going to have to side with the dragon on this one," Ellowyn says as she waddles over to us. Her hand is resting on her belly. Her expression is one of amusement. "You're welcome to play merchant in my shop any time you want, Azrael."

Azrael beams at me. "See."

"It's Pete," I tell Ellowyn. "Just Pete. He's a regular old *Pete*."

"Pete the dragon? I like it," Rebekah says as she saunters in. "I walked past Confluence Books and it's *packed*."

"We'll head over there right now," I tell her. I say goodbye to Ellowyn and baby and then motion for Azrael to follow me.

"You know, you can go back to Wilde House," I tell him. I even put on my airy, dreamy smile for him. "Take a break. Have some lunch. Enjoy yourself."

I think mention of food will sway him, but he frowns down at me as we walk over to Emerson's shop. Where he stops with me outside. "I do not like this little act of yours," he tells me.

He opens the door to Confluence Books and gestures me in.

"What act?" I return, frustrated that he knows I *have* an act.

I walk under his arm and into the shop. It is teeming with people and immediately gives me a sense of claustrophobia. But I wave and smile at Emerson directing traffic in and around the counter, and don't give Azrael the chance to respond.

When I make it through the throng of bodies to Emerson, she leans close to my ear. "Can you put the children's section to rights? One of those damn Blanchard demon spawn tossed every stuffed animal into the canopy and knocked at least half the shelved books to the ground."

"We're on it," I assure her. The Blanchard children are indeed demons, figuratively anyway, and I do not allow myself to think too much about the last time I saw their mother, Cailee.

Heaving about on a couch with my boyfriend.

But I'm here to help Emerson, not brood over my so-called romantic life. And the children's section *is* in shambles. There are at least two toddlers throwing tantrums and one baby screaming its head off. I smile at everyone anyway, and begin to tidy up while offering the occasional reading suggestions, the careful redirection of a wild toddler, or an answer to a frazzled parent's question about the parenting section.

After a while, I realize that Azrael has followed me, but

he isn't talking to anyone or apparently exuding any charm whatsoever. He's putting books back on shelves and giving threatening looks to any child who dares reach for one. Before I can scold him for that, an unholy screech pierces the air.

A child—one of Cailee's blond-haired, blue-eyed terrors—thunders over to a rack of books. He reaches out, shoves it, and the whole thing goes toppling over.

With only seconds to spare, I manage to snatch a little girl out of the way.

The boy turns, clearly looking for another rack to topple. I send out some magic that will keep all the books in place and hand the startled little girl off to her mother, but before I can do anything else, Azrael has plucked the Blanchard boy up and off the ground by the back of the collar. I leap forward. "You can't—"

The child starts screaming and struggling. Azrael looks like he's going to eat him.

"Azrael, put him down," I hiss, all the while internally muttering magical words so any humans in the store think they're seeing something else. Anything else.

And then I forget about magic, because I hear a familiar piercing voice. "Rigsby!"

Because of course this is actually happening. Here. In a crowd containing a dragon.

"Put him down," I say to Azrael. Firmly.

On a heavy sigh, he does just that as Cailee approaches. The offensive *Rigsby* runs right into her and throws his arms around his mother dramatically, sobbing and carrying on.

I can see Cailee is about to yell at us. Until her gaze finds mine.

Then she gets kind of . . . wide-eyed.

Satisfyingly wide-eyed, in fact, though the memory of her Daffy Duck tattoo is emblazoned on my mind, and it's all I can think about for one dazed moment.

"G-Georgie. Hi. Hello." She's patting her son's back as he wails into her side. Her eyes keep getting wider, and I don't know that she looks *ashamed*, exactly, but there's certainly embarrassment.

For the both of us. Even though *I* have nothing to be embarrassed about.

Except, I suppose, that a dragon was about to eat her child. I swallow my discomfort and summon a sunny smile.

"You'll have to excuse my friend Pete. He doesn't deal with children often."

"Particularly ones with absolutely no manners." Azrael affects a slight British accent. Then he places his arm over my shoulders, much the way Jacob did to Emerson last night.

Cailee stares at the both of us for a long, ticking sort of moment.

"You brought a *friend* home from England?" she says to me.

"Uh, well. Yes."

She shakes her head, but she's smiling now. She leans close to me, and I'm too stunned to react. "I *told* Sage there wasn't any way you were off in England being faithful. So it's okay. We're all okay. And no one has to go . . . spreading any unfavorable stories around town."

Cailee beams at me, as though with enough hope and cheer she can force me into agreement. But there's something genuine about it. It's not affected, it's . . . her.

It occurs to me that this is how she views a relationship. Affairs and infidelity are *of courses* as long as we can keep the public embarrassment to a minimum. And maybe for her, that's true. Maybe that's a deal she and her husband have struck, and it's absolutely none of my business.

But it was *not* the deal Sage and I had.

So, no, I don't smile at Cailee. I don't agree with her about anything. I just say a polite goodbye and turn back to Azrael.

Who is glaring at me like I've done something offensive.

"You can't *grab* children like that," I say beneath my breath. "They're not snacks. They're precious."

"Why haven't you told your friends?" Azrael looks thunderous. His words don't make sense.

"Told them what?"

"That your little wheat cracker crumb of an ex was cheating on you."

I blink at him. Children and parents—human and witch alike—are milling about, and he's . . . just saying that. Out loud.

"I . . . It's none of your business." I look around, worried about who might have heard.

"I have spent the past *year* listening to you lot go on and on about working together. Trusting each other. And these scant few days of being back in my own body, what I see is you holding yourself apart. Why?"

"What you're *seeing* is me third-wheeling it through coven life." I don't know where that comes from or why it sounds so raw. I point a bright, unconcerned smile at him to cover it.

To no avail. "Think better of yourself," he growls.

I balk at that. "I think *greatly* of myself, thanks."

"Then think better of them."

"You have *no* idea what I think."

No, Georgina? Because here I am in your thoughts.

You're an impossible asshole, do you know that? I shoot right back at him on this channel we shouldn't have open between us.

But before he can answer that, I turn away.

Dramatically, I can admit.

And I pay for it, because I nearly smack right into the horrible duo of Carol Simon and Maeve Mather, two of the Joywood's most powerful and exceptionally vile witches.

10

"GEORGIE." CAROL'S VOICE, AS ALWAYS, MAKES my skin crawl. Particularly because she always smiles in that creepy way of hers. It's almost as unnerving as Maeve's bedraggled familiar, a moth-eaten-looking blind pigeon she carries around with her in a panda-shaped purse. "You're back early from your travels."

I try to recalibrate. Quickly. Let my emotions go, or at least hide them while I play up the ditzy smile. I know it's the only thing they see—and really, I prefer not to be noticed by any members of the Joywood. It's safer that way.

"I came back for Thanksgiving," I say dreamily, as if the holiday itself called me, personally, from across the ocean. "Was I supposed to stay away until the actual Cold Moon rises?"

I laugh merrily at that, though as I say it, I wonder. Did they plan to keep me away all this time? No one else had to go off on a quest, just me. Is this part of some new, horrible Joywood plot?

Or am I just trying to make myself feel better because that might make me a special target like the rest of my friends? *You need to get over the idea that you are somehow special*, I can hear my mother say.

Inside I feel nothing but a roiling sense of *ick*. And not just because of my train of thought or the fact of these two awful women standing right in front of me.

"I'm not surprised a Historian like you would be so quick," Carol says, and anyone around us would believe she's being kind and genuine, but I know better. "You always were a smart one, weren't you?"

I am *beyond* creeped out. The last time I saw these people, they literally disappeared with a bang after assuring every voting witch they would see what a mistake they'd made in choosing the Riverwood over the Joywood.

"One of the smartest," a smooth British accent says from behind me. And then Azrael's arm is around my waist, pulling me to him. "Are you going to introduce me to your friends, babes?"

I have to put every last ounce of energy to work to keep from pulling a face or shoving his arm off me. Why is he *purposefully* engaging with the Joywood? Does he want us all to die?

And why did he call me *babes*, of all things?

I make myself smile, though it's hard. "Carol. Maeve. This is my . . . friend. Peter. We met in England."

He beams at them, then at me. "Once she described the beauty and charm of St. Cyprian, I couldn't resist following her home." I feel his eyes on me, and wonder how no one sees that dangerous thread of gold all but *seething* in his gaze. But he doesn't sound angry. He sounds besotted. "Or maybe that was just . . . her."

Carol studies Azrael with a frown. I notice that her trademark frizzy hair is looking a little more healthy and wavy while beside her, Maeve is standing there open-mouthed, and it appears she's missing a few teeth. She's gazing at Azrael like she can't believe her eyes, and I think she's figured it out—

But she hasn't. "A *human*?" she whispers to Carol, but not quietly enough for us to miss it.

Azrael cocks his head. "Were you expecting a werewolf?"

Maeve blinks, and Carol's expression grows tight. But only for a moment. Then she smiles, right at *Peter*.

"Welcome to St. Cyprian, Peter. I hope we'll see you at the Cold Moon Ball." She glances at me and delivers one of her pointed sniffs. "Georgie always likes to bring her little friends to our events."

If he's offended by *little friend* or the *always*—I think Carol is trying to say I'm a bed-hopping slut, as if that would offend me or him—Azrael doesn't show it. He just keeps beaming like he's a ray of British sunshine, and his arm around my waist tightens.

"I wouldn't miss it."

This is all beginning to feel like torture, so I try to remember the world outside this conversation. The bookstore. Small Business Saturday. The fact that I am in the ruling coven now, and they are a disgrace.

"Did you all come in for something specific?" I ask sweetly. I gesture toward the nearest table. "All the fairy tales are buy one, get one free. And there's a fifty-percent-off sale on—"

"As usual, Emerson doesn't carry what we were looking for," Maeve says, clucking as if she's deeply disappointed. From somewhere inside her purse, I hear an echoing gurgle. No doubt her poor pigeon.

I want to ask her why they're here, but I don't. I want to say all manner of things, but instead I just smile at them, bright and happy and as ditzy as possible, and offer no more conversation.

The silence stretches out. It's uncomfortable. But nothing can compel me to act like I notice. I keep right on smiling at them. Azrael beams.

If they want to break the silence, they can.

"Well," Carol says after an eternity. "It's good to see you back, Georgie. We can't wait to see what you can do."

That sounds like a threat, I think, as Carol flicks a glance at Azrael. But she only turns and walks away, dodging the sea of customers as she goes. Maeve gives another little sniff, hoists her panda purse higher like her feeble pigeon is a shield, and then quickly scurries along in Carol's wake. I swear a little chunk of hair falls off of her head as she goes.

I guess we know the spell worked, I say, and I wonder if Azrael heard that in his head, because when I turn to look at him, his expression is back to mad and disapproving, as if our run-in with the Joywood hadn't occurred.

"When will you tell Emerson?"

"About what?"

"Don't play dumb, Georgina. Nothing makes me angrier."

Which pokes at my own anger. "Then you need more things to be angry about."

"Why won't you tell her? She is your best friend."

Like I need a lecture on *my* best friend. I move away from him, around a small witch family who are staring a little too intently in my direction. I find a few more stray books, but Azrael is following, and I'm afraid if I don't answer him, he's going to make a scene.

"It's embarrassing," I say quietly. "Now, can we—"

"So what?"

My temper snaps. Just like that. I whirl on him—human and witch families around us be damned. "*So what?* I don't want to be embarrassed. Who does?"

He crosses his arms over his chest and shakes his head. "Your mother really did a number on you."

I feel a bit like I've been slapped. My *mother*? "What do you know about my mother?"

"Enough," he says with a kind of dark menace that makes *zero* sense for a dragon who's been cursed into a newel post for something like a century.

I remember myself enough to cast a quick spell to make sure no one can hear what I say to him, because there are already too many curious eyes in this store. "My mother hasn't been alive long enough for you to have known her before you were cursed, Azrael. So how could you possibly have an opinion on her? Or her effect on me?"

His gaze gets a little shifty then. Some of the anger turns into that sly distance someone uses when they're lying. "She used to make . . . Wilde House visits. And as established, I saw and heard plenty while in my post."

"Visits?" That makes absolutely no sense. My mother likes to talk about the Wilde family's *prominence* and *position*, but they live next door to each other and barely interact. "What? Why?"

He starts to walk away, down the stairs toward the front of the store where Emerson is checking people out. But he talks as he does it.

"There was a time, before you were born, that your parents were quite good friends with the Wildes," he says, casually, like that's well-known information. Like magical creatures and true covens.

But I have literally *never heard this*. Not that I ever thought that they were enemies. Just that there was always a careful and polite distance between Emerson and Rebekah's parents and mine.

I trail after him. "Friends? What kind of friends?"

Azrael cuts through the crowd as if it's a figment of my imagination, making his way to the front of a long line of people waiting to check out. He earns a few dirty looks and muttered remarks when he ignores all of them, leaning over the counter as if he's one-hundred-percent cutting in line.

But he's not. Or not to buy any books, anyway. He gets Emerson's attention instead. "I believe it's time your best friend tells you what *actually* happened between her and that Sage person."

Emerson looks at him like he's lost his mind. And I . . . have no words. Again.

Then Emerson's gaze slides to mine. She looks confused.

Hurt, even. But the customer behind Azrael is no longer *muttering*. He is loudly proclaiming the fact that he is a local author who has come to sign his books, and *he* could wait in line, so why *some people* are too good for that is a mystery—

I try to shoot an apologetic look Emerson's way as I grab Azrael's arm, then drag him away. Or, more factually, I grab his arm, he looks amused, and then he *lets* me drag him away.

But I immediately drop his arm once I can, once I've tugged him over to the door where we're out of the line and no one is paying attention to us any longer. I tell myself that's because it's the smart thing to do and because I'm mad at him, not because touching him makes me feel so . . . *shimmery*. "Now that you've ruined, I don't know, *everything*—will you just go back to Wilde House?"

Azrael scowls at me, his eyes glowing dragony gold, and I'm almost afraid he'll shift right here, right now, and *really* ruin everything.

Instead, he says nothing. Not even inside my head. He doesn't call me *Georgina*. What he does is turn and leave.

I'm relieved.

I tell myself I'm *relieved*. And if he gets into trouble out there, that's his problem. *Not* mine. He's a powerful being. An ancient myth. A dragon. He should be able to take care of himself, surely.

I go back to helping Emerson with the Confluence Books crowd. She's watching me with too-close attention, despite the fact she's got a store full of people, all din and demands. But once the crowd dwindles and I can leave Emerson without her feeling like I've ditched her in the middle of so much chaos, I do.

I can tell by the look she gives me that I'll have to confess to her later.

And I don't *want* to. I can't believe Azrael has . . . *betrayed* me like this.

I don't walk back to Wilde House. I just transport myself back, but my magic must be a little wonky from all my emotions, because I don't land in my room like I wanted. I land in the foyer.

Azrael is sitting on the stair—next to the newel post now glamoured to look like there's still a dragon in it—but immediately rises to his feet when I arrive.

He opens his mouth, but I am not about to let him say anything, because he still looks angry and has no right to. No right at all. None of this is his business.

Including me. *Feelings* are not *facts*.

"Don't talk to me. Don't come in my room. Don't even *look* at me." I shove past him on the stairs, ignoring the fact that he must have *let* me, because he certainly could have blocked me if he wanted to.

"Good thing I don't want to do any of those things," he returns at my retreating back.

We sound like children. I know this, and still I storm off to my room. I even slam my door, because why not? Maybe I am childish, and maybe that feels good.

I flop onto my bed. I stare at the ceiling. I want to cry, but no tears come out, and I feel tied up in a million knots. I reach out for my crystals, trying to organize them into some formation that will *fix* this.

But nothing happens. No magic. No hum. They might as well be gravel. I want to hurl them at the wall, but that is hardly a healthy expression of anger.

I set them down. *Gently*. I pull out my journal, deciding I will stream-of-consciousness journal my feelings. Then organize them. Process them, once and for all.

I put pen to paper, and then just . . . stare.

I try to write a word—any word—but none come out. The only thing I actually want to do is stab the pen to paper a few hundred times.

A bath, I think, maybe a little desperately. A good, cleansing spiritual bath. That's what I need.

But before I can even *sit up*, there are suddenly three people in my turret room. Emerson sits at the end of my bed. Rebekah is sprawled out on the window seat between the turret windows. Ellowyn arranges herself on my chair, being careful with her belly.

I can see immediately that it's time for a reckoning.

Damn you, Azrael. I hope he hears it. I hope he *feels* it.

I beam brightly at everyone. "So, what were our end-of-day Black Friday tallies? Record-breaking, I assume?"

No one takes the bait.

"Georgie, I am so confused," Emerson says. "Why does Azrael know something about what happened with Sage that we don't? What *happened*? You said it was mutual?" She's searching my face for clues, and I hate that. "Did he hurt you?"

She seems so concerned. So worried. I don't want her to be. I don't want anyone concerned or worried over *me*. I am fine. Don't I seem fine?

But now I have to drag out the corpse of something I was getting over—or would have been in the process of getting over once I had time to think about it—and rehash the whole thing. *Maybe the dragon should have stayed cursed.*

The wind chimes outside my window crash around, and I scowl at the noise. I don't have to *see* the curl of his massive dragon tail to know he's responding to that thought. But I don't take it back.

"It's not untrue that Sage and I grew apart," I tell them. "There was just . . . an inciting incident when I got back."

"Like?" Ellowyn demands.

Maybe I'll come up with a dragon curse myself, I think, doubling down.

I swear I can *feel* that dragonish grin of his like he's pressing it into my skin. *I'd love for you to try.*

With his voice in my head, I focus on it and use my magic to create a block. He won't be able to talk in my head anymore until I let him in.

I hope.

"I came home early and went over to Sage's to surprise him," I tell my friends, trying to sound calm. Because I don't want to explain that if I sound upset, it's not Sage I'm upset with right now. That feels far more complicated. "Turns out the surprise was he was with someone else."

There are three different sounds of outrage, so I rush to explain. "I think the shock of it was more about the fact he was actually *doing that*, not that I was hurt." That is actually true, though I hadn't planned to advertise it. But now it feels like I don't have a choice. I look at each of my friends in turn. "I didn't love him. I tried to. I tried very hard to, but I didn't. So it really isn't a tragedy. I'm not hurt. I was surprised, maybe a little offended. But I'm fine."

"Then why didn't you tell us?" Rebekah asks.

I want to throw a tantrum or challenge a dragon to a duel, but instead I smile. Gently. "Because I know none of you liked him."

They all exchange those usually-behind-my-back glances that make me want to scream. But I don't.

Rebekah is eyeing me. "So that means you couldn't tell us he's a disgusting, cheating, lying worm?"

"Why does it matter?" And some of my frustration must leak through then, because Emerson moves from the end of the bed to sit next to me.

"Because it means we don't have to be nice to him if he's a lying cheater," Rebekah says, as if that's obvious.

"Because it means he's not just boring, he's *slime*," Ellowyn adds.

Emerson reaches over and wraps her arm around my shoulders. "Because it happened to you."

I have never once doubted my friends. I love them. I know they love me. But I don't love the feeling of people . . . *having feelings* about what I do or how I do it. I don't like them *having reactions* I have to deal with.

Azrael's voice from earlier echoes in my head. *Your mother really did a number on you.*

And I hate that in this moment, it makes sense. Because I know my friends don't judge me the way my mother does. But because she *did*, I don't want *any* reaction to what I am or what I do.

It's why *I* put up the mask and walls. Not because I don't think they'll react kindly, but because I want zero reactions.

"It doesn't matter." They start to protest, but I refuse to let them. "It really doesn't. It sucks because it's embarrassing, not because I lost some great love of my life."

"Let's come up with a curse."

"Rebekah," Emerson scolds, but she's smiling.

"Just a tiny curse? Like on his penis," Ellowyn says, then grins. "Get it? Tiny."

And I'm able to smile a little at that. It's not that I feel better. But they know, and they're supporting me without piling on how much none of them liked Sage. How much they knew better. That's preferable to waiting for them to find out on their own.

Not that this ever *had* to happen, much less because of an interfering dragon.

Still, it did.

And I've dealt with it.

The end.

"No curses. No rituals. None of that is necessary." I give them all a stern look, and because I am never all that *stern*, they actually seem to listen. "It was a relationship. It ended. I'd like to focus on opening the archives at the Cold Moon Ceremony next week."

Rebekah and Ellowyn look a little surly at that, and I feel certain there will be a round of *Curse the Cheater* teas at Tea &

No Sympathy by morning, but eventually I get a promise from them that they won't *actually* curse Sage.

Not that I want to protect him, but we *are* the ruling coven now. We can't go around enacting revenge curses. That's what the Joywood are famous for. We need to be different. We *are* different.

But when Ellowyn and Rebekah head off, back to their own lives, I can't seem to dislodge Emerson.

She's quiet for a few minutes, and that is worrisome. I know what she's about to say is going to be heavy. Important.

"I have always given you space when you wanted it," she tells me eventually. "Or I've tried to. You're the only one I've ever managed to do that consistently for."

I know she's right, and it means more than I can express. So we just . . . lean into each other, there on my bed.

"But I don't want you shutting me out on stuff that actually *means* something," she says. "We don't need a heart-to-heart every time you have an emotion, but you need to at least *share*."

I stiffen a little at that, though I try not to. "I'm an only child, Em. I don't like to share."

"Don't make me steamroll you. I hear it's very painful." She smiles again. "You've heard what people say about me. You know it's true. Everyone should hate me, I'm a raging narcissist who bullies everyone, blah blah blah."

I manage a laugh, because right now I wish any of that *was* true, so I could hate her and dismiss what she's saying to me as the closest thing to a sister I have. "I don't want to waste time talking about him, hating him," I manage to get out. "He was a mistake. *My* mistake."

Emerson sighs. "Sometimes we have to share our mistakes, you know. Just like we share our successes."

I know this is new for our fearless leader—who very much preferred to succeed and fail on her own not that long ago. "You're *so* evolved," I tease her.

I expect her to laugh, but instead, she nods. "Weird thing is, Georgie, a really good, loving relationship will do that to you."

She's being too serious for my liking, but I smile. I let her hug me. And when she finally leaves too, I can admit that I feel a little better.

But there's still a dragon-shaped pit of anger and frustration—and still that same scalding-hot *recognition*—in my stomach that isn't going away anytime soon.

And maybe I don't want it to.

11

I DO NOT SPEAK WITH AZRAEL FOR THE NEXT few days as we lead up to the Cold Moon Ceremony.

I pretend this is because I am *just that busy*. Which is not entirely untrue.

I spend my days at the museum, dealing with the transfer of my old duties to my replacement and going through what I can find of Happy Ambrose's to figure out what my new role will be, since I can't trust anything the Joywood tells us. And I spend my nights up in Frost's library, researching fabulae and true covens, because if I fall asleep there in one of the big, cozy chairs, so what? That happens when pulling all-nighters.

And if I expect Azrael to come charging up the bluff or break through the block that I put up to keep him out of my head, well . . . that's between me and my active fantasy life that I've been trying to suppress for the whole of my existence.

He was in the wrong. That's all there is to it. I will not acknowledge his existence until he apologizes.

But I also avoid that existence, because somehow I get the feeling that dragons aren't the sort to hang around, *hoping* to be acknowledged.

On the evening of the ball, all the members of the Riverwood get ready on our own, but we decide to meet at Wilde House to head to the Cold Moon Ceremony together. Because it's always a good idea to show everyone that we're a unit. And, bonus, we're more powerful together.

There are two components to the Cold Moon Ceremony tonight. First, the town element, fit for witch and human alike. An actual ball with fancy dress and champagne and over-the-top Christmas decor and music—thanks to Emerson and her event committee, of course.

The second component happens at midnight and is the first ceremonial act of a new ruling coven—according to what little we've been able to find on what happens *after* the ascension trials. According to the lore, the voted-out coven is supposed to help and guide the new coven through the transfer of power. Hence the time between the trials and the solstice when we actually gain full power.

You can imagine how helpful the Joywood have been in that regard.

Nevertheless, we've managed. I've collected everything we need to open the archives—the first step toward our assumption of full power. Access to the full archives means knowledge. Not just of rules and law and coven matters, but *everything*. Family trees, as Azrael mentioned the other day. Histories that I know the Joywood have obscured from us, that they don't want us to know about. And no doubt all manner of things I don't even know I don't know.

Maybe I'll even get to the bottom of Ellowyn's ghost's obsession with crows, and why they seem to show up in that warning fairy tale.

I have only encountered one other thing in this life that makes me as giddy as the prospect of finally *knowing all the things*, and I'm not speaking to him.

I go to pull the dress I'm planning to wear out of the closet, but on my way, I catch sight of the fairy-tale book on the corner of my dresser, where it definitely wasn't a few moments ago.

I pick it up and look at the cover. It no longer shows Azrael bleeding, or the sweeter cover I remember from my entire childhood into adulthood. Tonight the princess and the dragon are wrapped up together.

In what can only be described as a steamy embrace.

For a moment, I can only stare. Then, as if scalded from the outside and inside at once, I put it back on the dresser. Face down. *I don't think so*, I tell the universe and all the watchful goddesses, while that terrible ache inside me shifts to longing before settling low in my belly.

Then pulses with a whole new kind of heat.

I march to my closet, pull out my dress, and ignore the strange butterflies in my stomach and any *pulsing*. I remind myself that the last cover was Azrael bleeding and falling, and it hasn't happened.

No reason at all to suppose the current cover will come to life either.

If I know anything about the universe—and any attendant goddesses—it's that they love their little jokes. I decide that's all this book is. Because what else could it be?

I force myself to concentrate on getting dressed instead, though my hands are shaky.

I have always loved to dress up, something that was frowned upon in the Pendell house because it was *showy*. This means that events like this are special. A reason to put on a fancy outfit, even if it does sparkle, because even a musty, dusty Historian should be in a pretty dress for a Christmas ball.

I study myself in the mirror. I look good. Maybe a bit more like the princess from the fairy-tale book than I find comfortable, considering my current standoff with Azrael, but hey, who doesn't want to go to a ball looking like a princess? Complete with a tiara.

I turn to leave my room because we're meeting up downstairs—

But Azrael is standing in my doorway. I stop short.

He says nothing. Just stands there, his dark gold eyes making me understand at last that all that *ache* inside me is nothing more than longing. He holds up a hand, and a gold chain full of sparkling colorful jewels unfurls in a line that swings like a pendulum. It takes me a moment to recognize that it's a necklace.

A *gorgeous* necklace.

He still says nothing.

I order myself not to think about that book cover. It is, therefore, all I can think about.

"Am I supposed to take that?" I try to sound cool and sophisticated, like I am proffered jewels from ridiculously attractive men on the daily.

Those dark eyes gleam. "That is commonly what a person does with a gift, yes."

I stand taller. *Primmer.* "You didn't say who it's for. Or who it's from."

He scowls at me. "Do you want the gift or no?"

I do. I *really* do. I like all rocks, but semiprecious and precious stones are a great personal weakness of mine. My hands itch to reach out and grab the necklace, but I have set a boundary and I will not cross it. I will *not*, no matter how pretty a bauble.

"No," I say firmly, then make myself walk past him.

But as I'm charging down the hall—in no way *running away* from him, I try to assure myself—I suddenly feel a weight around my neck. I look down, and the jewels are fastened there. He magicked the necklace onto me.

I whirl back to face him and he's *right there*. "What is *wrong* with you?"

"I don't understand why you're angry."

"I don't understand how you've lived hundreds of years *at least* and can't comprehend something so simple."

I should probably take the necklace off. I don't.

Azrael sighs, but impatiently. As if I'm the problem here. "You should tell your friends the things that happen to you. This is common knowledge. I solved this problem for you."

"It isn't up to you to tell anyone anything. Or to solve a problem I didn't ask you to be involved in. It's up to *me*."

"But I am right, and you were wrong."

I remind myself that smiting other beings is wrong, no matter the justification. "Forget it."

"You admit I was right, though."

It's like arguing with a brick wall. I turn to walk away, but he appears in a puff of smoke in front of me, blocking my escape route.

He looks annoyed, but . . . indulgent? I don't like it. No matter how it winds its way inside me, joining that hot, deep ache. "Very well, I am sorry for . . . doing the right thing that you did not want me to do."

He's impossible. I tell him so, and not very nicely.

Azrael only shrugs. "I am a dragon."

It shouldn't be endearing. I shouldn't want to smile. I certainly shouldn't forgive him.

Then again, he *did* apologize. And he's wearing a tuxedo. A very elegant, fashionable tuxedo. I thought it was bad enough when he was walking down the street in his casual clothes. No one who has ever lusted after a man in any form is going to be able to handle him like this.

I am not particularly able to handle him like this.

And it is clear from that hungry look on his face that he knows it. "We should go," I tell him. Like a warning.

"Have you forgiven me?" he demands, clearly ready to keep barring the way. And we don't have time for this.

That's why I say, "Yes."

Expediency, that's all.

There's that gleam in his gaze again. "Let me back in."

I frown at him. I've already forgiven him, but that doesn't mean I want him in my thoughts again. "Can't you just break in, if you're so mighty and powerful?"

He grins. "I could."

There's something about the fact that he *could*, but hasn't, that I assure myself means he's growing. Understanding boundaries better. I close my eyes and picture turning a key in a lock—essentially undoing the block I put up.

"Excellent," he says, and then he puts his hand at the small of my back and leads me toward the stairs. As if nothing ever happened and we're the best of friends.

Or something more than friends, *maybe*, a voice inside me whispers, but I'm not about to acknowledge what else we might look like, walking down the stairs in elegant clothes like this, his palm a shocking bolt of heat against that tender place on my back.

Wilde House is full-on decorated now—a product of both Emerson's and my magic—for the historical home tours I'll be giving this weekend. We went with a 1950s vintage look. Plenty of bright colors and tinsel and grinning Santas.

Everyone else is already waiting in the bright and sparkling foyer, even Jacob, who got a last-minute Healer call earlier to deal with a small, random attack that reeked of black magic.

"We clean up nice, don't we?" Emerson beams at all of us like she dressed us herself—an offer she made that was declined.

I feel like everyone is staring at my necklace, but if so, they don't mention it.

Emerson switches modes and starts instructing us on what's to come as she herds us out of Wilde House and we head over to the ball. Zander and Ellowyn wave down one of the horse-drawn carriages that are out tonight, creating a nice vintage feel to the cobbled streets on such a cold evening. Zander shoos away three crows that have been perched on the back of the carriage as he helps Ellowyn climb inside. Rebekah and Frost flag down their own.

The rest of us walk, and we all arrive at the same time to go inside together. Emerson is waylaid by members of her committee almost immediately, and I look around at the winter holiday wonderland she's created in the community center. It looks like half of St. Cyprian is here already, with more pouring in the doors by the minute. We know almost everyone, because small towns are like that. The difference is that these days, everyone wants to make sure they know us too.

As we make our way through the crowd, we notice the Joywood contingent, huddled together in one corner. They're dressed up, but they don't look . . . quite themselves. Festus has one pocket hanging inside out, which is just strange from a fastidious man like him. Maeve is wearing mismatched shoes and an overlarge hat, as if trying to hide her hair. Felicia Ipswitch has a bandage around her hand in a way that almost appears as though there's no hand beneath it.

It's creepy.

Creepier still, Carol is the only one who looks the same, if a little more shiny and resplendent than usual.

"I don't like it," Ellowyn says, and it's what we're all thinking.

Emerson catches up to me and looks at them while pretending not to, like all of us are doing right now. She leans in close. "I think their power is dwindling," she says in my ear. "Their influence isn't as strong. They've lost, and it's showing."

I want to believe she's right, but I don't like how *pleased* they seem, despite all the dishevelment.

They smell smug, Azrael says in my head. Unhelpfully.

"Stop staring," Zander orders us all in a low tone while grinning at a group of humans as we pass. "They live for that."

"Besides," Frost says in his icy way, "it's unseemly for the winners to appear to *gloat*."

He's not wrong, so we move as a group toward a table where we can set down our things and maybe grab a plate of the appetizers being passed around on trays. Emerson stops and talks to all the different people who flock to her, looking every inch the leader people respect and lean on—just as she always has. Even before we beat the Joywood.

Even when she thought she was human.

Before we can make another move, the Joywood descend upon us. Except they seem to be missing Felix.

"Another Cold Moon Ball packed to the gills," Carol says cheerfully. I can't stop staring at how happy and bright she looks, especially when she beams at Emerson. "Another festival triumph for you."

"You look like a big, ripe peach," Maeve coos at Ellowyn and her big belly. "Aren't you darling."

Ellowyn freezes with an expression on her face that would have anyone normal running for cover, but this is the Joywood. I watch her visibly control herself, and somehow not punch Maeve in the face.

Instead, she gets that familiar, faraway look of hers. "Did you know that during the 1600s, men were the ones who started wearing high heels? Women only started wearing them to seem more masculine."

Felicia turns to me as Festus frowns at Ellowyn. "You're the big star of the show tonight, dearest Georgie, and *don't you* look pretty."

Dearest Georgie? I stare at her for a full moment before I manage to squeak out a "Thank you."

The Joywood complimenting us and attempting endearments when they've been actively trying to murder us all year is too weird. I don't like it. I can tell that everyone else is equally unnerved. Zander puts himself *between* the ripeness of Ellowyn and the other coven. Frost looks cold and dangerous. Azrael is wearing a frown that a wise man would take as the warning it is. Jacob, Rebekah, and I hold ourselves like we're ready for an attack.

Emerson, on the other hand, nods as if these are really compliments and are exactly our due. She always has been better at politics.

"Enjoy yourselves tonight, gang," Gil says merrily.

Having never called us *gang* before. Ever.

Carol lifts a glass of champagne as if in a toast. "I'm sure everything will go swimmingly."

They all laugh gaily—it's blood-chilling, frankly—and then they turn and leave just the way they came. In shuffling half-disarray.

"Something weird is going on. I don't think I've heard them say anything overtly menacing since Georgie got back," Ellowyn says, glaring at Maeve's back. "That's not like them."

"Not even the usual dirty looks," Rebekah adds, watching with great suspicion as Felicia leans over to whisper something to Festus.

"Maybe it's just an act so everyone thinks they're fine with the transfer of power after their temper tantrum on Samhain," Emerson says, but her nose is wrinkled like she doesn't quite believe it.

You need your fabulae for the spell, Azrael says in our coven channel. I don't recall anyone inviting him to it, but here he is. *And they know it. They're expecting you to fail the spell tonight*.

He sounds bored, likely because he's busy plucking three pigs in a blanket from a tray that moves by us. He tosses all three into his mouth at the same time and chews with obvious satisfaction.

We all turn and stare at Azrael. He hasn't talked to us like this before, and he isn't *officially* a member of the Riverwood, as far as I know, so he shouldn't be able to.

But his ability to appear in all our heads says otherwise. And I suppose we don't really know *how* one goes about becoming *an official member* when a coven has already won the ascension trials.

He looks back, unfazed. "I thought that was obvious."

And now that he's pointed it out, it sure *seems* obvious. I'm not sure why I didn't think of that myself.

I'm sure it had nothing to do with being distracted by soaring flights and the hottest man I've ever laid eyes on.

So if we do the spell and succeed, the Joywood will know we've unearthed a magical creature? I ask.

Azrael nods absently, his attention on another waiter bearing a tray of what look like cheese puffs. *Maybe they won't know. But they will surmise it, and with their black magic affinity, probably get to the bottom of things. Because the spell can only work with a true coven.*

But if we do the spell without Azrael and fail, everyone will think we're as weak as the Joywood have always claimed we are, Emerson says to us, darkly, while smiling at another local business owner and asking after her restaurant.

"You know I love your new lunch menu, Corinne," she says out loud, with a laugh. "I may or may not dream about your eggs Benedict sandwich nightly."

Beside her, somehow looking as if the only thought in his head is this party, Jacob smiles too.

The rest of us try to look like we're not shocked. Though maybe we're not, not really. We're so used to roadblocks that at this point, anything easy would feel like a trap. This is almost a relief. A nice Joywood is *terrifying*, and I, for one, find it a comfort that they're just being dicks.

I can tell Emerson is considering a bunch of different options as she continues to chat with all the human and witch citizens who come to say hello to her. I can see Ellowyn's mouth move the way it does when she's devising new tea and potion recipes, her fingers twitching, which is a good indication she's putting potions together from afar.

Like me, I imagine we're all dismissing any ideas we come up with, because this is such a complicated situation.

But clearly we can't do the spell in front of the Joywood.

And just as clearly, I think as Emerson and Jacob turn back to us, we can't let anyone guess that we're having a feverish private discussion over here.

"I'll take the fall," I offer.

"What do you mean?" Emerson demands.

I ignore the golden-black eyes that immediately light up the side of my face.

I'll dramatically realize I missed something. I'll say Happy Ambrose's notes weren't clear. Big smile. Silly laugh. Dumb Georgie.

"No one thinks you're dumb," Azrael says, with heat. Maybe with disgust—enough that everyone else kind of . . . blinks at him. Then exchange more of those glances I hate.

"That's the point," I hurry to say. "Everyone thinks I'm airy and dreamy. It's easy to believe that I just missed one of the keys because I was off in fantasyland. Because when am I not?" Just ask my mother. She'll tell you I live there. "It buys us some time."

"But how much time?" Emerson shakes her head. "We have to do the ritual tonight."

We could do it in secret, I respond to all of them.

Emerson frowns. I can tell she doesn't like the idea, but it makes sense to me. We *have* to hide Azrael from the Joywood. There's no option there.

Or, Azrael says, drawing the word out lazily, *you could refrain from hurling yourself on an unnecessary sacrificial pyre and do the sensible thing.*

He is now sipping from a champagne glass I'm not sure how he got. I didn't see anyone offer him one. It's festive, festooned with cranberries and little sprigs of mint. It should look ridiculous in his huge hand.

It does not.

"I'm afraid to ask what *you* think is sensible," I manage to say from between gritted teeth. Gritted teeth in the shape of a smile, that is. I'm not an animal.

The artifacts, Azrael says in all our heads.

What artifacts? Ellowyn asks. *Georgie is the artifact expert around here.*

Azrael waves down another passing waiter and simply liberates the woman's tray. *Even before we were killed, cursed, and the like, there were witches who liked to collect things from magical creatures. Unicorn horns. Dragon tears. Fairy wings.*

He pops the appetizers into his mouth without offering any around, or even acting like what he's doing is strange. If asked, I plan to shrug and remind folks that he's a Brit, supposedly. Who knows what they do over there?

Frost begins to slowly nod. *Yes, I remember something about an adze fang someone I knew claimed to have seen. Among other things.*

I straighten because I heard a rumor about an adze fang when I was in Ghana, gathering one of the keys.

We procure one of these, claim it has the magic of a fabulae imbued on it, and then the spell can go off without the Joywood suspecting a thing, Azrael says, sounding even lazier, probably because that's actually malice and aimed at Frost.

But it's also a great idea.

Wouldn't they suspect something since even knowing we need an artifact means we know we need a magical creature? Zander asks.

Georgie will tell everyone she's been researching. Azrael sounds impatient in our heads, but all I can think about is how strange it is that he called me *Georgie* instead of *Georgina*. It makes me feel funny.

I don't like it.

As she has, in fact, been lost in her research, she can simply say she discovered references to the powers imbued in these artifacts. That's the sort of thing that's in Frost's library, isn't it? Azrael looks at me, almost accusingly. "Everyone knows Georgie's penchant for fairy tales and other such stories. Why wouldn't she discover these things?"

I don't like him calling me *Georgie* any better out loud, I find. So much so that I barely have time to worry over the fairy-tale reference and the image of that new cover in my mind.

Goddess, what I would do to feel his mouth on my—

But we don't have time, Jacob says, snapping me back to the here and now. *How can we find out where these artifacts are, go get them, and bring them back so fast?* He shakes his head. "The ritual must be done tonight."

"*Hello,* we could lie." Rebekah rolls her eyes. "There are no points for purity in a fight for the fate of the world, are there?" *We conjure something up. Have Azrael give it some magic. Done.*

"I support this plan completely," Ellowyn says, her eyes narrowed in the direction of the Joywood.

But I'm shaking my head, because we don't need to go to such lengths. "It's okay. I know where they are."

Everyone's gaze moves from Rebekah—and Azrael—to me, and suddenly I wish I still felt that sense of dislocation. Instead of being in the hot seat.

Every single library or archive I visited to get the keys had its own rumor about magical artifacts. That's how I tracked them down so quickly. I just mapped out all the ones that I could find rumors about and went there.

But it dawns on me that when I mapped them all out, my travel route formed an eight, an infinity . . . with St. Cyprian at the center.

I thought it was just a number then, but now I realize it's not. It was a message. One about true covens.

The Joywood are watching, Zander points out. *They'll notice if one of us leaves. Worse, they'll follow, and we don't want them figuring what we're up to.*

But we have a secret weapon, don't we? I look up at Azrael.

"They'll pay attention to *us*, but not to Pete from London."

Azrael's grin is slow, and maybe only I can see the dragon flickering behind it. "I'm a tiny Anglo-Saxonish human, pale and wan and easily overlooked as I wander about, doing incomprehensible British things."

Zander laughs, then frowns like he didn't mean to.

All right. We'll split up, Emerson says, laying out the plan. *Do rounds. Dance. Enjoy. Azrael will slip away once he's sure no one's paying attention to him, get an artifact, and bring it back before midnight.*

We all nod in agreement, then begin to pair off. Jacob and Emerson go out and dance. Zander heads off to get Ellowyn food before she incinerates someone with her hangry gaze—or her inability to speak anything but the truth. Rebekah sits with her while Frost stalks about the perimeter, clearly intimidating everyone he passes.

It occurs to me that he enjoys it, that this is what Rebekah means when she claims he's funny. He's like Darcy at the country dance and everyone flutters about in his wake—and he knows it.

I'm almost smiling myself when my scan of the party leads me to my parents.

I haven't spoken to them since I got back. I could pretend I've been busy. I *have* been busy. But more importantly, I've also been avoiding them.

Tonight's a good night to approach them, I think. We're in public, and Pendells don't draw attention to themselves in public.

"My parents are here," I say to Azrael. Excuse me, to *Pete*. "I should go say hi."

Azrael gets that shifty sort of look on his face, the way he did when he talked about my parents' friendship with the Wildes. "I'll take the opportunity to wander off and then not return for a bit."

I'm frowning at my parents, but I turn it on him. "Are you sure you should disappear so soon?"

"The sooner I'm off, the sooner I can be back." He shrugs, but that grin tells me he's looking forward to his mission tonight. "Who knows what trouble I might run into?"

I frown harder at him, but his gaze is on my parents as he bends over and brushes a kiss across my cheek.

Because that's the ruse, I remind myself as my entire body shivers into wildfire and longing. We're supposed to be a couple. And couples kiss. There is no need to *ignite* in the middle of the holiday party.

No need for wild daydreams about *fate*.

My fake boyfriend looks down at me, a flash of another fire, like something is confirmed. Then he prowls off. And when I turn to look back at my parents, I can see my mother heading toward me in her usual forthright, prow-of-a-ship way, my father trailing behind.

I fix a bright smile on my face. "Mom. Dad."

"Georgina," Mom replies, and there's a very distinct difference between the way *she* says my full name and the way Azrael says it. *She* is full of cold disdain, not all that lovely spark and flame.

But there's no point thinking of dragons who aren't in the room. "It's good to see you."

Mom's smile is frigid, as usual. "Is it? It seems to me that if that were true, we would have seen you before now."

She leans forward, and there's that brittle anger swathed all around her that I haven't seen in a while. Mostly because I avoid it—and her—but also because being part of the lead coven is kind of a big deal. Even to her. I was beginning to imagine that she might actually be proud of me for once.

"Did I just see you . . . kissing a *human*?" she asks in a horrified tone.

I stare at her blankly. Azrael *barely* kissed my cheek.

"I'll have to introduce you to Pete some other time," I say. "He wasn't feeling well. Too much American food, I think. Did I mention I met him in England?"

"*Pete*," my mother echoes. "Of course it's a *Pete* from *England*. I need a drink."

But when she marches off, Dad remains. I give *him* a real smile. I may not understand why he stays with my mother, but he's always been my soft place to land. I'm grateful for him.

"I already met my reading goal for the year," he says, as if the entire interaction with my mother didn't happen. "Isn't that something?"

I rest my arm across his shoulders. "It is quite the achievement. What was the best one?"

He tells me about some thousand-page tome from the fourteenth century, and normally I would listen intently, but I'm thinking about a million other things tonight. Azrael and magical creatures. Artifacts and spells. Cold Moons and long, dark nights, some of them spent high in the sky, surrounded by stars.

Dad gives me a little squeeze. "I should head back to your mother. It was good to catch up, princess."

"You too, Dad. Once we're fully ascended, you'll have to come by and see the archives."

He nods, but pauses. And he doesn't leave or take his arm from around my waist. "Just remember, when you get all those facts you're so fond of, not to forget that facts are not always the *whole* story."

I stare at him. "What does that mean?"

Dad squeezes me again, an odd expression on his sweet face. "You'll always be my little princess."

He says this like he's saying goodbye. "Hey," I say. "Is everything okay?"

"Of course it is." But he looks sad now. I'm sure he does, even through the smile. "I'm proud of you and your coven. It's making me sentimental."

I guess that makes sense, but the interaction still leaves me feeling . . . off.

As my father shuffles off to find my mother, I see Dane and Cailee Blanchard walk in, arm in arm, wreathed in smiles. I bet that to everyone in the room they probably look like the perfect, happy couple—if you like that kind of smug blondness.

But I know they're not.

Everything in me feels tight, constricted. I know Azrael has flown off to hunt down some *artifact*. The Joywood are watching our every move. And my mother is performatively nursing the one drink she will allow herself all night, the better to watch everyone else and shred them to pieces—with facts, only the cold, hard facts—when she gets home.

I need some air. The Joywood might think it's fishy, but if they follow me out the side door or send one of their sickly familiars, all they will see is a woman in desperate need of some breathing room and solitude.

I make my way outside, ditzing my way past anyone who wants to talk to me. As soon as I make it outside, I gulp in a deep breath of the icy air. Once. Again.

Everything is going as it should. Everything is *good*. We will get the artifact, do the spell, and I will *finally* have access to the archives reserved for the ruling coven only. I will finally have *all* the knowledge.

My father's words about facts and truth and stories come back to me, but I don't want to think about that. About complications and difficulties.

Truth is the answer. Always.

I take a deep breath and look out into the early December night. Moonlight dapples the surface of the river. In the distance, I can see the pulse and twining of the other two as they braid together into the confluence, brimming with magic and light. That's the reason we're all here, fighting to make it the way it should be.

Not the way it's been for as long as I can remember.

And the longer I stand there, the more it's like the rivers are singing a little song. But I can't quite hear it. The melody is haunting, and I think that really, I should get closer and then maybe—

"Georgie."

I turn and there's Sage.

12

I KNEW THIS WAS A POSSIBILITY. WITCHES IN St. Cyprian don't tend to skip the Cold Moon Ball. But I didn't really think Sage would . . . come find me, alone or otherwise. I didn't think he'd bother.

He looks at me with *great import*, a look I am actually delighted that I no longer have to respond to with feigned interest. "We need to talk."

"About *what*?" I cannot fathom what there could possibly be to discuss. "You can magic anything I left at your place back to Wilde House. I think I left my copy of *A Portrait of the Artist as a Young Man* behind."

Although, on second thought, he can keep that. I don't ever want to pretend I care about James Joyce again.

"Georgie." And I always heard that faint note of disapproval in his voice. Maybe I wanted it there, because I've always liked a project I could, with effort, get high marks on. But tonight it grates. "Who were you with back there?"

My eyebrows rise so far up it feels as though they might shoot off my head. "I beg your pardon?"

"That man. Kissing your *cheek*."

He is not kidding. He looks dead serious. He looks *affronted*.

I stare at Sage, and now that he is not half naked and bucking about on Cailee Blanchard, I really take him in. The tall, reedy frame. The ridiculous bow tie he thinks makes him look important and interesting. The wire-framed glasses I know he doesn't actually need. I think of every lecture he gave me on the environmental impact of beef when I just wanted to eat a damn hamburger, or why *Jane Eyre* shouldn't really be considered a classic because it's *actually* regressive and not at all feminist when he knew it's one of my favorite books anyway, or why the discordant, experimental music he listens to and claims to be inspired by was far, far superior to any music I like—the kind with a melody.

I realize in this moment that I put up with him simply because I thought he was someone my mother would like. Someone who would earn me a certain kind of response from her. An acknowledgment, almost. *See, Mom, I do not in fact think I'm special if I think I belong with this man.*

My mother. The project I've been working on all my life, with only low marks to show for it.

Yeah, my mother really did a number on me.

That gross, sick feeling in my stomach gets worse, because Sage is still standing there, and I am . . . so stupid. Just so stupid. I didn't listen to my friends because I didn't think they understood. And they didn't.

Because they love *me*, not who they want me to *be*.

"Sage, this isn't the time or place," I say, as kindly as I can manage. After all, there's no point making a scene. That much of the family code I agree with. "I have an important ceremony to prepare for, and I needed a little fresh air to center myself. Go back inside."

He does not do that. Instead, he moves closer to me. "I think we have an opportunity here, Georgie."

I'm so confused by that, I make the mistake of saying, "What?"

Instead of telling him to go to hell.

"We've hit a rough patch," he says in that way he has, like he alone can see across the expanse of my foolishness. And like he deserves a medal for having to work so hard. "We both made some mistakes, but I think that gives us an opportunity to be mature. To *grow*. Together. We'll only be stronger once we deal with this."

And the way he smiles catches at me, deep inside. Because he thinks that's all that needs to be said. He thinks he's got this. Me.

He thinks he's got *me*.

"*Once we deal with this*," I repeat, slowly. "And, to clarify, the *this* you're talking about is when I caught you *inside* another woman, Sage? A *married* woman? When you and I were still together and had decided to be exclusive? Is that what you think will make us stronger?"

He looks around a little guiltily, like he's worried someone's out here listening for his secrets, and I kind of hope they are. I'm pretty sure Dane Blanchard would beat Sage into a bloody pulp if he got the urge, and certainly if he'd seen what I saw.

Obviously deciding we're in the clear, Sage looks back at me. "We can learn something from that, can't we?"

"I *did* learn something from that," I reply, with the earnest nod I perfected and used to give him during his insipid lectures, usually brought on by someone else's words. That he heard or read somewhere, or saw on the internet. So desperate to think the right things and be seen as *correct* by the right people—and I guess the joke was on me, because I thought someone like that would get me right too, in the eyes of all those people.

And *ouch*. The self-realization in a breakup is *not* fun.

"I don't want to be with you, Sage," I tell him, because I am actually an adult. No matter that I doubt it sometimes and feel that everyone else does too. "Even if you hadn't cheated on me, this would be over. I don't want a relationship with someone who could betray me like that and act like it never happened."

He looks at me like I've broken his favorite toy, or maybe insulted James Joyce outright—hurt, but also indignant. And I almost feel sorry for him, because I can see now, with all that lovely hindsight, that he doesn't have real friends or even an inner life. He has nothing to help him see how pointless it all is, desperately feeling around for a sense of importance or propriety from other people.

A lesson I've taken a long time to learn, but I'm determined to finally learn it. I'm about to be *the* Historian, and I can't have mommy issues. That would make me no better than that weaselly Skip . . .

The last name escapes me, a memory that becomes hazy and as I try to grasp for it, slips away. Like a spell, but I forget all about that because Sage lurches forward and puts his hand on my arm. I don't like the way he grips me—and I don't want Cailee's leftovers, thank you.

Yet when I try to yank my arm back, he doesn't let go.

I yank again, and he holds on, and the thing is—he's not that strong. I shouldn't need to use magic to push him off me. I've never known Sage to have a *grip*, and I stare down at his hand—

But that's all the reaction I have time for.

Because there's a flash of *something*, and it smells like burning. Smoke twirls around in the moonlight, and then Azrael is here.

And Sage is dangling about a foot off the ground.

That dangerous dragon gold has taken over Azrael's gaze, and his hand is around Sage's neck. It's as though Sage weighs about as much as a feather.

Sage struggles against the hold, his usual superior expression giving way to red everywhere and panic around the eyes.

But I'm not that concerned about Azrael *choking* Sage, because it looks like he's about to incinerate the guy on the spot. That's what has me intervening.

You can't kill him! I shout into his head.

"Why not?" Azrael says to me out loud, and notably without a British accent. "He put his hands on you."

I have similar hard feelings about that, but I'm not a member of the Joywood. "It's against the law, for one thing."

Maybe for witches. But if you recall, I'm a dragon.

"*Pete*," I throw at him from between gritted teeth, because as much as I can admit I'm not hating this—it feels a lot like justice, and it's even a bit thrilling—we have appearances to keep up. More importantly, we aren't evil. "Put him down." *You're supposed to be wan and British, remember?*

He sighs. "Very well." The accent is back.

Sage falls in a heap on the ground, gasping and panting. He looks from Azrael to me, and his gaze darkens.

"Cailee was right. You *were* cheating."

I'd love to maintain my innocence, but what's the point? My innocence doesn't really matter to him, any more than his cheating mattered to me. That's the part that's really sad. "You can call it whatever you want, Sage. It's over."

Sage gets to his feet, brushing dirt and grass off his pants. He looks at me with more anger and even hate than I would have imagined he had in him. And it's hard for me to understand why a guy who cheated on me would care what I do, when here I am, setting him free with no fight or even an unpleasant scene. He should be thanking me.

Instead, he looks darker than I've ever seen him. "I should have known it was all an act. At heart, you're nothing but a dumb, dirty—"

Azrael leans forward. Sage scrambles back.

"Think very carefully what word you want to use in front of me, friend," Azrael says, all dragon and warning. But also with his British accent, I'll give him that.

Sage lifts his chin, but it's not really the show of courage or defiance I know he imagines it is, because he's backing toward the door that leads inside. "I'm not your friend."

"In what universe would you imagine you could be?" Azrael asks, laughing in a way that raises the hair on the back of my neck.

Then he lifts an eyebrow, that's all—and Sage practically falls all over himself to scramble inside.

It would be incredibly satisfying to let Azrael play with him a little, but that's unworthy of me. Or so I tell myself. And I almost mention it, but I hear that song from the river again, faintly.

I turn my head, straining to hear it.

"What are you doing?" Azrael demands, scowling down at me.

"Nothing." I'm looking out at the confluence, like maybe I can *see* the song if I look hard enough. "I came out for some fresh air, and there was Sage. You know the rest."

What *is* that melody? I swear I've heard it before. I know I have. I can almost hum it—

"What crystals are you wearing?" Azrael demands, sounding angry.

I pull my attention away from the song. I put my hand to my necklace. "The ones you gave me."

"No others?"

I pat the pocket in my dress. "A few others."

"Which ones?"

"For the ceremony tonight. Smoky quartz, malachite, sodalite. The usual."

His scowl only deepens. "You need a better anchor." He glances out at the river, but only for a second. "You need to carry something for protection."

"Against Sage?" I laugh. "I enjoyed watching you step in and all, but I could have handled him if I'd needed to. He's not complicated. Trust me."

He says nothing, but he's glaring at me, and I don't understand why.

"Did you get the artifact?" I ask, worried that something

went wrong there and that's why he's so upset. He can't really be mad I stopped him from *murder*. Can he?

"I got it," he says, but darkly.

I'm going to ask him why he's still so grumpy then, but he produces a long, slim box made of glass. Inside is a golden horn.

Everything else in my head simply evaporates as I stare at it. It's real. I can tell it's *real*.

"A unicorn horn," I say on an exhale, mesmerized by the way the moonlight catches all that gold, which should seem unnatural but doesn't. "I can . . . *feel* it." It's not like Azrael's magic, dark and smoky. It's like a prism, and it hums around the box in a kaleidoscope of magic.

I look up at Azrael, excitement making me want to laugh or dance. *We did it*. But the *we* has me thinking of the coven, and remembering . . .

"This isn't the unicorn Frost . . . *maybe* . . ." I can't say it.

Azrael sighs deeply. "Of course not. The artifacts are not made from mutilated, murdered fabulae. That could only be dark blood magic. These artifacts only retain their magic if they're given of a creature's free will. Usually toward the end of their lives. That's why there are so few of them. Don't you think the Joywood would have a trove of them otherwise?"

I want to reach out and touch it, but the glass is protecting it, and more, I can feel the spells keeping watch over it too.

"Only magical creatures can move it, wield it," Azrael tells me. "Magical creatures, and those witches who are given specific permission to carry such an honor."

I manage to tear my gaze from the horn, to meet his golden, gleaming stare. My hands itch to touch, I want to *beg* him to give me permission, but . . .

"Emerson, obviously, should—"

But he's shaking his head. "Georgina, it's you."

I swallow at the sudden lump in my throat. At the weight of the responsibility he's just laid across my shoulders. It's not that

I don't want it, but it feels overwhelming for a minute. Like Felicia said, I *am* the star of the show tonight. This is about archives, and a Historian has to be a good, intuitive researcher to track down the keys at all.

Tonight is my domain.

And tonight is why the Joywood never had to target me the way they did my friends. There was never any need. They knew this ceremony was a fail-safe. Without a magical creature—or the knowledge that magical creatures were real and some had left artifacts behind in anticipation of their approaching deaths—they didn't have to come after me.

All they had to do was wait for me to fail tonight, and better yet, have no idea why—because they hid their tracks long ago.

But I'm not going to fail now, thanks to this artifact.

Thanks to Azrael.

"How do I ask for permission?"

"You do not have to ask," he says, his voice strangely husky.

He holds out the glass case to me, his gaze never leaving mine. I have to take a deep breath to steady my shaking hands. Then I reach out to take it from him.

For a moment, we're both holding it. I can feel magic pulsing around us. His. The unicorn's. Mine.

Inside me. Outside me.

If there's a song at the confluence, I can't hear it.

For a moment, it's just us.

A melody I know as well as my own heart, my own breath.

Then Azrael releases the case, and it's in my hands alone. I have to work to steady my breath. To do something about my heart rate.

"Send it to wherever you're keeping the keys," Azrael instructs me. "You won't reveal it until right before you start the ritual."

I nod. I'm feeling more . . . fragile. Like one wrong move won't just ruin everything, but will shatter the amazing magic I've been trusted with.

And I'm not sure which one would devastate me more.

Still, I close my eyes. I center my magic. And then I send the horn to stay with the keys until it's time.

When I open my eyes, Azrael is staring at me. The intensity isn't new. I've caught him staring at me like that before. It's more that I'm having a harder and harder time convincing myself it doesn't mean . . . exactly what I feel like it means.

What I'm no longer so sure I want to pretend I don't know it means.

Inside, I am nothing but longing and fire and *fate*. That same sense that my life was leading me straight here, to him, all along. That everything about this is inevitable. That the only reason he is not rushing in is that he already knows where we're going.

Even a few days ago, that made me feel uncertain, but it doesn't tonight.

It feels like confirmation.

"There's not much time left of this ball," Azrael says, and I'm not sure he's ever sounded so calmly serious. Like every move we make is weighty. "Let's go back in."

I nod again. Finding my voice seems impossible. So we walk back inside together.

I meet Emerson's gaze across the room. She notices Azrael, then looks at me expectantly.

We've got it, I send to her.

She gives me a discreet little fist pump, which eases some of the tension inside me. We've got this. I know we do. We were *meant* for this.

Azrael's hand is suddenly on my back, directing me not toward Emerson, but to the little dance floor.

"We should dance," he says in my ear, creating a cascade of sparkling shivers through me.

Suddenly, out of nowhere, a mental image of that book cover pops into my head. It is emblazoned on my mind as we move to the music. But maybe this was all it meant. A dance while we're pretending to be a couple, so no one knows what he is.

But I understand that's not what it meant at all.

"You know what we are, Georgina," he murmurs, making me startle in his arms. "You always have. You always will."

I let my breath out, a long, slow shuddering. Inside me are all those daydreams. Passion and wild sex and laughter and longing and *him*. Us. This. *You can't just go cavorting around my thoughts.*

"Think quieter, then," he says pleasantly enough, and I'm all but plastered to his body while we sway to the music, and nothing I feel is *quiet*.

Still, I endeavor to do just that.

I try to empty my head of all thoughts.

Because the clock is striking down, fate is real, and it will be midnight soon enough.

13

THE BALL ENDS AT ELEVEN THIRTY, AND EVEN if humans were tempted to linger, something is in the air. It's a magic prompt telling them to go home. I look meaningfully at Azrael, and he nods, because Peter the London Boyfriend is meant to be human too. He needs to make a show of leaving.

It would be embarrassing to admit how little I want him to leave, so I don't. I don't admit anything. Besides, it's appropriate for me to be nervous about the ceremony.

Azrael steps back from me, letting go of me and ending all that *dancing* I can't even begin to think about right now with a spell hanging over my head.

You won't see me. You won't feel me. But I'll be there adding my magic as well.

I don't know if he says this only in my head, or in the full group channel. He's looking at only me as he lifts my hand and presses a kiss to it.

It should feel chaste. Fake. Even silly. A gesture in line with one of Sage's bow ties.

It. Does. Not.

What it does instead is light me up and make me wonder what it would be like to *truly* feel a dragon's fire—

But that, I tell myself sharply, is not helpful. I am about to lead a spell to open the archives I've been waiting my whole life to see. It's no time for fairy tales, no matter how real they might be.

Azrael's eyes gleam, and then he slips away, threading in and out of the packs of humans until he's no longer inside. The witches are spilling out of the building as well, but the magic makes sure the humans don't notice. They're off to their homes or whatever else they do at eleven thirty at night, but we're all headed to the same place: St. Cyprian's first capitol building.

It's right on the river, an old-fashioned fort where the human archives have been housed for as long as history has been written down in this area.

But we don't go inside. We all come together outside along the riverbank.

Any human who had the wild thought to be outside by the river on a frozen December night would see nothing. Maybe they'd think they saw a shadow, but on further inspection, all they'd really see was a murder or two of crows.

Where's Azrael? Emerson asks in my head.

Proving that what he said earlier was, indeed, just for me.

Just for me seems to echo in my head like a portent.

He's around, I assure everyone.

Witches are gathered in little clusters, murmuring to each other. Emerson, as always, steps happily into the unknown and starts directing people where to stand. There are specific rules for this ceremony. Rituals often have extensive requirements—that's part of the price of magic. But no one remembers the last time this was done, so we all require a little guidance.

One more thing we lost, I think, gazing over at the Joywood as they too assemble here as the outgoing ruling coven. I'm certain *they* know what to do, why we stopped doing it, and when.

I'm equally certain they're the *why*. I also know that, despite their strange appearances, they're here to witness the failure of their successors. A failure they set up a long time ago.

They stand here on the bank of the river they tried to use to flood the whole town last spring, looking incredibly smug. And are still without Felix.

They're also ignoring Emerson's instructions. She rolls her eyes at me.

Let's not belabor the point. Let them huddle at the river's edge, Jacob says in our heads, clear and calm, as usual.

Maybe it'll sweep up and take them under. Zander's suggestion is dark.

A girl can dream, Ellowyn offers.

Rebekah laughs, out loud, as Emerson takes her place in front of us and addresses the crowd.

"Welcome," Emerson begins, her politician smile in place. "We're so glad to have you here, witnesses to the first Cold Moon Ceremony in some time."

Maeve titters at that, like Emerson offered some great joke, and the sound carries through the air and the trees. Some people look at her, but Emerson doesn't give her the satisfaction.

"It makes sense to us that the first step in our final ascension is acquiring knowledge," Emerson says. "Knowledge that has been difficult to come by for some years."

She still doesn't look pointedly at the Joywood, but others do.

"And since this is about knowledge, about facts, about our history and all that will inform our future, I will not be leading this ceremony. It will be the Riverwood's incomparable Historian, Georgie Pendell."

She gives me a nod, and I smile at her, then the crowd. I've never minded public speaking. It's another lecture, essentially, and I've always been good at a lecture for academic purposes. If people get rowdy, I only need to smile blankly at everyone like I don't notice and it doesn't faze me.

Ditzy Georgie has her uses.

But new sorts of nerves are thrumming through me tonight, and for so many different reasons. I don't see Azrael, or feel him, and I don't like that.

I notice my father in the crowd, smiling up at me in that new, sad way. My mother is nowhere to be seen, which feels odd, considering this should be a big moment for her. For the Pendells. Then again, it isn't a major ceremony—because no one can remember it ever happening before, thanks to our evil predecessors, and no one's attendance is necessarily required.

Still, when I meet my father's gaze, his words from earlier come back to me. *Facts are not always the whole story.*

For a moment, I forget everything I've practiced saying. What I'm supposed to do. My mind goes completely blank.

I might panic.

Just a little.

But then I see a little gleam of gold up in a tree.

Azrael.

He's letting me know he's here. He's okay. And that means I'm okay too.

I pull in a breath and address the crowd. "As many of you know, I was tasked with gathering eight keys housed in some of the most remote or bespelled archives in the world. By collecting these and completing the Cold Moon Ceremony, we will formally transfer access to the full witchlore archives from the Joywood to the Riverwood."

There are some more mutters from where the Joywood sit, but I don't allow their words to penetrate. I focus on the crowd of people I know support us. Ellowyn's mother, Tanith, and her partner, Mina. Holly Bishop, who has the coffee shop on Main Street. Corinne, who runs the Lunch House. Emerson and Rebekah's mother, Elspeth, who I thought was still in Germany, on what I consider *my* leather armchair.

"At every stop, I found a key. Eight in total," I say to the crowd. I lift my hands, close my eyes. I picture what I need, whisper the words to bring it to me.

A large, ornate box where I've been keeping everything magicks its way into my hands.

I keep going, murmuring the spell to have the box hover there in front of me so I can pull out all the keys, one by one, and keep the unicorn horn hidden until last. I know there's the possibility that some people will *feel* that magic and wonder what's going on, but they won't be able to guess.

Except maybe the Joywood. But I ignore that thought too.

Because sometimes doing what needs to be done means knowing all the potential pitfalls and worrying about what might go dreadfully wrong, then doing it anyway.

"The first key, made of amber, came from my stop in Sydney." I pull it out of my box. Each member of my coven will wield a key during the spell. This one has been assigned to Emerson.

I hand her the key, and she goes to stand at what will be the metaphorical head of our table, a slight adjustment from the ceremonial instructions we originally found—no doubt left for us by the Joywood—but it's right.

I know it.

Then I hand out the rest of the keys—black agate from Colombo to Jacob, peridot from Tokyo to Rebekah, opal from Juneau to Zander, citrine from Buenos Aires to Ellowyn, sugilite from Accra to Frost—and, one by one, they each take their places in the arrangement of a true coven.

I can see the Joywood exchanging looks of concern, and that brings me some joy.

Okay. A lot of joy.

"The seventh key is for me, an amethyst from London," I tell the crowd, holding it up.

And I have to give credit to my neighbors and friends, and some vocal critics, in the crowd tonight. Maybe no one remembers this ceremony from before the Joywood—assuming there ever *was* a *before the Joywood*—but here in St. Cyprian, we take our ceremonies seriously.

They all applaud wildly, like they've been waiting for this moment none of us knew about for all their lives.

I don't go to my spot at the metaphorical table with my amethyst key, not just yet.

"The thing is, there were eight keys," I tell the crowd. And I want, more than anything, to look for that comforting gleam of gold—but I don't. It's too risky now. "I spent some time trying to discern what this meant. What we should do with an eighth key when there are, as we've all been taught, only seven members in a coven." There are murmurs in the crowd, but they sound more puzzled than anything else. I keep going. "And in my studies, my research, and my own personal fondness for tales of the old magical creatures that used to roam this earth with us, I discovered something called . . . a *true* coven."

The Joywood go dangerously still.

Along our private channel, there's a kind of mental intake of breath. Like we're all bracing for impact. Or schadenfreude.

I want to grin, but I don't. I keep my ditzy, fairy-tale Georgie smile in place. "It's possible it's an old wives' tale," I allow. "Or maybe something we've evolved away from simply because our magical creatures are all gone now. But I had eight keys, and I knew that while there are no longer any magical creatures roaming our world—"

Is that so? Azrael shouldn't be there in my head, sounding dark and lazy and too tempting. It's asking for trouble, but it makes me want to laugh all the same.

I don't. I keep going.

"—there were whispers I'd heard in my travels. Of artifacts, freely given by those magical creatures before they died, still imbued with their magic." That comes out sounding a little too assured, I think, so I make myself look dreamy. I tilt my head so my red curls go everywhere, because I know they're distracting. That this is a trick I learned from Carol Simon and her trademark frizz is something I have kept to myself since I was in middle school. I try to look as guileless as possible. "So I just figured, what can more magic hurt?"

I lift the unicorn horn in the glass so that everyone can see.

A wave of reaction and awe goes through the crowd. Mostly positive, I think—

But Maeve Mather is stomping her feet like a troll beneath a bridge. There's a strange, rodent-sounding squeal coming from over there.

"You shouldn't be able to wield that!" Maeve shrieks.

I look at her, wide-eyed and confused, an act I am *excellent* at. "What do you mean, Maeve?" I look at the horn, then back at her. "I seem to be wielding it just fine."

"It's common knowledge that magic artifacts can only be wielded by witches who were given permission to do such a thing," Gil Redd, the Joywood's tedious Praeceptor, blusters.

"Common knowledge?" I survey the crowd. "Has anyone ever heard of such a thing?"

There are murmurs. Shaking of heads. But not one person agrees with Gil.

Because if it was ever common knowledge, they took it from us.

It does my soul good to use that against them.

"Funny," Frost says in that cut-glass voice of his that seems to etch itself into the bones of anyone who hears it. "I've read that worthy witches can always wield these artifacts."

This time, the murmuring is louder.

Carol says nothing, but I can *feel* her fury undulating out of her and toward us. So I figure it's best to move this along. Careful not to shake, I whisper the words to open the glass case.

For a moment, nothing happens, and I think we're doomed—but then it opens.

I finally let myself glance over at that golden gleam in the trees again.

It seems to . . . wink at me.

On a deep breath, I pull the unicorn horn out of the glass with one hand and hold the key made out of malachite, designated for our fabulae, in the other. I move over to where my coven is arranged and set both where Azrael should be, letting them hover there above the ground.

Then, with my own key, I take my spot.

"We better hurry," Ellowyn mutters.

And she's right. I can feel the Joywood scrambling to find a way to stop us. Their magic is slithering around us, and it seems to get blacker and more ugly as the seconds pass.

But they're not having any luck getting through the protected unicorn horn. It's almost enough to make me giddy, but not yet. We have a spell to do. Anything can happen.

We can't be the only ones who can feel that magic almost *pulsing* all around us.

My coven holds hands, grasping each other to create the rectangle of the table. In the middle of us, our keys form a figure eight.

Frost and I both hold an end of the unicorn horn. It has its own magic, and that no doubt helps, but I can also feel Azrael's magic twining around my hand.

When we all say the words, I can hear him deep inside me, saying those same words.

So it feels like magic, and a vow, all at once—but I concentrate on the spell.

Our magic blooms and pulses, becoming its own figure eight. The keys begin to vibrate, then lift into the air. *"With keys collected, unlock the knowledge meant for us. With magic twined, we reach out to the confluence, the pulsing power of leadership, that begins with truth. Show us how to unlock the truth."*

I can *feel* an oily black entity just behind me, and yet it cannot penetrate. Whether it's our power, the unicorn's, Azrael's, or the fact the Joywood are weakening, I do not know.

But I know we're winning.

The keys crash together with a great boom that shakes the earth under us, but we hold tight to each other so it doesn't shake *us*. Then the keys break apart into a million little floating pieces, and for a moment, I begin to think I've done something wrong.

Could I have messed this up after all?

But as I think that, they begin to swirl, together, into the shape of another key. This one isn't made of a single crystal. It's made of many—and it's threaded through with gold.

Just like a dragon's eyes.

And once it's complete, the key falls into the center of our imaginary table.

"Protect the keys, the knowledge, the truth. Give us the strength to wield all of this. Confluence, be our light, our protection." We close the spell and end the ceremony, still holding hands.

I look up at the tree again, and the gleam of gold is unmistakable, but I seem to be the only one who can see it.

I hope I am.

We bow our heads, release our hands, then turn to all the witches gathered here with us. I move forward and pick up the perfectly solid, warm gold key, shimmering with magic.

A magic I can feel inside me like a kind of map.

And I know what it is. I have opened the witchlore archives.

We opened the witchlore archives.

It makes me want to cry, shout, dance. Throw my arms around my friends. But we look out at the awed crowd. And I can't help but notice the Joywood are still here, but . . . worse for wear.

Maeve is actually missing a shoe. Festus Proctor's face doesn't . . . look right, like it's deforming in front of us. Gil appears as though he might actually be turning into a toad.

And Felicia Ipswitch seems like she's aged three hundred years in the last hour.

Carol, somehow, looks just fine.

Still, I think Emerson must be right. Their magic, their power, must be fading. Carol's is probably just taking longer because she's the most powerful.

Maybe our ascension is stealing it from them. Because they're not just decaying in front of us. They're also not pretending to *look* happy anymore.

They hate that we succeeded.

Which reminds me of the rest of what I want to do tonight. The most important part, in my mind. I address our citizens.

"The witchlore archives are not just for the ruling coven," I tell everyone gathered. "While it will be my responsibility to keep them organized and safe, we will not shut the world out from knowledge. That time is over. The truth is for everyone. Access to knowledge is for *everyone*."

There's a murmur in the crowd. Surprise, I think. Maybe even wonder.

There's also what feels like fury from the Joywood contingent, but I expected that.

I continue on, as if I don't notice. Or more like it doesn't matter if they're mad or not, because it shouldn't. And maybe I'm bold enough to believe it doesn't, not anymore.

"I've been developing a system, and soon I'll put out a call for Historians who'd like to work with me in the archives to help facilitate this," I tell the crowd. "Once the Riverwood have fully ascended, anyone will be able to request information, access resources, and get help finding answers. It's *our* history. We all deserve to know it."

At that, we actually get applause. Better still, the Joywood disappear in one of their dramatic bursts, but almost no one notices because it's muted. Weak. Sad.

Just like them.

The rest of the crowd stays around for a bit, congratulating us and asking me questions about what *access for everyone* will mean for the most random situations.

"Access means access," I keep saying, as patiently as I can. "No one gets to judge you for what you want to know. That's not how knowledge is supposed to work."

And then, as the crowd finally filters away, I turn to the building.

It's glowing. The key in my hand is hot. "I can't wait to dive in. I feel like I could run a marathon. There's so much to find."

Emerson laughs and gives me a squeeze. "You were great, Georgie. But I don't have any marathons in me. Can't we get some rest and start fresh in the morning? We still have over two weeks before the solstice."

"I'm with Em," Rebekah says with a yawn.

"Dead on my feet," Ellowyn agrees, rubbing her belly.

I look at all of them. I can *feel* the archives pulling at me, but they all want to go home. How will I sleep if we go home? How can I possibly leave without—

"I will stay with her," Azrael says, melting out of the shadows in his man form but with eyes completely dragon gold. "A Historian must see her treasures before she can be expected to rest."

Emerson surveys him with some suspicion. But her next words are genuine. "Thank you for your help, Azrael. We could not have done it without you."

He looks . . . not quite offended. "Of course you couldn't have. No thanks are needed. I have done my duty as the Riverwood fabulae, as I always will." He shifts his gaze to Frost. "That is what a true coven does."

Frost only looks back at him with apparent mildness, but I think we can all sense the implied middle finger in his gaze. Azrael laughs.

"I can stay too," Emerson begins to say, but I shake my head.

"It's okay." I smile at my best friend. Even as that melody that's *Azrael* dances inside me. As I imagine where that dance might have led if we hadn't had the ceremony to worry about. As I acknowledge that I want him in a way that should scare me even more than it does.

I can handle the dragon, I tell Emerson.

She still looks at Azrael suspiciously. At the necklace around my neck, then me. Her lips are pursed, and I don't know that it's disapproval, exactly. Worry, I think, is more accurate.

But then she smiles. "All right. But if you need us . . ."

"I know." I always know. Even if the world ended right now, Emerson would find a way to have my back.

We exchange our goodbyes, and there's some reluctance in leaving me alone with Azrael that amuses him, but eventually everyone is gone. It's the two of us.

The melody of the river is back, and I almost look over my shoulder at where it's coming from, but the song between us is louder—

"Go on, then," he says to me, nodding at the building. "You've been waiting your entire life for this. Unlock it."

He isn't wrong, and it makes me forget about the music. It makes me want to hug him.

Because long before I dreamed of ruling covens, I dreamed of having access to the witchlore archives. To all that knowledge, all that history, hopefully untouched by the Joywood's dark magic.

And if I can find clear-cut evidence of the Joywood's misdeeds, then maybe this long nightmare can really be put behind us.

I move up the path. The building is glowing, but nowhere more so than the door I usually unlock first in the mornings. It's a small one in the back, facing the river, and once inside, you can either go up into the museum or down into the basement.

But suddenly there isn't just one keyhole in this door I know so well. There are two. One is dark.

One is gold.

I put the key into the gold one, holding my breath, and the door opens. It looks *almost* the same as it would normally, but the stairway down to the basement is bathed in more bright, shimmering gold.

I can hardly contain myself as I run down the stairs, Azrael behind me.

When I wave my hand to turn on the lights, the basement looks almost like it usually does—until I cross the threshold and all those old boxes and shelves *shift*. Every step I take, another part of the room resolves or dissolves itself.

It's like Frost's library. Things move and change, expand and retract.

As the Riverwood Historian, I'll have more control over it, unlike when I'm in Frost's library.

The idea of control immediately vanishes though, because as I step forward, there on the gleaming table at the center of everything is my book. That stupid fairy tale once again. Complete with that clinch cover.

I can't think of a single reason it should be here amidst all these important tomes I am itching to get my hands on.

Before I can reach out, or send some magic out to make it disappear, Azrael steps around me and picks it up himself. He studies the picture of the dragon and the princess intertwined, then looks at me with a raised brow. "Interesting."

I try to sound unbothered, but I flush. "Is it?"

"What do you suppose this one means?" he asks, but his smile is hungry. And knowing.

I laugh, but why does it sound so . . . shaky? "Who even knows? It's not a fortune teller, Azrael. You have yet to fall bleeding from the sky."

"Because it gave me a warning, and I heeded it. The cover

changed because you lot had the good sense to save me from myself. Had I gone charging after the Joywood or exposed myself as a dragon, that would have likely been me."

My heart is beating so hard in my ears, I'm certain I didn't hear him correctly. "What?"

He looks impatient. "The spell? That makes everyone think I'm a human? It worked. The book warned me and I listened. Now we're on to this next part."

"It's a book, not an oracle," I argue immediately. Even though I can feel all that song and shimmer inside me. That longing, that recognition.

My body is still humming with the magic of the spell, the archives of knowledge are all around me, and I'm Historian enough to find that exciting. But he's *more* exciting, and that should scare me.

It does.

Because I know that there is nothing casual here. Nothing between us that doesn't matter.

No thread in me that fate can't pull tight and make sing.

I try to argue myself out of it. I am a witch. He is a dragon. There's no *sense* to any of this. My life is *not* a fairy-tale book.

Though there must be something wrong with me that I've always wished it was. That I was really that princess. That I could live in a turret and lose myself in books, and imagine whatever I liked where no one else could see it or hear it or know.

He shakes his head sadly, like I'm a failing pupil—and while I have always played up the *Georgie is in the clouds* narrative, I never failed a class.

The longing in me feels heavy, like spun gold, but I make myself ignore him. I reach out into the archives. *Archives, strong and true. Keeper of fact, of knowledge, of truth. Show me, what have the Joywood been up to?*

But nothing happens.

I close my eyes and try to focus more on books than the dragon standing behind me. But once again, nothing happens.

Because it couldn't be that easy. I rub my hands over my face and catch a hint of his scent from the dancing. It goes through me like a shattering. "I suppose I'll have to work harder at it."

"I suppose," Azrael agrees, and I *don't* appreciate the agreement.

"Maybe it will show me something else. Something important. Something . . ." I turn and Azrael is still holding my fairytale book, the cover pointed at me. Like nothing could possibly be more important than that embrace.

Something inside me uncoils at that.

My heart seems to leap into my throat. I swear I can see . . . some vision that feels like a memory, though it isn't mine. It's the princess in her dress, holding her sword, her heart a song I already know.

It's been singing in me since Thanksgiving.

Before that.

Right now, here in the buttery light of the archives, it's the loudest it's ever been.

And I understand that my resistance grows stronger when I'm most afraid that I'm about to dissolve into him the way the archives do around us. Because once I do, there's no taking it back.

This thing between us has been a vow since the start.

Since I sat on a staircase and whispered my most private thoughts to a banister.

The uncoiling thing in me seems to laugh at that. *That is nothing like the start.*

"You still don't understand, Georgina," Azrael says, and there is some rare gravity in his voice while all that fierce dragon gold stares *into* me.

"Understand what?" I ask breathlessly.

But inside, I keep going back. Back to my own history, for

a change. I let myself remember all the dreams I used to have of dragons. *A* dragon. Walking together in a foggy wood. Flying high over places that were not *here*. Waking together in a warm bed, a cozy cave. Fighting, side by side, for right.

For love.

Every time.

My mother tried to charm that away too. Because those dreams did not become me, she would say. They were a sign I was too silly, too foolish, and we couldn't have that.

"Understand *what*, Azrael?" I ask, because I can feel the great *knowing* inside me, *just there*. On the other side of this cliff I've been dancing on for far too long.

He doesn't explain. Not in words.

His huge, solid arms come around me. "You already know," he tells me in a low voice.

Then his mouth is on mine.

And it's like I've never been kissed before in all my life.

That great, wild song inside me swells.

And every last one of the million dreams I've had—both specifically dragon-centered and generic daydreams alike—comes true in the searing heat of his mouth on mine.

The way he kisses me like he has tasted me a thousand times before. Like he already knows me so well, knows the secrets of my body and the key to my soul.

Everything is foolishness and fairy tales and kisses that change everything.

Everything here is meant to be, and it's like I can see our souls twined together through time, through different bodies that are still this, still *us*.

Us. Us. Us.

I think, *This is it. We'll just incinerate each other. Everything will be over, and maybe that was his plan all along? Maybe he is my end.*

But the kiss only keeps going.

It is wild and free and astonishingly carnal. It's like flying, even with my feet firmly planted on the ground, though I try my best to twine myself around him, because this is new and this is memory and *this is it.*

Something inside of me . . . *lets go.* In relief.

Finally.

His voice or mine?

Our voices, or something else?

I don't care, because everything around us pulses. Magic and need. Hope and desire. And the overwhelming feeling that I've been waiting centuries to feel this again. Like I once was a princess, riding a dragon who couldn't be mine. Not in that time.

But in this one . . .

I can feel him pulling himself together to fly us somewhere else, and I have lost any and all resistance somewhere along the way to this marvel of a kiss—

But then something makes a *slamming* sound, deeper in the archives.

We both startle enough to break the kiss. To look at each other, dazed, and then look at where the sound came from.

"What was that?" I ask, trying to move toward the sound.

Azrael growls. "Ignore it."

But clearly the archives want to tell me something. Something that isn't in a fairy-tale book, and I can't ignore that, no matter how I feel on the inside.

Or you want an excuse to stop the unstoppable.

I don't know if that's my own voice or Azrael's, because I see a huge leather-bound book on the floor. On the cover is a big unfurling tree.

Then it slams open, pages flying everywhere, as if there's a great wind in the room, though there's not. When the hubbub stops, an ancient-looking and carefully inscribed family tree is on the open page.

I lean forward, peer at it. "A family tree. A Wilde family tree."

"Georgina."

I don't like the way he says it. Sort of a warning, but a soft one. A *you won't like what you're about to see* warning. He hasn't let me go, but he hasn't pulled me away from the book either.

If the book wants me to know, how can I look away?

Besides.

I see my name.

14

"I DON'T UNDERSTAND," I WHISPER. NOT TO Azrael. Just . . . to the page.

Because this is the *Wilde* family tree. My name shouldn't be anywhere near this.

I push Azrael's arms off me, and while I can feel his reluctance, he lets me. I turn toward the book, crouching down and squinting at *my* name on a Wilde family tree—certain I must be misreading something.

Still, his large hand stays on my arm.

I barely even feel the heat there, because this Wilde family tree doesn't only show *my* name. The line leading from me goes up to my mother, which would make sense if this was the Pendell family tree. And it can only be her, with that name. *Cadence Hilaria Morgan.*

I trace the line from my mother to another name, where my father's name should be. It should say *Stanford Pendell* in the same dark ink, but instead it says . . . something else.

A name I recognize, though it doesn't belong here.

Desmond Wilde.

Emerson and Rebekah's father. Not *mine*.

"This is wrong." That's the only explanation. I actually laugh. "This is . . . the Joywood's dark magic, I guess. A really weird choice, but I never pretended to understand them."

I turn back to Azrael, and there's even a smile on my face. Because it's just . . . wrong. Fake. Nothing else makes any kind of sense.

But Azrael is standing there, his arms crossed though he's still dressed in his finery, and he looks . . . sympathetic?

It's not an expression I imagine has often been on his dragony face.

And suddenly, I can't really feel my body. Like I've gone entirely numb.

Too many things are hitting me at once.

My father looking sad, talking about *facts* and *stories*.

Azrael saying with such confidence that my parents used to be friends with the Wildes when I never knew them to do more than exchange a polite nod, then move on quickly—and his shiftiness about it. Not that he was lying, I understand now. That he didn't *want* to lie to me.

The Joywood at our ascension trials telling me I didn't even know my own past.

And if I go back farther in my memories, I can suddenly remember an old picture of Lillian Wilde that used to hang in the guest room I often slept in. Emerson and Rebekah's grandmother treated *all* of us like grandchildren when we were growing up, even giving me her brownie recipe when I was just the neighbor's kid.

In it, she was a young, happy bride.

With flowing red curls.

The kind of red I've never seen anywhere in any of *my* relatives, but see in my mirror every day.

Everything goes a little dim then. Like all the lights went out, all that magical gold.

And in the center of the remaining gray is my name on a Wilde family tree.

My. Name.

"Georgina, you must breathe."

It's only when he says this, and actually sounds concerned, that I realize I've been holding my breath, like I'm trying to make myself pass out. I suck in a tortured gasp, then let it out on something like a sob. "I don't understand."

I lift my gaze to meet his. I stare at him. I can't make sense of any of this, least of all Azrael.

Because . . . "You knew?"

He looks uncomfortable. It's the first time I've seen him anything but totally confident since he exploded into his actual form in the foyer of Wilde House.

"I overheard some things in my time as a newel post," he says.

Far too carefully.

"What things?"

"Georgina."

He doesn't have to say *you don't want to know*. I can read it all over his face.

So I have to say it myself. I have to stitch it together myself. This horrible, impossible thing the archives wanted me to know.

The thing the Joywood certainly knows.

My mouth is so dry it hurts, but I force the words out. "My mother and Desmond Wilde had an affair."

He does not deny this. And when I only stare at him, he gives a very slow nod.

Holy Hecate. Blessed Soteria. This is real.

I feel like my knees are going to give out, but before they do, a chair is shoved under me, and I collapse into it.

The family tree lies in that book at my feet.

Wilde family tree. Desmond Wilde.

I cradle my head in my hands, like I need extra support as my mind whirls and whirls and whirls. But what I keep coming back to is my dad tonight.

He knew I'd be getting access to the archives.

He knew what I would find.

Facts are not always the whole story.

"My dad knew," I hear myself say, muffled because my mouth is buried in my own palms. "It's why he was sad tonight. He knew I'd find out. He knew the truth and he knew I'd find it. But how did he know? How long has he known?"

I'm not sure I'm really asking that as a question so much as thinking aloud. I think back, trying to pinpoint a moment. But in my memory, my parents have always been what they've been—the way they are now. Not happy. Not terrible. My mother too sharp, my father too soft.

Just . . . them.

Why would he have stayed if he knew what she'd done? Why would he have kept up this fiction?

Why did he . . . treat me like his own?

"This I do not know," Azrael says quietly, and he could be answering any of those questions. "After a certain point, your father never returned to Wilde House."

"And my mother?"

"There were certain discussions."

I stand then. My weak knees are replaced by a restless need to *move*. I pace back and forth, and on one pass, I shove a finger in his direction. "You have to tell me. *You knew.*"

He clearly doesn't care for being pointed at. Just as he clearly prefers to be *making* the demands. It's stamped all over his gorgeous face.

If only I'd kept kissing him.

If only I could rewind time and kiss him all night, and not have to know this.

When Azrael speaks, it is gentle, and somehow that's worse. "Desmond refused to acknowledge you. At first, this enraged your mother, but then, I suppose, she accepted it. Either way, she never graced the door of Wilde House again."

I'm thinking about all of those years. My whole *life*. Emerson's and Rebekah's whole lives too. Emerson and I used to say we were as close as sisters, especially in the years Rebekah was in exile. And all that time we *were*. We *are*.

We have all been raised in a *lie*.

I guess this should feel old hat by now. The Joywood sold all of us lies for too many years. I still don't know how many.

They also knew about this, I remind myself. About me. They had access to this very same book.

It makes me feel almost like they're in here with me, their oily magic on everything and all over my skin.

"I was only an observer," Azrael tells me in that same disturbingly quiet way, when I have never heard a story about a dragon caring for the petty little concerns of mortal witches. But then, Azrael has cared for me even when *all* he heard were my petty concerns, my sleepwalking truths whispered like prayers in the dark of a sleeping house. "I know what I saw and heard, but I do not know the full truth. That would have to come from the people who hid this from you."

Still, he knew. All this time. Like my mother, like my father. Like my enemies.

"You should have told me," I say in a pained whisper.

"Why?"

"I had a right to know."

"I cannot argue that point, but why was it up to me?"

I stare at him. I have no quick answer. Only a cascade of twisted, complicated emotions I can't make sense of, but seem wrapped up in all that gold in his onyx gaze.

"You know your coven, your friends," Azrael says, and some of that gentleness is starting to turn to impatience. Perversely, that makes me feel the slightest bit better, because it's him. It's normal. It's the first hint I have that I might actually survive this moment, the weight of this knowledge. "What is it you're afraid of? I would wager considerable riches on Emerson being nothing but overjoyed that you are her sister."

I am *actually* Emerson's sister. I am living in Wilde House and I am *not* an interloper. I belong to it. And to my best friend.

"Emerson will celebrate, but she'll also be deeply hurt by her father." And I can't accept it. I can't *be okay* with it. Her father *had sex* with my mother. It makes my stomach hurt. "Rebekah, on the other hand . . ."

"Will hate her father more, if possible. That has little to do with you."

Why is he being so reasonable when *everything* is wrong?

The worst part, I think then, is that I will be tasked with setting it all to rights. Because I'm the one who found out. *I'm* the one who's going to break the lie that we've all been living under, and as I know from this last year, no one likes that.

But I don't know *how* to fix this. I don't know if this can be fixed. It's so complicated and twisted, I don't even know who I should speak to first.

No one, I think. I want to tell *no one*. Once again, I want to go back in time.

For a moment, I'm actually tempted to try it. But time is a dangerous thing. If you steal time, you lose time, just like the nursery rhyme taught us.

Then again, I *want* to lose this.

Azrael grips my arms then, and not gently. "Georgina, get a hold of yourself."

I look at his eyes, black and gold. For a moment, it's like I can see a million years reflected back at me. Riding dragons and fighting the darkness, always the darkness. Crows in the air and around us. Endless wars and a great, bright sword.

But that's just that stupid book again.

Isn't it?

He rubs his hands down my arms. Then he pulls me close, into an embrace that is not less affecting for being a simmering fire instead of a blaze.

"Let us return to Wilde House. I will draw you a crystal

bath." I feel his breath move through my hair, and something relaxes, deep inside, at being in his arms again. I get the impression that touching me, holding me close, calms him. Like he needs this too. "You can invite me to join you, of course."

I think he is trying to make me laugh. To lighten the mood. But with the earlier kiss and this strange connection between us, he has miscalculated.

And with my entire world upended tonight, I have to make this clear.

I don't want to wish for too much. I can't *let* myself be wrong, not about him.

I push him away, just enough so I can look up at him. "I don't know what life was like before you were cursed, but I doubt witches and dragons were . . ."

I trail off because I don't know what word to use for that kiss, for what I sense waits for us there, in all that wildness and sweet fire.

His gaze is so intense that it should hurt. "Have you not read your own book?"

"It's a *fairy tale*, Azrael."

"It is a history of who our souls once were."

"You can't honestly think—"

"I don't think. I know. I am a *fabulae*, Georgina. I *know*. And so do you. Have you not dreamed it? Always."

Always.

It echoes inside me, deep and loud. I recognize it. I remember it. But I have never let that echo control me. "A Pendell knows when to draw the line between fairy-tale foolishness and facts. Cold, hard facts."

Yet *facts are not always the whole story*, my dad, who is not my father, said only tonight.

And my mother has been lying to me since the day I was born.

"But you are not a Pendell," Azrael says, with a quiet ruthlessness that slices through me like a stab wound.

I laugh then, a little hysterically. Even when I wasn't living up to the name, I lived my life with the understanding that this Pendell Historian would have to accept who she was someday. Boring and drab and *reasonable*, even if in the ruling coven. Oh, I like my bright colors and flowy scarves and fantasies, but the truth of me was the scholar of books, the devotee of research.

Because that's who Pendells are.

And now that's been taken away from me. It should be a relief. Maybe at some point it will be, but right now I can only feel betrayal. "You're right. I'm a *Wilde*." Desmond Wilde's *secret child*. I laugh again. "I don't even *like* Desmond Wilde. Does anyone?"

I can feel—and see—the frustration mounting in him, and that hardly seems fair. *His* life didn't get upended today.

I ignore the fact that he did spend a long, long time cursed into that newel post.

"It doesn't matter what name you use," he growls at me. "Names don't matter. Don't you see? *That's* the point. Who cares who you are in this time?"

"This time?" I ask, though something in me is shaking. Like I am coming apart, from the bones on out.

He knows. Maybe he feels it. I can see it in the way his gaze searches mine. In the knowing, demanding gleam in all that gold.

"We are bound together, you and I, in every time." Azrael says this like prophecy. Like fact. And he is not done. "There has never been a moment in all of eternity that you have not been mine. You have lived many lives, and I am in all of them. This is who we are."

For a moment, I'm frozen. In sheer terror.

Because I want it to be true, even though I know it can't be. Maybe dragons can live in every time, in many different lives, but witches get the once. This is common knowledge. That's why we have ghosts.

This is who we are.

Even though it can't be, I want it to make sense of everything I've ever felt and denied.

I want to be the princess in that book.

I want everything I was told I couldn't have because I was a *fucking* Pendell, and Pendells do not get to shine like that.

But I am not a Pendell.

I never have been.

"Okay, then," I manage to get out.

Because in this moment, where my entire life has been upended, I don't want to ask the questions. I don't want to *fix* anything. I don't want to pore over the *facts* and go drop this same bomb on my friends.

I want to be his. I want him to be right, and this feeling inside me to be true. For once, I want everything I feel to be the only truth I hold on to. If dragons can exist, why can't lifetimes? He was right about true covens and fabulae, so why shouldn't I let myself believe it's possible he's right about *this*?

Now it's my turn to reach out to him, to pull his mouth down to mine, to pour all this . . . whirling, confusing *mess* of mine into him.

And he takes it and turns it into wildfire.

Magic sparks against magic, desire against desire. We are nothing but flame—and I need it. Goddess, how I need it.

To sear off all these confusing things I don't want to know.

I want it to roar through me and wash it all away.

I want to be purified in his *this is who we are* until I believe it too.

His hands are as hot as his mouth, rough and deliriously mobile. Our mouths are greedy, until there is nothing but us.

An us that does not seem to be tethered to my outside body, but to something far deeper.

Then we're in the air.

The stars press in all around us, and we're not flying the way we did before. This is something else.

"How are we . . . ?" I ask in part wonder, part desire. "I'm not a . . . ?"

"Dragon magic," he tells me.

Because I am flying with him, but my body is not my body. We are both smoke and swirling, rush and plummet. I stretch into scales and stars, wrapping myself around him, my arms wide like wings. Maybe I really do have wings.

And everything is a building, blinding pleasure. Everything is magic.

"I don't know what to do," I tell him, and the heavens.

"You do," he tells me, his mouth at my neck. "You have done exactly this too many times to count."

And I know it's true. I know it's all true. I know it's fate and longing, passion and joy.

His magic makes me a dragon in the air, just like him. Crafted specifically for him and the press of his immensity within.

There is no name. There is no time. There is only *us*.

And a dizzying culmination that is more than just any moment. It is every moment.

Souls meant to come together, no matter what time they find themselves in.

Then we land in my bed, breathless and pulsing, in the shape of a man and a woman.

"Now," Azrael murmurs as he crawls down my body and settles himself between my legs, "dessert."

And when the fire comes for me then, I arch up and cry out. It's brighter and hotter and louder than any other I've known.

Azrael laughs. It's a deep sound I can feel between my legs, into my skin, deep into my bones. Again and again, until we roll together and I climb on top of him. I prop myself up against the wide expanse of his chest.

I look down at him, and I know.

This is ancient, this power we have over each other. For each other.

This is forever, this passion without borders or bounds, beyond life and death.

I am his. He is mine.

His gaze is gold and black and fire straight through.

It's *him*.

He is *mine*.

We have always been this. Us. *Fate*.

It takes me a long, hot little struggle—even though I am something far more than merely *ready*—to take all of him deep inside me. To breathe until I can move, then lose myself in the slide and catch and the sheer perfection of the magic we make together.

Over and over and over again.

Until we can do nothing but breathe into each other, wrung out and still perfect, and *us*. Here in my bed, like we have always belonged here.

Azrael pulls me close, tucks me against his body, my head in the crook of his arm.

I hear him growl against my neck. *"My own."*

But as my breathing steadies, I'm forced to realize that as wonderful as that was—too spectacular to believe, in fact—it really didn't *solve* anything.

I feel so much joy and *wholeness* that this sadness shouldn't still be sitting there in the pit of my stomach. It should have been wiped away. At least for a little while.

Azrael presses a kiss to my temple. "Go on, then. Let it out. You'll feel better."

So I cry.

And I let my dragon comfort me, as he did when he was my sleepwalking daydream.

The way I want to believe he always has.

15

I WAKE UP IN MY BED. ALONE.

Well. Not entirely alone. Octavius is curled up at my feet. His eyes are open, and he is studying me with a certain kind of knowing I do not wish to parse.

It's a relief not to have to have a conversation with anyone just yet. I need some time alone to sort through . . . everything. In the light of day. In the comfort of my own thoughts.

You're welcome.

So much for my own thoughts.

But I smile in spite of myself. Azrael's nearby, but also giving me what I need. Because I may not understand the exact *hows* yet, but I understand *this*.

Our souls belong together.

I don't *want* to believe it, in the light. I just do.

I stretch. I don't feel called to commune with my crystals, not just yet. So I simply move over to the window seat and curl up there. I look out at the pearly light of another cold morning. It's early yet, and unusual for me to be up without an alarm, but I suppose that makes sense too.

After all, a lot of things happened last night.

And I *want* to handwave it all away, like it was a long, complicated dream. I *want* to tell myself everything that happened last night—and I mean everything—is confusing if not impossible, but . . .

Trouble is, it makes a little too much sense.

We've always been told that a witch's soul is a one-time deal. Witch to death to ghost, if you can master the energy in the afterlife. But we've also been told magical creatures went extinct and the Joywood aren't evil.

So.

I let that thought roll where it will, and I hit more questions.

Why has Wilde House always felt like home? Emerson like a sister, Lillian like my own grandmother? Why did moving over here at eighteen and talking to a carved dragon head all night long seem so *right* even when I was constantly trying to convince myself—or my mother was doing it for me—that it was wrong? That I should shuffle back home and act more like a Pendell and less like my friends. Less like I might be *special*.

What I can't really fathom is my dad's role. Not *Desmond Wilde*—I still can't face that head-on—but the man I've always *thought* was my father. If he knew, and what he said to me last night suggests he did, why did he go along with it? I need to talk with him.

But I also know I need to talk with my coven.

And Azrael.

I have to deal with *everything* and that's unfortunate, because what I *want* to do is get back in bed, pull the covers over my head, and sleep for a year, getting up only for snacks and a good book.

Octavius makes a graceful leap up onto the seat. It's an impressive feat for such a big, chunky cat. He crawls into my lap, and I scratch his throat until he purrs.

And the more he purrs, the less I feel the bed calling me.

In the light of day, this moment is not too big for me. I won't let it be. Something *special* is blooming inside me.

Because no matter the thing about Pendells, or my mother, or anything else, the Riverwood *is* special. And I am part of it.

I pick up Octavius and cradle him like a baby, just the way he likes, until his purring vibrates within me like my own contentment. It makes me smile, and more, fills me with a kind of determination. Or maybe it's just that I understand myself and my place in all this better this morning, having finally learned my own history.

I can identify as a Pendell because I was raised by them. I can identify as a Wilde because apparently I have that bloodline in me.

Or I can just be *me*. A soul that has been around the block a few times, apparently.

And has found Azrael in every one.

I sit with that for a moment, Octavius's purr like a rumble in my own chest. I used to have dreams along those lines, past lives and past adventures, and every single time, my mother told me I was delusional and it was *worrisome*. She charmed my sleep to keep me from dreaming.

But all these years, I was right to believe, to hope, to *dream*.

I put Octavius down, then set about getting ready. I have historic house tours to give today, as part of one of Emerson's holiday initiatives. Nothing about yesterday changes that, except I have more connection to this particular historic house than simply living in it.

I slide on a labradorite bracelet, a nod to my imagination and the dreams that brought me here. Some rings with honey calcite and iolite for when I can get to the archives later, one of which I bought in Sri Lanka when I got the key in Colombo.

I'm reminded of what Azrael said last night, and while I have no fear of Sage, I consider my collection of black jade. There's one in the shape of a crow, but it has eyes made of amethyst, and that's not what I want. So I grab the black jade carved in the shape of a little rodent I picked up in London because I thought it was cute. I slide it into my pocket for protection.

I leave my room, but I hear something in my library down the hall. Frowning, I magic myself inside because the door barely opens thanks to all the books in there. And because anything that messy repels pretty much everyone, especially Emerson, giving me privacy without my having to ask for it.

I weave my way through books, trying to find the source of it. It's faint, but I can hear it, and it tugs even harder. It's that melody again, and it wants to fill me up.

I want it to fill me up.

I make it to the window and toss it open, leaning out into the crisp morning air. I can see the river out there, dark and dotted with ice. Is it singing to me? Does it want me to—

Octavius is meowing at the door, and I look away from the window. He's stuck one paw inside, but he's pretending he can't get the rest of the way in when he could magic himself inside if he pleased.

I sigh and go back to the door, move some books out of the way, and open the door wider. But he doesn't enter. He just keeps meowing at me, louder and more pointedly.

"I don't know what your problem is, but I guess we should go down to breakfast," I tell him placatingly.

He stops meowing, then takes a few steps toward the stairs. He even looks back at me like he's making sure I follow. I shake my head, because cats are cats even when they're magic, and I follow him downstairs. I hear the murmuring of voices and the smell of breakfast coming from the kitchen. When I step into the cozy room, everyone is already here, sitting around a table and eating another elaborate breakfast Emerson no doubt put together.

But Azrael is where my gaze goes first. He's leaning casually against the counter, mainlining food and coffee, as usual. When his gaze meets mine, his smile turns dragony, and his eyes are hot and gold.

"Good morning," he greets me. "I have called a meeting."

I wait to be horrified by that, or at least a little frustrated. I never said I was ready to discuss *any* of this the moment I woke up. Or at all. Just because I can maybe accept that this is happening between us, that doesn't mean there shouldn't be good, healthy boundaries where he doesn't just swoop ahead and *decide* things.

But at the same time, this was going to fly out of my mouth the moment I looked at Emerson. I know how to keep myself hidden from people. I know how to hide from the truths that make me feel small.

What I don't know how to do is hide from the fact that Emerson is my half sister. That Rebekah is too. That we are *actually* family. There's no smallness there, just sadness about other people's choices.

I smile back at Azrael, because he was right to call it.

"Were the archives everything you hoped they would be?" Emerson's smile is wide, her eyes eager. "Can we make a very long PowerPoint presentation on all the Joywood's misdeeds?"

"Not yet," I say carefully, piling my plate high with food. My stomach has started to jitter with nerves, but I don't let those nerves win. I *won't*. "The archives are finicky and won't give me everything I want right away, apparently. It'll take some work, but I'll get there."

Emerson smiles at me. "Of course you will."

And I am caught by the overwhelming *reality* of this. She is my *sister*. And I know it doesn't matter, because she always has been, whether we knew we shared blood or not. My ultimate champion and supporter and *friend*.

"There was something the archives did . . . Well, some things have changed," I say.

I look around for Azrael, and he's standing behind me. Like support.

If support was also guzzling down every flavor of muffin.

I look back at my coven. My friends. My *family*, and I take the empty seat next to Emerson. Then, as we sip our coffee and eat our breakfast, as we have so often this last year, I start at the beginning.

I tell the story of two keyholes, the golden light. The way the room shifted and changed.

I do not leave any details out. I talk about the book, the changing cover. When I get to the kissing part, I lay it all out there. The menfolk are various shades of horrified. For different reasons, I'm sure. Jacob likes his privacy. Frost is no fan of the dragon, his ancient enemy. Zander looks disappointed, then slides a twenty-dollar bill across the table to Ellowyn.

"I *knew* it," she says, waving the money in the air.

"You had a bet?" There is a mix of surprise and censure in Emerson's tone.

"And you didn't let me join in?" Rebekah shakes her head. "Because I'd definitely be a winner too."

I frown at both Ellowyn and Rebekah. It's not the bet that surprises me, exactly. It's more that I'm surprised they saw what I kept talking myself out of seeing.

"I mean, he's clearly got the hots for you," Ellowyn says, and smiles because if she says it, then it's true. "And you're flustered by him." Also true. "It was only a matter of time."

Again, true.

"I do not know if I like this characterization," Azrael grumbles.

"Welcome to the Riverwood coven and the Ellowyn truth

bomb," Zander says, not exactly in a friendly way. But not like the knives are out, either. "You learn to deal with it."

Emerson puts her hand over mine, her gaze concerned. "But none of what you told us is a change, is it? Except your level of access to witchdom's history."

"True." I take a deep breath. Then I tell them about the book interruption. The way it opened itself up to the Wilde family tree. "My name was on it."

Emerson's grip on my hand tightens, but she's grinning. "Oh! Are we long-lost cousins? One of those you go back far enough and we're tenth cousins twice removed type things?"

I shake my head. "A little . . . closer than that."

"How much closer?" Rebekah asks darkly, like she knows where this is going. I can't imagine she does, not just yet, but she's definitely picking up more than Emerson is.

"My mother's name was there." I don't mean to drag this out and make it more dramatic. But it's so hard to find the words. "Stanford Pendell was not listed as my father." I suck in a deep breath, then look at Azrael. He gives me a reassuring nod, all gold eyes, and that helps me say the thing I won't be able to take back. "Desmond Wilde was."

A heavy silence fills this room I know so well. This happy kitchen where Emerson and Rebekah's grandmother used to putter around, singing little songs to herself, always far more aware of what we were up to than we liked to believe.

Maybe I'm not the only one remembering Lillian Wilde and her brand of magic that sometimes wasn't *magic* at all, but love—and thinking about the fact that she was *my* grandmother too.

It all settles on us, hard and irrevocable and yes, ugly. I wish I could say something else, something to fix this and make it less . . . *huge*.

I wouldn't say Emerson looks *devastated*, exactly, but she's clearly thinking about her parents and their marriage. Maybe about the *details*, like what Desmond had to be up to that year if he got three daughters out of it. About what it means that they all kept this lie *this* long. Wondering if everyone knows but us.

She looks at me, a little desperately. "Maybe the Joywood changed something and . . ." But she doesn't finish the sentence.

"Em. I don't think the Joywood can change what's inside the archives. Hide it, maybe, but make actual changes to the lore? I don't think so. Too much adds up. The way my father was acting, things the Joywood have said, the red hair, like your grandmother's." I can't call Lillian *mine*. Not yet. Not *out loud*. No matter what that family tree said. I take a deep breath, hold her gaze and her hand. "I don't think it's wrong."

"We can't really be surprised that Dad's an even bigger dick than we already thought he was, can we?" Rebekah asks darkly.

"I don't know the details," I tell her, with a great calm that must come from somewhere, though I have no idea where. "Azrael . . . observed some things, overheard some things, during that period."

"Did our mom know?" Emerson asks him.

He lifts a shoulder. "I'm not sure. The only thing I saw or heard was Desmond and Cadence speaking. There was fighting between your parents, but that was hardly new. I do not know if anyone else knew. If they did, it was not spoken of around me."

Emerson nods, and then she looks back at me. Her smile blooms, even if it's a little wobbly, and I can still see those worries in her eyes. "That means you're our sister."

I feel my own eyes starting to tear up. I nod. "Yeah."

"Georgie." She shakes me by the shoulders, and even though a tear spills over that she quickly dashes away, she's grinning from ear to ear. "We're *sisters*."

It makes me laugh. And for the first time, I'm really able to feel the *joy* at that. My best friend in the world is my sister. My *sister*.

"Thank Hecate," Rebekah says, and she's smiling too, though there are no tears. And no darkness or bitterness when she reaches over to squeeze my hand too. "Now we can share the load of having to be *Emerson Wilde's* little sisters."

"I am *honored*," I whisper back, past the knot in my throat.

"Did you find anything else out?" Frost asks. "Perhaps the next step in fully ascending?"

He's trying to sound dry and like he doesn't care, but I don't believe that. I think maybe he's protecting Rebekah's feelings.

"I was a little distracted," I say. But that's not really the right word. "Upset. It's not easy to accept that you're not who you thought you were."

"Nothing about *you* changes, Georgie," Emerson tells me fiercely. Her arm is still around my shoulders.

"I think maybe it does, but in a good way," I assure her. "The whole last week—or year, or maybe my whole life—I've been trying so hard to be *realistic*. Scholarly and rational. The perfect Pendell my mother wanted me to be. But I'm not a Pendell, and she's not perfect herself. So maybe . . . maybe this is the last straw, and I can finally let all that go."

Emerson squeezes me again. "You could have come and told me last night. You didn't have to sleep on it."

I glance at Azrael. I could lie. I could say it delicately. But why bother? I have my dragon, and he has me. "We were . . . not sleeping, Em. First we were not sleeping in the air. Then we came back here and continued to not sleep in my bed. And the shower. Or beneath my crystals in the trees in the back garden, which you might think would be cold, but not with a dragon."

Zander puts his fork down and runs a hand over his face. "Why? Why would you say all that out loud? *I* didn't need to know that. I *never* need to know that."

Frost looks like a statue. Jacob looks like he's exited his body.

I realize that I'm happy. Just . . . happy, despite everything. Or maybe because of it.

"I needed to know *all* of that," Ellowyn says emphatically. She leans toward me, grinning. "Details, please."

But before I can offer any, just to see how all the men—including Azrael—will respond to *details*, Emerson's phone alarm starts trilling.

"That's the five-minute warning before I have to leave for the store," she says, glaring at her phone. "And the historic home tour starts in fifteen. Do you want me to call off the tour? I can."

"No, of course not. I can handle it."

"But you don't *have* to."

I think about sacrifices, and the difference between the ones forced on you and the ones you choose. I think of the responsibility we've been handed by our entire community. It's a weight, but it's also a gift. And so is this.

"No, I don't *have* to," I say. "I want to. I love giving the tours, and we haven't let anything that's happened this year get in the way of living our normal lives. Why start now?"

Everyone begins to move. Zander says goodbye to Ellowyn with a kiss for her and the baby, then is off to the ferry. Jacob magicks himself off to a Healer call.

"Once I finish the tour, I'll head back to the archives and see what else they have to tell me," I assure Frost.

Rebekah stands with him, then pulls me into a rare hug. "I guess you belong in this house after all," she whispers to me.

I want to cry again, but I know Rebekah would recoil at that, so I just squeeze her back and release her, so they can head back to Frost House to continue the ongoing research into any and all details on ascension we can find.

Then it's Emerson's turn. She pulls me into an even harder hug.

"This doesn't change who we are. Not really. Everything before this moment still happened, and everything we're facing still has to be overcome," I tell her, but I hold on just as hard to her.

She pulls back, just a little. "We didn't need blood to be sisters, but it's . . . it's amazing, all the same."

I nod.

Then Ellowyn and I eye each other.

"I'm not particularly tactile," she says, but then smiles and gives me a quick hug too—which might just be a greater miracle than a staircase accessory turning into a dragon lover.

Then the two of them head out onto Main Street to walk down to their shops together.

Azrael slides his arm around my waist and tugs me closer into him. Easy. Like this is just who we are. A unit.

Like all those little gestures Jacob and Emerson have been doing for months that make my heart *ache*.

I thought I was jealous, and maybe I was. But maybe I also knew I had this out there somewhere. That it wasn't *Sage*, no matter how much I told myself it should be.

I lean into him and let his strength replenish my own. It's a lot. This year has all been a *lot*. And there's still so much more to come.

But for today, I need to give one of the tours of the historic houses on Main, all dressed up for the holiday. The first tour group will meet here in just a few minutes. Then I'll take them around Wilde House before moving them on to the next. The Pendell house.

It's not really the morning for a dragon.

"You could tag along with Ellowyn to Tea & No Sympathy," I suggest. "Flex those merchant muscles."

He's silent for a moment. "Trying to get rid of me?"

"Unless you want to pretend to be human in a group and learn about the history of this house—which you probably already know—I think helping Ellowyn out might be more fun for you, and more helpful for Ellowyn than it would be for me."

"Are you calling me a distraction?" He grins down at me.

And I remember, in my mind's eye and every inch of my body, just what last night was like.

"Yes," I say.

Emphatically.

He laughs, but then sobers. "What are you wearing for protection?"

"Black jade."

He makes a considering sound, like this is acceptable, but not enough. He takes my hand and slides a ring, black tourmaline twisted with gold, onto my finger.

My left ring finger.

Suddenly everything that I've rolled with well enough over the past twelve hours seems to crash inside my chest, a little like panic. "Azrael . . ."

"You've worn it before," he says, lifting my hand and pressing a kiss to the top of it. His eyes so gold it hurts. It reminds me of what it was like when he was inside me. "Because in every time, you are you. You are my own. And in every life, I claim you as best I can."

"Claim?" I echo, a new kind of song rising in me.

"I will always claim you," he tells me, and he sounds almost formal. "With fire and fury, as suits a dragon's woman." Then he flashes that grin at me, as if he's not making my head spin. "And my favorite princess."

"Tell me," I whisper at him, not sure where this desperate longing comes from. "Tell me about us."

His expression saddens, and that hurts more than the desperate longing.

"I cannot tell you what our past lives were, Georgina. It is not what magic or time or my soul will allow. Your soul might be old, well traveled, *mine*—but it is in a new body, with a new life, and you must live the current one. Not relive the past ones."

I suppose this makes sense, though I don't *love* it. Especially considering my entire life is dedicated to the past, essentially. Also . . . "Why do *you* remember, then?"

His response is as grave as I've ever heard him. "Dragons always remember."

He doesn't say, *It is our curse*, but it hangs in the ether, like something I once knew.

Before I can ask more questions, the doorbell rings. And Azrael disappears in a dramatic puff of dragon smoke. I think it was supposed to make me laugh, but I'm stuck on *dragons always remember* . . . as if the memories are not always *good*.

16

I REGRET SENDING AZRAEL OFF THE MINUTE I open the door to the first tour group.

Usually, these groups consist of more humans than witches. If we do get witches, they tend to be from out of town. Interested in the lore of St. Cyprian, the center of the witching world, and eager to soak in their own history.

But today, Carol Simon herself is part of the group standing on the porch. I'm not sure if I'm more shocked by her presence or the fact she's wearing a very dramatic brooch in the shape of a weasel.

That looks a little too much like the little rodent of black jade in my pocket.

Yet this is hardly the most pressing matter at hand.

Emerson took care of the "company" spell that every witch knows, to make sure the house looks its best when guests arrive—but I add a little extra to it with a muttered word—*sparkle*—to withstand Carol and to hide things like the ring I'm wearing.

I don't want to find out if she's seen it before too.

Then I work on that ditzy smile and offer a broad, historical welcome to Wilde House as I beckon the group inside. I launch my well-rehearsed spiel about when the house was built, charmed with the usual spell, so that the humans just hear dry human history while the witches hear about the flight from Salem, the search for a place where three rivers meet, and the founders' decision to hide one of the rivers to protect this place that must stay hidden.

I'm halfway through when I realize that Carol is not only not paying attention, she's studying the chandelier in the entryway with suspicion. Like she's worried that the mermaid is free and helping us out.

Oh *shit*.

I don't glance back at the dragon newel post, even though I want to. We fixed it and glamoured it back to looking how it should, but will she know that he's not in there anymore?

I think you have to get in the newel post, I shout frantically to Azrael in my head, putting my hand around the necklace he gave me like it's some kind of safety blanket, tangled there with the one I usually wear. No doubt he's already at Tea & No Sympathy, but his voice is in my head almost immediately.

I think you have perhaps lost your entire mind. I blame the sex.

Carol is here.

He says nothing to that, and I have to stop worrying about *him*, and start worrying about the crowd of people I've just ushered into Wilde House.

I go deeper into lecture mode. I talk about the history of the house. What's original—like the woodwork, some of the flooring—and what's been added on over the years—like the chandelier, the glass, the modern amenities. Luckily, it doesn't seem unnatural for me to stand in front of the newel post while I do this with everyone crowded into the foyer. I can see Carol trying to angle herself so she can look at it more closely, but I do everything I can to block her while also trying to make it look natural.

I talk about the decorations. Each historic house on the tour gets a historical period and must decorate like that period would have, so I go on a long lecture about how our bright, colorful decorations evoke the period of the 1950s.

Then I point toward the kitchen, even though usually I'd move into the living room and the library. I feel like it's easier to lead them away from the newel post this way. "From here, we'll move into the kitchen. A more modern addition, but with some interesting historical touches."

"Don't we usually head into the living room at this point?" Carol interrupts as I make a move to take them toward the kitchen—away from the staircase.

Why is *she* interested in the living room? I thought she was here to spy on the newel post?

Then I remember the *nachtkrapp* on the rug in the living room. She isn't focused on Azrael. She's looked at the mermaid, the newel post, and now wants a look at the rug. She's essentially checking up on anything cursed in Wilde House.

I smile wide, because this is actually a relief. She might suspect something, but she doesn't know what. She can only guess.

I can work with that.

"Usually," I say brightly. "But I decided to change it up this year. The kitchen is the heart of the house, and I think to understand the rest of the house, you have to understand that."

I can tell there are no cursed magical creatures in the kitchen because Carol looks bored and irritable, though she's still *gleaming*. There is something alarmingly *youthful* about her face, which is not something I've ever noticed about Carol Simon before.

Once I've said absolutely everything I can think to say about a kitchen, with anecdotes about the warmth of Grandma Lillian Wilde—which, yes, I know will annoy Carol, who never liked her much and had a hand in her early death—I move through the rest of the downstairs, always watching Carol to see if there's some other cursed magical creature I've never noticed before.

When we're in the living room, she stands right on the rug. I see her dig her heel into the bird's heart.

When we head upstairs, my nerves pick up. Because I don't know for sure if Azrael is in the newel post, and I don't dare look. I'm worried it will cause Carol to pay far too much attention.

But, in a move born out of habit more than purpose, I run my hand over the newel post as I start my ascent up the stairs. It's warm again, that impossible heat I used to tell myself was my imagination. Now I know better.

Azrael.

But I can't linger. Maybe it's him. Maybe he's simply sent his magic into the post. But he's there in some way. I glance back and see Carol do the same thing I did.

Then she snatches her hand away, as though she's been zapped with electricity.

I have to smother a smile.

Upstairs, I go through the same process. I answer questions from eager humans and keep my eye on Carol. There's a lamp in the shape of a Piasa bird in the second-floor hall, but she seems more interested in looking out any windows that overlook the river.

I think back to this morning in my library. I thought I heard that same song that's been teasing me lately floating up from the river. Does Carol hear it too?

And . . . is that good, or terrifying?

Maybe I need to find the source of it before she does. I should mention it at our next coven meeting.

When I finish the tour of the upper levels of the house, all securely magicked to be as impressive and anodyne as possible no matter who happens to be living here at any given time, I lead everyone back downstairs. Carol gives the dragon newel post a wide berth, but also a little smirk. As if she's won.

I'm glad she thinks so.

Personally and strategically.

I herd the group out onto the sidewalk outside. "And now you'll all head to the next stop on the tour, the Pendell home," I say, and point toward my father, already standing out on his porch.

He waves. I wave back. We've done this for the past five years. I always follow up my wave by proudly telling the crowd my father is a *fantastic* historian—witches know this means his designation is Historian, not just that he likes to research arcane topics as many humans do in historic villages—and will have great information for them about the Pendell house.

But that man . . . is not my father. I don't know what he is to me.

Knowing *who I really am* is tricky and hasn't gotten any easier overnight, but I can't even really sink into all the ramifications of that, because Carol stands right next to me.

"Did you enjoy your first foray into the archives?" she asks, as if we're good friends and she's deeply interested, not just evil. This close, I notice that her forehead is entirely smooth, like she finally succumbed to the spell version of Botox.

I play up that smile I've spent my whole life perfecting. "I did."

"Do you still think the entire witching public should have access to *everything*?" She nods over at my father, who's greeting the tour group.

I'm glad for all the years I spent pretending I don't know what anyone's talking about. Because her purposefully pointing out my parentage hurts, and I don't like it. I haven't figured out how to deal with it yet, and she's known *all along*.

I'm a mix of furious and hurt and uncomfortable.

But my smile is sunshiny bright, because there's a reason Carol has not used this secret against me—or Emerson, or Desmond, or whomever. I don't know what it is yet, but I know it exists. "Yes, of course. Knowledge *is* power, Carol."

"Say the power hungry." She snorts, as if she's made some

hilarious joke. "I can just picture Emerson charging into those archives thinking she'd be able to get all sorts of answers."

"Maybe she did."

"Don't *lie*, Georgie. It makes you look dimmer than usual. I know how the archives work. Only the Historian . . ." She trails off. There's a moment where Carol Simon looks thoroughly shocked. Then furious.

"Only the Historian can what?" I ask innocently enough, but I think I know. *Only the Historian can wield what's inside the archives*, something in me asserts, as if I have always known. I think back to last night and how Azrael . . . touched nothing. Only I did. Only I *could*.

That means Carol couldn't either in all her long reign. And she didn't want me to know that.

Which is maybe why I say the next thing, even though I know I shouldn't poke a wounded animal. Because she might be losing her place as leader of the witching world, but I am *not* dim, and I know that there's something in Carol that's still dangerous.

But I don't stop myself. "Then why did you kill your Historian, Carol?"

Her eyes narrow. Magic snaps in the depths, but it feels . . . weird in the air between us. Staticky and garbled.

I want to believe she's truly weakening. I want to be amused by this pathetic attempt at being intimidating.

But there's an unhinged desperation in her eyes, deep, deep down, that still manages to scare me.

"No coven really needs their Historian, Georgie. Don't you know that by now?" She shakes her head as if she pities me. "Who needs *knowledge* when you control everything either way?"

I'm not sure that tactic ever would have worked on me, but it's interesting how she keeps trying to use it on the women in our coven. So sure that if she can make us feel *less than*, we'll cower.

We haven't yet.

"This coven does," I tell her. "Because our history, our knowledge—it's going to be for *everyone*. And that is going to be *our* power. Not control. Not fear. Not *lies*."

Then she smiles at me—my own tactic used against me. She leans in close, pats my arm. "Of *course* it will, Georgina. Of course."

The way she drawls out my full name feels like a curse. Particularly when she walks away, whistling like something out of an old horror movie.

Then she just straight up cackles and disappears.

For a moment, I'm frozen. But I'm not just stiff. I'm *cold*. I want to go inside and sit by the fire. Or my dragon. I turn, but glance once more in my father's direction.

Except the porch is empty and the door is closed. He's inside, giving his tour. And I . . .

I don't know what to do, or how to feel. All the determination I felt this morning feels off-kilter now that I've had a Carol run-in.

I walk back into Wilde House and still don't feel any warmth. Even when I close the door behind me and lean against it.

Azrael swirls out of the newel post, this time with only a slight shaking.

He leaves it intact behind him, all that blue-and-green smoke pouring all around me, moving all over me like a caress.

Then he's a man, rolling his shoulders and moving his neck from side to side, like being in the newel post was uncomfortable. He frowns down at me.

"You're shaking."

I hate that I am, but I like that he notices. That he notices everything. Though I can't ignore the fact that Carol *still* trying to play her mind games really does make me feel a bit *dim* and slow, since we haven't figured out what's next. Sure, weak people use threats to feel powerful, but she still *feels* powerful.

Even though we won. We beat her and her cronies fair and square. So . . .

"Why does it feel like it isn't over?" I ask him as he comes closer. I lean against that hard wall of muscle that he calls a chest, trying to find some comfort in it. And I realize how often I have done this, come to my newel post for comfort. Not because I didn't want to be a burden to my friends, or even honest with them, but because this always *was* comfort.

But his words aren't comforting at all, even as his arms come around me and he tucks me in close.

"Because it isn't," he tells me, and I can feel the truth in the words the same as I can feel the rumble of them in his chest. "As long as they have access to dark magic, it's not just *not over*. It's dangerous. For everyone."

17

I SPEND THE NEXT FEW DAYS IN THE ARCHIVES, but it's not like that first night. The archives are being decidedly difficult. No more books appear and show off for me. I commune, I ask, I *beg*.

But they give me nothing.

I try to find information about next steps, about what happens on the solstice, and how to make sure the full power exchange happens.

I try to find books about dragons, past lives, and most importantly, dark magic.

"Maybe it's a test," I suggest to Octavius, who's curled up in the middle of the table in the center of the room. A little shaft of light shines on him from the skylight above, and he's basking in it.

He doesn't offer anything in return, not even a feline show of support.

I don't feel *tested*. I feel thwarted. Like the Joywood are dancing around in the stacks, hiding everything I need. Which makes it easier to pack up at night and head home.

I have no desire to dance with the Joywood.

Tonight, I decide to change my way home. Maybe I'm not

getting anywhere in the archives because I'm following the same old patterns. Maybe I need to take a page out of Azrael's book and upend everything.

The thought makes me smile, and I decide to take the longer walk back to Wilde House along the river path that humans—mostly—use to jog and cycle on.

I watch the river as I walk, my hands in my pockets against the cold. I've forgone the black jade rodent that looked a bit too much like Carol's weasel and switched it out for a disc made of fluorite that I bought in Juneau. I curl my fingers around it now, still seeking that spiritual crystal guidance I've had trouble feeling since I returned from my trip.

My crystals and I just haven't been on the right frequency ever since. Everything has felt off since I came back. I frown a little, trying to think back to anything that might have happened to ruin my balance. Sage and Cailee, obviously—except I felt off before I walked in on them. I went to Sage's house because I *already* felt strange.

I hold the fluorite disc more tightly, but I still feel nothing. Nothing comes to mind to explain it. I stop walking, though, because what *does* come to mind is that melody.

Faint and just out of reach, as always.

But calling me, tugging me.

I realize then that I forgot to tell my coven about this. About Carol watching the rivers from the windows in Wilde House when she was there.

How did I forget? It feels imperative now.

If Carol hears this melody too, then surely I need to get to the source of it. I step off the paved path and take a few steps on the hard, cold ground. I frown down at the river and feel a shiver of fear when I see the water looks black again, the way it did before Emerson dived into the confluence and fought off the flood that would have killed us all.

This is a very bad sign. I should hurry home and tell everyone.

I'm sure that's what I'll do, but my feet take another few steps toward the water anyway. Because that melody is *so close*.

If I could make out the words, would that be the answer to everything? I just need a few words. Then I can—

My feet slide out from under me. I let out a screech. My butt hits the ground *hard*.

But then . . . nothing else happens.

I let out a surprised, relieved sort of laugh. I get my bearings, a little confused, but it was just a slip in the mud. I'm fine. Shaking my head, I try to push myself to my feet. Muddy and a little wet and feeling silly.

I'm just hoping that no one saw me bite it on the riverbank. That's hardly the sort of dignified behavior witchdom is looking for in its newly elected—

But I can't get up.

I struggle to move, to get my feet under me, but I can't.

I can't.

And the water is suddenly creeping up and over my legs. I try to shove myself back on my butt since I can't seem to get to my feet, but the mud not only won't let me go, it's sucking me closer and closer to the water.

All that waiting black—

And maybe it's an overreaction, but I try to reach out to my coven.

Only it doesn't work. I can *feel* the magic deep in the center of me . . . stuck. Like something is blocking it from moving out.

Fear sinks its claws into me, because this is more than a slip in the mud, more than rising waters. I reach into my pocket, frantic for something that will help. I touch the fluorite disc, but it *burns*.

All of the crystals on my body begin to do the same. Pulsing and burning hot, but not in warning, not in comfort or guidance, not in anything *good*.

They are actually *burning* me.

Every single crystal on my body is like a fire, and their singing as they blaze through me, that same, terrible song—

Except the ring Azrael gave me.

I decide it's my only hope. I hold it out, away from the water. But I know almost at once that it's the wrong move, it's not the answer. I have to *use* it.

With my ringed hand, I begin to slap at the black water as it seethes in closer. It doesn't seem to *do* anything—

But the water isn't rising anymore.

And then, deep inside that black, dangerous water, I see glowing eyes.

I freeze, because those eyes remind me of something in a cage—

But the memory is dim. Still, I know this is bad and wrong, as black tendrils of water begin to wrap around my legs and pull. Hard. I'm sliding in the mud, into the water and the vicious black.

Something in me screams. Maybe I do.

Then a roar thunders through the air above me.

I look up at the bright sky, and there is Azrael in his full dragon form, like he should definitely not be if we're trying to keep him a secret.

But that's only a fleeting thought, because I'm getting sucked into the water again. Azrael's eyes blaze gold as he swoops down low along the surface of the water.

Fire roars out of his mouth in a dazzling dragon display. Something deep in the water screams in pain, but ribbons of black shoot out of the water and wrap around one of his wings. He shoots more fire, and the ribbons fall into the water with a *slap*. But then another band slithers up over my leg, pulling me so that I'm neck-deep in black, oily, churning water no attempts at swimming or magic can seem to disengage.

Azrael lands on the water, dragon claws flashing. He's grappling with something, and then there's a loud *boom*, almost as loud as Azrael's roar.

I hear something high-pitched mixed in with the *boom*, like the crescendo to a terrible song, and then I can feel something *break*.

At last I'm able to scramble away from the water.

Which is just its normal brown again. I look around frantically and see my coven charging in. Azrael lands next to me, still in his dragon form.

His wing is bleeding. My lungs are burning.

"What happened?" Emerson demands, skidding to a kneeling halt next to me. She's immediately whispering a spell to get me dry.

"It got away," Azrael says disgustedly. When Jacob approaches his wing, he jerks it away. "A witch Healer can't help me. See to Georgie."

Jacob pauses, then turns to me. He kneels down next to me too. "Are you okay?"

I nod. "I'm fine. It just . . . tried to pull me in. Into the water."

"She's burned," Azrael says flatly.

And only then do I remember the crystals. I hold out the hand that tried to grab the fluorite. There is indeed a burn there.

Jacob sets about to healing, and I would try to speak, try to understand what has happened, but a crowd has appeared. Made up of witches—Joywood and Riverwood supporters alike—who live in St. Cyprian and must have heard the commotion.

And who are now staring at Azrael, *full-on dragon Azrael*, with a mix of awe, shock, and fear. Mostly fear.

This isn't the worst thing in the world, I tell myself. It's fine. It's just a dragon. We all wield magic, and a dragon is just a step away from that.

Everything is okay, I tell myself.

Until the Joywood charge through the middle of the crowd, right at us.

18

AZRAEL.

He looks over at me. There is a kind of resigned fury in his gaze. As if he knew this would happen, and more, that there is no stopping this moment.

As if we have lived this life before.

And there is only ruin ahead.

My heart plummets, hard and fast. I don't believe it. I *won't* believe it, and yet my emotions don't seem to get that message.

Maybe the giant fire-breathing dragon could change back into a regular guy to seem less alarming to the crowd who thought dragons were extinct, Zander suggests in all our heads.

Azrael fixes him with a glare that would have most witches shaking in their boots, but he also changes. Right there in front of us. With smoke and the rumbling of distant thunder, he shrinks down into his more palatable-for-a-crowd form.

When he's back to a very large man, but a *man* instead of a *dragon*, there's still a long, ugly gash on his arm.

It hurts me to even look at it. Jacob has healed most of my burns, so I nudge him away and point at Azrael's arm. "Jacob . . ."

Jacob nods. He gets to his feet and walks over to Azrael.

"It's no use," Azrael growls. "A witch cannot heal a fabulae."

"Maybe I can't fix it," Jacob says evenly. "But let's see what I *can* do."

Please, I send out to Azrael and Azrael alone.

He shoots me a long, dragony look, then gives Jacob a faint nod. But I can't focus on whether Jacob can actually heal him, because Maeve is screeching as if Azrael is currently chomping on her with his full-size dragon teeth. Their little group is missing Festus and Felix now, but the rest of the Joywood coven are in the throes of a veritable fit.

"Explain yourselves," Carol demands, cutting through the screeching. Her eyes are bright, and compared to Maeve and Felicia, she's downright glowing.

"What would you like us to explain, Carol?" Frost asks her in frigid tones. "It seems one of our coven was once again attacked, and the sort of dragon you have taught your people doesn't exist saved her. Imagine that."

"Dragons are *dangerous!*" Gil shouts. His arm is hanging at an odd angle, like it's fallen out of its socket. One ear is much lower on his face than the other. "Everyone knows this!"

Which is funny, because how could anyone know it when we were all taught they went extinct centuries ago?

"How *dare* you hide such an unpredictable monster from us," Carol says, and she almost can't hide the utter glee in her expression as she makes sure her voice carries to every last witch standing here on the riverbank. "This is not the *Riverwood way* we were promised."

We were hiding Azrael from the Joywood, specifically—not witchdom as a whole—but I don't think there's any point in mentioning that.

"Dragons aren't dangerous," I reply instead. Ellowyn and Rebekah are on either side of me now, acting like they're ready to hold me up at a moment's notice. I can tell the whole coven is worried about me, but I feel fine. I'm mostly just filled with fury and anger that Carol is trying to warp an attack on *me* into an example of bad behavior by *us*.

"What was that hideous display, then?" Felicia asks, throwing a dramatic hand in the air toward Azrael. Three of her fingers are just bone. I look around, but no one aside from my friends seems to recoil at the gruesome sight.

"He saved me," I tell everyone, searching the crowd for friendly faces. For awe and understanding instead of fear and worry. I refuse to take the mug Ellowyn is trying to push at me. "From something dark trying to pull me under the water."

"And yet two of *our* coven are missing," Carol says, rolling her eyes. "*You* are all here and accounted for. You can pretend to be a victim all you like, but those of us with even an ounce of intelligence can see right through you and your melodramatic fake threats. The water is fine. Have a look yourselves."

A couple of witches move forward and peer down at the river, using muttered light spells to show the water in the quickly falling dusk, and a murmur seems to go through the crowd. Because the river looks normal. Cold and brown, as it should look on a frigid December night. Whatever attacked me and then escaped Azrael's grasp hasn't just retreated. It's taken away all signs it was ever here.

I don't know why I bother being surprised.

"She was burned," Jacob tells the crowd in his steady, serious way, and surely that has to turn the tide. "Burns I've only seen on people attacked by black magic. The dragon clearly saved her from it being worse."

"They will use this dragon against you," Carol counters at once, watching the ever-multiplying crowd the same way I do. "He's their paid muscle. *We* never trucked with ginormous magical creatures who are *known* to prey on children."

"No, you prefer biddable rodents," Frost says coolly, and gets the full force of her glare.

"This is getting out of hand," Emerson says then, wielding her powerful voice and unshakable certainty. "Azrael is not going to hurt anyone, I can assure you. We're not sure why or how he was freed from the curse that jailed him in our newel post, but he's not a threat."

"Says *you*," Carol accuses, her voice echoing out through a crowd that only grows larger every time I blink. I see Sage with a couple of other teachers, looking entirely too smug, and I want to hurt him.

"Yes, says me," Emerson replies in a tone that suggests Carol is unhinged. Carol *is* unhinged, but we've all learned that making direct statements about such things will backfire. No one likes a direct woman. The horror! Emerson keeps going, sounding almost soothing now. "If Festus and Felix are missing, we can look into that, but it has nothing to do with the dragon."

"I thought you wanted everyone to have a say, Emerson." Carol smirks. "I thought the Riverwood was built on everyone working together to form the best community we can." She's quoting something Emerson said at the ascension trials. Everyone seems to know it. And then she titters. "Not sure *death by dragon* is best for any community."

Emerson doesn't say anything for long, ticking seconds that I can measure by the pounding of my heart. She surveys the crowd. Carol has gotten most of them worked up. There are a lot of fearful gazes in Azrael's direction, even though all he's doing is standing there, arms crossed, in his human form. Jacob didn't fully heal his injury, but it's no longer actively bleeding. And it's been stitched up in some way.

But people don't see any of that, I realize. They don't care that he's been hurt, that he's done something brave.

They're afraid.

"You must destroy him!" Maeve shrieks. When she stomps her foot, her heel crumbles straight off. The actual heel of her foot, not her shoe. She reaches down, picks it up, and shoves it into her purse.

No one besides us seems to notice.

Did everyone see that? Rebekah asks quietly.

Maybe she's found a new way to feed her weird bird, Ellowyn replies.

"We will *never* rush to end someone's or something's life," Emerson is saying, loud enough so the whole crowd can hear. "What we need to do is find out why we thought magical creatures were extinct in the first place, only to discover that many of them have been cursed into the everyday objects in our homes. Give us some time to do that before we rush to judgment, with our assurances that Azrael will bring no harm to anyone."

Carol staggers back as if Emerson took a swing at her, and *cries out*, "You can't let a fire-breathing dragon cavort about the town! More people might go missing!"

"You're engaging in hysterics, Carol," Emerson says, bright and inordinately patient. She moves her gaze out to the crowd again. "I said we take responsibility for him. I meant it."

"I don't feel comfortable with this!" Joanne Walters yells. Not a surprise, as the woman loves to complain.

"Our *kids* walk these streets," Cailee adds from where she stands next to her husband. She's wringing her hands together, and she looks suitably terrified.

"None of you have kids," Dane blusters, right on cue. "Yet," he adds as an afterthought, gesturing at Ellowyn's belly. "You don't know what it's like to worry for your children."

I could tell them I am innocence personified. It does not matter, Azrael says in our heads. *Don't waste your breath*.

"Emerson is right," Holly Bishop says then, pitching her voice to carry through the crowd. "Even if we have concerns, we can't just *kill* him. That's over-the-top."

Carol's gaze is sharp, magical, a direct contrast to her crumbling and missing coven. "Imprison him, then."

A murmur of something too close to assent goes through the crowd.

Emerson nods. "If you think Carol speaks for you, and you'd like to see the dragon imprisoned, raise your hand."

"That isn't fair, Emerson," Corinne Martin says, a little too calmly for me to be able to dismiss her outright the way I'd like to. "Carol doesn't speak for me, but I have concerns about what I saw with my own two eyes. Fire-breathing. Huge claws. If he wanted to take us all out, he could."

"He could burn down the whole town!" Joanne cries. "Who would stop him? Who *could*?"

It's all right. I'll agree to another one of their prisons. Azrael's voice is in our heads, and we all turn to look at him—except Emerson. She's still gazing at Corinne. Not in betrayal, exactly, but certainly with some hurt, as I know she thought the other woman was a friend.

But then, things change when you're the friend with all the power.

No. I say it firmly so everyone in my coven can hear it reverberate in their heads. *We're not bowing down to mob mentality. To the Joywood's manipulations. What was the point in winning the election if we're still genuflecting to them?*

Azrael's eyes are pure gold, and his voice is only in my head then. *Trust me, Georgina.*

It isn't fair.

No, he agrees, and offers nothing else.

"I accept these conditions," Azrael says to the crowd before Emerson has a chance, and he does it in that lazy way of his that I'm sure riles up as many people as it comforts. "I won't fight you. Lock me back into the newel post."

"Oh, no, not in Wilde House," Carol says at once, with a hint of her former titter. "We can't trust these sympathizers with a dragon in their home. We'll imprison him at my house."

"We're supposed to trust *you* with access to a dragon you want destroyed?" I demand of Carol. "I don't think so."

She smirks at me. "My, my, Georgie—we're awfully touchy

about it, aren't we? For a woman who was only moments ago very seriously entangled with one of our honorable high school teachers."

I don't look at Sage. I won't give him or Carol the satisfaction.

"The cemetery," Frost says, interrupting whatever Carol is trying to get at. "It's across the river and safely apart from St. Cyprian. Off the bricks, yet sacred. No one *should* be able to do anything untoward there." But he raises a brow at Carol, as if already accusing her of something.

"How could we possibly trust your spell?" Felicia asks, her canny gaze on the crowd, gauging their responses. She's wearing an overlarge hat, and I find myself wondering if she has any hair under it.

"We're supposed to allow you to do it?" Rebekah asks with a laugh.

"We'll each choose three people *not* in either one of our covens," Emerson says. "Anyone here in the crowd can nominate and vote on a seventh. Then they'll speak the spell that imprisons the dragon across the river in the cemetery until we can prove to you all he is not a threat. Because he isn't."

"And how will you determine this, Emerson?" Carol asks, her voice a slithering thing I can feel down my spine. "With your feelings?"

"The way we intend to determine everything that matters to this town," Emerson replies with that admirable calm when *my* blood pressure is skyrocketing by the second. "A vote where all voices can be heard. And tracked by everyone in witchdom. As the days go forward, we'll endeavor to communicate all the reasons Azrael is not a threat to you. If your minds change, and you wish to see him freed, you only have to send me your change of vote. Once we have a majority, he'll be freed."

Felicia sniffs. "And if you never reach a majority?"

Emerson looks at Azrael, and her expression is hard to read. This is the leader she is, I know. Always fair—but fairness isn't always easy. And being a good leader isn't always doing the thing you feel is right the second you want to do it.

I hate it.

"If the tide has not changed by solstice and our full ascension," Emerson tells the crowd in the same calm way, "we will have a meeting to determine his fate."

Azrael does not have any reaction to this. Not like me. I want to tell Emerson she's out of her mind, but I can't do it here in front of a crowd. It's never been harder to keep my mouth shut.

With everyone's agreement, our two covens choose three people each to do the spell, with the crowd nominating the seventh. Emerson picks Jacob's sister, Ellowyn's mother, and my . . . well. The man I grew up thinking was my father.

Carol picks Joanne—no surprise there—then Dane Blanchard, and *my* mother.

I stare at her as she takes her place with the Joywood's choices. She doesn't look at me and I think, *Okay then*. I guess she has nothing to say to me now that I know the truth. Not just who my real father is, but who *she* is.

Cadence Pendell isn't as good and respectable as she wants the world to believe. I could ruin that for her, couldn't I? I could do it right here, right now.

There are a lot of lives I could ruin with a few words, I think, and the desire to do just that washes over me when I see the smug way Sage is watching me from his little group of teacher friends I never liked.

But Azrael comes to stand beside me. He puts his hand on the nape of my neck in a way that is not likely to quell any rumors about us, but I love it. I lean into it. The heat, the strength, the certainty that all these lives have come and gone, but *we* remain.

And he says nothing out loud or in my head, but I somehow know not to speak.

The Riverwood choices stand in a line facing the Joywood

picks—Ellowyn's mother, Tanith, and mine in a sort of face-off—and then the seventh choice, calm Corinne, makes them a circle. They begin the simple containment spell, joining hands and chanting the familiar words together.

Easy but effective words. A good, clean spell. Magic swirls in the air, and I want to *sob*.

Not sobbing hurts, like that horrible burning all over again, but this is nothing a Healer can cure. This is witch justice, exactly as we promised, and Goddess help me, but I *hate* it.

Azrael squeezes my neck, then reaches down to move the ring around my index finger. *Be safe, Georgina.*

And then he's gone. Not in some grand puff of smoke, nothing dramatic or dragony.

Just not *here* anymore.

Imprisoned, once again.

All because he saved me.

19

"GEORGIE—"

But I'm not listening to Emerson or anyone else who calls my name just now.

I immediately fly across the river to the cemetery. Most of the coven are right behind me, but Emerson has to stay and deal with an angry mob. I'm sure I'll feel bad for ditching her and leaving her to it later.

Maybe.

I land outside the cemetery with the determination to *do something* pounding in me—

But I stop short.

Because just behind the iron gate marking the entrance to the cemetery, where there are usually a few trees, there is now a *giant* dragon statue. As if he's guarding the entrance to the local dead, and it's suitably terrifying. It's a gigantic display of stone, showing off towering teeth and sharp claws.

It is *meant* to terrify.

"Those assholes." But there's barely any heat behind it. That's how truly outraged I am.

Zander lands beside me and shakes his head. "That's a bit much."

"A very purposeful bit much," I return darkly. "I can't believe . . ."

But I don't have words for all the things I can't believe. I want to *cry* that he's stuck again. *Cursed*. Because he revealed himself to save me, which feels like a kind of deep echo inside me, like he's done just that before. Then, as now, because people want to see the worst in him.

And in everything, no matter how much we work to try to make things better.

Because, in this time, the damned Joywood makes sure of it.

Even now when they shouldn't be any kind of a factor.

I move toward the statue then. But before I can put my hands on it, the mass of stone . . . shakes a little. Like it is having its own quiet earthquake.

And then Azrael, in man form, appears at the side of the stone.

Relief swamps so deep, my knees almost give out. "You can get around the spell."

"Not exactly," he says, pausing at the cemetery gates. "The statue isn't my confinement. The cemetery is."

His eyes are gold and on mine in a way that feels like a touch. I take a breath. Then I make myself take stock. Not of what I feared across the river, but what is happening *here*. Azrael can't leave the cemetery grounds. That's not great, but it's better than being stuck in a statue, unable to communicate.

I'm clinging to whatever silver lining I can.

Until this moment, I don't think I knew *how much* I have come to depend on this man. My dragon. My newel post confidant brought to beautiful life. It isn't just the book. Fate. The lure of other lives, hard losses, and a love so deep I sometimes imagine it's threaded into my bones.

I just like him.

I really, really like him. This man who is funny and irreverent and so dangerous—while always being a safe place for me. This man who pretended to be a human and helps us whether we want it or not and happily took his place in our coven—in our lives—before we knew he belonged here.

This man who taught me how to fly like a dragon, and that was only the beginning.

Like doesn't begin to cover it.

I can't remember him through other eyes. I'm glad I can't, because I like this view so much.

This dragon is definitely worth being tied to throughout time.

"Did the Joywood fail to imprison him in stone on purpose?" Frost asks in a musing sort of tone, his icy-cold gaze moving from the statue to Azrael and back. "Or is this because their power is fading?"

I don't care. I launch myself forward, through the gates, directly at Azrael. And he catches me. He's sturdy and warm and *here*.

He wraps his arm around me and holds me like no one's cursed or ever could be. And I can feel that he is holding on to make sure *I* am okay, the same way I am holding on to make sure he is.

Like really isn't the word.

"I'm betting on the latter." Azrael looks out over the stones, and the statues of familiars. "Though I wouldn't trust that the power fading will last."

"How would they get it back?" Zander demands.

"Destroying you lot." Azrael looks down at me. "Something attacked her, and then me. They have power somewhere, still. Black magic, at a guess."

"I tried to reach out to everyone," I say.

"They blocked you. Isolated you in the hopes of picking you off." Azrael looks at me, his eyes gleaming with that hot gold. "The usual Joywood playbook."

"If she couldn't reach out to us, how did you get the message she needed help?" Rebekah asks him, her eyes narrowing in suspicion.

But I already know the answer. I look down at the ring on my finger. "What you gave me are the only crystals on my body that didn't burn me."

Frost frowns at that. "The burns weren't from the water?"

"No." They hadn't been on my legs, where I was getting sucked in. That was bad but didn't *burn*. That had been the crystal I was holding, the crystals in my pockets and on my body. The necklace I always wear—the prehnite from my mother at pubertatum—but not the crystals on Azrael's necklace. There was only one burn on my neck, right between my collarbones. "It was my crystals."

"Take them off," Azrael says darkly. He has taken his arm away from me. He points to the ground, then grunts in frustration. "My magic does not work here."

I pull the crystals out of my pockets. Take the prehnite necklace off. Hold them out in my hands. I stare at them. They look and feel like crystals. How could they burn me? How could someone get to crystals I have cleansed and charged and worn?

"Put them in something," Azrael orders me. I'm not sure I've ever seen him like this. Darkly furious, but with a very tight lid on it. I want to reach for him, but clearly the focus is on the crystals, so I magic myself a little bowl to put everything in.

Azrael nods toward Frost. "Take the bowl outside the cemetery. Destroy them."

I don't know what to think about the fact that Frost does this immediately. He doesn't question it, either. More telling, he doesn't balk at Azrael giving him orders. He doesn't even shoot the dragon one of his *I'm the first Praeceptor* glances.

Like this is so serious nothing else matters.

Rebekah and I exchange a wide-eyed look.

Frost strides through the cemetery gates and keeps going, almost to the path that leads through the woods and down to the river. A few crows sit on a branch and seem to watch him. He mutters a spell, and there's a small explosion in the bowl. A flash of light, a loud, crackling kind of flame, and then dark smoke billows up.

When Frost comes back through the iron gates, he holds the bowl out to the rest of us.

My crystals are shattered into violent shards. *All* of them.

And something oily and black oozes out from each of the broken pieces.

I'm not the only one who recoils.

"Black magic," I whisper. There was a vile, nasty blackness in the middle of my crystals, and I didn't even *know*. Then it dawns on me. "Those are almost all new crystals. I got each of them in the places I traveled to find the keys. I thought it would give me luck in the archives to wear crystals I got while gathering the keys to access them, but—"

"They were traps," Frost says, not unkindly.

Which is actually deeply kind, for him, and yet . . .

I feel small. Stupid. They set a trap and I fell right into it. They knew I would find the keys. They banked on it. I thought I was so smart and all the while, they *wanted* me to find those keys. They know me and my love for crystals. They knew exactly what they were doing.

And what I'd do too.

And I did it.

But it's not Azrael whose arms come around me to comfort me. It's another rare show of affection from Ellowyn. And I need it so badly I don't even make a joke of it.

I can't even think of something to say to release all this tension. Because my dawning realization is worse.

It wasn't *only* the crystals I picked up on my travels that were the problem. It was the necklace my mother gave me at pubertatum, and I suppose it became a habit to wear. A weird lifeline, if I think deeper about it. Maybe if I wore it enough, I could finally be what she wanted me to be.

And instead it's been infused with black magic for all these years.

Before I can really delve into how I feel about all of this, Emerson and Jacob appear. They both look grim, and that's *before* they take in the dragon statue, Azrael standing apart from it. A pile of crystal shards with black magic oozes in the bowl Frost is holding.

There is no battle gleam in Emerson's eyes, and that's unusual. She looks *tired*—and that's almost unheard of—as we catch her up on what we've discovered.

"What was it like with all the pitchfork-bearing villagers?" Rebekah asks. "I mean, our friends, neighbors, and fellow citizens?"

Emerson shoots her sister a quelling look, which is at least more normal. "People are uneasy. We need to explain what a true coven is and the role of the fabulae that's been kept from us all too long." She nods as if she's come to a decision. "We simply need to put together a presentation of the facts."

"It will not work." Azrael says this with no heat. Just a grim kind of certainty.

"How do you know?" Emerson asks him. "I don't think you understand the power of a good presentation to change minds *and* hearts."

"It's a passion of hers," Jacob says to the dragon. Deadpan.

This is one reason we love him.

Emerson is winding up to give one of her speeches, but then it dawns on me. "The fairy tale."

Everyone looks at me.

"That book?" Emerson asks. "What about it?"

"There are two crow armies in the story. One with the good crow leader, honest and true." Just like Emerson, the more I think about it. "She's defending the fairies, and she has a bunch of crows on her side. But the *other* side won't listen to reason about the fairies. She tries and tries. They refuse to listen."

"It's just a story," Zander says. "I know it had Ellowyn's Revelare stuff in there, but it's still not a historical text."

"No, but it's also not *just* a story," I counter. "There's historical fact buried in there. There's *our* story buried in there. And it's magical because the story keeps changing. Which means there are other stories too."

I look over at Azrael, and I don't like what I see on his face. A *guardedness* I don't recall ever being there before. "You all must focus on the future," he tells us. "On the solstice and your ascension. Not fairy stories and not me."

I don't understand that kind of response. Not from him. "But you're what makes us a true coven."

He's not looking at me. His gaze is on a grave to his right. It's a Wilde, with a stone raccoon sitting on the top of the headstone.

"I knew him," he says as we all peer at the carved name. LINUS WILDE. "He was a Historian, I was his protector, and I failed." There are layers in his voice then, like smoke and fury, but when he looks back at us, his gaze is cool. Onyx more than gold. "This time around, I have not failed. But I *almost* did."

I can see how that weighs on him. The *almost* of it.

I move to him, and he doesn't push me away, but there is still a distance he has put up. A wall, even as his arm comes around me and he looks out at my coven.

"You all do not understand the role of the fabulae yet. It's not the same as yours. I add magic to spells, to ceremonies, but I do not have to have a say in all the goings-on, the day-to-day. You must go on as you did before I showed up."

I don't like this at all. "Why would we do that?"

But he remains calm. Too calm. "Trust me. I have not led

you all astray." Then he smiles, but it has none of that dragon certainty, and I hate it. "Yet."

"Azrael—" I begin.

He looks at me, and I think he's trying to hide all the old pain in his eyes, but I can see it. "You must all go and focus on full ascension. On making sure the Joywood do not have access to the archives, to your crystals and homes and so on. You must be vigilant. You can deal with me once all is said and done."

I can tell no one is quite buying this, but no one *says* anything. No one argues with him. So *I* do, clenching my hand tight around the ring he gave me.

"You don't really think we should just . . . leave you in a graveyard and worry about ascension like you're not trapped here, do you?"

"I don't *think* you should. I *know* you should," he says gently. Almost like he understands what he's asking of me. Of *us*. He looks like himself again, for a moment, when his gaze meets mine. "Trust me, Georgina."

I want to. I really do. But this is leaving him behind, and that is not what I stand for. It's not who *we* are.

"How about we regroup," Emerson says then. And I know this is directed at me, even if she's ostensibly addressing the coven. "We'll all go home and sleep on it. Then we'll meet back here in the morning and discuss plans."

Azrael makes a frustrated sound. "You need not come back here. Have your meetings and plans in Wilde House where they belong."

"We'll be back here in the morning, Azrael," Emerson replies. Firmly. "Whether we need to or not."

He says nothing to this. He turns back toward the grave he pointed out instead. Behind me, my friends take off, talking quietly amongst themselves.

Emerson comes to me and gives my arm a squeeze. "If you

decide to stay here tonight, let me know, okay? I don't want you alone after what happened."

I nod. But I don't promise. I think alone may be just what I need. But I won't put myself at risk again. There will obviously be no more walking along rivers.

She and Jacob leave then, choosing to walk over to his farm.

I don't watch them go. I watch Azrael's back instead. Of *course* I should stay here, with him—

But when he turns back to me, he looks so remote. Walled off. Not like the dragon I've come to know at all. Not even like the newel post version of him.

"You should go back to Wilde House," he tells me stiffly. "Or the archives. There is much to do, and those are the places where you will be best protected."

"Do you think this *act* is going to work on me?"

He sighs at that. "This is not a game, Georgina. It is not . . ." He trails off. Then some of that intensity I know so well shines through in his expression, making everything in me feel comforted and furious at once. "I need you to understand me. To believe me."

"What I can't believe is that you suddenly don't want to be in the middle of this."

He looks at that Wilde grave again. Sad. Guilty. "This is not about wants. It is about what is right." He says this as if the words and feelings are brand-new to him, but with a dollop of self-recrimination that I'm not loving. "It is about the future. Not the past. I have been trying to re-create the past, and you almost died for it."

"Don't be ridiculous. The Joywood are behind the black magic attack."

"Yes," he agrees, but doesn't explain.

Maybe he does actually need time. Maybe this mood of his will blow over. Maybe this is what a bad reaction to something he can't burn looks like on a dragon—and Hecate knows I would be having a whole private opera if I found myself *imprisoned* in a *graveyard*.

Then he reaches over and touches my face. "My own," he says, and I can tell he is trying to smile. Trying to lighten this up between us, but he can't manage it. "They have taken away my ability to protect you by putting me here—something I was almost not able to do today anyway. So you must protect yourself. You *must* be careful. They have made you a target because you are the one who can find the truth, and the past. I think we both know the truth and the past can be dangerous weapons. You must focus on the present, the future, instead. So you are safe."

And then I realize what this is. Worry. Deep concern. Over *me*.

But he doesn't seem to understand that's a two-way street. I grip the hand on my face. "What if something happens to you here?"

He gestures around the cemetery with his free hand. "Frost was not wrong. This space is sacred. I'm not saying the Joywood wouldn't try to pervert the sacred, but they will find it incredibly difficult. I am safe here. You seven are the ones who are walking in a world without safety. You must not spend your time here. You must not let me be a distraction. I accepted my imprisonment because I can handle it. Focus on your coven. Focus on *you*."

He's trying to get rid of me. He's trying to *manage* me. He's never done this before, and I have no idea what to do with it.

"Azrael, *you* are part of *me*."

He stares at me then. There's gold in his gaze, but also something else. Something has changed. From the moment he saved me from that water, something *changed*.

He presses a rather chaste kiss to my forehead. Squeezes my hand with the ring on it. *His* ring. *Our* ring. "Do not take it off. It is protection, Georgina." His gaze meets mine, serious and focused.

"I won't," I say, as honest and real as any vow. "But you must promise to reach out for help if something goes wrong. You must promise—"

"Georgina," he interrupts, decidedly *not* promising. "You must go. And focus on the real problems at hand." He holds my gaze, gleaming and determined. But there's an odd kind of desperation there. "The past does not matter. I need you to understand that."

It's such a strange thing for him to focus on. I have the terrible notion that he means . . . all of our pasts. Not just what he's been doing since he escaped his curse.

But I'm a *Historian*. Of course the past matters. I would think so even if he hadn't said it himself.

There's no point arguing with a dragon who's made a decision, though. Might as well go pound my head against the snarling stone version of him instead. So I hug him, hold him close, and he does the same.

I put my hand over the gash on his arm. I am no Healer, but still I whisper words of healing, hoping it offers *something*.

When I pull back, his expression is careful, unreadable. But he smiles. "I will see you tomorrow morning. *Not* before."

I want to scowl at him, but . . . This is what he wants. And *he* is the one imprisoned, so I should give it to him.

Reluctantly, I leave him behind. Alone. I *hate* it. I know if I go home to Wilde House, I will only stew, and likely convince myself to return against his wishes. So I go to the one place I know I can be distracted enough to forget he is *imprisoned and alone*.

I go straight to the archives.

It feels different immediately. It's more welcoming.

There are stacks and stacks of books already on the table. A book on the history of dragons, three tomes on the dangers of black magic, and every other book I asked for before. Still nothing on the history of the Joywood, but it's progress.

"What's changed?" I ask out loud, frowning around at all the golden light. "Azrael being imprisoned? Being attacked like that?"

Then it dawns on me. It was the black magic in my crystals.

The archives knew, clearly, and they could not allow me to have any information about power, about covens, about ascension or black magic, until I was free of it.

If Azrael wasn't stuck in a cemetery right now, I think this understanding might have defeated me. That's how close I was to ruining everything for everyone, because I had no idea *I* was the Joywood's latest attack on my coven.

I thought Carol had kept my true parentage a secret because of some grand plan, but it was just this—a distraction. The Joywood use the personal to distract from the political. And everything they do is about power.

I should have understood they would never give it up so easily.

I stand here, in the middle of historic texts and all our *pasts* laid out to learn from. Why doesn't Azrael want me to do that? It makes no sense. What is he trying to hide?

No, he's not one to hide. I know that much. He's trying to protect me from something. Something that connects to the attack today—and I frown at that.

What about *today* made him worry about the *past*? About me, a *Historian*, finding the past?

But I should focus on the Joywood's past.

"Thank you for this important information," I say, addressing these archives, this body of knowledge, that knew enough to protect the witchlore from me. And who can tell the difference now. I raise my hands and tip my head back, like I'm free-falling into all that *knowing*. I connect with the magic that makes me a Historian, the magic that has always led me through my research. The magic that is why I'm here. "Show me the Joywood's black magic."

The room shifts now, and I hold my breath—thinking, *This*

is it. Finally. I freed myself from the cursed crystals, and now I'll get my answers—

A large box appears on the table. I rush forward, ready to dig in. But it's empty.

I frown at the box, then the golden magic around me. I don't think it's a trick, but I'm not sure what it is. It's not the information I wanted, I know that. I let out a long sigh.

"All right then," I say, wondering how to shift tactics. On the night I opened the archives, they showed me the family tree of their own accord. Maybe that's the key. It's not what I want. Maybe I need to ask the archives what *they* want to show me.

I reach inside myself and make that connection once again. "Show me what you will, if you will," I say, giving myself over to the bright magic that fills the room, and me.

The room shifts all around me once again. Light reflects off different surfaces, as if different parts of the archives are talking to each other the way I have always believed books do, and then a book floats down from the ceiling onto the middle of the table.

I peer down at the title. It doesn't connect to anything I've asked for before. Nothing about the Joywood then or now, but I know this is for me.

A Fabulae's Guide to Past Life Regression.

My pulse picks up at *past life*. I immediately flip through the old pages, letting the book make a case for itself, and it doesn't take me long to know what I need to do.

Because no matter what Azrael says, no matter what he's *afraid* of, the past *does* matter.

I tuck the book under my arm, but underneath it is the fairy tale, once again. *Our* story, but the cover has changed again. No more embracing. The dragon is in the background. I don't like that at all, how far away he is from the princess. How small he's drawn, like he doesn't matter.

You're wrong, I want to shout at it. But in the foreground is the princess. She's asleep in a deep, dark wood. A crow sits at the end of her bed. It reminds me of Ellowyn's dream that she told us about on All Souls' Day. There was a crow at the end of it, with violet eyes. And something about . . . crows being freed. Above the princess's head, in a little dreamlike bubble, are four versions of the princess in different kinds of dress.

Like she's dreaming about different lives for herself. *Or old lives*, something in me whispers.

Just like the dreams I used to have. The ones that my mother said were dangerous delusions that needed to be nipped in the bud.

This is confirmation that she was wrong. And that I'm on the right track.

When I leave the archives, I head to Zander and Ellowyn's house on stilts next to the river, but I don't risk walking. When Ellowyn answers the door, there's concern on her face as she beckons me inside and closes the door against the night.

"Everything okay?" she asks.

"You can reach into the past."

"Sure," she says, as Zander comes up behind her, sliding an arm around her waist and over their baby.

I hand her the book the archives gave me. "I want to do this."

Ellowyn and Zander both look at the book. Then at me, with twin looks of concern on their faces. "Georgie . . ."

"Any risk is mine to take, not yours," I say with certainty, because I know this is right. Not just right, but the only path. "It says so in the book. You and the baby will be fine."

Zander and Ellowyn exchange a glance, the kind of glance born out of their years. Their new, improved partnership and the trust they've built along with the baby they're growing.

And all that love.

It makes me *ache* all over again for this strange partition

Azrael has put up between us. But I'm certain the answer lies in the past he doesn't want me to find.

"You're not a fabulae, Georgie," Zander says, gently enough.

I smile, with only the faintest hint of ditz. "A minor technicality. I don't think it matters."

"It might," Ellowyn says, but she's flipped open the book to the first page.

"Azrael said that we need to focus on the future," Zander argues, because he wants to protect literally everyone, always. "Don't you think we should listen to the dragon who knows all this stuff we don't?"

"I think those who do not understand the past are doomed to repeat it." I raise my brow at him. "As you should know very well. Personally."

Zander lets out a sound like I punched him in the stomach. Which I guess I did. "Ouch."

Ellowyn closes the book. "This should be a full coven thing, Georgie."

"Great. Let's gather them."

"A full, *true* coven, meaning Azrael too."

I hesitate, then I shake my head. "No. We got this far with only the seven of us. We can do this with only the seven of us too. And I think we have to do it. There's something he doesn't want me to find in the past."

"Then maybe we shouldn't find it," Zander argues, but more carefully. "Particularly *today*. A day when you've been *attacked*."

I keep my gaze on Ellowyn. Because I know she's on my side, and if she is, Zander will be eventually. "Would you stop trying to find what you knew you needed to find just because someone told you not to? Or, worse, if someone tried to *stop* you?"

She's caught, because we all know telling Ellowyn what to do is a useless enterprise.

"Did you know," she murmurs, "that when you put a certain number of men—"

"Wynnie," I say, dropping that nickname she only allows rarely as a bomb.

She sighs. "Let's head over to the North Farm," she mutters instead of wowing us with misdirection in the form of facts about men. "Get everyone to meet us there."

20

IT DOESN'T TAKE LONG TO GATHER EVERYONE in Jacob's cozy little farmhouse. This afternoon's attack and *baying mob* have left everyone on edge, or that's how it seems when every single one of my friends—including Frost—makes a big deal over me and how I'm still standing when I haven't had time to think about it.

When I'm not sure I *want* to think about it—that song, the burning crystal, the slick and greedy tug of all that black, the moment before Azrael descended when I thought all was lost—

I focus on the farmhouse instead, because we've spent a lot of time here over the past year. It's looking far less like a single, solitary man lives here these days. There are lots of colorful, *organized* touches from Emerson everywhere I look. They've melded their lives into one life, and that will only become more and more a thing.

Once they get married. Take all those next steps.

For a moment, I'm struck by that idea. A future *beyond* ascension. Beyond this longest year. My friends will get married, have babies, live very adult lives—all while we run the witching world.

You know, if we can get past all this dark magic business.

And where will I be? I wanted the future to be Sage because that's what my mother told me I was destined for. I gave it my very best shot.

But *I've* always known, even when I didn't want to, that I was destined for dragons.

I think all these *doubts* are the same doubts she planted in me when I was small. Maybe all mothers try to make a fortress against fear, and end up jailing their daughters there. Maybe that's a kind interpretation of what my mother did with a child she intended to lie to for the whole of her life.

But I believed those doubts. I internalized them, one after the next, like *facts*.

Facts that made Sage seem like the best prospect, no matter that I had more feelings for the fictional characters I read about. I was taught so well. Fiction and feelings were for silly little girls. Grown women who wanted to fight the ruling coven needed facts and rationality.

But the dragon *is* a fact, and so is what needs to be done.

"We need to do a past life regression on me," I tell the assembled group once everyone has settled and I've answered all the questions I intend to about *how I feel* in the wake of the attack. I hold out the book the archives gave me. "This tells us how to do it. Ellowyn has to lead it, but we all need to help."

There's a beat of silence. And one by one, everyone looks to Emerson. Our leader through all of this, every step of the way. The one all final decisions go through. She's made a lot of tough, fair choices this year. Maybe soon I'll be able to consider that agreeing to imprison Azrael was one of those. Maybe.

Right now, though, is the first time I've ever seen an expression on her face that makes me think she doesn't actually *always* want to be the one deciding.

Because she doesn't want to agree, but she doesn't want to hurt me either.

"I know the Joywood have lied to us and skewed our pasts beyond recognition, but some things remain true," she says gently. *Kindly.* I brace myself. "Witches and past lives . . ." Emerson sighs. "It doesn't make sense. We've dealt with ghosts. We might not know everything that happens on the other side, but we know that's the next destination."

Meaning we don't do reincarnation dances through the ages.

"I *know* I've had a past life because I *know* I've been her." I point to the cover of the fairy-tale book that I set on the coffee table. The one that currently shows a dream the princess is having. "If that's not a sign to do a past life regression, I don't know what is."

Emerson picks up the book and studies it, looking like she *wants* to agree with me.

Which isn't the same thing as actually agreeing.

"The past life regression outlined in this book is for a fabulae," Ellowyn says, not looking at me, as if this is a betrayal. And I certainly feel it like a betrayal, so she's not wrong there. "Not a witch. And we're just now learning about fabulae. Magical creatures. We don't know that they'll react to magic the same way we do, which means this is risky until we do some tests or research or something."

She looks at Frost, as if hoping he'll know how to test what needs to be done.

Somewhere in my rational brain, I know that my friends are being cautious because they care about me, because they don't want me hurt. But it's hard to absorb that right now when I *know* this is the next step.

Frost is standing by the fireplace, looking at the crackling flames as if they are revealing the mysteries of the universe to him. "Unless . . ."

I stare at his back, holding my breath. I can't convince all of them, but if the first, original Praeceptor is on my side . . .

"The archives showed Georgie this book about past lives," he says. "And this fairy-tale cover changes, as if sending her messages. This is a true fact, yes?"

Everyone nods in agreement, but no one does it more emphatically than I do.

"Let's say this fairy tale is true. Or could have been true or has some truths in it." He looks up from the fire. "We know it does, because Ellowyn is, in fact, a Revelare."

We all look at Ellowyn and her gemstone eyes that mark her a new—or rather, old but Joywood-obscured—designation. The book led us to that revelation. The book and some ghostly help.

Frost is looking over toward Emerson and the book from the archives that she's still holding. "In this fairy tale, we have a dragon and a princess with magic having a romantic relationship." I am about to jump on that, but Frost's cool gaze slides to me, and I bite back my words. "What if that means they could have had children together?"

That sends a kind of shiver round the room, or maybe only through me. I think about that night that started in the archives and catapulted us into the stars—

But Frost is still talking. "If that's possible, why wouldn't other witches and magical creatures have done the same? And if they did, that would make some of their descendants part witch and part fabulae."

We all stare at each other. This is something we were all explicitly led to believe was not possible, even while also being encouraged not to believe magical creatures could exist. It's hard to take in even if you haven't been cavorting about with a dragon.

"That seems far-fetched," Zander says with a frown after a minute. He looks at Ellowyn and her enormously pregnant belly. "Wouldn't we know if we were part magical creature?"

"We didn't know magical creatures existed, much less were cursed and murdered in the Joywood's time," I point out. "How would we know if we've got fabulae in us?"

"It could be just another thing we've lost," Frost says, frowning. "Not really any more far-fetched than your resident half witch, half human having a three-quarter-witch child."

"Blood."

Everyone looks at Jacob, who is not prone to just *blurting out words*. He looks up at all of us as if he didn't mean to say that out loud, a thoughtful expression on his face.

"It's in the blood," he clarifies. "Just like humans, witches have blood types. Healers have lots of theories about how and why these blood types developed, and there's not necessarily an ancestral link between people with the same types. Zander and I have the same type. Frost's and Ellowyn's witch side are also the same. But Emerson and Rebekah and Georgie all have the same blood type, and we know there's a genetic link between them now. It could mean nothing, but theirs is more uncommon than the rest."

"What are you saying?" Emerson demands.

He holds her gaze steadily. "If Frost is right, if Georgie is right, then . . . there might be evidence of fabulae blood in the Wilde line, in the blood type you three share. We'd have to do a much deeper study, but it's possible."

"Wouldn't the family tree you found tell you that, Georgie?" Ellowyn asks.

"If I researched it, I could confirm it if it's true, but the tree is just names and dates—not designations or any other information." I look around at my coven, thinking about blood and friends, family and magic. But my gaze lands on Ellowyn. "We have to set up the past life regression. If I have fabulae blood, that makes sense. It's *why* I had these previous lives with him."

"It could still be dangerous, Georgie," Emerson says, putting the book back down on the table. "Think of all the spells that nearly took Ellowyn out. *And* Zander."

"They were thwarted by the Joywood using her blood against her."

"Who's to say the Joywood might not use yours against you? They know we know about fabulae. Maybe they know about this. It's too risky." She tries to smile encouragingly at me. "I know you're upset that Azrael is imprisoned, but *he's* okay with it. Let's take our time. Let's breathe and think."

Emerson and I don't fight. We don't argue. Even when we were girls and all our other friends were having all those typical girl gossips and backstabbings and dramas, that was never *us*.

But I'd fight her now. With everything I am.

And it's not that Azrael is more important to me than she is. It's not because everything is changing. It's not because I feel left out.

It's because this is the most basic truth I know: We *have* to do this.

I feel it in my bones.

"It wasn't too risky when Ellowyn and Zander and the ghosts fought off the blackness. Or when Frost sacrificed his immortality. Or when you dived into the middle of the confluence when it had been compromised by black magic." I am growing more heated with every example. "You had to do it. They had to do it. *I* have to do *this*."

Emerson stares at me, that same thread of hurt in her expression that was there when Corinne disagreed with her, even if Corinne was right.

It's like I stuck a knife in her, and I can't stand it.

"I have to do this," I tell Emerson, not as my friend. As a Historian speaking to a Warrior. "I wouldn't insist on it if I didn't believe it."

For a moment, there is only silence. And it feels like the entire room, the entire decision, is hanging there between us. Emerson and me.

Her leadership against my needs.

But I know that even if she says no, I'm going to find a way to do it anyway. No matter what it takes.

Maybe she sees that too. "Should we go to the cemetery to do it?" she asks quietly. "Azrael—"

"This is just us," I say firmly. Because I am pretty sure he would not approve of this, and anyone who's not in can get out, as far as I'm concerned.

And I can't let myself sag in relief that Emerson has agreed. I have to keep charging on.

We read through the book and arrange ourselves just as it says.

Me in the center, Ellowyn in front of me.

We sit, cross-legged, knee to knee. It reminds me of the ritual we did at Confluence Books back in the spring. When we discovered Emerson was a Confluence Warrior.

I don't let myself think about how the dark magic reached in and nearly got Emerson that time. I won't let myself think that way.

The rest of the coven arranges itself around us. The indoor familiars fill in any holes. I can feel Octavius at my back.

"First, we all need to relax," Ellowyn tells us. "This is a very calm spell. We're not trying to change anything or stop anything. We're gathering information, and we need to go in with an objective observer's mindset."

I think this isn't aimed *just* at me, though it feels a little pointed. But I'm not the only one on edge. I can feel it all around me. It's been a *day*, and now I've convinced everyone we can do this thing. Or that we have to, anyway, when we're witches who have always been taught that there is a clear progression from life to afterlife, with very few alternatives.

Past lives have never been on the witch's menu of possibilities.

I feel a moment of regret then. Or maybe it's a hesitation, because I suddenly feel all the things my mother has tried to impress upon me my entire life. Why *do* I think I'm the only one who knows these things, feels these things, *is* these things?

Why can't I be content just being a quiet Historian witch from a long line of Historian witches?

Because I'm not a fucking Pendell, I think savagely.

Because the dragon is real. The necklace he gave me full of crystals that did *not* burn me sits around my neck, because he is mine, and I am his.

Because the book keeps changing, and I know what I feel.

I always have.

So I follow Ellowyn's instructions.

"*Spirit, moon, air. Past, present, wild, tangled before, open to us*," Ellowyn murmurs. She places her hands over mine on my knees. "*Find a well-traveled soul, and show her well.*"

At first, it's hard to understand what I see as I soar deep into that kaleidoscope of images, all of them not the same me, but me. There are too many versions of myself. Too many versions of Azrael as dragon and man. I can't connect to what I'm seeing.

It's too much, too fast.

No matter how I try to center myself, it whirls around me. I can't put the timelines together. I can't make sense of it.

It pours over me and all around me, like it's that river again, pulling me in. And everything is caught up in the rush of it.

Except one thing.

One thing I see repeated again and again and again.

One red thread.

The magic begins to release its hold. The river is calm again, no rush and no whirl.

And when I open my eyes to Ellowyn's violet and sapphire Revelare glow, I don't know what I was supposed to get from that, but I know why Azrael didn't want me to see the past. All our beautiful chances spread out behind me.

I look at the members of my coven here with me, save one. They're sitting around me in a circle, looking worried and tired, because they don't know what I saw. Only the energy it took to show me.

"Well?" Zander asks.

Emerson's gaze searches mine. "Did you find what you wanted?"

My throat is so tight, it almost feels like I'm being strangled. "I found information," I say. "They were all very different lives, except for one thing." I make myself keep talking. I make myself say it. I follow that red thread. "Azrael dies. Or I do. Violently. In every single one."

21

EVERYONE TRIES TO COMFORT ME, BUT I'M not comforted. Though probably not for the reasons they think. They *think* I'm scared, knocked back, sad.

Maybe I am a little.

But mostly I'm wondering why Azrael is suddenly afraid of a past he already knew. Because there's no possibility that he didn't already know this. That he wasn't fully aware our stories always end in violence and blood.

It did not stop him from acting like I was his.

Or from putting that ring on my finger.

What I'm wondering is, what changed? What about that black magic attack and the Joywood's insistence on imprisoning him made him suddenly so afraid of the past? Afraid of working *with* us?

It's getting late, and Zander and Ellowyn make their excuses. Rebekah and Frost head out not long after. Before I can collect Octavius, Emerson puts her arm around my shoulders.

"I don't want you going back to Wilde House alone."

I am about to say what I always did, that I'm never alone because there's a dragon in the banister, but I can't. He isn't there anymore.

I wish I sounded less shaky when I reply, "I'm fine, Em. It was the crystals that put me in danger. They're gone now."

"You were attacked today," Jacob says in that no-nonsense Healer way of his. Like there's no argument I could make to that.

But there is. "Yes, but—"

"You can either spend the night here, or Jacob and I will follow you back to Wilde House. I'll leave the decision up to you." Emerson smiles at me.

I scowl at her. Because she knows that even if I took a stand and flew back to Wilde House, making them follow me, I would feel guilty. I would end up sleepless and awash in apologies and regret.

"Fine," I grumble.

Emerson links arms with mine and starts pulling me toward the stairs. "I'll make up the guest room for you." Octavius takes his time following us. Cassie, who almost always sticks close to Octavius when I bring him out here, is right behind per usual.

Upstairs, Emerson takes me into the guest room. She flings a hand up and murmurs the company spell, and magic flows out so that everything is instantly dusted, straightened. The bed is turned down, with a stack of fluffy towels and a robe at the foot. Anything else I could possibly need, from hand-milled soaps made right on Main Street, St. Cyprian, to a selection of shower gels and bath salts, is set in a happy little basket on the desk.

But she doesn't leave me to it. She takes a seat on the corner of my bed, looks right at me with that Emerson battle light gleaming hot in her gaze, and asks the question I don't want to answer. "Are you really okay?"

We're alone. Two best friends. This isn't coven business now. It's us.

I let out a breath. "I don't know what I am."

"That's fair." Emerson frowns a little, reaching for the fairy tale, which has apparently magicked itself to the end of the bed beside her. "This book really loves to follow you around, doesn't it?"

"Yes." I stare at the book. "I'm being stalked by an unhinged fairy tale."

Emerson flips through it. "I still feel like there's an answer in here we haven't figured out yet."

I don't want to look at the book right now. I don't want to think about dragons at all. But then Emerson kind of jumps to her feet, holding the book open like it bit her.

"Georgie, did you . . . ?"

She doesn't finish. She just hands me the book. It's opened to a page in the front that has always been blank. There are only two words there now, small but unmistakable:

For Georgie.

It doesn't make sense. There's never been a dedication before.

Certainly not to me.

Then again, it's a stalkery, magical book. The cover changes all the time. Why *shouldn't* there be a dedication page?

The bigger question is, why do I see it now? Why have I never seen it before?

I think of the archives giving me what I needed today. I think of the necklace I've been wearing since I was sixteen that Frost destroyed not that long ago at Azrael's command.

But before I can really sink into all those terrible feelings surrounding my mother giving me a black magic necklace, I notice that Emerson is gesturing for me to flip the page, so I do.

And pause.

It's the title page. Where there's more new information.

There's an author and illustrator listed when I don't recall there ever being one before.

Particularly this one.

Lillian Wilde.

My gaze snaps to Emerson. My breath seems to be stuck

somewhere between my lungs and an exhale, and I think she's struggling to breathe too.

"That has to be wrong," I say, though part of me wants to sob. Because Lillian would have been *my* grandmother too, but if she wrote this to me . . .

Does that mean she knew? And never told me?

Emerson is shaking her head. There are tears in her eyes, and I know how much she misses her grandmother. We all miss her, but Emerson is the one who walks into her bookstore almost every day. Emerson is the one who took that Wilde family responsibility on her shoulders.

Even when she didn't know she was a witch.

Emerson reaches out for my arms. "Of course she wrote it for you, Georgie. Of course she did. She's your grandmother."

There is something about the way Emerson keeps that in the present tense that makes me want to sob, deep and hard. But there's a bigger issue here. "If she wrote it for me, that would mean she knew I was her granddaughter while she was alive . . . and she never told me."

I don't like it any better out loud than I did when it was only in my head.

Emerson doesn't look away. "I won't tell you how to feel. But I would just say . . . we don't know. What she knew. What she didn't. She was the best, but I'm not saying that she couldn't have made mistakes. I'm just saying that if anyone deserves the benefit of the doubt, it's her."

Emerson is right. But how will we ever know for sure? Lillian has shown up for Emerson and Rebekah upon occasion, but that's been rare. It takes considerable energy for a ghost to reach out to the side of the living.

And Lillian has never reached out to me.

I look down at the fairy-tale book in my hand, thinking about all those changes. And no doubt more changes to come. Maybe this *is* Lillian reaching out.

Emerson says good-night, then charms the guest room for deep sleep on her way out. I can feel myself getting sleepy immediately, despite everything, and I'm grateful for it. I'm not sure I have the energy to find a charm for myself.

And I sleep well. Deep, no dreams.

When I wake up, there's no evidence that I was burned yesterday. Nothing to indicate I was attacked. I look, but there are no marks on me. There's also no hangover-like feeling from seeing all my past lives whirl all around me.

There's just a rested feeling, and a big, fat cat curled at my feet. He glares at me a bit when I get up out of bed, but I give him a nice long pet until he purrs. Then I get dressed. I have archives to search today. Work to do.

I want to bury myself in books, just like the good old days. It's the first day of Christmas Around the World. Saturday morning we'll have a parade, but the crowds will start today. The bookstore and tea shop will be packed, so I'll be helping Emerson and Ellowyn as needed.

Focus on the present and the future. I frown at Azrael's words. Because he's wrong. He's just *wrong*. There are *answers* in the past, and not just us bloody and dead, trussed up in the red thread of our sad destinies, but real answers hidden somewhere in there.

And I have to find them.

I walk down to the kitchen to find Jacob and Emerson almost done with breakfast preparations, and I can tell that they did their own cooking. They move in the kitchen like a perfectly oiled machine. It's beautiful to watch.

Emerson sits me down, piles my plate high with food I won't be able to eat all of but I know will taste like my feelings anyway, and then chatters happily about St. Cyprian things.

Like she knows I need an Azrael-free conversation first thing in the morning. And she *does* know that, because she's not my best friend for no reason.

With breakfast done, the three of us walk back to the cemetery together. Cassie is bounding ahead on the path. I see Jacob's stag familiar, Murphy, watching from a winter-empty field.

Octavius, naturally, opted to stay inside the warm farmhouse.

We meet up with Zander and Ellowyn on the path, walking up from their house closer to the river. Ellowyn looks flushed and annoyed, and I don't ask why. We all know she's furious about how hard it is to get around with her pregnant belly and incredibly touchy about it too.

Zander walks beside her, looking proud and indulgent, like her crankiness is the best part of his day.

Like they fit together in every possible way.

Rebekah and Frost are ahead of us at the cemetery gate, no doubt having flown over. As we walk closer, I study the way they stand so close together. Rebekah smiles up at him the way she smiles at no one else, and Frost smiles only for her.

More things that hurt.

More things I want.

We all come together just outside the cemetery gates, that big statue of a dragon grinning dangerously down at us.

Or snarling, I guess, depending on your perspective.

I look past it, into the cemetery. Azrael is standing in man form in the center, and he's not alone. He's surrounded by the ghostly apparitions of many a witch and familiar.

I can't hear what he's saying from this distance, but his expression is grave.

"Mom," I hear Zander breathe out. He moves forward toward the ghost of his mother, Zelda, and Ellowyn isn't far behind. I realize that all my friends are rushing to their lost loved ones.

Except Frost. And me.

We remain outside the gates. I can't tell what Frost is doing. Thinking about all his dead, wherever they might be in space and time, at a guess. But I can't focus on that because I'm still looking at Azrael. Studying him.

Like if I stare at him long enough, the way I would any piece of lore I can't make sense of—a string of dead languages or indecipherable images—I'll be able to figure this out. Figure *him* out.

I don't know how long I stand there, trying to come up with a way to read a dragon like a great historical tome, when I hear a voice say my name. A familiar voice, though I haven't heard that particular wavering melody in years. For a moment I wonder if it's the river again, but something in me knows better.

I turn my head just enough to see Emerson and Rebekah bracketing a small woman.

Lillian Wilde.

She has her ghostly arms around Emerson and Rebekah, but she is looking at me. Her misty eyes shine, and I . . .

I am looking at my grandmother.

Who was always there, even when I didn't know who she was to me. Who called me special when everyone else told me I was regular.

Maybe she was telling me all along.

With halting steps, I move forward. Into the cemetery and toward this woman who was always so kind to me. Who was the antidote to my mother. Who took every sling and arrow that came at me next door and turned them into warmth, funny stories, anecdotes, and belonging.

The thing about Lillian is that she was always there.

When I reach her, she pulls her arms away from Emerson and Rebekah and reaches out to me. She's not corporeal, so it just feels like a cool breeze, like goose bumps down my arms.

"Did you know?" I whisper.

She looks at me and runs a see-through hand over my hair. I don't feel it like I would a living hand, but I still feel a disturbance in the air around my curls.

"Not in a direct way. I knew there was something there. A connection." She frowns slightly. "Maybe I didn't want to know." Because, of course, that would tell her things about her son, Desmond. My real father—though I don't want to think about fathers now. She smiles at me. "What I knew—and know—beyond any shadow of a doubt is that you're special."

You aren't special, Georgie. My mother's impatient voice. *You're a Pendell. Act like one.*

Lillian sighs, like a patch of fog. "Once I crossed over, I saw more of my son's mistakes than I wanted to. But you were blocked to me. It has been so hard to reach any of you, but you especially."

Blocked. It dawns on me, hard and cruel. "The necklace my mother gave me."

She nods sadly. "Among other things. The Joywood do not want you all having access to the dead."

"Then how is this happening?" Emerson asks.

Lillian turns to look at Azrael, who is leaning against the statue of his dragon form like he hasn't a care in the world. But I can see that he does. It's in the set of his shoulders, that haunted look in his eyes.

"I may not have the magic to *do* things, but that does not mean there is not magic to be used," he says, still in that stiff way I don't understand or like. "They made the mistake of putting onyx in the statue. It might make it look that much more terrifying, but it gives me access to energy. Energy enough to reach out to my fellow cemetery residents and help them . . . appear, shall we say."

His gesture encompasses all the ghosts around us.

"It never fails to amaze me how little you lot know," a woman in somewhat Victorian garb says to Ellowyn. When Ellowyn only grins at her instead of getting offended, I realize this must be Elizabeth Good. Ellowyn's ancestress who showed up in ghost form before Samhain. She helped us. Saved us, really.

And that means her husband, Zander's ancestor Zachariah Rivers, is who stands beside Elizabeth.

Dreams and books and fairy tales. Ghosts and crows and dragons. True covens with fabulae. For a moment, I really stand in that. All these things we've been told don't exist, don't matter, aren't for us.

And at every turn we prove them wrong.

Because we *are* special.

It turns out we have been all along.

Emerson turns to the crowd of magical beings and creatures and asks for their advice.

"Anything you know," she says. "Anything you can share. We're grateful for it all."

There is a lot of commotion, then, on this misty December morning. Lots of theories about how to defeat black magic. Lots of dark muttering about the Joywood. Zachariah insists we need to find the crows, as if there aren't crows just about everywhere. Emerson is magicking all the practical suggestions down into a notebook. I'm doing the same, sending queries to the archives so I'll have the appropriate books waiting for me.

No stone will go unturned—we'll all see to that—but it's clear no matter how many ghosts or familiars offer suggestions that no one *really* knows how to beat black magic.

Which makes sense. I don't think even Frost knew when he could remember everything, and he's been around forever.

Still.

"I'll research all your suggestions in the archives and see if we can't find an answer there," I tell the crowd of magical things.

"And you'll have all our help, should that be what you need," Lillian says. She's clearly the de facto leader of the ghosts. Echoes of Emerson, and that makes me smile.

It gives me hope.

We begin to say our goodbyes because we still have real lives on this side to see to. But it's hard. For all of us, I think, not just me. I really don't want to let this moment with Lillian go.

But some of the ghosts begin to disappear. One by one.

And soon enough my coven begins to head off to those real lives too.

"I have to get to the store," Emerson says to me regretfully, but she doesn't leave. She's waiting to see if I'll ask her to stay.

Because she never opens that store late, but for me, she would. That's best friend love.

But I'm looking at Azrael. "It's all right, Em. Go. I'm headed straight to the archives after this."

Emerson glances at Azrael, then me. She nods once, and then she's off.

And it's just Azrael and me again. He stands with yards between us and makes no move to close the distance. It gives me a shiver.

"You should get to the archives," he says. "You have much work to do."

For a moment, I can only stare at him. I see him, bloody and falling, over and over again. I see myself, pale and lifeless. Death, death, and more death.

The red thread that connects us, time after time.

I get why he didn't want me to see it, but I don't understand why it suddenly *matters*. "Why wouldn't you just tell me?" I ask him.

And I don't know why it hurts. It's not like I *asked* him.

But at the same time, he's the one with all the knowledge. He *remembers*.

He studies me, and something has gone cool in his gaze. "You should not have done that ritual," he says flatly.

I shrug. "I had to do it. The archives and the book told me to. Maybe if you'd told me yourself, I wouldn't have had to."

He looks *wounded* by that, but it's only the truth.

"Did you note how often it was *your* painful death?" he asks a bit dryly—but there's a hint of *something* in his tone. Something with fangs. "And how close that was to happening just yesterday?"

"I was the one getting pulled into the water, so. Yes. Noted."

"And *I* was the one who pulled you out." He moves forward then, and he grabs me by the shoulders like he wants to shake me, but he doesn't. "You must let me save you this time. You must trust me. You must *listen to me* this time. Promise me that, Georgina."

I wish I could. "I do trust you, Azrael," I say gently. I put my hand on his chest, hoping he understands. "But I have to trust myself most of all."

He steps away so that my hand falls too. Everything about him goes cold as he crosses his arms over his chest. "Very well."

I move toward him. "Azrael—"

But before I can say anything, he just disappears.

And the dragon statue shakes a little, so I know he's gone in there. Purposefully and by choice gone into the prison the Joywood made for him.

Leaving me out here, all alone.

22

A DAY IN THE ARCHIVES WITH NOT MUCH TO show for it feels a bit like the good old days, pre-dragon. Pre-ascension. Pre . . . this year of learning too much and sometimes wishing I thought ignorance really could be bliss.

There's a dull ache behind my eyes from reading page after page in one musty old tome after the next, but it's a good ache. Whatever else it might signify—like that maybe I need glasses—it's also a sign of work being done.

It's the only sign of progress I really have.

I read a lot about black magic. Mostly treatises about why it's against the law, dire accounts of its use and its effects, and example after example explaining why it's subject to the harshest punishments in witchdom. And while I understand the historical context of St. Cyprian staples like our enchanted bricks, offering safety—and no black magic—to all, it's not enough to move forward with anything that might help us *now*.

I keep the stalkery fairy-tale book—written by my grandmother, for me—with me the whole time, thinking it might give me a clue as to where I should look next and what might be coming.

But it doesn't change.

I'm determined to stay in the archives until I figure everything out and can go back to my coven with spells and a plan, but Emerson starts sending me messages as the hours drag by. About brains without food.

So when I close up the archives, it's dark and cold. A fully December sort of night, here in a river town in Missouri all decked out in holiday lights. A faint snow is falling as I head outside and shiver into my coat. I feel a pull to walk back to Wilde House, to wander down Main Street and soak in the lights set against the darkest time of the year—

But that *pull* reminds me a little too much of being sucked into the river, so I magic myself over to the front gate of Wilde House instead. I want to scratch the itch of holiday perfection by looking at one of the prettiest houses around, all done up in the snowy moonlight.

Instead of having a moment to breathe in the cold air and get right with the Cold Moon, I immediately notice that my father seems to have done the exact same thing.

Except he's *not* my father, I remind myself. He's Stanford Pendell, and he's no relation to me. He never has been.

It makes my heart hurt.

We're both standing in front of our respective gates, gazing up at the house I grew up in and the house I live in.

If we weren't so close, I might have hurried in and pretended our paths hadn't crossed, because I have no idea what to say. Or do. Or feel.

But there's no hiding in the moonlight. Not with snow on my face and his gaze steady on mine from yards away.

He smiles that same sad smile from the Cold Moon Ball, illuminated only by the flickering streetlamp and the stars above. "Working late again, princess?"

I swallow at the lump that's suddenly lodged deep in my throat. I realize that I'm staring at him. Because he's so . . . familiar. He's so *dear* to me.

Yet he's not mine.

He's always called me princess, even when my mother berated him for indulging me in my chronic daydreams. I walk over to him, propelled by something I can't quite name.

Maybe I can fix the distance between me and *somebody*.

It's a pull that feels far more elemental than a melody or a river. It seems to come from the depths of my own heart.

When I get up close, the only word I can manage is, "Why?"

He aims that smile toward the cold ground between us. "You could be asking a lot of different whys."

The night is frigid and getting colder as we stand here. The snow is coming down harder, small flakes that speak of future snowdrifts and snow days. No one should be standing out here like this for too long, no matter how heartbroken we might feel.

We should go inside, I think. I should invite him in for tea, have a mature, adult conversation, and work through this in some kind of healthy way.

But I feel rooted to this spot, on a sidewalk with my nose growing colder by the second. And the lobes of my ears. They both sting. "I wasn't yours. You *knew* I wasn't yours."

He studies me in that quiet, patient way of his. I used to find this annoying. I used to think that when he was deep in research mode, he only ever saw me as a problem to be solved.

But I wasn't his problem. I never was, and he always had time for me anyway.

"I suppose, in a matter of blood and whatnot, that is true," he says in that careful way of his that I have spent my life trying and failing to emulate. "And I did know it."

"So," I say, and I don't sound as careful as he does. Or as careful as I should. *"Why?"*

"What I also knew was that you were here. A perfect little baby girl with all that red hair." He shakes his head. "I knew that Desmond was not going to admit any involvement, and your mother was ashamed. Of her own actions. Of her own mistakes." He smiles again, and it's even sadder this time. "She's never been good at making those and dealing with the consequences."

He understands her better than I've given him credit for. Certainly better than I ever have.

I want to tell him that, but it's like I can't speak. Like this time, my own history has me in its grip, so hard around my throat that all I can do is stare at him through the snow.

"I'm not sure I've ever seen your mother really love anyone," he tells me in that same quiet way. "Perhaps it's not in her." And then he shrugs, like that's . . . just life. Some people don't *love*. "It seemed to me, or it did when I saw an innocent baby, fresh and new and with old souls in her eyes, that someone should love her. And if it wasn't going to be her father or her mother, it might as well be me, because I loved you from the moment I saw you, Georgie."

He makes it sound so simple. A choice he made. Like that's all love is, in the end. A *choice*.

Like he's always known about *old souls* and never thought them foolish, or that I thought too highly of myself to imagine I might have an old soul myself.

He made that choice to love me, day after day. Maybe he never stood up to my mother in any real way, but much like with Lillian, I knew I would always find a soft spot to land with this man. He was who I ran to when I was little.

And maybe I did let my mother get to me, finally. Maybe I had too much of her in my head as this year unfolded and it became clear that we were going to take on the Joywood. When it became obvious what that could mean for me personally.

Still, for a whole lot of years, I got to daydream as I pleased. I got to retreat into my fairy tales and enjoy them as I liked. Because of people like Lillian Wilde, Emerson and Rebekah and Ellowyn—all of my best friends.

But it started here. With him. All because Stanford Pendell

thought *someone* should love the baby his wife gave birth to after an affair.

A few tears fall onto my cold cheeks, and he reaches out and brushes them away. Just like he always did, that achingly familiar brush of his gloves against my skin. "Nothing has changed for me, Georgie. It's as I told you—facts aren't the whole story. You of all people should know that you get to write your own as you go."

It makes me think about past lives. New lives.

And the thread that moves through all of them, no matter the ending.

A thread that isn't red and terribly painful.

Love.

Maybe none of us can choose *who* we love, but we can certainly change *how* we love. This man is living, breathing proof.

I move forward and envelop the only father I've ever known—and the only one I imagine I'll ever acknowledge—in a hug. "Thank you for loving me . . . when you didn't have to."

He squeezes me back. Hard. "It's no great sacrifice to love you, Georgie. I can't think of a single reason why anyone would ever do anything but."

I think I knew that, deep down under all the confusion that family tree kicked up, but I needed to hear it. I needed to do this. Maybe I still need to deal with my mother and Desmond at some point, but this is the person who matters the most to me.

Because this is the person who showed me what love is, every single day of my life.

How can I pretend I don't love him in return? As wholly and completely as I always have?

"Dad," I say, because he is my dad. Maybe he's never been my *biological father*, but he is, and always will be, my *dad*. "I'd like you to come help me in the witchlore archives. I know I can't officially deputize you yet, so it might mean a lot of sitting around being a wall I can bounce ideas off of until we get past Yule, but I think . . . I think that's what we need."

The people we love and who love us, no matter the circumstances.

No matter the difficulties.

Hasn't that been the lesson we've learned over and over again this year? Love is magic.

Love is the antidote.

To everything.

"I'd be happy to," my dad tells me. We release each other and smile at each other, wider than ever, maybe because now we *both* know that love is a choice. That this love is *our* choice. "Come in for tea, princess. I've got a new book I want to tell you about."

And I might be hungry, I might be tired, but that's just what I do. I follow him into my childhood home. I sit with my dad in the parlor and discuss books over tea while a fire crackles in the hearth. Octavius senses me over here and magicks himself into my lap. If my mother is somewhere, she doesn't make an appearance, and that's a good thing.

It's just us. Just like before.

And it's what I need to really believe what he said.

Facts *aren't* the whole story.

After a while, my father falls asleep in his chair, and I head back outside. I walk through the snow, the porch lights of Wilde House beckoning to me. I carry Octavius cradled in my arms like a baby.

Inside, it's dark and a little cold. It still feels like home, but it also feels emptier than it should when I've been living here alone more often than not these days. I look down at the snoozing orange cat in my arms.

I suppose him being here means I'm never *really* alone.

But there's no dragon in the newel post, or in my bed. So all that new, wild warmth is just kind of dull and cold now. A big stone statue outside of town, in fact.

Love is the answer, I tell myself. It's a voice that doesn't sound like mine, though it comes from deep inside me. And I know it's true.

A love that has existed between Azrael and me across lives.

Through too many deaths to count, and yet we always find each other again, following that red thread down through the ages.

Maybe it's not so much reincarnation as a chance to get it right. In every other scenario, one of us died violently. Maybe we keep coming back until . . . until we don't.

Until we find the answer.

23

THE NEXT MORNING WE'RE ALL UP EARLY AT Wilde House before the Christmas Around the World parade. We all have our assigned, volun-*told*, and occasionally chosen roles.

I'm dressed up like Saint Lucia, complete with white dress, red sash, and wreath of candles on my head. I leave Azrael's necklace that he gave me in my jewelry box and ignore the little pang it gives me.

When I get downstairs, Emerson is dressed up like a Victorian Mrs. Claus, and—in a surprising twist—somehow got Jacob to dress up like Victorian Santa.

I do not ask how. I suspect it involves very *private* promises.

He looks a little gray, and I have a bad feeling that means another black magic attack. When Emerson gives me a brief nod, I know I'm right. It's a concern. There have always been hints, here and there, that black magic has reached out and swatted at people this way, but the continual attacks every few days feel like a ticking time bomb.

But what can be done if the archives won't give me answers?

I try to push this disappointment away and focus on the happy festivities at hand.

Zander is dressed up like Scrooge, which took only a little pleading from Ellowyn—the kind he never would have succumbed to before this year, no matter how many secret Beltane trysts they shared. Ellowyn herself got excused from the usual costuming on account of pregnancy. This year she'll just ride on our float, decked out in a dramatic cloak decorated with evergreen and berries, embodying Yule and the upcoming solstice while tossing candy to the watching kids.

Frost refused any and all costumes as a matter of course and dignity, as he put it—but that only means he and Rebekah got put in charge of walking next to the float and handing out *pamphlets*.

Emerson, Rebekah and I worked hard on them. My historical knowledge, citations, and ability to translate both into simpler, more straightforward explanations work well with Emerson's uncanny ability to know just what kind of questions people might have. And Rebekah makes everything visually pretty with her graphic design wizardry.

Humans who get their hands on a pamphlet will only see a sweet rundown of the different floats and Santa Clauses—or comparable winter solstice figures—from different countries and traditions.

Witches will see a thorough explanation of fabulae, true covens, and how we intend to proceed with this knowledge. Freeing Azrael, yes, but also finding and freeing other magical creatures. Working *together*.

It's been the Riverwood promise since we were nothing but a group of friends.

Emerson was keeping me updated on the votes about Azrael's fate on an hourly basis until I asked her to stop. Last time she told me it was close, but still in favor of keeping him imprisoned. I told her to just let me know when he's free.

When, not *if*. I'll deal with him then.

Today, I'm focusing on St. Cyprian. On a *festival*. I always love this time of year and all the different holiday festivals Emerson manages to pack into a few short weeks. How no matter the weather, people come out and support this little town of ours. How the Yule season—regardless how a person or witch or magical creature might celebrate it—is one of togetherness. Of braving the dark winter march toward the light *together*.

Emerson grabs me before we all head out for the parade. "Where's your sash?"

I look down. I could have sworn I put it on, but it is indeed missing. I try to magic it into my hands, but it doesn't appear. I frown a little, but quickly give Emerson a bright smile. She's on edge for a lot of reasons, hyped up on caffeine and what she always calls *festival adrenaline*. Best not to worry her.

"I'll be right back," I assure her, and magick myself upstairs to my bedroom. The sash is on my bed, tucked under a book.

The fairy tale.

Always the fairy tale.

"Do you have something to tell me, finally?" I mutter at it. I snatch it up and see that the cover has changed, but no matter how I stare at it, I can't make sense of it.

The princess is still in the foreground. The dragon is off in the back. Still there, still clearly watching, but not a part of the narrative.

"I'm not a fan of that," I tell the book, but I focus on the princess. And the parts I can't make sense of.

There are now *crows* everywhere around the princess. A circle of violet-eyed ones surround her, and it looks like a few of them are putting a necklace over her head.

I peer closer, at the princess and the necklace in one crow's beak. I blink, because it's . . . familiar.

I think—I *know*—I have a necklace like that. A swirling mix of purple, blue, and green in one teardrop-shaped crystal.

I drop the book and walk over to my jewelry box. Since time is limited, I mutter a quick spell to reveal the necklace to me. It lifts up out of all the other crystals and jewelry, so I grab it and slide it over my head.

The book has not led me astray yet, and this necklace has been in my collection so long I don't even remember how it got there—if someone gave it to me, if I bought it, if I found it somewhere, the way I sometimes do. It's just . . . always been here.

I decide—I *hope*—that means it's only made of good magic and supportive energy. Even though I'm a little leery about trusting in my crystals again.

I hurry up and tie the red sash around my waist, then transport myself downstairs so Emerson doesn't become totally unglued. She immediately grabs my hand. "We'll magic ourselves over to the assembly area."

She doesn't even give me a chance to help. Propelled by her own magic and one of Ellowyn's energy teas, she's got us all to the courtyard, where the parade people are assembling and getting ready to start.

Emerson immediately marches away, but I stay where I am, facing the river. It's a bright, sunny day, making you think the sun might *just* fight off the frigid air. The snow from last night's storm clings to the trees and rooftops, and there are lingering patches of snow and ice on the bricks. Across the icy river, I can just barely see the archway of the cemetery. And the new dragon statue that glints in the light, like a threat.

That pokes at some of my cheer. Something about what the Joywood did to him that day has changed everything, and I hate it. If he wasn't imprisoned, he'd be with us. Though he'd have to be pretending to be a human still. Pete from London.

I wish he was part of this, but *really* a part of it. Not as a dragon hiding in a human spell, but as himself. Dragon or man form.

Free, and safe to be who he pleases.

But I don't want to be mad at him, worrying about him, pining over him today. I want to enjoy this damn parade.

"Where's Gil?" I hear Emerson ask.

I turn to look at the Joywood contingent. They've got their own float, a whole Charles Dickens thing, though several of them are missing. Not just Gil Redd, who normally helps at things like this. And I recoil a little bit as I look at them, because every single one of them except Carol looks like *they* should be residents of the cemetery.

As in six feet under.

"Gil isn't feeling well," Carol says tersely. Her hair is a honey shade of blond in a beautiful, wavy twist—instead of its usual frizz ball, but considering the rest of the Joywood all look like dressed-up zombies, I wonder if that means both Gil's legs disintegrated or something equally problematic they can't magic their way out of.

I make a mental note to see if black magic can rot a witch from the inside out. It seems not just plausible, but more and more possible. Especially considering they're now missing three of their coven members.

Maybe we don't need to defeat them at all. Maybe we just need to wait them out. I eye Carol's youthful appearance.

Or not.

We assemble on our float, taking our places as explained to us in the usual intense detail—complete with charts—by Emerson. The parade begins at the exact time she planned. The floats begin to move. We sit and wave as we slowly proceed down the street, while Rebekah and Frost walk a little ahead of us, handing out their pamphlets.

Emerson and Jacob are supposed to sit and wave and maybe toss out some candy to kids. But as ever, Emerson can't help herself. She's on her feet in no time, walking next to the float, then stopping at every group of witches that gets a pamphlet to talk to them.

I watch her, and more importantly, the witches' reactions to her. She makes eye contact, she grasps hands, she holds all the babies and makes a fuss over all the little kids. It's very *politics,* maybe, but there's a genuine light that shines out of Emerson when she does these things.

Even dressed up like Victorian Mrs. Claus.

I can hear her voice, certain and sure. "Think of all the things that have changed in the past year, all the things that we've learned have been hidden from us. Is that how we want to go on? Hiding from the *truth*? We saved St. Cyprian from the flood and the dark magic in the confluence by *not* doing that."

The way she says *we* clearly makes people think they were included. Like they were part of everything we did. I expect someone to point that out, but they don't. The fact she wants to include them clearly wins some people over.

The Joywood—whose float is right in front of ours—are scowling. Rotting and scowling. Though I still think only we can see it. Every once in a while, I see Felicia wave a hand, and some of the pamphlets go flying, or spontaneously combust.

But not many.

They just don't have the all-encompassing power now that we've been voted in. They're dwindling in numbers. They're literally losing body parts.

Yet I have absolutely no doubt they're planning something. Something Carol-centered, maybe. Knowing them, something devastating.

I just wish I knew *what*.

The parade finishes up, though Emerson is still doing her thing. The rest of us mill about at the end of the parade route, waiting for her to be done. Jacob is talking with some of the volunteers who are dealing with breaking down the float itself. Zander is making noise about getting Ellowyn off her feet, even though she was sitting the whole time and is looking as if she'd like him to sit down and shut up for a change.

I find it comforting that their spiky dynamic remains unchanged at its heart, despite the fact they let themselves show the affectionate part too these days.

I sigh happily and absolutely do not think about Azrael. Mostly because I hear a bird making an ungodly racket somewhere near me. I turn, searching for the sound. I expect to see everyone else turning to look too, but I seem to be the only one who hears it.

Just like that haunting music from the river—

But then my eyes land on the perpetrator.

And I know this is nothing like that melody.

A smaller black bird is standing in a narrow alley, almost perfectly framed by the sunshine and shadow.

Is it a crow? Like in the book?

I can't tell, but one thing I *can* tell is that it has violet eyes.

Just like that damned book cover.

24

ELLOWYN IS CLOSEST TO ME, SO I REACH OUT, grab the sleeve of her cloak, and tug.

She turns her head toward me. "Wh— Oh, shit." She immediately reaches for Zander's hand. "Remember that dream I told you about from All Souls' Day?"

"Not real— Oh, *shit*," he says when he catches sight of the violet-eyed raven. "Yeah, I remember."

"I think we need to follow him," I say, not taking my eyes off the bird as he hops once, then twice, each time moving deeper into the shadows of the alley. "Can you get everyone?"

"On it," Zander says, then disappears.

I take a step forward, but I'm still holding on to Ellowyn's cloak, so I don't get far.

"Georgie . . ." she says in warning.

"We can't lose him." I know this the way I know that Azrael is wrong to stay away from me. I take another step, and Ellowyn steps with me. "Do you remember anything else from your dream?"

"He was just there and . . . Well . . ." It isn't like Ellowyn to trail off and get quiet, so I risk taking my eyes off the bird and look at her. She makes a face. "I'm just not entirely sure the *bird* part was a dream. I'm pretty sure I woke up from the dream and he was in the window."

"Pretty sure?" I ask.

She looks at me with her bejeweled Revelare gaze. "He was in the window. He was real."

And she can't lie out loud. So that means it's the absolute truth.

We stare at each other. Then at the crow, who is standing there, half in shadow with his head tilted to one side, staring right back.

Rebekah and Frost appear then, and Zander reappears next to Ellowyn. "Jacob is trying to maneuver Emerson out of an impromptu speech. Apparently the vote has almost gone in Azrael's favor. She just needs two more," he says, his gaze on me. "Then they'll catch up."

He'll be free. He'll be *free*. Once he is, I can deal with all the Azrael-ness of it all, but for right now, I have to think about this violet-eyed bird.

I hurry a few steps forward into the alley because the bird has started hopping again. He's almost out of sight.

We reach the end of the alley at a fence line. On the other side of the fence is a parking lot. It's not the most beautiful setting—except, when we arrive, something sparkles around us.

Magic, but not a magic I recognize.

If I have to describe it in terms of anything I've seen, it's a little bit like Azrael's smoke.

And a little army of crows sits along that fence line, there at the end of the alley.

They're not just *sitting*, I realize. Not the way crows do all the time, all over the place. There's a certain *intent*. A *purpose*, even, as if they *arranged* themselves there—

My breath goes a little shallow. Are these crows magical creatures? A different sort of fabulae?

But how were they freed if they are?

The biggest bird among them flies forward. It has something in its beak. It sets the envelope down in the middle of all that sparkling magic, on something like a tiny podium. Then it simply . . . flies away. And the others follow, one after the next.

Like a parade of crows.

And then there are no more birds and no more swirling magic. Only the end of an alley and an envelope. I move forward to touch it, but Ellowyn holds me back.

"This feels like an epically bad idea, Georgie," she mutters.

"Cosign," Rebekah agrees from behind us.

"By all means," Frost says with scathing sarcasm, "pick up the magic envelope delivered by a full murder of crows in a dark alley in midwinter. What could go wrong?"

"I hate agreeing with him," Zander practically growls. "On anything. But give me a break, Georgie. At least wait for Emerson and Jacob before you jump into the next suicide mission."

But the script on the front is a looping, fancy calligraphy. And it says my name.

Not my nickname.

Georgina, it reads.

Jacob and Emerson appear. Emerson is clearly worried, but she's listening. "It was on the book cover this morning," I tell them.

I describe the scene in detail and the necklace the crows gave me in that picture.

"I know this is an envelope, not a necklace," I say before anyone else can, "but I think I'm supposed to read it. It has my name on it, after all." I look back at my coven, especially Emerson. "This book has been nothing but a positive force for us," I remind her. "Your—*our* grandmother wrote it."

Eventually she nods at me. A green light.

I pick up the envelope and open it carefully, then pull out a card.

It's ornate. Beautiful drawings of trees and many crows, with purple-and-green gems along the top. Along the bottom, there's an intricately painted scene from the cemetery across the way.

Complete with a dragon statue.

"What does it say?" Emerson demands.

"It's an invitation," I say. Carefully, as I read the words in dramatic calligraphy, and not in English. These are old spell words. An ancient vocabulary I have previously only read in very old books. "It says, more or less, *'The Most Holy Cornix, First of Crows, is Commanded by His Royal Highness the King to invite Georgina Pendell into the great compliment of His Royal Presence at the St. Cyprian cemetery. Immediately.'*"

For a moment, we all stand there very quietly. Rebekah studies the invitation over my shoulder. "Whoever made that has some serious skills."

I'm studying that dragon statue. It doesn't *feel* like a threat, but I'm worried anyway. "We have to go."

Emerson pauses, and I think I am either going to have to argue with her . . . or just fly away and argue with her later. But she finally nods. "Let's go."

So we all fly across the river and land, together, at the cemetery entrance, still in our ridiculous costumes. Azrael is standing in the archway, the statue rearing up behind him. His arms are crossed, something like a puff of smoke billowing out of his ears as he stares not *at* us—

But behind us.

We all turn.

Across from him, outside the cemetery bounds, sits a man.

Though *sits* and *a man* are not actually accurate descriptors for what I'm seeing.

He's tall and lean, languid and yet pulsing with power. He's dressed all in black. His face is shrouded in shadows and the suggestion of jet-black hair. He lounges in a tree, sprawled out on a low branch like it was made to be a bed.

"Hello, Riverwood coven," he greets us, his voice low and

powerful. His leg swings lazily to one side of the branch. "A pleasure to make your acquaintance, though I believe I only invited *one* of you."

"We're kind of a package deal," Emerson says, eyeing the man carefully.

"I suppose I can overlook this lack of manners. You are *witches*, after all." He sniffs a little. "And you come with a *dragon*."

I look back at Azrael. Fury pumps off him. But he's within the square of the cemetery, and we're standing just out of his reach.

I honestly don't know what to think. I'd jump to *this is bad*, but the book led us here, and well, it's not like Azrael hating someone is fully something to go by. He hates Frost.

I look back at the new guy. He jumps off the branch and into the snow below with a kind of grace that reminds me of bird flight.

"I am Gideon Wulfram, better known as the Raven King." He looks down at us, violet eyes glowing. "You may bow, curtsy, faint. Your choice."

"Not real big on any of those things," Zander grumbles next to me. He has himself slightly angled in front of Ellowyn, but Ellowyn is staring at Gideon Wulfram, the Raven King, in a way that makes me wonder . . .

Could this have been her violet-eyed post-dream crow?

"Witches never did have any *flair*," the *king* says in a conversational sort of way that makes Frost's languid wave of a hand seem stuffy by comparison. "Despite these bizarre *costumes*. But that is an age-old complaint with no cure, and we have real problems at hand. It has come to our attention that one Georgina Pendell, regrettably also a witch, can free magical creatures from the Joywood's evil curse."

"Don't let your guard down until the crows are free," Ellowyn whispers. Her eyes are wide, her hand splayed over her belly. "That was in my dream."

Gideon gives a little nod, as if agreeing with what Ellowyn's saying. Then his violet eyes focus in on me, and everything in me . . . stills.

I know deep, ancient, unmistakable power when I see it. But there's something else humming there. A kind of recognition. I have to wonder . . . Did I know him in a former life?

"How would such a thing come to your attention?" Azrael demands. But he's stuck there in the cemetery, and the king smiles as if he knows this. As if he *enjoys* us all being *just* out of Azrael's reach.

"Not all of us were so weak as to be killed or imprisoned by the curse of a rogue coven," Gideon says with another bored wave of his hand. "*Some* of us know how to handle ourselves when black magic is about."

"The phrase *birds of a feather* comes to mind," Azrael says darkly.

"Be careful with these dangerous accusations, dragon." Gideon's violet eyes glint with malice as he looks past us toward Azrael. "You may have burned my people once, but you won't again."

"You deserved it," Azrael retorts. "You're a dick."

Gideon smiles. It is . . . not pleasant. "I believe there is a saying amongst the witches and the humans, is there not? You should know it, having enjoyed so many of their witticisms while in the guise of a bit of furniture. *Takes one to know one*, asshole."

All this *we* and *us* talk makes it clear. "You're a magical creature, aren't you? Not just a bird?"

The Raven King gives me a withering violet look. "What in this world or any other is *just* anything?"

Fair enough, I suppose.

But the king is still staring at me, and something . . . changes. In the air, like back in the alley. A kind of sharp, edgy sparkle.

He moves close, though I'm not sure how. It's like the world around us has gone a little fuzzy. The only thing I'm aware of, beside the two points of violet in his eyes, is a faint racket that

DRAGON FIRES EVERYWHERE

I'm pretty sure is Azrael back there spontaneously combusting, especially when Gideon reaches out and touches my neck.

I barely notice, though. Because there *is* something here. Not like the connection Azrael and I have, but still. This is strange, deep, but it is also . . . important.

Gideon pulls the chain around my neck, so the teardrop gemstone appears from beneath the collar of my white dress. He looks stormy and not quite so *languid*. His eyes meet mine.

"My grandmother had a necklace identical to this," he says.

He stares at the necklace another moment, then drops it and steps away from me. The magic that swirled around us seems to dissipate.

The real world comes crashing back down—

Complete with Azrael growling threats and Ellowyn trying to talk him down.

But I don't look at him.

I keep my gaze on the Raven King. "I don't remember where I got this necklace. It's just . . . always been with me."

I remember that Jacob said the Wildes might be part magical creature. And if crows might be magical creatures, if my soul has gone from body to body—

"You must tell me how you freed your dragon," Gideon says, putting this strange development aside. I have the feeling he's doing it deliberately.

And I don't think I'm ready for any more familial revelations, so I let it happen. "I honestly don't know how I freed him. I read from a book. And then . . . there he was."

He nods. "You will read to me from this book."

"Like hell she will," Azrael growls, and there's that dragonish gleam of gold in his gaze and fire burning loud in his throat, but he can't do anything from where he stands.

He knows that as well as we all do. As Gideon clearly does too.

"I thought you said you weren't cursed," I say, because if he's not cursed, why do I need to read to him?

"I said I know how to get *around* a curse." His frown deepens, and his violet eyes glow. "Read to me from your book."

I shake my head. "I don't think it's that simple."

"I didn't ask what you think, Georgina."

I swear I hear Azrael growl.

Gideon is unfazed by the dragon, and focuses on me. "I *told* you to read to me from the book."

"You may be *a* king," I say to him, smiling brightly. "But you're not *my* king."

He nods toward the necklace. "Am I not? Because as far as *I* know, it's only *my* people who wear dragon tears."

Dragon tears. I feel the weight of the necklace around my neck. I look back at Azrael. His expression is grim and stormy—and it's fixed on Gideon. "Because only *crows* would be sadistic enough to wear another fabulae's *tears.*"

"I forgot," the Raven King says with a silken disdain. "Dragons prefer trophies of the dead fabulae they murder in cold blood. So noble."

"If the Joywood cursed you, won't you all be freed once the Riverwood takes over?" I ask, because surely that's a compromise. A sensible solution. Once we're in charge, no one will be cursed. It's only a week away.

"He didn't wait," the king says, jerking his chin toward Azrael. "Besides, we don't know what will happen. The Joywood are evil. I presume their curse stemmed from a deep and unnatural understanding and use of black magic. Is your full ascension going to magically make *that* go away?"

"We're working on it," Emerson says immediately.

The king rolls his eyes. "Of course you are. For *your* people. What about *my* people?"

"I didn't know your people existed until Georgie accidentally freed a dragon from a newel post," Emerson shoots back with more impatience than usual. "I am doing the best I can with what I have."

She takes a minute, looking from the Raven King to Azrael, then over to Frost.

And she seems even less patient than before. "How about those of you who have been around the proverbial block a few times stop fighting old wars and start focusing on the current one? How can we all work together to get rid of black magic and nasty, evil curses? For good. For *all* people."

"Maybe I'll tell you," the king says, smiling once again. "But you'll have to lift my curse first."

Emerson frowns. Azrael scoffs. But I . . .

"It's okay. I'll read him the book," I tell my coven.

"No, you fucking won't."

And I'm shocked that it isn't just Azrael who says this, loud and clear and furious.

It's Frost too.

25

I AM NOW FACING DOWN AN ANGRY AZRAEL *AND* Frost, the ancient dream team no one wanted.

"Why not?" I demand of them at the same time Emerson and Ellowyn do. Emerson because she's in charge. Ellowyn because she takes immediate affront to a man—any man—insisting it's his way or the highway.

"Magical creatures, every last one of them, are mercurial and untrustworthy, with no regard for laws or rules," Frost says darkly.

"Sounds an awful lot like every immortal *I've* ever known," Rebekah offers offhandedly, earning her a glare from Frost. Though she only has to smile for him to soften.

"I suppose those feelings about us are why you spent centuries reveling in the killing of these mercurial, *beneath you* creatures?" Azrael asks Frost, and his tone isn't offhanded at all. It's vicious.

"If I reveled in it, you'd already be dead," Frost returns coldly. "We cannot give in to the opaque demands of whatever random dom fabulae managed to *get around* the Joywood curse. It sets a dangerous precedent."

"Besides," Azrael adds, his wildly golden gaze shifting back to the Raven King, "this one in particular is a murdering, thieving upstart."

"I take great offense to the *upstart* part," Gideon offers lazily, apparently fine with murder and theft. "Are the immortal and the dragon agreeing simply to thwart me? What interesting bedfellows we keep when we're afraid of the truth."

"The only truth I am having trouble taking on board is that *you* are the only magical creature I know of that found a way around this dark magic curse," Frost says.

"And why should we free you from it? So you can turn your dark magic on us?" Azrael demands. "I have no need to taste the petty vengeance of blackbirds in this lifetime."

I study Gideon. I have no reason to trust this man—or raven, or *whatever* he is. I have every reason to trust Frost, and more reasons than not to trust Azrael.

Still, there is also something about trusting my own gut. If I don't believe in my own intuition, what is there to believe in?

"We want everyone free," I remind dragon, ex-immortal, and the rest of my coven alike. "From *all* curses. It's not our job to tell anyone what to do with that freedom or hold a *Joywood* curse over anybody's head. That is not our role. That's not what we do. It's what we're trying to get away from."

I turn to Emerson, who is nodding along. She even offers a subtle fist pump, always and ever the highest possible compliment from my best friend.

And neither Frost nor Azrael has a retort to that.

I take a few steps toward Gideon, ignoring Azrael's warning growl. And anyway, there's nothing he can do about it from his side of the cemetery gate.

There is something *familiar* about this Raven King, and I can't figure out what. Is he in the book? Have I dreamed him?

It doesn't matter. A curse is wrong, and if I can undo it, I will.

"I'll read the book, but I don't think it will work the way

you want it to," I tell him, carefully, because he's the kind of being that makes every word feel like a vow. "There's more to this, but I will try, because the Riverwood doesn't want to see *anyone* suffering under a curse."

"Yes, he certainly looks like he's suffering," Azrael mutters.

But I ignore him. I whisper a spell to bring the book to me. This in itself feels like a bad sign, because if we really needed it—if this was *supposed* to work—wouldn't the book appear on its own?

Still, there's no harm in trying. The book materializes in my hand. I'll read the Raven King what freed Azrael and hope it does the same for him.

As if this is all the boring frivolity of the peasantry, Gideon is once again sprawled out on his tree branch, appearing almost half asleep.

But I know better than to believe the way powerful creatures *appear*.

The dragon tear is warm against my collarbone. I feel . . . fractured, and yet it's not bad. Just like the pieces of myself have detached into multiple sections and are standing next to each other.

Not a *loss*, just a rearranging.

I shake the thought away. I look down and begin to read the same passage I read Azrael only a few weeks ago. Maybe I don't say the words with as much bitterness as I delivered the words during that post-Sage debacle, but I try to imbue each word with *some* kind of magic.

But for all the strange connection I have to Gideon, I know nothing is happening. No curse is being lifted. Nothing is being *changed*.

When I'm done, I look at him, and he is scowling. His violet eyes seem to glow with an unleashed violence. I can see each and every one of those things Frost warned of—mercurial and untrustworthy being the least of them.

And yet I am not afraid.

"Do it again," he demands.

I lift an eyebrow at him, a look I have perfected for use on young people running amok in the museum on field trips.

His scowl deepens, and his violet eyes are nearly pulsating with that *glow*, but when he speaks—through clenched teeth—I can tell he is *trying* to not be *quite* so demanding. "Try it from the beginning." He pulls a face. "Please."

I don't need anyone to tell me that the Raven King does not use that word often.

If at all.

I nod and do it again. When it fails, I try yet again. Emerson and Ellowyn have to head to their stores, Zander to the ferry, and Jacob leaves two different times to attend to Healer matters. But Frost and Rebekah stay through the duration.

We do it a few different ways. I even try a dramatic reenactment of how I first delivered the words to Azrael-as-newel-post.

But nothing works as the afternoon slogs on. Nothing changes. No curses are lifted, and magic barely ruffles the breeze around us.

The sun is beginning to set. I see Gideon eye it with frustration. Then me. With a lot more than frustration. "So much for *everyone* being free, Georgina. I do not *truck* with liars."

"Doubtful, as one must *truck* with oneself," Azrael mutters, but it doesn't matter, because in a sparkle of magic, Gideon is a violet-eyed raven, flying toward the confluence and leaving us all behind.

I look up at the pieces of my coven still here. "I really did try."

Rebekah puts her hand on my shoulder. "You tried harder than anyone else would have. It wasn't the book, and you knew that. Come on, we'll take you back to Wilde House and—"

But I shake my head. *I need to have a private conversation with him.*

Rebekah gives Azrael a distrustful look. "When you're done,

head right to the farmhouse. Or Zander and Ellowyn's," she says. "No flying over the river alone."

I nod, the memory of the black in the river trying to take me under too vibrant to even *want* to argue. Rebekah gives me one last look, delivers something closer to a scowl to Azrael, then steps over to Frost. They disappear together, hands clasped.

I turn to Azrael. I can see he's trying to adopt a very *I don't care about anything* expression and demeanor, but he's failing. A million frustrations exist in his eyes, brighter than the black or the gold.

Part of me wants to stay outside the cemetery limits, so I can keep this fence between us and hurl as many accusations and bombs as I want.

But arguments are not the answer. Only knowledge is. It might be frustrating, but I will continue to work toward information, answers, and solutions. And no one—not even my beloved—will get in my way.

I walk through the cemetery entrance. "Why do you hate each other?" I ask him.

"I cannot tell you."

I roll my eyes. "Honestly, Azrael, it is ridiculous how much I have to fight against you to help your own people."

"Georgina, I *cannot* tell you. I wish I could."

I realize then, this is what he told me before. Our past lives are not something he can discuss with me. He is saddled with the memories, and I must live without them. Even *knowing* they're there.

So many curses, restrictions, lies, and wars. So much foolish disagreement and pointless infighting. I know in my heart we can't win anything worth having like this. With anger and distrust and *curses*.

But why can't I figure out what we can do instead?

"I saw my past lives, Azrael." I don't mean to say that. Or the next thing, but I do. I can't help it. "I saw us die."

"Yes, but did you make any sense of it? Do you know how many bodies your soul has had? Or was it just a whirling jumble?"

I frown at him. I don't think I told him that. But he is correct.

"You are not meant to know your past lives, Georgina. I have *told* you this."

"Then why does that damn book keep trying to show me?"

He shakes his head. "You don't understand."

"You won't let me!" And okay. Maybe that came out louder than I meant it to.

Not that it gets through to him.

"Your soul is important, precious, and it has learned many lessons, but it must also inhabit the body it is in," he says in that same weary way. "You must be the person you are in *this* time. Being cluttered up with old lives that no longer matter will not aid you. That is why I told you to leave it behind. That is why, when faced with a memory of the past, I told you to let it *lie*."

I stare back at him, but it makes sense, I suppose. Still, I think of all the knowledge I would have if I could remember. If I could *see*. If all those pasts weren't a whirling jumble, but *facts*.

The kind of facts one finds in an archive.

Maybe he can't tell me, but does that mean I can't find out who I was?

"Go to your coven. Your archives. Fight the Joywood and their black magic. Stop . . ."

"Stop what?"

He takes a breath and fixes me with a detached kind of expression. It reminds me of Emerson in her politician mode. Any traces of his own feelings are hidden behind this mask.

"You did not listen to me before. Will you listen to me now, when it matters the most? We must not fraternize with the crows. They are dangerous. They are not to be trusted. They will betray you."

I am already shaking my head before I realize it. "That isn't true, Azrael."

"It *is* true. I have *lived* this truth." He pounds a fist to his chest. A show of emotion. Of desperation.

But I know he's wrong, and it hurts. Being at odds seems to make all of those lives pointless, surely. I want to tell him that we can both be right on this.

Until he says, "If you cannot listen, I cannot be who you want me to be."

I feel as though I've been struck. "Is that a threat? Some sort of manipulation technique?"

"It is how it must be."

"I can't ignore the Raven King when he's in my book, when I feel . . ." I wrap my fist around the necklace. The dragon's tear. "You're wrong, Azrael. You must trust *me*."

We stare at each other for a long time in nothing but a throbbing, painful silence. At an impasse. Neither of us willing to give an inch.

Fairy tales might be stories of princesses and dragons and people being saved by courage and love . . . but they are not without the dark, the loss.

Maybe this is ours.

Maybe in this life, we survive, and *this* is how I lose him.

"I will give the Riverwood my magic when the time comes, if I can," he tells me, almost solemnly. "I will be the Riverwood fabulae, but that is all. You must accept this."

He's so serious. So determined. And I do not *understand*.

"I guess you should take this back, then?" I slip the ring off my finger. My heart beats painfully against my chest. It's a bluff. A desperate one. Because what if he takes the ring back? I don't want that any more than I want him imprisoned here.

He stares at the ring but doesn't immediately take it. The tight band around my lungs eases a little. He won't do it. I called his bluff and—

Azrael reaches out then and takes the ring from my hand. He stares at it for a moment, then snaps his fingers. It disappears.

It's just . . . *gone*.

I feel like I've been *impaled*. "So, that's it?"

"If you insist on dealing with the crows? Yes. I will save you, if you will not save yourself."

"No explanations? I don't do what you want and you just decide our souls *don't* belong together."

He studies me for a long time. "If that's how you see it? Yes."

His lack of emotion is maddening. It's . . . unacceptable. It's a *tragedy*. "You are the most useless, selfish asshole of a fabulae or soulmate I could ever imagine." He only looks at me like these words don't matter in the least to him. "Have you ever cared about anyone else in your entire set of lives? Have you ever been anything more than a selfish bastard?"

"No," he says simply, his eyes too hot to bear.

Each accusation hurts me more than him, apparently. Everything hurts *me*, and nothing hurts him.

And that's fine. Better to know it now. And hey, he's not pulling his Riverwood support, right? So what does *this* matter? Old souls meant to find each other—and we did.

Maybe all we're really meant to do is die. Or break.

Maybe our fate is that instead of dying, we realize this was never meant to be.

"Emerson said the vote was getting close," I tell him. I don't sound like myself or anyone I recognize, but I can't care about that. I only care about the way I look at him now, pitiless just like him. "Should you be freed, don't come to Wilde House."

And then I fly away.

26

I KEEP MY HEARTBREAK TO MYSELF FOR THE time being. It doesn't help us any, and the solstice looms ever closer. We have no answers, no matter how I want them, and even though the Joywood seems to simply be melting away in a horror show scene of rotting corpses, I don't trust that their end will be that convenient or have so little to do with us. Especially considering Carol's current resplendence.

So I will find the answers however I can. Even if that means consorting with a raven king.

I spend the night at Ellowyn and Zander's, fussing over baby things and making them a dinner with my own two hands. I crash on their couch, and then in the morning, I go to the ferry with Zander and ride over the river on it like a human.

A highly protected human with a glowering Guardian watching over her.

When the ferry docks, I walk quickly away from the river and head toward the archives. Zander doesn't start the ferry moving in the opposite direction until I am safely on the bricks. I can't decide if I feel protected or smothered, but it's too cold to ponder that one too closely.

I brave the chill and dreary day with my neck bent against the wind and don't see the person outside the archives' doors until I'm shoving the key into the lock.

"Dad."

He's sitting on a bench with his nose in a book, as usual. He's bundled up, but the tips of his ears are red. He blinks once, the way he always does when he has to reorient himself to reality. "Good morning, princess. You did say you wanted my help today, didn't you?"

It feels like a hundred years since I told him that. But he's here. "I did. And I do. Come inside and warm up."

We head into the archives—the magical ones. Down the stairs and into all that gold and light. I unwind my scarf, then do the same for Dad, because otherwise he'd forget.

I glance at the table as I shrug out of my coat, to see what the archives have given me today—if anything—but the only thing sitting there is my fairy tale.

I rush to grab it up, thinking the cover will be new. Another sign. But in what feels like the strangest turn of events yet, it's back to the original cover. The one I grew up seeing. The one that never changed until Azrael was freed from the newel post.

I sigh a little.

"Ah, your old friend," Dad says with a chuckle, and despite everything, I like the way he characterizes the book as a friend. He holds out his hand, and I hand it to him. "You used to make me read this to you over and over and over before you could read the words yourself," he tells me fondly. "It's why I got to calling you princess."

I smile at that. At him. A mix of nostalgia and pain at how little I knew then waves through me, but I try not to let him see it. I go to the table and call the archives for one of the books I was reading yesterday. It lands in front of me with a thud, opened to the page I left off reading.

Dad's still riffling through the fairy tale, so I let him.

"You know, I never noticed . . ." He's muttering to himself, as he often does when he's deep into reading something. "Surely I would have noticed."

"Noticed what?" I ask absently, frowning at the book before me. I still have so much to read about black magic that Dad's take on the fairy tale doesn't seem that important.

"Well, the princess character dresses in eight different outfits," he tells me. "And each outfit is emblematic of the fashion in each of the witchdom eras, or time periods."

At first, I don't really think much of that. He's talking about costume changes, and I'm reading about how to block your very eyes from the allure of black magic, lest it set your soul to festering.

But there's something about the words he's using. *Eras*, for example. *Time periods*, *princess character*, and *eight*.

Eight is a meaningful number this year. Eight is Azrael, making us a true coven whether he breaks my heart or not.

So I turn away from a treatise on black magic and study my father instead. "We're only taught six time periods in school." Ones that mostly align with human history, though we place a little bit more importance on human witch hysteria than a simple read of *The Crucible*. "Why would there be eight?"

My father looks chagrined. "Six is the accepted version of historical events, yes. That's why it's what's taught in school."

Accepted. "There's an *un*accepted version?" I have never heard this in my life, and I have studied a *lot* of history. Theories and proven fact alike.

He hesitates, then gestures to my large, boring tome. "Perhaps we should focus on—"

But there's something here. Humming inside me. Maybe it's a misguided hope that there's an answer somewhere, but this *feels* important. "Dad, I need you to tell me your unaccepted version."

He blinks at that. "It isn't that I don't want to tell you. It's just that it's complicated." But he's gazing off into the distance, and that humming inside me gets louder, because I can tell he'll keep going. "The two missing historical periods are something I first wondered about as a child. All throughout my schooling, I tried to find proof, thinking I'd make some great historical discovery. But I wasn't alone in that."

"Other people believed you?" This is new. Even amongst Historians, my father presents as, well, a little odd. Not *too* odd, since he's a Pendell. Just a little. Just enough.

"I was studying it, trying to discover the proof with . . . Desmond Wilde."

I press my fingers to my eyes, wondering if every single revelation will *hurt*. "What?"

"That's how we got to be friends. We both had this theory. Years and years ago, long before you were born." He shakes his head, as if he's as baffled by this information as I am, hearing it for the first time. "We were working together, not exactly in secret but not openly either, before we were married. We had both made separate discoveries that led us to believe there were two missing historical periods from the teachings. We wanted to prove that. And then we wanted to determine why these periods were being kept from us."

I stare at him.

I know I should form words, but I can't quite get there.

"Desmond had discovered a few books in the Wilde library, ones that Lillian had charmed and locked up," my dad tells me in that same musing way of his, as if he's reading me another fairy tale. "He got to them anyway. They were about fabulae, crows, all sorts of magical creatures we had been led to believe didn't exist in our timeline. But we thought they did."

That shocks me into speech. "You believe in fabulae?"

He tuts at that. "Of course. I didn't need your coven to tell me that there's more than just *us*, Georgie. Though a dragon is also very convincing. I voted to free him, of course. No one should be imprisoned out of everyone else's ignorance and *fear*."

I can't think about Azrael and votes. But it does make me wonder. If the vote is *close*, are there more like my father? Witches who suspected this long before we brought it to light? Did they hear Emerson at the parade and think, *Finally*?

My head is spinning. I don't know how to take any of this on. "So . . . you and Desmond Wilde studied books on magical creatures, including crows, and determined . . . ?"

My father sits a bit straighter, the way he does when he's in full possession of his facts, and thus in his happy place. "There are two periods erased from our history. The first covers a civil war amongst the fabulae, before any of our witch trials began. Witches were involved, and *I* think they took sides."

I wonder if this is where Frost's and Azrael's animosity stems from. They both would have been around, even if Azrael had been in a previous life. And as he told me, dragons remember.

"The second lost period sits in between witch trial movements," he continues. "Similar, but it was a crow-specific civil war then, which most of the other fabulae stayed out of but witches . . . didn't."

"Crows are fabulae?"

"Yes, there are two kinds, you see, and even those who thought they went extinct agree on this. Magical creatures like your dragon, which become myths and fairy tales and are largely magic on their own. Then the animals with magical powers that roam the earth and support witches and even some humans. Your familiars, for example. Desmond's and my theory was that crows were a third type. A bit of a mix of both. But any proof of this was lost somewhere along the way."

In my readings the past few days, I had seen the two different types, but never something that put crows in a third type. But the fairy tale sure keeps them front and center, doesn't it?

"The books we found outlined everything that had gone on between these groups, and Desmond and I found clues that led us to believe the events occurred long after the dates we had been told magical creatures went extinct, but nothing is that straightforward, unfortunately."

I try to work through the implications of this. Civil wars amongst magical creatures. With witch involvement. This has to be where all the animosity between immortal, fabulae, and crow stems from.

My father sighs, that gleam of *facts* in his gaze dimming. "I used the accessible archives to attempt to create a timeline, but . . ."

"But what?"

"Not long before your mother . . . fell pregnant, Desmond said it was all for naught. We'd just been young and stupid, and it couldn't be true. He shut me out. Turned me into a bit of a pariah while he was at it." He smiles a bit ruefully. "I suppose I set it aside because . . ."

Because it was all mixed up in betrayal and infidelity. And because it was, even though I know I need to focus on everything that might help my coven, I ask him the question I couldn't before. "Why did you stay with her?"

He doesn't answer right away. He seems to really consider this, and I feel a helpless surge of love at how *him* that is. Never an easy answer. Always the weight of that *consideration*. "Your mother takes care of things. She's particular and certain about all sorts of details I don't care about. Staying with her meant staying with you, but it also meant I could lose myself in books and not have to worry about much else." He shrugs, like it was an easy enough choice.

Maybe for him it was. I'll never understand it, but then, maybe I don't need to. No one says you have to understand your parents' lives. If you're lucky, you'll understand them a little and the choices they made *for* you, assuming they made any of those.

I know he did.

And what I really do need to understand—here and now—is fabulae and crows and undoing curses. I need to understand how to wipe out black magic and all the ways it threatens not just me, but everyone. All of St. Cyprian and the witching world beyond.

Because they were hidden from us for a *reason*, and I will get to the bottom of that reason.

I turn back to the fairy-tale book. The princess is dressed in eight different outfits over the course of the book, and while I am no historical fashion expert, I know enough to agree that it showcases each of the historical periods—and I realize this is what's new.

Instead of the cover changing, the illustrations inside have changed.

I used to have all her costumes memorized. Some are the same as I remember—particularly those representing the older historical periods. Beautiful dresses, flowing cloaks, intricate scepters.

But in the later pages, her dress gets more modern.

On the last page, when all is won, the princess is wearing a dress that has me just . . . *staring*.

It looks *exactly* like the dress Emerson has been looking at for bridesmaid dresses. She hasn't made any final decisions, but still. *This* is the dress she liked the best.

A little chill skitters down my back. This has to be a sign . . . but for what?

I've always been a firm believer in the idea that knowing our history will help our present, but the book is supposed to be a *story*. Even with all its changes, I prefer to think of it as *suggestions* . . . Or do I?

It has led me everywhere I need to go, or at least I think it has. Either way, I need more.

I frown at my father. "These books Desmond found that you guys used. Are they still in his library?"

Dad looks away from me, rocking back on his heels. "Not exactly."

"What do you mean, not exactly?"

I'm thinking they've been destroyed, that they're locked away or lost to us forever. That he ripped them to shreds when he found out what Desmond had done—even though I can't picture my father having that kind of emotional response to anything. Particularly if it involves destroying his beloved books.

He clears his throat. "The last time I set foot in Wilde House, I—uh—*borrowed* a few of the books without Desmond's knowledge," he says, as if making a confession. And he's not done. His gaze slides away from mine. "And *perhaps* I also magicked fake versions of the books into place, so it appeared they were still in the library. I was afraid he would do something drastic and destroy them, so I *had* to save them. History is meant to be known, not hidden." He intones that the way he always has, my whole life, but then he coughs. "And he never said anything, so I assume the fakes worked."

I can only blink at my father. "You *stole* his books?"

Dad shrugs at that. "Just because Desmond decided he didn't believe anymore didn't mean I was going to let him destroy the possibility that someday we might have answers. I knew the books would be safer with me. They're in our library at home. I've been through them backward and forward, but not in a long while." He nods at me. "Things have changed now. Maybe something will jump out at you if you go through them."

"You have to magic them here."

He shakes his head. "I have always been incredibly careful with these books. I'm not sure why Desmond turned so hard against this idea, or why it's all been concealed from us. But I think it's best if we don't arouse any suspicions. Moving them next door from Wilde House was one thing. Moving them to the archives—a place you rightly want to give the public access to—well. I think we should proceed more carefully."

Maybe he's right. The archives don't have these books or haven't given them to me. So maybe there's a reason they aren't here.

"Let's go." I don't wait for him to agree or disagree. I just reach out for his hand, and I take us over to my childhood home. Directly into the Pendell family library, which has always been my safe space.

Except today, my mother is here when we arrive. Which feels ominous.

Because *she* is the perpetrator of that necklace I was wearing that was infused with black magic. *She* is against me in more devious ways than I ever believed, including her vote to imprison Azrael.

I want to be furious, but it hurts. And keeps on hurting to stand here, looking at her and seeing the slight physical similarities while she studies me with pursed-lip consternation.

"What are you two up to?" she asks.

"Research," we reply in unison, like we always have.

This causes her to scowl deeper.

"Stanford, I'd like to speak to Georgina in private," my mother says stiffly.

My father looks up at me, smiles a little sheepishly, then shuffles away. He has always been *there* for me, a soft place to land, but he never fought for me. It doesn't fill me with the same kind of anger I feel toward my mother, though. I'm not even sure *anger* is the right word. He loved me when no one else would. Or did. And maybe I didn't have parents who would fight for me, but I had a best friend who would. A best friend who, it turns out, is my half sister.

So there's that.

"Georgina, I do not know what that display was the other day," my mother says sternly. "Or what you think you're doing, cavorting with *dragons*, but this is unacceptable. Maybe your new, power-mad coven won't tell you this, but the job of a Historian is to proceed with caution. To advise with *facts*. To carry oneself with a *quiet* dignity."

I've heard these same age-old lectures since I was small, and the offense given was the state of my appallingly red hair. I can recite them in my sleep. What I can't believe is that she's seriously standing here, doling it out again like nothing has changed.

She has to know that I know everything. Desmond. The necklace.

"Speaking of unacceptable displays," I say coolly. "What were you thinking, giving me *wearable* black magic?"

She looks at me like I've spoken one of the few foreign languages she doesn't speak. "I beg your pardon?"

And she actually *sounds* shocked, but how can I believe someone who was involved with black magic crystals?

"That necklace you gave me for my pubertatum. It had black magic *inside* it." I shake my head. "And go figure, it's been working against me ever since."

At the word *pubertatum*, my mother stills. She stares at me, looking more . . . upended than guilty, but not unmoved. Not confused any longer.

After a moment, she shakes her head. "I didn't."

"I remember it distinctly," I say in a harder voice, because I can't believe she's trying to lie about this too. "You gave it to me yourself."

"It was . . . not from me." Her hand is at her throat, and I have never in my life seen her so rattled. I didn't know it was *possible* for her to get rattled. "Someone else gave it to me to give to you."

"You can't honestly think I'll buy that? When you've lied to me my entire life about who I am? About . . . *everything*." I look at her, try to rationalize this new story. "Surely you have more brains than to take a gift from the Joywood, even back then."

"It was Desmond."

She clears her throat as if it hurts, then slowly lowers herself into a chair like she can't bear her own weight anymore.

Desmond. "You mean my father?" I shoot at her, and I think this is more lies, but—

Mom closes her eyes and sighs, and I've never seen her look *defeated* before. Not ever. "Right before your pubertatum, he told me he wanted the daughter he couldn't claim to have something of his family's. But he couldn't give it to you without arousing suspicion, so he asked me to do it. And I did."

I swear I don't breathe. I can't even think. All these years I've thought of Emerson and Rebekah's father as an asshole, sure. But one too self-absorbed to cause any real trouble. Even finding out he was *my* father too didn't change that estimation.

But right before I took the test to determine if I wielded enough power to be considered a witch, and before Emerson and Rebekah were given different forms of punishment for not having enough magic—when, really, it was because they had too much—he gave me a necklace imbued with black magic.

The Joywood specialty.

"Georgina. I did not know," my mother says to me now, forthright and earnest in a way I've never seen her before. "I have no interest in dealing with black magic. It's *wrong*."

But she doesn't argue about what happened. Which means she isn't *surprised*, really. Which means she knows this is something Desmond *would* do, even if she wouldn't.

She gets to her feet and crosses the room to stand in front of me. "You must stop," she says to me with this new earnestness that makes me uneasy. Because she isn't lecturing or demanding. There is desperation here, and I don't know what to do with that—not coming from her. "Stop all this pushing, prying, fighting. Dragons aren't what we need. Dramatic battles aren't what we need. We need peace."

"By capitulating to the most evil force there is?"

She makes a face. "I thought you would understand once you had access to power. I thought you would be *better* than this."

I know there's real fear in her, not some put-upon thing. And maybe how she's always harped on me is all born of her own fear, as I let myself imagine before.

But it's the coward's way out. I know this deep down, like sinew and bone. "You thought wrong."

She sighs, and there's some of that control back. In the way she frowns, in the way she steps back from me. In the sorrowful way she shakes her head. "Don't say I didn't warn you," she tells me softly.

And I don't think I'm imagining that she *hurries* to leave the room, like I'm contagious.

I want to sink into a chair myself. Have a little cry, or maybe a nice long one. But there's no time. I need those books. I start scouring the titles, wondering what I'm looking for.

A few minutes later, Dad peeks his head around the corner, as if worried my mother is still here and he'll be seen. But she's gone, and I'm . . .

There's no time to wallow in all my feelings. I gesture him forward. "Show me the books."

He nods and leads me to a little corner shelf. It's where he keeps his oddly shaped books about fungi, or so I thought. With a swipe of his hand, the fungi books disappear. In their place are two thick black leather-bound tomes.

"I'll keep watch for your mother," Dad says, frowning toward the door. "She shouldn't know we're doing this."

I don't ask him why. If it's because she's never liked the so-called *nonsense* he liked to fill my head with or something more insidious. Like that maybe her loyalties are suspect?

Maybe I don't want to know the answer.

"You look through them," Dad urges me. "See if anything pops out as important."

I nod and take the heavy books to a chair. I don't know where to start, but while everything with Azrael is a painful *ache*, that meeting with Gideon yesterday actually haunts me. Like a dream I vaguely remember, just out of reach. An itch I can't scratch.

I want to know why. I have to know why. If this is what's to come between me and my dragon, I'd better understand it.

I open the crow book first. I get to know the book, running my hands over the cover, the spine. Testing the weight and strength of the pages. I whisper soothing words, hopeful words, about what information it will let me have.

And it likes me. It blooms open for me.

I learn about an island of crows. A civil war. A fight with a dragon. I find myself oddly drawn to a crow queen. And if I trace her family tree, she has a grandson.

Named Gideon.

Is she the original owner of my necklace?

The book is filled with interesting, not-taught-in-school facts about ruling fabulae families, wars that include magical creatures, and witches forever taking sides.

I want to sit and study the pages forever, but I can't. Because it's not giving me what I need so desperately. Nothing on how to save the fabulae—all kinds—from a Joywood curse. Very little about black magic, except suppositions about who might have been wielding it.

I get to the end of the book, frustrated with how little this helps.

Maybe I'm going about it the wrong way. Maybe I need to

be studying the Joywood themselves. Maybe, regardless of the fairy-tale book, I am looking in the wrong place.

"The problem is, while this is all presented as real historical fact, we found no proof of it," Dad says from where he watches the library door. "No proof of the existence of crow shifters, or dragons or unicorns or fairies. No access to this crow island, wherever it might be. I believe it was written down because it's true. I believe these books are important because what's in them is true, or was. But there's no way to make the connection between *this* and the reality of it. Or at least, none that I found, with or without Desmond. I made a vague timeline. Even that isn't *proof*."

My father has limits. How he acts around my mother shows me that. That's who he is. His strength is books, analyzing. Noticing things like *eight* costume changes in a book.

He is not brave.

I am.

And it's not only me. My coven is brave. My dragon, that bastard, is brave. Blinded by old fights and wars, sure, but brave.

I focus back on the book. I will find something. I will find some avenue to walk down, no matter how dangerous or scary.

I flip through and find myself focusing on a chapter that has my heart leaping into my throat.

The Night of Dragon Tears.

I begin to read, half skimming in impatience because . . . what?

There's a battle between two different crow factions. A royal group and a revolutionary group. A crow woman in the revolutionary group, who is royalty herself. A princess who doesn't believe in her family's rule. She believes in the revolution.

She enlists the help of a small pod of dragons, falling in love with one of the dragons in the process. My heartbeat kicks up. A princess. A dragon. So much of it is like my fairy tale. Down to the Revelares and their contributions.

But there is no happy ending here. Though the revolutionaries win the war, they do not lead well. With his newfound power, the leader of the revolutionaries crowns himself king. He uses black magic to kill the dragons who helped him and takes the princess for himself, imprisoning her in a marriage she does not want but must endure for the safety of her people.

It's a sad story, told in the way of historical battles. Factual, with little emotion. And yet I feel all the emotion swirling around inside me as if these are my memories. I want to weep.

This was not the happy ending I was promised in my fairy tale. The difference between fact and fiction, I tell myself—but it feels like an indictment of every happy-ever-after I've ever wanted to believe in.

And Azrael knows all this because . . . he lived it. He cannot trust crows because they killed him. And yet, if that really was *him*, the princess was *me*. Or she had my soul. Or however this whole thing works.

I *was* a crow. If I was the soul in that princess, does that mean Gideon is my *grandson*?

How can I turn my back on that?

I can't dwell on these horrible, contrasting feelings. Feelings are not facts, even mine, and I have to press on. I have to find out if there's anything to learn from this horrible war. Anything I can use for *now*.

But no matter how I flip through the book, letting it lead me, there's nothing. I'll have to read it again more closely to see if I missed any details. But nothing major leaps out at me, and this is a disappointment.

I'm about to switch it for the fabulae book, but something catches my eye. A little . . . ripple on the back cover. Like the light playing tricks on me, but that shouldn't be happening, unless—

"Reveal to me, what I should see."

The ripple intensifies, the warmth of the dragon tear against my skin becoming a pulsing kind of heat.

Books have been our salvation time and time again in this long, strange year. They told us Emerson was a Confluence Warrior, Rebekah a Chaos Diviner. They introduced us to Revelares, and the cover on my fairy tale has warned us and guided us with each of its changes. They have led us every step of the way.

The answer is in *books*—texts, written histories, grimoires and ancient spells and even fiction. Maybe especially in fiction. In the metaphors and the *emotion* behind what we're doing here and why.

I close my eyes and wrap my hand around the dragon tear, letting myself really *feel* the power inside it. I think of Azrael and what it feels like to fly together, his hungry smile, the way he saved me, the way he held me when I cried over my parentage.

And still he took his ring back. Because we both have to do what we each think is right.

We are each drawn to complicated choices and harder sacrifices.

"Reveal to me what I must see," I say again.

I feel something shimmer in the air—much like in the alley yesterday.

"Georgie," Dad whispers.

I open my eyes to a room full of sparkling light. Sparkling magic. Like the alley, but more. Bigger, brighter, pulsing with its own power.

The magic of the books unleashed.

The two books in question hover above me. The pages are flying like there's a great wind moving through them. Then they're . . . merging, almost. A new book seems to morph together in the destruction of the other two.

It falls into my lap. The title is written in pretty gold script.

A Study of the Failures in the War that Came Before: A Case for How to Fix It

By Morgane Wulfram, the Raven Queen Consort

27

I SPEED-READ THROUGH THE BOOK, KNOWING I'll read it again and again, slower and more carefully each time. But right now, I need the gist before I take the information to my coven so we can put it to use immediately.

Every time I turn a page quickly, my father grunts from where he's reading over my shoulder. But he doesn't mount an argument.

It's written a bit like an academic paper. There are sources cited—though they aren't like any I've ever seen before, so I can't quite follow them. Some of the information is a repeat of what I just read. The events of the crow war, bringing the dragons in, a king's betrayal.

And then, as I get toward the end, some of the writer's emotions slip in.

> We were so close to success. So close to peace. I have spent my days since the moment the king chose black magic over the peace we fought for going over what we could have changed, what we needed that we didn't have.

I watched the king fail, again and again. I watched my son learn from the mistakes of his father and do better, but he shut the world out. There must be more to this world than the machinations of crows, and now it is someone else who wields black magic against us.

We must stop it, so that my grandchildren have a choice.

I have witnessed much, and I have learned. I have dreamed of times before and the intervention of well-meaning witches. My son has dreamed of times to come.

And so I put pen to paper, hoping that the right beings will find my advice, my belief, my lessons, learned the hard way.

In order to beat black magic, once and for all, we must first have a group of leaders, not just one. No one leader can rule. Power is a dangerous drug that needs its counterbalances, or black magic will always filter into the cracks, drowning out whatever good was meant to be done. We must be ever diligent to fight the urge of ego, to remember the good of all.

If there is any hope that we defeat black magic, it cannot be done in factions. It cannot be done separated from one another. I have seen it. It must be done through a group of powerful beings who embody the following:

A leader with unshakable belief and endless determination. Support from quiet, determined strength and power. Someone who has dabbled in the worst that can be done and learned to do better. Someone who has lived apart and has returned with new perspectives. Someone who has a foot in multiple worlds. A protective presence with unbendable loyalty. Someone with an unquenchable thirst for knowledge and the creativity to apply it. And someone who has seen multiple lives and remembers them all.

Eight creatures, making infinity.

They will need to work together, love and live together, and then bring together all of us magical beings under one common purpose.

No one can be left out. No one can be locked away.
This is our only hope.

But that's exactly what the Joywood have done, I think. Separated us. Made us forget magical creatures even *existed*. Cursed the crows and the fabulae they couldn't kill. I'm breathing a little fast, because this is *an* answer, but it isn't *the* answer.

Togetherness and unity are an abstract, not a battle plan.

But it's clear that the only way we move forward is with everyone uncursed. And Azrael must come to accept the crows are part of it.

I reach out to my coven immediately, calling an emergency meeting at Wilde House, and only then do I read the rest.

I believe that this is possible. I believe that this is coming. If the good among us continue to raise our children to believe in hope, love, and unity, we can dream of a day when black magic is no longer a threat.

I take a deep breath, let it slowly out. This might not *feel* like a concrete answer, but it's an answer all the same. It's forward movement, looping in the past. We *have* to find out how to uncurse the magical creatures. We have to bring us all together.

"I have to go, Dad," I say, getting to my feet and hugging the book to my chest. I turn to face him, and he's nodding at me.

"I'm very proud of you, Georgie," he says, in that careful, serious way of his that makes me feel loved no matter what. Even now. "I have all the faith in the world that you and your coven can make this right."

I swallow at the lump in my throat. "If we win this, you were part of it."

He smiles. "It sounds as if, should we win this, we must all be a part of it."

I squeeze him tight and then don't bother to walk. I magic myself right over to Wilde House, pausing in the foyer to glare at the makeshift newel post that isn't Azrael, and to feel the quiet of the house all around me.

Everyone is coming, but it'll take some time yet. Not everyone can drop everything at a moment's notice for a meeting, not even the meeting queen herself, Emerson.

I go to the kitchen and Octavius appears, weaving through my legs with a hearty purr.

Emerson is, unsurprisingly, the first to arrive despite likely having to rush out of her store without completing all her preferred closing rituals. "What did you find?" she demands.

But I shake my head. "I want to say it one time, Em."

She grunts in frustration and looks like she might argue until Jacob arrives—looking a little gray. Emerson instantly focuses all her worry on him. "Is everything okay?"

"Jaqui was attacked on her way to her waitress shift at the Lunch House," he says. "It was black magic. She's doing well, but it took a lot." He looks at both of us. "She said the attacker kind of looked like Gil Redd, but only kind of."

Gil, who has supposedly been missing. I don't know how to make sense of that.

Rebekah appears with Frost then, and they exchange a look, as if deciding how to tell us something. I mutter a spell that adds more frosting to the cupcakes before me.

"Apparently we can add Felicia to the missing Joywood members," Rebekah says. "When I was at Holly's coffee shop this morning, I heard some of the teachers talking before their classes, and she hasn't shown up for work in days. Not a good look for the principal." She catches the look on Jacob's and Emerson's faces. "Another attack?"

Jacob nods, and Rebekah curses softly, then looks at Frost again. For once I don't need a translator—I can see how concerned he is all by myself. Either he's getting more mortal or I'm just getting used to him.

"I'm here, but I'm sitting on this couch and I'm not moving," we hear Ellowyn yell from the living room.

Rebekah and Frost move for the living room. Then Jacob and Emerson do, arms around each other's waists. Maybe Emerson's arms more around Jacob, given how grayed-out he looks after a long session of Healing.

As I finish the food, I magic it out to the living room. And once I hear Zander's voice add a low rumble to the conversation humming in the room, I head there myself.

Everyone's in their usual spots and everyone's eating, which brings me some comfort. Another black magic attack is bad, but at least we have some kind of *progress*.

"All right, Georgie," Emerson says—*not* in her usual place, because I've called this meeting, which means I'm leading this thing.

"If this is a coven meeting, shouldn't we go to the cemetery and get Azrael involved?" Ellowyn asks, stretched out on the couch, a plate balanced high on her belly.

I think of his ultimatums about crows, and how much this involves crows. "Eventually, yes," I say. "But I think a lot of what I'm going to tell you guys is not news to him, no matter how little he likes it."

"So our magical creature has been holding out on us. How surprising," Zander mutters. He's sitting on the floor, leaning back against the couch Ellowyn is sprawled out on.

"Not holding out, exactly," I say, not sure why I'm defending the very dragon who stomped all over my heart with his giant claws, but here we are. "Living through something makes it hard to see the forest through the trees, I think. It can take a very wise creature, who understands all the different worlds at play, to show us the right path."

I explain the time periods, my father's books that he technically stole from Desmond—who technically stole them from Lillian. Who was hiding them herself.

"It's like Zachariah," Ellowyn says, eyes wide. "His obsession with crows."

I explain the charms and the first reading, and then the *ripple* on the back of the book. And all that wild magic once I revealed it. "Then the two books sort of melded together and became one. One that has some suggestions on how to beat black magic for good."

"You're wrong, Georgie."

I look at Ellowyn. Octavius is curled up on her chest now. She's petting him while both of them look at me intently. And I frown at her, because I'm just recounting what I read in a book. I can't be *wrong*.

"We need Azrael for this," Ellowyn says firmly.

"Not yet. I—"

Octavius hops off Ellowyn and trots over to me, weaving in and out of my legs.

"I'll fill Azrael in when it's . . . pertinent." And when I don't feel like he took a hammer to my heart.

So also maybe never.

"It's pertinent. He told me so." She points at Octavius, and I wonder if she's having some sort of pregnancy hallucination.

"Wynnie, he doesn't talk."

"I know," Ellowyn says, studying Octavius. "It came through me . . . all weird. I don't know if it's a Revelare thing or a being pregnant thing. It wasn't like how Ruth talks to me, how we talk to each other, but it was him. And he keeps saying what sounds a lot like *Azrael*. Insistently."

I open my mouth to argue with her. We don't need an imprisoned dragon with absolutely no desire to help. We don't need an asshole more interested in holding old grudges rather than solving a problem.

But Ellowyn is in my head then, a channel between only the two of us. *I don't want to be a dick—*

Don't you? I interrupt, because she usually does.

She laughs inside my head, but it fades quickly. *I think if I could stand hip to hip with Zander for ten years, you can do this.*

That feels *awful*, because of course she's right. For their ten-year breakup full of anger and loathing—of themselves and each other—Zander and Ellowyn came together for the good of Emerson and then the coven. Over and over again.

Then there is a kind of crash at the window, and we all look over.

To see a very large violet-eyed crow.

Who caws at us imperiously and then flies away.

Ellowyn gives me a smirk as if to say, *See*, and she isn't wrong.

So.

"I guess we need to go to the cemetery," I mutter.

We gather and then head over to the cemetery. Ellowyn brings Octavius—who can apparently *talk* to Revelares or pregnant ladies or *something*.

Gideon is already there, though like the last time, he is standing outside the cemetery boundaries. He is not lounging quite the same way. In fact, he's holding himself almost stiffly—

And then I see a little trickle of blood coming out of his nose. I rush forward, compelled by a strange twist in my heart I'm not sure I fully recognize or understand. "Your nose is bleeding," I say, stopping myself *just* short of touching him.

He lifts a finger to the drip of blood coming out of his nose, then shrugs. "Outwitting curses has a price." *Hurting is part of the price*, I think then, remembering something Ellowyn said a long time ago. "Is there a reason your *cat* wouldn't stop *meowing* in my head until I had to accept that painful price?"

I blink at Octavius in Ellowyn's arms. So, not just Revelares or pregnant women, but *crows*? And *not me*.

I try not to be hurt by that, but it doesn't work. "I have some things to talk about, and Azrael needs to be included, apparently. Come inside the cemetery, Gideon."

His expression is defiant, his crossed-arms pose even more so. But I give him a *look* I remember Lillian giving us girls when we were being a little too rowdy.

He scowls more deeply but moves toward the cemetery gate.

We all go inside the boundaries, and Gideon finds himself a seat. Right on poor Zachariah's grave. He smirks at Zander, who is scowling at him.

But it has nothing on the scowl that currently graces Azrael's face. I think he'd be breathing fire if he could. It's a good thing he can't. Still, it's best to get this started—and finished—before the chance for a fight breaks out.

"Gideon," I say, almost formally, "your grandmother . . . she was a crow princess who fought with revolutionaries to end her father's rule."

"I don't know why you think old wars are going to solve the problems of now," Azrael says darkly.

I want to *punch him*. "Maybe if you'd shut up and listen, you would."

"Yes, this is my grandmother's story." Gideon sounds suspicious. "How do you know it?"

"I found a book. About the crow war. Written by your grandmother."

Gideon looks affronted. "Witches should not have this book."

"What about those who are only *part* witch?" I ask him.

He blinks once, as if surprised by this revelation.

"And," I continue, frowning at him, "I happen to believe *everyone* should have *all* the books. Any book they want. If we are to learn as one unit, we must not have hidden pieces of our past. And it is *our* past. Witches helped."

"We would not all characterize it as *help*," the Raven King says dryly.

I ignore this comment and push on. "The crow princess brought dragons and witches in to help with her revolution because she believed that in order to build a new, better way of life, we *all* had to work together."

"And then every last dragon who helped was slaughtered," Azrael says with deep disgust. "What togetherness."

"That's an interesting way of saying the dragons betrayed our leader and were punished accordingly," Gideon replies in the same tone. "And the crows have since learned a lesson about dealing with fabulae *or* witches."

"Dragons betrayed your leader?" Azrael demands, a dangerous gold fire in his eyes. "Are you a liar or a fool?"

I stand between them and hold out my hands. The facts laid out in the book did not account for two different versions of the same history, but maybe I should have foreseen that. Maybe it's all . . . connected.

We cannot move forward if we're always sure our version of the past is not just *correct*, but the only possible version. And maybe that echoes a little too closely to the fight Azrael and I have been having.

But I can't deal with that now.

"Gideon, whose story do you believe?" I ask him. "Your grandmother's, or your grandfather's?"

Gideon refuses to answer this question, no matter how I glare at him. I decide we'll come back to that.

"The book is clear," I tell both raven and dragon—and everyone else. "We must learn from our history or we are doomed to repeat it, again and again and again. The humans are right about one thing. Absolute power corrupts absolutely, and this is exactly what the witches have done."

"In the past, maybe," Emerson says now, hotly. "But not now. Not us. *We're* not about power. *We* are about giving everyone a voice. That's why we won the ascension trials."

"But that's just the witches," I say patiently. "We have a whole world of magical creatures who we didn't even know existed, so we couldn't serve them. We couldn't give them a voice. Now we all have to come together and build a new power structure *together*." I look at Azrael and Gideon. And then at Frost. "You three represent old wars, but you need to understand that they—*you*—are what's holding us back."

It's probably wishful thinking that I see some little hints of chagrin in their closed-off expressions.

"I will work night and day to undo this curse," I promise Gideon. "I will not rest until you are all free. And when you are, we must all be ready to work together to defeat the darkness that has kept us apart all this time—cursed and ignorant." I turn to Azrael then. "You too. All of us means *all of us*." He starts to snarl something, so I raise my voice. "You do not have to hold hands and skip. You don't even have to agree. But you must be willing to work *together* until this is done. Until we win, once and for all."

I glare at Frost too, since he's part of this three-way ancient war. Hell, he was probably there too.

It must be a great glare, because Frost is the first one to give in. "There will certainly be no *skipping*, but I would sacrifice my life for this coven." His brow rises. "As I have proven already. And as I will continue to prove, even if that includes working hand in claw with fabulae and crows."

I look at Azrael. He looks away.

He huffs out a puff of smoke. Everyone is looking at him now, and he is staring at his own terrifying statue. "I fought with the crows once and was rewarded for my sacrifice with a knife to the heart." His hands clench into fists. "I mean that literally." He turns that dark glare on me. "This curse, and the people who used black magic to imprison my people, are my only enemies still living. I will see them all dead this time or die trying."

"What a rousing vow of fealty," Gideon murmurs, earning a sharp glance not just from Azrael, but from me as well. I soften almost at once, because the trickle of blood has not gone away. If anything, it has intensified. He needs to return home.

I cross to him. I put my hands on his shoulders, and I see a baby in my arms suddenly. I feel an overwhelming wave of warmth that I shouldn't. I don't know what he sees or feels, but he looks at me with a deep suspicion, so I know it's *something*.

"There is no fealty here, Gideon," I tell him. "There is only cooperation. There is only working together to end the curse that holds your people even now."

I feel the dragon tear heat against my skin, and I somehow know my next steps. I take the dragon tear necklace off. It was his grandmother's. A symbol of her love that was taken away from her. But she did not crumble. She did not give up. She loved her children and her grandchildren—something I think is evident in the way Gideon speaks of her now. And something I know is evident in the hope she had for the world, for our future.

The words come to me as if they have lived my whole life right there on my tongue, waiting for this moment. "We cannot always change the world. Sometimes we must change ourselves, and our own bitter hearts, and hope that in so doing, we plant the seeds that will change futures we can never see."

Gideon's face shifts, into something not quite wonder. Not fully hope. "My grandmother often said those words to me in her last days."

I nod. I may not remember my past lives, but there is a *knowing* inside me. A piece of my soul was there. A piece of my soul loved him as a little boy. I put the necklace around his neck. "Go home and stay there. Do not hurt yourself anymore. We will free you when we can. And when we do, Gideon, you must be prepared to work with us. Because you're not alone anymore."

He stands very still. His eyes are a gleaming black.

And my heart aches, an echo of the soul I once was.

At last he steps away from me, the dragon tear sparkling at his neck. "You do not *rule* Crow Island, Riverwood coven. But we will work together for the best of all, even so."

He slides one last look in Azrael's direction, then nods.

"Even dragons," he says quietly.

Then a gust of wind moves through the cemetery, and he is

a giant raven in flight, winging his way toward the river and the confluence. A sparkling dragon tear hanging around his neck.

I'm not the only one who watches him go.

"So we're working together," Rebekah says. "We've got dragons and crows, and once we figure out how to uncurse everyone, a whole slew of magical creatures. Do you really think that will just . . . erase black magic? That it's really the answer?"

"No," I say, because unfortunately, I don't think that. "But I believe the answer will find us. If we take the right steps, if we believe. If we work together." I turn to Azrael then, chin lifted. "You're the lone holdout, dragon."

He sneers when I call him *dragon*.

"These pipe dreams are almost cute," he says, and he pretends like he's addressing all of us, but I know it's just me. "*Togetherness*. You're the first to think of it, I'm sure."

It takes everything I have not to scowl at him. "We'll be the first to make it work."

"We tried that once." And now he makes no bones of staring at me and only me. "I believed in it. Once. And I was killed for the trouble."

"How noble," I say, pulling out my bright, bubbly Georgie smile.

A lick of flame shoots out of his mouth, but his imprisonment keeps it from being more than the end of a lit match.

"Why don't you fly after your little crow friend, since you have become so close?" he suggests, but it's in a vicious tone that hurts more than fire or claw ever could. "You can tend to his wounds. Listen to his crow lies. There's a reason they're called an unkindness at best. A murder at worst. But do not take my word for it."

It occurs to me he must misunderstand the connection I feel to Gideon. "You don't have to be jealous."

Azrael snorts at that. "I am not *jealous*, Georgina. I am worried for your welfare. And *mine*. The last time we trucked with crows, we were both punished for it. *I* remember it well. You do not."

"Maybe not, but I know how to learn a lesson, Azrael. Do you?"

He steps forward, and I recognize that there is a deep well of hurt here, one I did not fully understand before. But he is projecting it onto the wrong people, and for that, I'm angry instead of sympathetic.

Also, I'm hurt myself.

"I would not have cared if I had died in the blaze of war, or in saving you—or who you once were. I would not hold a grudge against this king if we had died on the battlefield." He shakes his head. "But I was his brother-in-arms. And he betrayed me."

I hold his angry gaze. I see a million hurts in his onyx-and-gold eyes that I realize he has never dealt with. His soul might remember all the lives he's led, but he tries to leave them—and each death—behind.

Perhaps that was why it was so easy for him to jump into *life* with me in the beginning.

And so easy for him to pull away when he was reminded how it ends.

How it always ends.

"We aren't talking about the king you knew, Azrael," I remind him. "We are talking about his *grandson*."

I don't say *mine*, because Gideon isn't *my* grandson. I know that once, he was. But I don't *remember* past lives—it seems I can only occasionally feel them. And while a piece of my soul was there, it does not make up who I am, or at least *all* of who I am. I have more lives, including this one.

"You have a world to save," Azrael tells me. "If my brethren are freed, I will not stand in your way. I will not decry your ill-advised alliance with the crows. I will not be a hindrance." He leans a little closer. "But I will not be a part of it."

"You're our fabulae."

"You can find another."

If *I* could shoot flames from my mouth, I would.

He moves closer now, lowering his voice so only I hear him. "It would be best for you all. I have lived this life you're trying to re-create, Georgina. I was killed, and you lived with that monster till the end of your days. Do you wish for history to repeat itself?"

I study him and realize what I'm *really* seeing. Not stubbornness for the sake of stubbornness. Not even old grudges.

Fear.

And it all started at that river. When I was harmed. And even though he saved me that time, he has lived through failing to save me. And not just me, but the Wilde Historian who came before me, old Linus, who walked into the river himself one morning. He even failed to save *himself* in the crow war.

For a moment, all my anger softens. Because I remember how lost we all felt when Lillian died. How Zander became a shell of himself when he lost his mother. Grief is a terrible thing to bear, and Azrael's had to do it over and over again.

We both have, but mine is wrapped up in the forgetting, and feels like longing. His, I see, stays sharp. Because he *remembers*.

"Azrael." I try to find the words to get through to fear. To hurt and grief. I'm not sure I have them. "There are risks we must take in this life. And in my life—no matter how short or long—I want to know I did the right thing. So all you're doing right now is hurting me."

"Will you always do this? In every life? Put everyone above yourself? Have you not finally learned, Georgina, you really are *special*. But it means nothing if you *die*."

I don't remember every life, but I know he's wrong. "Sacrifice for the right cause is not a mistake, no matter the outcome. When will *you* learn that?"

He scoffs disgustedly and turns away from me.

I realize something with a harsh pain. It has not occurred to me until this moment. We might be soulmates, that red thread tugging us from life to life, and I might like this current version of him—hell, I'm in love with him, for all that matters right now, but . . .

"This is not love," I say.

He whirls around, looking stricken. Then furious. "I remember every second my soul has loved yours. I know what love is."

"No, you don't. *I* don't need to remember to know. I just know." I reach over to thump my finger into his chest and instantly regret it, because touching him just makes me want to touch him more. But I don't. I make myself go on. "You are only worried about *you*. How *you'd* feel if I die. How it will hurt *you*." I am so tired of crying in front of this dragon, but I can't stop myself. I am so tired of letting him hurt me, but he can't seem to stop either. "What about if I live knowing I failed my coven? I failed myself? If I am *special*—"

"I have roamed this earth waiting for your soul to return to me again and again," he roars. But he calms, quiets. Serious but fierce. "And I will not be a part of watching you throw that life away *again*. For *crows*."

But it isn't for crows, or him, or me. It's for . . . everything. "You're really cutting me off because I won't sacrifice *everyone else* to save myself?"

He is decidedly quiet then.

"You're pretending this is about a crow who did nothing to hurt you, even if his grandfather did. But it is nothing but selfishness." I thump him again, and say it. "Cowardice."

Still he says nothing. I want to think the words are penetrating, but I can tell from his stubborn expression they're not.

"Maybe our souls were meant to be in some other lifetime, but if you think I can be the woman who would turn her back on what she knows is right because it's dangerous, because there might be suffering or sacrifice, you don't know me at all. And you really *don't* belong in the Riverwood coven."

Something flashes in his eyes, but he says nothing. And I'm not going to wait around and see if he will.

I walk out of the cemetery, realizing when I see my friends standing near that tree that they must have retreated outside the gates when Azrael and I started fighting.

But they didn't leave me. They're waiting for me.

I don't look back at Azrael, because I know I'm right.

This is love. Right here. Standing up for one another, with each other, time and time again, no matter how things get tough. No matter how we disagree.

Because love is not about *outcomes*. It is not a weapon or armor.

Love is the answer.

28

I THROW EVERYTHING I AM INTO UNDOING the black magic Joywood curse on the magical creatures. They're imprisoned, erased, hidden. So I research anything that might connect, spending long hours in the archives and up in my own library and room while everyone else comes in and out.

Sometimes it's Frost or Jacob in the archives with me, as they both have a patience that the others don't. Sometimes Ellowyn and Rebekah sit with me on the top floor of Wilde House, playing with crystals, considering herbs. Sometimes Zander comes by with something new he remembers Zachariah telling him about the crows and we note it down, trying to build a full picture.

Just about every breakfast, Emerson sits with me, and we eat and discuss what I found—or didn't find—the day before. She worries over those last two votes to free Azrael that remain just outside her reach, though we pretend that is not a personal conversation.

We don't see Gideon again. I steer clear of the cemetery.

I dive deeper into the witchlore archives and try to come

at the same questions in different ways. Instead of looking for evidence of what the Joywood changed, I look instead for the history of the Joywood coven themselves. Like . . . when did they come into power? What was their ascension like? When did this curse on fabulae actually happen?

Information that should be readily available, but isn't.

The archives don't seem to want to fork over much related to the Joywood. Is that a decision the enchanted archives have made on their own? Is it another Joywood curse?

These are things I would love to be able to ask Azrael. Dragons might not keep to strict witch calendar years, but I bet he could give me an idea of a *before* and an *after*.

No matter how I look, I can't seem to find anything. I begin to wonder if black magic has been woven into my clothes.

All the spells I cast to find out claim it hasn't, but I still wonder.

Because anything and everything feels possible these days. Especially when I wake up every morning a little bit more unlike myself: frustrated, impatient, and curt with those around me.

I decide I can lay that at Azrael's feet too.

With only a few days before the solstice, our full ascension, or a total disaster to end all disasters, Emerson and I are sitting at the Wilde House kitchen table one morning. She is bright-eyed and talking a mile a minute. I am bleary-eyed and scowling into my coffee. Jacob is standing at the counter and lands somewhere in the middle. Awake and alert, but he doesn't even try to get a word in.

"Maybe we need to go back to the beginning," Emerson suggests, flipping through the fairy-tale book that hasn't changed again, as far as I know. The cover is the cover from my childhood. The princess embodies all eight timelines in her dress. It's all depressingly the same.

Maybe books *aren't* the answer, I think . . . and that's how I know I need to shake myself out of this funk. Books are *always* the answer. If they're not, you have the wrong books. "What beginning?"

Emerson holds up the book. "You read this aloud to a newel post, and a dragon was magically uncursed."

"Yes, and we tried that with Gideon. It didn't work, if you recall."

"Maybe it wasn't the book. Maybe it was the place," Jacob says thoughtfully.

"The cemetery is sacred. Why wouldn't it be the place?"

"Maybe *because* it's sacred. A curse is the most unsacred thing there is, so . . ."

I don't think that makes any sense, and I don't think Emerson is on board either, because she's frowning, still flipping through the pages. She gets to the last page, the page where I—where the *princess* is wearing the dress that's almost identical to the one Emerson has flagged for her bridesmaids.

She studies it for a few moments, a lot like I did the first time I saw it. "It's kind of like a vow, if you think about it," Emerson says. "What happened when you freed Azrael, I mean. You were saying words of love out loud to your . . ."

I know she wants to say *soulmate*, but with the current state of things with Azrael, doesn't want to hurt me.

So I focus on the reality of what happened, regardless of *souls*. "Except I was furious at Sage, and not in a very *vow* place. I didn't even know Azrael was real." That's not entirely true. "I certainly didn't know about the past lives thing."

"Maybe not," Emerson says carefully, still studying the illustration. "But maybe it doesn't matter. Maybe it's not about you knowing on a conscious level. Your souls have always loved each other, if nothing else. So the words had your old lives and all that love behind them. The magic freed anyone who heard it."

I frown. "That doesn't explain why it didn't work with Gideon. Azrael was *right there*."

Emerson ponders that, still studying the book. I magic myself more coffee. I have a long day of trying to get the archives to cough up some Joywood dirt for me, and I haven't been sleeping well.

We don't need to talk about how many times my dreams star a certain dragon. Maybe I should work up a spell to block them. But the thought makes me sad, because at least in dreams he's *there*.

You're pathetic, I tell myself, though even that lacks heat, because believe me, I already know.

"What if . . ."

Emerson has an idea. A big idea—I can see it in the way her eyes gleam then. It's the same look she gets when she's revamping a festival or in her hyper planning mode. But something holds her back. She looks at Jacob, raises an eyebrow, and it's clear they're having a private conversation in their heads.

I try not to scowl. I stab a blueberry on my plate with a fork while I wait for them to clue me in.

Jacob laughs softly. "If our wedding *wasn't* in service of beating the Joywood, I'd be surprised."

My eyebrows furrow. "Your wedding?"

Emerson leans forward, her eyes shining with a gleaming new plan. "We have it on Main Street. Outside Confluence Books. Our vows are parts of the book—the parts you read Azrael. Readings from you guys can be the other parts too, just to cover our bases. We broadcast it out for anyone who wants to hear. It should reach any magical creature in St. Cyprian, and it might not free *everyone*, but it'd be a start."

"And if it doesn't work?"

Emerson shrugs. "Then it doesn't work. Jacob and I will still be married. We can still have a wedding that's part of a festival."

"Her dream come true," Jacob remarks dryly, but his mouth is curved, the love evident. He's just happy to marry her. However, whenever.

I want this to be the answer. I want my best friend marrying the perfect man for her, that *love* they share, to be the key. If we do this, everyone will be free, and black magic will be done. Over at last.

But I don't think it's going to work. It's not enough. It's too simple. When nothing else has been simple this year. *Especially* when we thought it should be.

That means it's up to me to figure out what happens when *simple* doesn't work. Like Emerson said, they'll be married anyway. So I guess there's no harm, no foul on that end. And it won't be the first time I go along with one of Em's plans but make backup ones of my own. This is how I got through ten years of her thinking she was a human.

I shake my head. "That only leaves you three days to plan your wedding, Em."

"Give me a real challenge," she says with a laugh.

And it's my first genuine smile in days.

Later, as we're walking through the foyer on our way out into our respective days, I look up at the chandelier. "Wait. If your theory is right, wouldn't Melisande have been uncursed when I said those words to free Azrael? It's possible the rug in the living room couldn't hear me, but she's *right here*."

I gesture up at the mermaid chandelier, and I swear it gleams back at me. Balefully.

Emerson squints up at the glittering crystals. "Maybe. And maybe this doesn't work. But it won't be you alone. It'll be all of us—so extra love and vow power there. *And* it will be on the solstice—so supercharged magic there. It will be a real wedding, so *actual* vows will be said. From a magic book. No matter what else happens, we know the book is magic."

This is true, of course, but I'm still looking at Melisande. And realizing that the lights on the chandelier, which weren't on, are now flickering.

"I guess you've figured me out," a melodic voice says, pretty and tinkling.

The gold of the mermaid is . . . *slithering* almost, and then changing. Evolving and emerging. The tail of the mermaid moves with a flick of gold, and then it sounds like something *splashes*—

And a wall of water seems to fall in front of us.

But it isn't water, really, and it evolves into a woman.

Melisande the mermaid is standing in front of us. Her green eyes sparkle like emeralds. She's breathtakingly beautiful, and somehow flesh and blood. She has wild hair that even outdoes mine. She's dressed in shells, and her long tail looks sleek and shimmery.

It's amazing that these things can still surprise me.

"You . . ." But I don't have the words. Did I really uncurse more than just Azrael all those weeks ago? I look up at the chandelier. "But . . ."

"Oh, I haven't stayed in there. I've just been careful about coming and going." She waves an elegant hand. "I wasn't about to let Azrael know I was free too. God knows what idiotic scheme he'd drag me into." She flashes a flirtatious grin at Jacob. "*Dragons.* Always scheming."

But for long moments, none of us can seem to find our words.

She studies each of us in turn. "He hasn't been around much, so I figure it's safe to tell you that you're right. At least, I think you must be. I felt the locks of the curse fall off me when Azrael exploded out of that newel post. The only difference between that day and any other day was the princess reading the book to her dragon."

That categorization—me as the princess, the fact this mermaid called him *my* dragon—is a piercing pain in my heart, but I'm getting used to those by now.

Even Emerson is largely speechless.

"I don't trust dragons," Melisande continues, eyeing the newel post with a sneer. "But I've seen enough of the Riverwood coven to trust *you*." She's back to smiling brightly at us. Gorgeous and effervescent, and magnificently breasted, shells or no shells. "If you free my people, and not just dragons and crows, we'll stand with you. *All* the river creatures listen to me."

There's something about her that's so mesmerizing, none of us say anything. We're just *staring*.

As if that is nothing but her due, she inclines her head. "Now, if you'll excuse me, I need a swim."

And she just . . . disappears.

"Did that really happen?" Jacob asks after a few moments of continuing shocked silence.

Emerson shakes her head, as if to shake away a lingering spell. "Yes. And she confirmed my idea, so I think I like her." She nods then, decisively, a sure indication that she's taking this as a good sign. Then she smiles at me. "Good luck at the archives today, Georgie. And get ready for a wedding-planning-all-night kind of night. Don't worry, I should have a binder to you by lunch."

Then she's out the door and off to the bookstore. Yet I have no doubt she'll come up with a wedding binder, run her store, and handle any number of St. Cyprian and witchdom-related issues before noon. That's Emerson.

"I was skeptical, but if the mermaid thinks it will work, who am I to argue?" Jacob laughs from beside me.

As if that's *that*.

Then he's off too, and I am standing in the foyer where I unleashed a dragon. And apparently a mermaid as well.

We have the crows, if we can free them.

We have a mermaid, and supposedly all the river creatures, if we can break their curses.

Maybe we don't need a dragon, freed or not.

I want to believe that.

But I don't.

And I believe even less that he will come around. Because

he is steeped in fear, and I realize, in the strangest way it is not unlike my mother. Who wanted me to shrink and hide and never be *special*. Now Azrael wants the same, so I'm not hurt or targeted or betrayed or worse.

But I won't do it. That's the thing I realize as I stand in this foyer that is now empty of everything magical but me. It doesn't matter what the reasons are.

I won't shrink myself ever again.

29

IT IS NO SURPRISE THAT EMERSON IS A MIRAcle worker. She always has been, though what she pulls off this time is truly next-level, even for her.

The night before solstice, everything is ready as if she's been planning it for ten years. She has a gorgeous white dress and veil. We have bridesmaids' dresses that fit us perfectly, and the men all have their suits and ties and shoes. Main Street is decked out in its usual winter holiday decorations, plus what Emerson is calling her *winter white theme*.

The snow hasn't cooperated, so she did it herself, decorating the old town with a lovely, magical dusting of snow that is all charm without the iciness and bitter cold. Plus no cleanup afterward. Humans will marvel that it all melted away in the night.

Assuming we win. But then, Emerson always assumes we'll win.

Tonight we send the men away so we can have a little bachelorette party of sorts. Only it's Emerson. And it's us. So it's no raging party. It's just an old-fashioned sleepover like we had when we were young. Before the pubertatum. Before everything changed.

It feels a bit like the sentimental goodbye to our childhood that we never got. Melisande even crashes the party for a bit and has us crying with laughter at her tales of men she's literally and metaphorically caused to crash upon the rocks.

"Deep down," she tells us with that smile of hers, "men are fools who *want* that crash. It's all in how you frame it."

We nod sagely. It might not be traditional prewedding talk, but we enjoy it anyway. When she retires to the chandelier for the night—*because I look good in crystal, thank you*, she tells us—Ellowyn flops back on her couch. "We just partied with a mermaid," she says with a laugh. "Zander is going to be *so* jealous."

Emerson yawns. "I know what Rebekah is going to say, but I think that's all I can handle. *Some of us* need our sleep for tomorrow."

"You were always such a sleepover killjoy," Rebekah says, but with that sisterly fondness.

"That's exactly what I knew you'd say."

Rebekah shakes her head. "All right, before bed, one last toast."

She magicks us all little flutes of champagne—sparkling cider for Ellowyn—and we hold them up to Emerson.

"To Emerson. Our oldest sister—in blood, and spirit," Rebekah says.

"Our fearless leader," Ellowyn adds.

"The best friend anyone could ever be blessed with and, no doubt, about to be the champion wife of all wives," I say, letting the tears fall.

Emerson sniffles but doesn't cry. "I do like being the champion. Which is why I *know* tomorrow is going to be the best. Because I'm marrying Jacob, and because we weren't just *meant* to lead. We were *forged* to lead, to unite. Tomorrow, the Riverwood coven ascends. And we will find a way to defeat black magic—before or after. No one can tell us what we can or can't do. I know we will succeed, because we're ready to do whatever it takes for *everyone*." She nods as if confirming it. "Some things are just meant to be."

She believes this. About Jacob, certainly. But also about the Riverwood and our eventual success. About her ability to bring everyone together, and serve them fairly.

The truth is, she has always believed this, no matter the setback, the betrayal, the heartache, the loss. She believed all of this, even before she knew who she was or what had been done to her.

"I thought you were tired, Em?" Rebekah reminds her as she gears up to say more.

Emerson huffs out a breath. "Oh, fine. No speech."

But then she holds out her arms, and we all move together in a big four-way hug.

"I love you guys," she whispers fiercely.

So we all hug, cry a little, and go to bed.

Or Rebekah and Ellowyn do, but Emerson grabs me on the way up the stairs to our respective rooms.

"I thought about not telling you, but . . . well. I saw the votes change a little earlier, at last. The majority is for Azrael being free. He can leave the cemetery, and we don't have to decide what to do with him."

"Can't the votes go back?" I ask, rather than think about what this means.

"I suppose they could until tomorrow, but that doesn't mean he can't walk free until then."

"Did you tell him?"

Emerson shakes her head. "I imagine . . . well, he should feel it."

"Right." *Right*. And if he felt it . . . he would be here. If he wanted to be.

He doesn't want to be. He isn't *ready* or *brave* enough to be, and that's fine. I tell myself this. All night. Sitting in my bed, wide-awake, Octavius asleep on my pillow, just . . . *waiting*.

He never comes.

Eventually, I hear people downstairs. Sounds in the kitchen. Breakfast being made and people chatting.

It's morning, and it's Emerson's wedding day, so I can hardly hide. I need to put on a happy face and celebrate my friend. Even if my heart feels blended into a terrible little pulp.

But it isn't hard to pretend otherwise when I get to the kitchen. Emerson has a floating to-do list that follows her around as she makes breakfast. Before I can try to take over, Rebekah waves me to the table.

"I told her I'd make breakfast, but she insisted she needs to move," Rebekah says from her seat.

"I just had this really disturbing dream last night that I need to work off," Emerson tells me.

"Join the club," Rebekah mutters.

They both look at me, but I shrug. I didn't sleep, so no dreams for me. Just the bone-deep worry that without Azrael letting go of his fear of my death—which is inevitable at some point—we can't win this. So as little as I like the idea myself, why not enjoy each other while we can?

"Was it Maeve drowning in a pool of black magic goo?" Ellowyn asks from the entry to the kitchen, a fuzzy blanket wrapped around her shoulders.

"Yes," Rebekah agrees. "In great, gooey detail."

Emerson frowns at Ellowyn, then her sister. "How did you know?"

"You all had the same dream," I say, puzzled. "The same dream of Maeve Mather drowning? What new evil is that?"

"If the rumors are true and our dream is true, it means that the only Joywood asshole left is Carol Simon," Rebekah says. "So not a new evil, just the same old one. I wish that made me feel better."

We all kind of pause. Carol *is* the leader of the Joywood, their Warrior, and arguably still the most powerful witch in the world. She's nothing to sneeze at, with or without her coven.

Still.

"Surely together we're stronger than Carol," I say. "We have beat her every step of the way this year. Even with black magic involved."

Emerson gives me one of her determined nods. "Exactly that."

We all sit down and eat, and there's a purposeful change in subject, from evil to dresses and shoes and flowers. Emerson is sending off missives to her wedding vendors, clarifying last-minute details for the solstice festival that always hums along beneath the usual Christmas celebrations, apparently finishing up the last of the year's chamber of commerce duties, and corresponding with governing bodies in other witch-heavy areas on this, the day of our ascension to full power and rule.

No big deal.

I message nobody.

And sooner than seems possible, it's time for all of us to get ready. There's a nervy kind of excitement in the air as we get into our dresses and then help Emerson into hers. I do Emerson's hair, a mix of my own skill and magic. Ellowyn handles the makeup.

Emerson's mother pops in for a little bit. It's the first time I've seen her since finding out her husband is my father. And I have to think about *that*. The fact Elspeth was never particularly *kind* to me, but not quite as cutting as she was to Rebekah and Ellowyn.

I guess I knew how to play a role after all.

Of course, it's also possible she doesn't know. My heart twists at that idea. That we're all keeping a terrible secret from her.

I am so tired of all these *secrets*.

Once Emerson is fully ready and Elspeth gets her fill of pictures, she makes a move to leave.

"I have some of the extended family to wrangle," she says.

"I'll see you at the wedding." She leans in and gives Emerson a kiss on the cheek. "You look beautiful."

I think that's it, but as she passes me, she gives me a *look*.

"It must be a heady thing to have access to the full archives," she says.

I feel speechless, but I can't *not respond*. I cough. "I don't take my responsibilities lightly."

She looks at me a little longer. Then she gives me a nod. That's it.

But I think that's all it needed to be. Silent acknowledgment that we don't need to make this a *thing*.

"If we're going to stick to the schedule, we better get to the bookstore," Rebekah says, and the fact she's even paying attention to the schedule is for Emerson and Emerson alone. A sweet gesture.

Emerson knows it. She's grinning as she stands up.

"We did it, you guys." But she's being generous. Sure, being a witch means that putting together events is a breeze, but it's still her *wedding*, and no matter how we helped, she did the bulk of the work. Just like with everything else.

Zander arrives, dressed in his wedding finery. He hesitates in the doorway, though he smiles. "You look great, Em," he says.

But there's something in his eyes, in his expression. Kind of a *forced* cheer.

"What's that look about?" Ellowyn demands, narrowed eyes of suspicion arrowing in on him. "You're not supposed to be here. The guys are supposed to meet us at the bookstore."

"Yeah, and we will. I just wanted to give you a little heads-up." He tries that smile again. "Uh, well. Jacob is just, uh, running a little . . . late."

"Then you need to go make him *not* late," Ellowyn is saying, with just enough malice and threat even *I'm* inclined to believe she might shank Zander right here, right now.

"There was another black magic attack last night," Zander

explains apologetically to Emerson. "It was brutal. A couple Healers tried to handle it themselves. No one wanted to bother you or Jacob this morning, but . . . it was bad, and they needed him."

Everyone is quiet at that. Our happy, excited wedding bubble is officially popped.

But Zander steps forward and puts his hand on Emerson's shoulder. "We'll head on down to the bookstore just as planned. He'll get there when he's done. It'll all be good. Maybe we start five minutes late, but that's not the end of the world."

"Have you *met* your cousin?" Rebekah asks, and I think maybe she's trying to lighten the mood, but it doesn't land.

Emerson reaches out and takes Zander's arm. "Will you go be with him? Just in case he needs help after?"

"Of course." He pats her hand, then disappears.

All of us are frozen for a moment. This was unexpected. I think maybe if it had been an attack *on* Jacob, it might feel more run-of-the-mill. We're used to that.

But this is a happenstance we weren't prepared for. It isn't evil, per se. Sure, it's black magic, and that's evil, but it's not *at* Jacob.

It's not aimed at *us*.

As far as we know.

"Come on, Em," I say, wrapping my arm around her waist. "Zander wouldn't make that up. Five minutes late, tops. Let's head over to the bookstore and get situated."

She nods, and so we magic ourselves over to the bookstore. Emerson doesn't even try to look outside to make sure everything is set up the way she wants it, which is how I know she is *Not Okay*.

"We'd feel it if something was really wrong," I tell her, giving her a squeeze.

"The black magic attacks getting worse *are* really wrong," Emerson says, pulling away from me. She goes to stand behind the bookstore counter. Like that gives her some kind of strength or makes her feel more in control.

"Okay," Rebekah agrees. "But that's not something we can fix right this second, so let's focus on what we can. Don't you want to see the chairs? They look great."

She points toward the outside.

Emerson shakes her head. "I'm sure it's fine."

We all exchange terrified looks. But after another minute or two of painful silence, Zander and Frost appear.

With Jacob, thank Hecate.

They're all dressed in the wedding suits Emerson picked out, but Jacob looks awful. Like he's barely standing, and with the way Zander positions himself behind Jacob, I wonder if he's holding him up.

Emerson magicks the big comfy chair over and pushes him into it. Ellowyn magicks him a tea and keeps shoving the mug at him until he drinks.

But he smiles at Emerson. "I'm not supposed to see you before the wedding."

"That's a human tradition, and we are *not* human," she says to him sternly. Then she kind of crumples into a kneeling position next to him and presses her forehead to his knee. "You have to stop giving so much of yourself, Jacob."

"You first." He runs a hand over her hair, careful not to mess with any of the pins. "I'll be okay. Promise. But, Em . . ."

She looks up. We all look at Jacob because of the grimness in his voice. "It was Evie."

It's a blow. Evie North is a Healer, and attacks on Healers are the lowest of the low. And Evie is also Jacob's *sister*.

I can see Emerson's grip on Jacob tighten. "She's okay," Emerson says firmly, like if she says it, it will make it true.

"Mom's with her. She wouldn't even stay put. Said she had to come to the wedding. She's okay, but . . ." Jacob trails off, as if he can't finish.

"But it's worse. It keeps getting worse," Emerson finishes for him.

Jacob's expression is grim. "She said the attacker was almost familiar. That the face of her attacker looked like some grotesque mix of Felicia and Maeve."

But before we can deal with this—really deal with these attackers who resemble missing Joywood members—someone clears their throat over a loudspeaker. A magical loudspeaker that treats each of us like we're our own sound system, like what comes through is directly *in our faces*.

We set it up ourselves.

"Good afternoon, St. Cyprian."

It's Carol's voice. We all move to the door to see Carol on the little stage in the middle of Main Street, with the perfect light dusting of snow framing her. Right where Jacob and Emerson are going to say their vows.

"I have received the *most* disturbing news that I'd like to share with you all while we . . . *wait*," she says, and she draws out the word *wait* like the wedding isn't on time because Emerson has set out to insult us all.

I'm outside before I know I mean to move. I can hear Emerson tell Jacob to stay put, but when I look back, he's followed her out of the shop too.

Zander is still behind him, no doubt trying to be a very conspicuous wingman while downplaying Jacob's injuries to Emerson.

"I have had news of a terrible attack done to one of our own." She surveys the crowd. "Poor Evie North, a *Healer*, was clawed, burned, and nearly *murdered*."

An echo of surprise and concern moves through the crowd. Carol's gaze finds the little knot of us in the crowd. She smiles. It isn't kind.

"I'm so glad Emerson can engage in a *wedding* while we're all being terrorized by a dragon," she says, making sure it echoes through that speaker so she's saying it to every single magical being alive.

"That attack was not done by a dragon, Carol," Jacob says in a dark, if tired, voice, but he also uses the same magical speaker. And Healers aren't known for lies.

Unlike her.

But she is unfazed, as ever.

"Oh?" she returns, with a raised eyebrow and fake surprise all over her freakishly younger face. "That's funny, because *I* heard that it was done inside the cemetery. Where, you might have heard, a dragon is imprisoned."

30

THERE'S A MURMUR IN THE CROWD. THE KIND of murmur Carol loves to stir up, especially when it comes to us. Fearful looks pass like a long, slow, insistently dark ripple across water. We can see it happen from where we stand.

On some level I get it. The problem is that Azrael and other magical creatures are the unknown. We've been taught not to believe in them, so any sign of their existence can easily feel threatening. No one needs to trust what Carol says to worry that a dragon might be a problem—a sign of something bad and scary that might also eat them.

She made sure to put on a show and build a scary statue.

And she's still entirely too good at what she does.

I worry the votes will turn back, and we'll have to imprison him again. I worry that's *exactly* why Carol is doing this.

Jacob moves past me, ignoring all of our protests. He's still pale, still so obviously hurting, but he is moving on his own two feet, and his voice is strong when he speaks.

"I was there. I healed my sister. It was no dragon attack." He turns to face the crowd. "My *sister*. I'd know if she was attacked by a dragon."

I realize I've only ever seen Jacob this furious twice before. Once ten years ago when Emerson was suddenly unable to remember anything magical in one fell swoop. And once again earlier this year, when Emerson was directly attacked.

"Why are you all so desperate to protect this dragon?" Carol asks, eyes wide and full of feigned innocence, like she simply can't understand this need of ours to consort with predators. "It does speak of a coven not entirely in touch with their community's needs and fears, I have to say."

"*You* imprisoned him, Carol. How did he have the magic to attack Evie, and what was she doing in the *cemetery*?" I demand. "Last I checked, Healers can't fix the dead."

"Who knows what these monsters are capable of?" Carol lifts a shoulder. She doesn't need to answer any of these questions. She's instilled the fear she wanted to. "Now, what are we going to do about it?" she asks the crowd.

"Enough," Jacob says. He grabs Emerson's hand and marches her up the aisle. She's whispering things about how he should sit, be careful, calm down—but he's not having it.

"I'm fine," Jacob says firmly. It's his brook-no-argument voice, and even Emerson doesn't try her luck with it. "We are getting married, Emerson. Now." He pulls her up onto the stage and stares Carol down, reminding everyone that Emerson might be powerful, but *he* is the man she leans on. The man who is not intimidated by her like every other person around. "We have something to do. If you're concerned about the dragon, perhaps you should be in the cemetery. Not here."

I hate that he would suggest such a thing, but Carol only smiles. Like she hoped he'd respond this way.

"Of course, your needs should come first," Carol all but purrs.

Emerson is unfazed, even as I'm huffing and puffing in outrage. She doesn't look at Carol. She turns to the crowd. She's ready to give a speech, even in her elegant wedding dress.

She's always ready to give a speech, Hecate love her. "I have outlined our feelings on the dragon, on magical creatures in general," she says calmly and even cheerfully, as if she sees no cause for concern here. "I have spoken with all of you about the important and *hidden* historical information Georgie found for us that *proves* the strongest covens have a fabulae by their side. We have shown you the *facts*."

"Facts?" Carol demands. "Georgie and facts?" She turns to me then, and I feel the gazes of many of the crowd on me too. "Anyone who knows Georgie knows that she'd rather believe in a *fairy tale* than facts. Princesses and dragons and *crows*."

The way she sneers those last few words at me makes me certain that she knows about the book. That it's some kind of threat toward all those things. But how?

"We let you imprison Azrael, even though we didn't agree with it," Emerson continues calmly. Her hand is still in Jacob's. "We have let your vote on the matter govern how long he stays, and just yesterday . . ."

I see it dawn on Emerson that Carol's timing is very specific.

Because the vote went our way. And Carol *shouldn't* know that since we haven't announced it. So she can't come out and *say* the dragon was free when Evie was attacked without ruining her case.

Emerson changes tactics immediately. "Solstice is coming. Does this not seem like questionable timing that stems from bitterness over losing a bid to keep ruling over witchdom?"

There are more murmurs in the crowd, but they seem less dark than before. Families and friend groups talk amongst themselves.

"Let them have their wedding, Carol," Holly calls out. "We can deal with the dragon after."

"After?" Carol screeches. I swear it seems like her eyes might bulge clear out of her head, but at least she's still intact, despite the condition of the other Joywood members the last time we saw them.

A lot of people in the crowd murmur their agreement. Maybe they don't trust Azrael, but they came for a wedding. They also trust Jacob beyond a shadow of a doubt. He's helped so many of them, or his parents have.

The last remaining member of the Joywood doesn't have the stranglehold on the crowd she used to.

Maybe no one ever trusts people in power completely, and they shouldn't. But they trust us more than Carol right now.

I'll admit that it feels sweet.

After more and more vocal support for the wedding from the crowd, Carol stalks off the stage. I watch her go since *I* don't trust her in the least. Particularly when she doesn't go far. She stands off to the side, arms folded, glaring at Jacob and Emerson on the stage while snow falls all around her but doesn't accumulate on the bricks.

I can't get past the fact that none of the other members of the Joywood are here. Not a single one. Have they all really died off? Crumbled apart or rotted away or drowned horribly like that dream I'm delighted I didn't share?

But then, why does Carol look so good? How can she wield so much power alone?

As I watch her, I notice something else. She is standing very close to a certain Desmond Wilde. He's seated, but not up front with Elspeth or any other member of Emerson's family. He's off to the side, in the middle of a group of people Emerson would likely tell me are deeply important to witchdom, but who seem random to me.

Maybe Emerson sat him there because she knows how much he likes to feel important—and it also keeps him away from her—but it just feels *off*.

I think about the books he stole from Lillian that my father, in turn, stole from him. The fairy tale that Carol apparently knows about when she shouldn't. I think about the archives, and the decided lack of any decent information on the Joywood.

And I am struck by a thought I maybe should have had sooner. Just maybe, the best and dirtiest secrets aren't *hidden* in the archives by the Joywood or black magic or my own failures. Maybe they aren't there at all.

Maybe Carol has a library in her house too. Like the Wildes, like my father. Maybe, *just maybe*, the Joywood's evil history is tucked up in the home of its most powerful and most evil member.

And here Carol is. Away from her house and focused on Emerson, as usual.

Meaning it's the perfect chance to find out.

I look back toward the stage. Jacob's parents are up with Emerson and Jacob now. They are acting as the priest and priestess who will lead the handfasting that witches use in place of human religious rituals.

Everyone is getting situated. Rebekah pulls me forward so I can take my place on the stage with everyone else.

But that idea of mine is poking at me. Even as Jacob's mother, Maureen, welcomes the crowd to this happy occasion.

Emerson. I think I need to sneak into Carol's house and try to raid her library.

Emerson's gaze whips to mine. Then she looks out at the crowd for a moment before turning back to Jacob. I put it out on the coven channel, so everyone heard me. They're all sneaking looks at me, but we're good at not reacting—though I can see the wheels turn in Emerson's head.

Eventually she gives a little nod.

Do your reading, then sneak away. With Frost—

No, just me. Frost can stay here and keep an eye on Carol. If she disappears, he can warn me and come after me. But more than one of us gone is too big a red flag.

The best friend being gone is, of course, in no way the same big red flag, Frost replies dryly.

I'm almost touched he's noticed that we always-mortals have

different relationships. But there's no time to study a man who's lived forever.

So make a projection of me, I say instead. *I'm the Historian. It has to be me.*

I don't think I'm being stupid or reckless. I'm warning everyone about what I need to do, not running off and doing it alone without letting anyone know, like some I could mention. The chances I'm the only one who can wield the books are too large.

But maybe I don't have to go fully alone, I amend, as I can *hear* everyone's reluctance. If Azrael was here . . . But he's not. *I'll take my father.*

There's quiet in the coven channel. Jacob's father is talking to the crowd about love and loyalty, devotion and steadfastness.

Trust me, I say to Emerson. Just Emerson.

She gives one last nod.

"Each of the friends of the bride and groom is going to do a reading. First is Georgina Pendell."

We agreed that there was no need to remind everyone of our positions in the coven. *That's the power move*, Rebekah said. *Only weak people introduce themselves with a title.*

Powerful people assume their title is self-evident, Ellowyn agreed.

I force myself to smile out at the crowd. I look down at the piece of paper where I've written my part of the book. Not the part that I read to Azrael—that will be Jacob and Emerson's vows to each other. This is something different.

Something that makes me ache all the same. Because somehow these words apply to my life, *my* love.

"Real love blooms in trust. In yourself and in each other. Sometimes the world and its wars ask too much. Sometimes you lose sight of each other along the path, but you must always find your way back. To love without limits. To joy beyond measure. Because to do otherwise is to let fear win."

It brings tears to my eyes as I read, even knowing what I

need to do next. Because Jacob and Emerson found their way back already, after ten years of Em not knowing who she was. I have no doubts about their happy-ever-after now. Not just because they love each other, but because they'll fight for it. Fight for each other. *Both* of them.

No matter what they give of themselves to others, they will always come back to their love, their *home*.

They *fit*.

And I refuse to let that land inside me like a new kind of grief.

Because I have shit to do. I don't have time to grieve.

When my reading is done, I walk off the stage and to my seat. By the time we're all done with our readings, Jacob and Emerson will be alone with the priest and priestess to give their vows, to bind their hands and ceremonialize what is already true.

I hope I'll be back in time to see it.

But right now I have to focus on more than this wedding.

Real snow begins to fall along with the lovely snow Emerson whipped up for the ceremony, but the magical warmers and actual heater towers keep us all cozy. Even out here in the middle of Main Street, St. Cyprian. It's perfect, just as Emerson wanted, and I wish I could enjoy it. I wish we could all enjoy it.

But as Jacob said, what kind of wedding would Emerson have except one that might free people from terrible curses and bring the Joywood and Carol down for good?

Nothing could be more *her*.

Now seated, I create the projection inside me, and then Ellowyn and Zander give it life. While they make the projection spell a reality, I let it go and then simultaneously magic myself out of the seat and off to the front of Carol's house.

I tried to land inside, but she's got enough wards and locks to keep even the strongest witches out. Plus I've never actually been inside, so there's no picturing it to project myself there.

I told my coven I'd bring my father, so I reach out to him.
Dad, I need you.

It's real winter on this side of town, and freezing, so I magic myself a coat plus one for Dad. When he appears, looking more than a little concerned, I hold it out to him, and he slides his arms inside.

"Georgie..."

"I need you to be brave," I tell him, staring at Carol's house. Not at him. "I need to get in her library."

The truth is there. I know it.

As ever, my father focuses on the puzzle, not the problem. "How are you going to get in?"

It appears to me like a flash. I am not just *a* historian. I am *the* Historian. And a key once unlocked many secrets to me. Why wouldn't it unlock this?

I call out for the key. When it arrives in my outstretched palm, it is warm and glowing, just like when I go into the archives.

Please work.

I move forward, past Carol's gate. I start walking toward the looming door. But I can tell Dad hasn't followed, so I look back.

"I can't pass the gate, princess," he says.

He stands there, pushing against something invisible that won't let him pass. But I'm so close. And the wedding is only so long. I can't wait. I can't worry about why I can get through and he can't.

"Stay right here," I tell him. "If you see anything fishy, reach out to me. Reach out to my coven."

"This isn't safe," he admonishes me. "You know it isn't."

"Maybe not. But I have to do it." I feel it like a pull. And it's a bit like the pull of the river, so maybe that should stop me, but the key is glowing...

And the key is not black magic. It is not *bad*.

When I reach Carol's door, I see gold shining from the keyhole. This is right. This is *right*.

I put the key in the door, and the lock gives.

My heart is beating like a hammer against my chest. The key feels like holding a hot coal, almost, and something in the shape of a circle burns around my finger where Azrael's ring once was.

Azrael. That grief swells up in me, but now is not the time for it. Except maybe one little thing.

You should be here, I reach out and tell him. Maybe he's blocked me. I don't know. But I feel better having sent that message to him anyway.

Carol's house smells like sulfur and rot, but it's *beautiful*. Gleaming wood and elaborate carvings. Every window is stained glass. Every light fixture is a glorious gold.

I peek in each room I see, looking for books. When I finally make it to the library, it's the biggest and most beautiful one I've ever seen. It puts full museums in Europe to shame, both in volume and the artifacts she's no doubt stolen. I should be disgusted.

But the Historian in me, raised in libraries, can't help a dreamy sigh all the same.

I scan the titles, keeping the archive key in my hand.

What am I looking for? What do I need to know? I ask the library, the same way I ask the archives.

I *feel* something move around me, but it's almost like it starts and then stops. As if it's hindered by something.

An outside, evil force.

No doubt more wards and locks. I look at the key, wondering if there's some clue here. But it's just a key. The room is just a library.

Still, something is *here*. I feel it. A dark, lurking presence.

But books are ideas. And ideas aren't dangerous in and of themselves. It's what people do with them that causes trouble.

That's never seemed like a good enough reason to restrict any and all ideas to me. I'd rather let the ideas go free and maybe work on restricting the people who try to use them to hurt others.

"*Reveal to me, what I should see,*" I say.

The world around me *ripples*, but doesn't quite change. So I do it again, and again, and *again*. Still there's no give.

I *know* something exists behind the facade, but my magic can't reach it. I keep trying, though. I have to do this. I have to succeed. Everything is up to *me*.

I'm pretty quickly spent. Sweaty and shaking. I've no doubt done irreparable damage to my hair, and if I have the energy to get back to the wedding, it will be on nothing more than my own two feet, not a flight or a *pop* of magic.

But I haven't succeeded yet, and I have to succeed. I squeeze the key in my palm. It got me in here. It must have the answer. I look around, searching for something. Not the books I'm after, but maybe some kind of sign—

Then, there it is.

A little metal . . . weasel? A lot like the one Carol wore to the house tour what feels like a lifetime ago.

It's screwed to one of the bookshelf joints, but if I touch it, the metal swings. And when I swing it out of the way, there's a keyhole.

With shaky hands—both nerves and exhaustion—I shove my key into the hole. Nothing happens. But then I turn the key, and . . .

The world beneath my feet rumbles. The shelves shake, move, twist, and then turn. They open up the wall into a dark sort of cave.

And in that cave are even more books.

A stack of books, bound in black leather. There are no titles embossed on them, no authors mentioned. But I *feel* the evil pumping off them.

I smell it. I taste it.

And still I move forward. I need to protect myself before I open them, I know I do, but—

"You didn't think it'd be that easy, did you?" a voice asks me.

It's a vaguely familiar voice. But only vaguely—

Until I turn and come face to face with my father.

Not Stanford Pendell, but my *biological* father.

Desmond Wilde.

31

FOR A MOMENT, I CAN'T SEEM TO FORM A thought, much less say something.

It's not the shock at being interrupted here. Why would *anything* be easy in this long, painful year? It's not even *that much* of a surprise that—*of course*—someone turned up to make this hard.

What stuns me is that this is *Desmond*.

Not Carol or one of her cronies. Not even some evil black ooze. My actual biological father.

He stands there, dressed in his crisp suit. He looks exactly the way a father of the bride should, but . . .

There is something wrong here.

Something *more* wrong than this man having an affair with my mother and keeping the fact that he's my blood relative secret for almost thirty years, that is.

"Are you . . ." I hardly know what to ask. "Are you really *working* with Carol?"

I can't fathom that this self-important man, someone who's always been so . . . pompous yet ineffectual could be . . . *actively engaging in black magic.*

But he's not the Desmond I'm used to seeing and dealing with, however distantly.

Today his eyes are a deep, terrifying black, and that's new. Is it black magic or . . . is this just a Carol-controlled husk in the shape of Desmond? I certainly don't remember his eyes being that black, or his smirk being *quite* that oily.

I definitely don't remember him giving much of a shit about anything but himself and how he might become more important in the highest levels of witch society. I never would have picked *him* to be a lackey.

Then again, he made sure to get that black magic necklace to me back at my pubertatum, didn't he? So working with Carol can't be *new* for him. Unless . . .

Desmond Wilde was a friend of my dad's. And my dad doesn't always live in the here and now, but he's never been a fool. If he thought they were friends, they were. They researched the secrets of the fabulae and the crows together when doing so was traitorous—and the Joywood have always been fans of swift and brutal "justice."

Why would anyone risk it if they didn't believe in what they were doing?

But then Desmond had a sudden change of heart. And followed that up with an affair with my mother and a lifetime of cravenly jockeying for status, which isn't the same thing as power. It's nothing but the *appearance* of power.

It makes me wonder if the thing that changed Desmond was Carol all along.

"You were a mistake, you know," he says to me, examining his hands, clearly expecting that almost casual comment to rip me to shreds.

But I laugh. "Shocking! A child from an affair was a mistake? Imagine that."

He gazes at me with those empty black eyes. Like a living corpse. Like a Joywood zombie. In spite of myself, I have to fight to restrain a shudder.

"I should never have let your mother keep you."

"So why did you?"

He frowns a little, as if he's not sure why. As if he doesn't quite remember.

Definitely a Joywood zombie, I think.

He indicates the cave with a tilt of his head. "Go on then. Have a look. Learn all the secrets of the Joywood."

I laugh again in spite of the fear moving through me. "Yeah, I'll go ahead and skip right into the cave of evil while you watch."

I call out to my *real* dad and my coven, but there's only an echoing silence.

And Desmond's smirk.

He moves closer to me. That's when I realize I have nowhere to go except into the cave.

I try to reach out to Azrael too. Maybe we're at odds. Maybe we don't—can't—agree. Maybe the real future for us is finally *not* indulging in the love our souls were meant to feel.

But I am not going to *die* here at the hands of Desmond Wilde without *trying* to get help.

"You can't reach them," he tells me, with fake pity. "Not your sad, illegitimate father outside. Not your friends performing their little farce. They think all is well, and they'll keep thinking that until it's too late."

He smiles wide, and if I'm not mistaken, lets out the faintest little . . . titter.

And that's how I know.

This is not Desmond. This is Carol. I *know* it.

So with no warning, I lash out. I shoot a blast of magic power that *should* knock Desmond over—

But he's not Desmond. Not totally.

His power is greater—stronger—and he doesn't even *budge* from the blow. Instead, he throws out a blast of his own.

And it has me skidding back, perilously close to the cave. I fight it with everything I've got, but it's all-encompassing. It's all over me.

Thick and black and oily.

It's like that river sucking me under, but this time it's pushing me into a cave, into *black*, into *evil*. And I've already spent so much energy just trying to get here.

We battle on in the same way. I manage some decent blows, but I never knock him back. And while I block some of what he throws my way, I am inching closer and closer to being thrown in that cave that *throbs* with evil.

I have one foot in, one foot out. I'm holding on to the side of the opening to keep the blast from taking me all the way in. Everything in me is flagging—every ounce of strength, power, magic.

It's a renewable resource, and mine has been depleted.

I guess this is me dying horribly again, I say in my head, going for a little rueful gallows humor here at the end.

Because hey, at least I know I'll come back.

And I'm going to fight until I can't.

I throw another blast at Desmond and grip the doorway with everything I've got. And as I do, I feel one of my fingers start to . . . heat. Like a strange, hot brand around my ring finger.

There's a deep, distant rumble through the house, kind of like when I turned the key to open the archives.

But this is angrier.

It isn't Carol-as-Desmond, because he looks up, shocked.

Then furious, and not in my direction.

With his attention diverted, I throw out what little magic I have left. It knocks into him, but at the same time, the roof seems to crash in on itself.

No. Not on itself.

Because a huge, pissed-off dragon crashes in and lands with a thud that rattles the entire foundation I'm standing on. I almost topple back into the cave, but I just barely manage to grab onto the wall and hold myself up.

Azrael.

Here.

In dragon form and breathing fire.

I've never loved him more.

Carol-controlled Desmond manages to hold off the fire blazing at him, barely. Azrael reaches forward with one fearsome claw and closes it around Desmond's body with no trouble at all.

And he roars, loud enough and scary enough to make me believe very deeply in genetic memories, because I am certain no breakable creature on this earth can possibly be chill in the face of a *dragon roar*.

But that doesn't mean I can let him do this.

I scramble forward. "You can't kill him!"

Azrael sighs, a plume of smoke erupting from his mouth. He slides me a wild gold look as he gives Desmond a little shake. "You are forever saying that to me."

Since I've said it all of *twice* now, I assume he means across our many lives. But I don't have time to mine that notion. "Carol will only use it as proof that magical creatures are dangerous."

The way he looks at me is downright ferocious. "We fucking *are*."

"But you're not evil, Azrael. You're not black magic. And I . . ." I look at Desmond hanging limply in Azrael's giant claw. "I'm not altogether certain *he's* actually in there. I think Carol has some kind of mind control over him."

Another round of smoke. "If she does, he let her."

A terrible truth I can't deny. But still . . . "We can't give Carol more ammunition. Not until you're all free."

He sighs. Then, with a flick of his tail—which crashes through lamps and walls like they're made of papier-mâché—magic erupts in the corner of the half-destroyed house. A statue appears, kind of like the dragon one in the cemetery. But instead of big and fearsome, this is a small and inconsequential little stone thing that looks like a naked rat.

He tosses Desmond's limp body at it, and with another burst

of magic, Desmond is gone. I realize that Desmond is now imprisoned like Azrael was.

Azrael takes his time turning that huge dragon's head of his back to me.

And for a moment, we stare at each other across the wreckage of Carol's once-pristine house.

My throat is so dry it hurts. "You came."

He studies me with that golden dragon gleam. "Did you know they are broadcasting that tiresome fairy tale all the way across the river? Directly into the graves. And there's no way to block it out."

"I did . . . not."

"Well, they are. And I heard you. Loud and clear. Then." He looks at the looming cave full of books that must be full of Joywood secrets. "Now."

That makes my throat feel tight.

He keeps going. "Then the rest of them. The Guardian. The Immortal. The Revelare and the Chaos Diviner. On and on about this *love* thing I apparently know nothing about. And maybe you are right, I don't."

That hits me even harder than any of Desmond's blows, but there couldn't possibly be a worse time.

"Azrael, I don't have time to fight with you. I can't do whatever this is." I'd magic myself right out of here, but I don't have the magical battery for it, and I need to deal with some evil books.

Not a moody dragon I needed *days ago*.

He scowls at me. "Your words freed me once, Georgina, but I suppose that was different. That was a very physical imprisonment. A curse. This time, it was my own choice." He shimmers bright and hot, and then he is a man, and that makes everything in me *ache*. "Perhaps you were right, and I was selfish. I did not want to feel that pain again. It is *unbearable*."

"Yes," I say. "I know. I don't have to remember. I feel it all the same."

His face darkens, but it's an intensity of emotion, not temper. I feel it inside me like a new storm. "I do not want to lose you. I cannot stand the thought, but you were right to call me out on how . . . I love you for the woman you are and always have been, always willing to be brave, to fight. You are special, but not just to me. In every time, you have been special to *all* who need you, and in *this* lifetime, like that damn crow lifetime, there are so many who need you."

My heart catches in my throat.

"I know how to love, Georgina. It is all I know how to do when it comes to you. But I have never been given the chance to live *and* love. We have been torn from each other in every time, and always too fast. Too soon. More than once by *crows*. Yet if you are the teacher, Georgina, I have no doubt I can learn to be better. To love you for who you are without *fear*. And maybe I can even learn to forgive. If it will save the world. If it will give me you, who must save the world."

My breath comes out a little shaky. I'm beyond tired. My magic is down to zero. I need so many things, but mostly I just need him.

I always need him.

Just for a moment.

I move forward and rest against his huge, hot body. I lean my forehead against the broad wall of his chest. "Azrael, we have to do the saving of the world part first."

"I have called in reinforcements." He nudges me toward the cave. "What do your books tell you?"

"They are most certainly not *my* books."

Still, I step toward the cave. We must do what needs doing, and then . . . then we can do this. *Us.*

This time I want there to be an *us*. A future. Not an *almost* ripped from us in the midst of yet another battle of right versus wrong.

I focus on the pile of evil books. I hold up the key. I murmur the simple spell that has never failed me and has led me down a thousand roads through otherwise impenetrable texts. *"Lead me where I need to go, show me what I need to know."*

The books shudder and shake. Then something... glimmers.

I realize there's a small book on top of the larger ones—or there is now. It's a slim paperback. I lean forward, afraid to step too close.

Then I forget everything.

Because it looks just like my fairy tale, but... not. The cover is horrifying. It's far too much like a vision Ellowyn projected to us during the ascension trials, showing us what the Joywood rule would look like. A mansion on a hill of gleaming gold—not all that different than Carol's house. Everything else black, dying, rotting.

But instead of the entire Joywood enjoying a feast through the window of the house, it's just Carol. She's youthful and thin, supple and pretty. Her hair is in beautiful honeyed waves, her smile sultry and satisfied. Bones litter the ground beneath her. Azrael's dragon head is on a pike outside the house, and she has clearly been eating a feast of birds. *Crows.*

There is a bright, gleaming sword leaning against the table. I recognize that sword because it's in my book too. The princess has it in her hands in one of the scenes, riding her dragon toward battle.

A scene Ellowyn also saw in her dream on All Souls' Day.

I'm hesitant to even touch the book, but I need to get back to that wedding. I've already spent too much time here. I mutter a quick spell to protect me from any lingering black magic, then pick up the book and flip through the pages.

Each one depicts Carol, or a version of her, murdering each one of her coven members—or versions of them. There are also magical creature sacrifices, each more grisly than the last. There's blood, blood, and more blood.

And with every death, Carol looks younger, more beautiful.

But she is alone on the cover, at the end. *Alone*, while those who remain are tortured and faceless as they suffer at her feet.

I know this will be her undoing. We've known it since the start of this wild year.

She can't beat us if we're united.

Then I turn to the last page, and everything inside me turns to ice.

It's a wedding that looks far too much like Emerson's. Except the wedding in the book has been ruined by a gruesome creature—some repulsive Frankenstein's monster stitched together from the pieces of people and creatures she's killed and ritually sacrificed.

Including the Joywood members she ruled St. Cyprian and the witching world with for years.

An untold number of years.

Some of them were her friends.

Like my father. Despite the outcome, I know that they were once friends.

"We have to go," I say then, shutting the book with fingers turned to icicles. "We have to hurry."

It hasn't happened yet, or I'd feel it. I'd feel my coven's reaction. I'd feel the danger itself. And even though I haven't felt it yet, I know we still have to hurry. There is only so much time.

I put the fairy-tale nightmare down on the stack of other books. I try to magic some sort of protective case around them, but I'm spent.

Then Azrael puts his hand on my shoulder. "Try now."

I feel his magic pump into me, and I'm able to do it. I make a safe holder for all the books, then magic it all to the witchlore archives. Before I can say or do anything else, Azrael shifts into his dragon form again.

It's a shimmering brightness, and then he surrounds me, gleaming scales and his *immensity*. And he simply lifts me up and, in a graceful maneuver, plants me on his back.

Then he rises up and flies out of the hole he made in the roof.

But he doesn't go to Main Street. He soars over the roof and straight down in front of Carol's house, where my father is at the gate, still fighting against whatever wall has kept him from getting into the house.

"How did you break through?" I ask Azrael as he lands in front of my father.

"Magic, Georgina. Of course." He inclines his giant dragon head toward my father. "Mr. Pendell."

"Ah. Mr. . . . Dragon?"

"Azrael. Azrael Evermore. Now, let's save the world."

He uses a wing to place my father on his back, right behind me.

"Oh, *dear*," Dad breathes, wrapping his arms around my middle and holding on tight.

Azrael jerks his head up at the sky then, so I do too. And I see . . . crows.

So many black birds, circling above us.

Reinforcements, he said. Azrael somehow got them to come. To help. They aren't *free* yet. I know that. But they are all risking *pain* for this. Risking whatever they can give.

Because we need to work together.

And because my dragon asked.

I hold on to him tightly. *Thank you.*

I wouldn't be thanking me yet.

But this is literally our last, best weapon. Maybe our *only* weapon. Working together, no matter how hard it is.

I can hear the voices echoing from the wedding. The readings must be over because I can hear Jacob's voice. The vows are starting. "We have to hurry."

But one of the big ravens flies in front of us and leads us down to the ground. He's violet-eyed and huge. He morphs into a man as he lands.

"You'd better be right, dragon," Gideon says darkly. Then he holds out his hands, palms up. And I realize with a start that . . . Azrael had to have gone to Gideon. Specifically. Found Crow Island, rallied them all *and* their king. No matter his pride or his fears.

Gideon mutters a few words in a language I can't quite work out, and a sword appears. He holds it for a moment. I understand that it is very heavy—and infinitely precious.

His eyes gleam as he offers it to me.

I've never seen it in person before, but I know it at once. The sword from the book. *My* book *and* Carol's.

"The sword of unity," my father says in awe. "It's supposed to be a myth. A—"

"Fairy tale?" I supply for him.

He chuckles. "Yes."

I lean down and take the sword from Gideon. It feels right in my hands. Not heavy at all.

"You may remember it," Gideon says, a touch of irony in his voice. "It was my grandmother's. Hidden on Crow Island for as long as I can remember. I'm entrusting it to you, Georgina Pendell, in the hope that you'll know what to do with it."

I raise the sword with one hand. A storm is rumbling in the distance. Evil is on its way, and we must fight it. "Hope, love, and unity," I say.

The words from Gideon's grandmother's essay.

Gideon murmurs the same, then bows. "Together we live or together we die, *princess*." There's a rumble deep in my dragon's chest when he calls me this. I think we can all tell from Gideon's smirk that he did it deliberately for that very response. But his expression is dead serious when he meets my gaze again. "We will fight for as long as we can. Until the curse is broken. That cannot be long."

There is a loud cawing then that fills the sky.

I hold the sword in my hands, sitting astride a dragon. The moment calls for a rousing speech, but I'm not Emerson. I *read* words. I make worlds in my mind.

Speeches aren't my thing.

So I raise the sword into the air, and I say the only thing I can. "Then let's go break a curse."

Azrael lifts into the air once more as Emerson's voice takes over on the speaker, reading the words I once spoke aloud to Azrael. Speaking them into every nook and cranny of witchdom.

Everywhere a cursed creature might wait, dreaming of deliverance.

"I am yours," she says to Jacob. To the world. To the people we hope to *govern*, not *rule*, because we aren't like the Joywood. We don't want what we could get only by black magic. We want a magical world filled with complexity and opinions, whether we like them or not, and all the people and creatures that hold them. "You are mine. Our souls intertwine. I would lay down my life for you, but even then I would not die. Because love cannot be torn asunder."

But before she can finish, the whole damn world begins to shake.

32

AZRAEL DROPS MY FATHER OFF ON THE outskirts of the wedding crowd in a quick, smooth move that I appreciate. He doesn't really slow down, but still manages to place my father outside the fray, near a growing snowdrift that might give him some cover. This is where he belongs.

The wedding situation has deteriorated, to put it mildly. Our coven stands on the stage in defensive positions. The onlookers have created a kind of circle in the audience.

And in the middle of that circle of people below the stage is Carol.

Her hair is wild. Her skin seems to be . . . melting. Black, oily swirls stretch out in coils from her fingers, which is nauseating. But much worse—*much, much* worse—is what's erupting from the ground as if it's being *pulled out* like some kind of dark afterbirth by those black tendrils.

It's that hideous creature from the book. That shuffling, disgusting patchwork of evil.

It's huge. Not only monstrous . . . an *actual monster*.

Not the *suggestion* of monsters we've fought off all year, but a real one, like the red-eyed horror show adlets that attacked Emerson in March.

And it seems to have a kind of gravitational pull. Chairs and heaters whip in the wind it kicks up, crashing against its immense body. It doesn't seem to care.

My stomach threatens to come out my throat, and my heart is clawing at my ribs. Some witches seem frozen in horror, not that I can blame them. Others are screaming. Still others are scrambling, running away, or trying to take cover in the alleys and shop doors along Main Street. Some braver witches are trying to fling their magic at Carol. It only bounces back.

But I am also brave. And I am part of the Riverwood. Brave or not, handling this is our duty.

Azrael lands us on the stage, and I rush to swing myself down from his back, sword in hand, until I'm standing there in all my state in front of my friends.

"It's like the book," Ellowyn says, gazing at me while holding a blast of magic, aimed at Carol. "It's like my *dream*."

I don't know what *brave* looks like on my face, but I do it. "Let's make sure that dream has a happy ending."

Rebekah grins at me, lazily, like this is a garden party instead of a horror show. "Badass, Georgie. I like it."

"Zander, Frost, try to clear the area of bystanders," Emerson belts out then, swinging back from what looks like a quick recon of the wedding guests. Of course she's calm enough to hand out assignments. "Azrael, does your fire do anything to black magic?"

He lets out a flare of it, like a test. Or a warning. "Not permanently, but temporarily it can break the bonds dark magic can make."

"Go, use it," she tells him. "Break whatever bonds Carol has formed."

And she keeps going. "Jacob, gather the Healers and help where it's needed. I don't see a lot of injuries, but I think the number is going to climb. We know she likes a body count. Rebekah and Ellowyn, find a safe place away from this mess. Try to come up with spells that can do damage from a distance."

"Potions are poison if used properly, and I know just the thing," Ellowyn says with a grim kind of glee.

"Georgie, you and I are going to get down to Carol." She studies me, then looks out over the destruction of her wedding. Still in her white dress, though while we stand there, she divests herself of the veil. "I think I should have a sword too. After all, I am the Confluence Warrior."

I try to hand her mine, but she shakes her head. She reaches up, pulls down a light from the sky. Like she's done this a million times before, when I know she hasn't. When I know the last time she wielded this sword was earlier this year, and it was Jacob's first.

But that's more sword-wielding than I've done.

Now we stand, hip to hip, with our swords before us like we've spent lifetimes wielding them with ease.

In front of us is what I can only call a black magic tornado.

And we see tornadoes in Missouri, but I have never wanted to hide from one of them.

This is much bigger, much blacker, like a swirling *wrongness* that *wants* to eat us all whole.

Behind it stands Carol, cackling like the twisted lunatic I've always thought she was while her giant zombie swipes its limbs about, throwing witches every which way. Like they're nothing more than broken bits of confetti.

It's sickening.

Zander and Frost are working to funnel people into the alleys and away from the main fray. They're getting some people out, but it requires a lot of magic and effort to block Carol and her zombie's attacks.

"We have to get through that tornado," Emerson says.

I look at it dubiously, but when Emerson charges forward, striking her sword directly into the swirl of evil, I move with her. I hack and cut away at it and the little tendrils of black magic that slither between the bricks at our feet, through the gathering snow, and up around our ankles.

When I look up again, I see Emerson's sword has somehow *melted* in the black magic tornado.

"That is . . . not good," she says grimly.

Then she grabs me, and we're flinging ourselves back. Away from that terrible, dark spiral.

But if the swords can't stop it, what can?

I look around again. Zander and Frost are still helping people. Jacob is healing folks as fast as he can. Rebekah and Ellowyn are hurling magic and what looks like various potions at Carol and the zombie from a spot on the roof of the bookstore, but it's barely penetrating.

"If we expend all this energy protecting people, we aren't going to have enough to stop it," I tell Emerson. "We need everyone."

We need unity, I think. We need more than *witches*.

A screaming missile of oily residue flings itself at us. I hold up my sword and throw out magic, and Emerson does the same, but it keeps coming—

Until Azrael swoops in front of us, blasting fire from his mouth and stopping it in its tracks. It falls to the ground with a nauseating splash.

He roars out his triumph and hovers in the air near us.

"Thanks," Emerson offers. "I don't suppose you can melt them all?"

"I would if I could."

"Could you try?" And she sounds a little less *upbeat* than usual, so I know she's scared.

Emerson scared makes me . . . *terrified*.

It's like Azrael feels the shift in me. He looks down at us, at me, his gaze a blaze of gold. "I have an idea," he mutters.

"All ideas are welcome," Emerson says.

Azrael shifts in a fury of light, and comes down to kneel

over me, his expression more ferocious than his actual dragon form. He takes my chin in his hand and presses his mouth to mine.

It's a hard kiss. Almost bruising.

It's the most beautiful thing I've ever experienced.

"Don't die while I'm gone," he tells me fiercely.

Then he leaps up, throwing himself into the air and changing back into a dragon as he does it. He soars high, bellowing and shooting fire down below.

"You still have your sword," Emerson says quietly. "You need to use it, Georgie. I'll make another one for me, but I think we should assume it will only be temporary."

And when she looks at me then, it's not as a Confluence Warrior. It's not as my coven leader. It's as my best friend.

My sister.

We're losing. I know we're losing. Too many witches are held tethered by black magic tentacles no matter how Frost and Zander try to get people free. Familiars have joined the fray, pulling people out of the tornado's pathway, giving Frost and Zander more time to cut away the black tendrils of evil.

But the tentacles keep coming. The snow keeps falling, natural and magical alike. And I think there must be some kind of *bubble* keeping us from reaching out to witches beyond St. Cyprian, because no one is coming to help.

If we're going to lose this, though, we're going to do it fighting.

Me and Emerson, like always, even back when our biggest concerns were that the boys got called on more in kindergarten than we did (Emerson) and that there was never a good recess-to-class ratio (me).

We give it our best. I go around slicing through as many black magic tendrils as I can, but it's useless. They grow back twice as fast. Emerson is on her fourth sword. I'm tired, and there's been no progress.

Only snow and screaming.

There's one hope, I think. One thing that can save us.

I strike through a few more black tendrils popping up through the bricks. I turn to Emerson and grab her with my free arm.

"You and Jacob have to *finish* the vows," I tell her desperately. "I'll try to hold Carol and that *thing* off. But you need to get on the stage. *Finish the vows.* It doesn't have to be pretty. You just have to mean it."

Emerson looks at me. She's used to calling the shots, but I don't think she fully understands what's happening the way I do. The crows. The fabulae.

"It's the only way," I tell her.

She nods—maybe because it's not like there's a better plan—and then she flies off to find Jacob.

Meanwhile, I am left to fight.

Not alone, exactly. The armies of crows, along with Zander's and Ellowyn's bird familiars, are diving at tendrils that get too high, clawing through ones that hold witches captive. It's a losing battle, and the crows are already weaker than they should be since they're working to get around a curse to even be here, but they fight.

We all keep fighting.

Melisande has joined Ellowyn and Rebekah. Their bombs are better aimed, but have little effect. Still, it just goes to show, if we can get *more*, we can get *better*.

Jacob and Emerson scramble up to the stage as Carol's scream echoes between buildings. She screams louder, and bricks start crumbling off, tumbling down facades. Windows are shattering. Jacob narrowly blocks Emerson from a hurled brick. Then she stops shards of glass from flying at both of them.

"They need guarding," Zander says, suddenly next to me, flinging out his own magic. He's left Frost and a few familiars to keep helping people out, but we're losing ground. Black tendrils of evil keep shooting up from the ground, grabbing more and more witches.

We need *more* than witches.

We need *everyone*.

I look up in the sky, hoping to see Azrael return—but instead my breath catches.

The largest raven of them all, violet-eyed and familiar, takes a dive at the tornado's center. *Gideon.*

But just as he's about to reach his target, the zombie's tail—which looks exactly like a weasel's—whips out lightning-fast and slams against his body, sending him hurtling down to the ground.

I reach out, trying to stop his fall with magic, but it's too far, and I have so little, and—

I watch my dad *dive* forward from the back of the melee. And then he blocks Gideon's inevitable crash to the ground by catching him.

In his arms.

As brave as can be.

I want to revel in that, but I can't, because something is creeping up my back. I whirl with the sword and manage to cut off the tendril before it latches around my throat—but that's all the warning I need. I have to pay attention to my own attackers or I'll be taken out.

Jacob and Emerson are on the stage, but they keep having to fend off attacks. They can't speak the necessary vows. I try to get to them, but it's not quick or easy.

There are too many tendrils, everywhere.

And the snow keeps coming, heedless and quiet in the face of all this chaos.

When I'm *almost* to the stage, I hear that mighty dragon roar in the distance.

Then Azrael comes into sight, and he's not alone.

He's brought ghosts.

All the ghosts I know and some I don't. I'm not sure how he managed it, but they all ride on his back or fly fanned out behind him, as if that's just . . . normal. Like the afterlife is all about dragon rides and air currents.

He drops them off at the stage.

"We can't do much, but we'll do what we can," Lillian tells me as I climb up on the stage myself, beating the tendrils off as they try to drag me back.

I point at Jacob and Emerson. "Protect them so they can finish the vows."

My grandmother—and it still makes me feel good to call her that—gives a ghostly nod, then rallies her ghost troops. They form a circle around Emerson and Jacob, and with whatever vestiges of power and energy they have left or can summon, they work together to block everything flinging itself Jacob and Emerson's way.

I want to help them, but I have to assume they've got it.

I need to put myself back into the fight.

I think of fighting spells. I think of every anti-evil speech I've ever heard. I try to feel all of that *right* inside me and propel it out toward all that *wrong*.

But as I do, I see Azrael fly low with fire shooting out of his mouth, and he's just a *hair* too close to Carol.

She suddenly has a sword, just like mine but fully black. She flings it upward, and it rips through Azrael's belly. I scream out, feeling that pain like I've been sliced open too. I want to fly toward him, but a tendril of black has gotten around my ankle. It burns, though I barely feel it.

I need to get to Azrael.

Maybe I scream that.

Zander's trying to free me, but then Emerson's voice rings out. Loud. Sure. "Because love cannot be torn asunder. Love will set us free."

Something cracks so loudly I nearly drop the sword and slam my hands over my ears. I don't. Somehow I don't, but I'm suddenly free of the tendril, and I can move.

To Azrael.

It's chaos now. An earthquake. Black magic explosions. A veritable war zone, but I rush to Azrael anyway, like my life depends on it. I know, deep down, it does.

And I'm not happy when I get there. He's bleeding dark and oily *evil* from the stomach, laid out on the ground while a few witch Healers try to help him.

Somewhat tentatively.

I skid onto my knees at his head. His eyes are closed, but his dragon chest rises and falls, so mine can too. I hear Emerson and Jacob in the distance, but I can't pay attention to them now. Not now.

"Well, at least it wasn't a fucking crow," he says when I stroke my hand along his face. "This time."

"No, Azrael. Not defeat. *Hope.*"

"Your witch Healers can't fix this, Georgina."

He opens his eyes and meets my gaze. He opens his mouth to say something I'm sure I don't want to hear. Someone interrupts us first.

"But *I* can."

I look up in the direction of the woman's voice. It's Melisande. She's holding . . . Octavius? "We both can," the mermaid says, gently pushing me out of the way. She murmurs words I do not know, or maybe she's singing them. Octavius curls up next to Azrael's rising and falling chest and *purrs*. His eyes gleam bright. And slowly but surely, Azrael's wound begins to stitch itself together.

"I am going to *hate* owing you a favor," he mutters at her.

She grins. Then she gestures around us. "I think you'll have quite a few favors to owe when this is done."

"But . . ." I'm still staring at Octavius.

"He was only a baby when he was cursed," Melisande tells me. "He never learned to communicate, but he's not your average familiar." She reaches out, scratches behind his ears. "Octavius is a fairy cat."

"A fairy cat."

Melisande nods. She gestures to someone, and Ellowyn appears with a mug that she hands to Azrael. With a huff, he drinks it, still in dragon form. Still healing as Octavius purrs next to him.

"Now that we're uncursed, he'll learn to talk to you," Melisande says, getting to her feet. She glances at Azrael. "But be warned, fairies and dragons have somewhat contentious relationships. Though this *particular* dragon should take an intense liking to mermaids and fairies, since he was saved by them."

Azrael only grunts, but I'm distracted, because she said *uncursed*. I look around and the war is still on, but it's . . . different.

The crows have amassed in bigger numbers, in all their bird and human forms. There are fairies and centaurs. Basilisks, griffins, and the Fenrir from Sage's spigot. Even the *nachtkrapp* from the rug in Wilde House. Witches that I saw Zander and Frost help out of the cross fire have come rushing back with weapons.

Crystals, swords, and athames of their own.

But there's only one way this could have happened.

Emerson and Jacob finished the vows. The magical creatures were freed—fabulae and crow.

We have *united*. Come together at last.

"It worked," Azrael says in awe.

As if he didn't quite believe it. But he fought for it anyway.

Because *I* believed it.

I want to sob. I *really* want to take the longest nap ever, but it isn't over yet. Carol is still *there*, even if her hair is starting to fall out and her zombie is smaller. She's still hurling out desperate black magic, but she is . . . surrounded.

Because we came together—not just magical creatures of all descriptions, not just witches, not just crows.

All of us.

Even the high school graduates who we befriended on our way to Litha are here. They saved us once already this year with their votes, using their powers for good.

As Azrael and I join the circle, I see Gideon across the way. His leg is bloody, his face bruised—but he's alive.

And he's adding his power to the magic—good, bright, light magic—surrounding Carol now. On one side of him is the fairy from my window growing up. On his other side are Ellowyn's mother and her partner, Mina. Next to me is Emerson, with Azrael on the other side. Witches, magical creatures, crows, and ghosts begin to surround Carol and her monster.

"Hope. Love. Unity," I whisper to myself.

Then louder.

And it catches on.

Slowly it becomes a chant. A spell.

So simple, when the world, and even our future free of black magic, won't be *simple*.

But sometimes you have to start with simple to get anywhere. Sometimes, no matter how complex the things you build on top of them, the foundations have to start with the most simple truths.

Hope.

Love.

Unity.

And people brave enough to fight for them all, no matter the cost.

Carol is screeching, but she's turning into a Joywood zombie herself. Her skin is melting away. Her hair is gone.

The creature she made is falling apart at the seams. Black

magic oozes all over the bricks, then is covered by the insistent snow.

Though he's still healing, Azrael begins to create a ring of fire around the black that remains, and another dragon flies in to help him finish the circle when his energy flags.

We chant until we have Carol trapped. She's dissolving before us. There is nothing but black ooze left.

"Now what?" Zander asks.

"I can think of several fitting ends," Azrael mutters.

"I am certain I know a spell for each," Frost agrees. They look at each other in a moment of perfect understanding, like they might one day be friends.

Imagine *that*.

My father rushes over to me with a book. It's one of the Joywood books from Carol's house—I recognize that smell. He holds it out, opened to a page.

"Containing black magic," he says excitedly. "There's a whole chapter on how to contain and dispose of it."

I take the book from my father, and it doesn't feel evil anymore. Because wiped of Carol's intent, it's just information. As intended.

"We need to contain it *in* something," I say as I read. "No one person can hold on to it, and it must be displayed for all to see at all times."

I frown a little. How are we going to come up with that?

"You must choose wisely," Frost says then, frowning as if this is a memory. "She must be contained by her own evil, or she'll be a threat again."

"I have an idea," Azrael murmurs.

Then, with a loud thump, the dragon statue from the cemetery lands in the courtyard at the end of Main Street.

We all look at Emerson. Her beautiful wedding gown is torn. She has a gash on her cheek, and she's holding her arm at an odd angle. She is clearly being careful to hide the majority of her injuries from Jacob, who is standing at the edge of the alley. He's trying to heal a sniveling Sage, who keeps crying out in a pain that is no doubt minor.

Save everyone else first. That's our Emerson. And I don't feel a pang of sympathy or hate for Sage. Just a delightful nothingness.

Because that's all he really was.

"Yes," Emerson says, nodding at the dragon statue. "How do we do it?"

I read them the book, the spell. And we all come together—not as our coven, or even the citizens of St. Cyprian. But as anyone who wants to be part of a new world, free of black magic and greed and evil.

Witches, ghosts, magical creatures, and crows all come together and say the words.

And the black, oozing representation of all Carol's evil solidifies into a little gemstone. On the last word of the spell, it hovers in the air, then is sucked into the dragon statue.

We all stand in silence for a few beats, just staring at it. Something's missing. I can feel it.

The sword will seal it. It will seal the black magic. It will be a sign, forever, that division and curses, greed and cruelty, cannot sustain a world.

I look down at my sword. What do I do? Shove it into a dragon statue's hand? Get a little King Arthur with it?

"It will seal it," Azrael agrees, even though I wasn't *speaking*. "But a dragon cannot wield the sword of unity."

I feel something brush against my leg then. I look down, half expecting to see another tendril of black magic.

It's my fairy tale. On the cover is a statue like the one before us. But instead of just the dragon, there's a princess on the dragon. Holding a sword up to the sky.

"Perfect," my dragon rumbles.

Azrael waves a hand, and I don't know how he has any energy left, except the magical creatures seem to have fared better than the witches and crows. Probably because they've had years upon years to store up magic and strength.

Now riding the fearsome dragon statue in real life is a stone woman that looks an awful lot like the princess in my book.

And me.

"Go on then," he says, nudging me forward.

The stone princess is holding out her arm, and inside the fist is a hole made so that the sword's hilt should go right in.

"Hope, love, unity," I murmur, more to myself than to anything else.

As the sword goes in, a ripple of magic flings itself out like snow.

And in the actual snow is something else.

A lifting. A lightening.

The curse we've *all* been under lifts. The Joywood's mind control.

I remember Skip Simon attacking Emerson.

I hear people talking excitedly.

"Remember when the Joywood . . ."

"My entire family was made into a pack of plague-stricken rats for a whole winter!"

"One of my best friends was a crow!"

"Did Carol really turn her own son into a weasel? Or a weasel into her son?"

Frost is rubbing his temple, with Rebekah's hand on his back. I can tell he's remembering things he's lost too.

I turn to Azrael, and just *lean*. I'm exhausted. But then Ellowyn starts doling out cups of her brew that will revive us. *All* of us.

As I lift my cup to my mouth, I see the ring Azrael once gave me on my finger. I don't recall him putting it there. I look up at him, eyes narrowed. "It's been there all along, hasn't it?"

He shrugs. "Perhaps."

But it has. I know it has. I've *felt* it, even though he hid it from me. I lean into him even more. "I always knew you'd come through. Even when I was afraid you wouldn't."

"That doesn't make any sense," he says a bit grumpily.

"Of course it does."

He snorts. "It appears we will have quite the long life to become bored with one another, Georgina."

I smile at that. "I don't know if you know this, Azrael, but a girl who enjoys reading is *never* bored."

"Witches, magical creatures, crows. *Friends.*" Emerson's voice booms out from the speaker, and I know it reaches everywhere in witchdom. Everywhere in the world. "I'll have a cleanup crew organized for first thing in the morning, but you know what we're going to do right now?" She lifts a fist and pumps it toward the crowd, the mess, the complicated and beautiful knot of *us*. "We're going to *celebrate*. Happy solstice, St. Cyprian. May we appreciate the coming light."

ONE YEAR LATER

ST. CYPRIAN TIMES

Happy New Year!
By: Emerson Wilde-North

Magical beings of St. Cyprian, we have made it through another fantastic trip around the wheel!

I wanted to look back at all of our accomplishments—thanks to the tireless work of your representatives in the Riverwood coven and, most importantly, the willingness of our community to see the hope in a new future of unity and connection.

Together, we are living up to the promise of this marvelous little town!

As the leader of the Riverwood, I know that we're not perfect, and I want to remind you that we welcome all *contributions to our monthly town hall meetings. No complaint, comment, or compliment will ever go unheard or unaddressed on our watch. Public investment in what we do as a coven is* how *we do what we do as a coven. Teamwork makes the dream work!*

We have done a great many things over the course of our first year, always with an eye toward improvements to the town and the wider magical world—as well as a great many things we can all be proud of as a community of witches, familiars, fabulae, and crows.

Mr. Stanford Pendell has finished his compendium of the true history of the witching world, sourced from his own lifelong research and full access to the witchlore archives. This will be the textbook witches and magical creatures will use in their high school classes moving forward.

Speaking of books, the Riverwood fairy tale that played such a large role in the defeat of our predecessors has gone to print. This fall we will host a celebration of the book, the statue, and its honorable writer, the late Lillian Wilde. Business owners—please see me for ways you can participate in what I hope will be an exciting new addition to our annual festival lineup!

We have welcomed many new additions to our community this year—many more magical additions than the last ten years combined!—including the Riverwood's own Zelda Good-Rivers, born at Ostara on her late grandmother's birthday. The happy parents thank everyone for their well-wishes.

We are continuing to hammer out agreements with the crows to honor all the history involved. Crow Island remains closed to witches without direct invitation, but we are happy with our progress toward a greater sharing between magical communities, not without awareness of our complicated histories, but with hope for a brighter future.

The Free Archives initiative has been a great success. Our esteemed Historian Georgie Pendell has worked around the clock to make the archives open for all. Thank you to the Historian workers and volunteers for getting us as far as we've come.

The Frost School for Fabulae has opened. Great strides have been made by our formerly cursed children catching up with their studies. As a bonus, Frost House no longer sits up on the bluff beneath its decrepit glamour, a great step forward for both the magical and human communities.

The fabulae wing of the witch hospital has also seen great success, though we are still seeking fabulae Healers to join the Norths in this endeavor. Remember, ask not what your community can do for you, but what you can do for your community!

As another new year dawns, we wish the same for all of you that we wish for ourselves:

Love. Hope. Unity.

And the best way to step into these wishes and make them come true is involvement in the St. Cyprian community. Our next town hall meeting will be at the end of January. Please join us and let your voices be heard!

Azrael puts the newsletter down on the nightstand next to him with a dramatic sigh. "And what, pray tell, do the humans read when they pick up such nonsense?"

I am sitting at my table, cleansing my crystals, Octavius curled in my lap. He was the first student enrolled in Frost's fabulae school, and he comes home exhausted every day. But he is learning, and we're finally communicating.

"Mostly just a recap of all the festivals, and Emerson had to assure them there was nothing *satanic* about including Yule decorations in the Christmas Around the World parade."

I finish what I'm doing, lift Octavius and cradle him like the baby he is, then gently place my fairy cat on his bed on the window seat.

Then I turn to my dragon. My love. He has healed up nicely from his injuries at last year's winter solstice. He still gives me his little gifts, only now I can thank him properly. I am, it turns out, *very* thankful.

But then, so is he.

We show each other all the time.

He surprised everyone, except perhaps me, with his committed involvement in coven business the past year. I think they all expected him to be . . . well, *mercurial* is the word of choice, and Azrael is nothing if not that, but he is also a stalwart supporter in bringing together the different factions the Joywood divided us into.

At last.

He has traveled the world searching out fabulae Healers for the witch hospital here in St. Cyprian. He has worked with a group of fabulae and witches to search the far corners of the earth to ensure all fabulae were released from their curses. And he has been an ever-vigilant caretaker of the dragon-princess statue that destroyed black magic once and for all, letting the bricks of St. Cyprian be a refuge once more.

But most of all, he has been by my side. The partner of my dreams I once talked myself out of.

The love of all my lives.

Tonight, he flashes that mischievous dragon smile at me, holds out a hand. "My own, my Georgina. Let's go for a ride."

And so we do, soaring over St. Cyprian and the confluence, our friends and family, and the marvelous world full of the people we saved. The unfiltered light and power of the confluence glows for us. A ghost waves from the cemetery.

Every day, our home looks more like the vision of this magical place that Ellowyn showed us at the ascension trials.

Higher we go, until I can see Crow Island winking in the river, revealed at last—until we are so far into the stars that we see nothing at all but each other. It's a real fairy tale, my dragon and me. It's a dream made real. It's something I thought I couldn't have just a year ago, and it didn't require that I compromise who I am to get it.

I just had to be me. Books and all.

He remembers all the lives we've loved in, and then lost. I can't remember the details, but I can feel the weight of them every time we touch.

And I know a secret.

This life is going to be the best one yet. Because *this* time, we're going to do the hardest thing of all and *live* our way into an ever-after. We're not going to *die* for love. We're going to *live* it all the way through.

I can't wait.

All those books have it right—we just have to be willing to fight our way to the good stuff. Because we're all worthy of fairy-tale endings, happy-ever-afters, and the love of a thousand lifetimes.

We're all the princess in our own story. Don't let anyone tell you different.

And it's up to you to pick up that sword and fight for your own heart, no matter how dark it gets along the way to a life full of light.

I'll see you there.

★ ★ ★ ★ ★